Faye Kellerman was born in St Louis, Missouri and graduated in Mathematics and Dentistry at UCLA. She began her career as a dentist but turned to writing after the birth of her eldest child in 1978. She has now completed nine novels featuring Detective Sergeant Peter Decker and Rina Lazarus, and one historical mystery. In between writing, she tries to find the time to indulge in her two favourite hobbies, gardening and music. She has four children and lives with them and her husband, novelist and psychologist Jonathan Kellerman, in Los Angeles.

Prayers
for the Dead

Faye Kellerman

Copyright © 1996 Faye Kellerman

The right of Faye Kellerman to be identified as the Author of
the Work has been asserted by her in accordance with
the Copyright, Designs and Patents Act 1988.

First published in Great Britain in 1996
by HEADLINE BOOK PUBLISHING

First published in Great Britain in paperback in 1997
by HEADLINE BOOK PUBLISHING

A HEADLINE FEATURE paperback

10 9 8 7 6 5 4 3 2

ISBN 0 7472 5231 9

Typeset by Avon Dataset Ltd, Bidford-on-Avon, Warks

Printed and bound in Great Britain by
BPC Paperbacks Ltd.

HEADLINE BOOK PUBLISHING
A division of Hodder Headline PLC
338 Euston Road
London NW1 3BH

To Jonathan for a quarter century of love, laughter and just plain fun.

To Jesse, Rachel, Ilana and Aliza; the keys to my heart — thanks for putting it all in perspective.

To Mom, my lifelong friend — love you, kid.

And to Rita — for all the inappropriate giggles.

Special thanks to
Dr. Isaac Weiner
Dr. Hillel Laks

Prologue

'This is a team effort, Grace. You know that.'

Even through morphine-laden stupor, Grace knew that. From her hospital bed, she looked up at her doctor's face – a study in strength. Good, solid features. A well-boned forehead, Roman nose and a pronounced chin, midnight blue eyes that burned fire, tar-black hair streaked with silver. His expression, though grave, was completely self-assured. Someone who knew what he wanted and expected to get it. Truth be told, the man looked downright arrogant.

Which was exactly the kind of doctor Grace had wanted. What she hadn't wanted was some young stud like Ben Casey or an old fart like Marcus Welby with the crinkly eyes and the patient, understanding smile. She had wanted someone bursting with ego. Someone whose superiority was touted, worn with pride like Tiffany jewelry. A self possession that spoke: *Of course the operation is going to be successful. Because I always succeed.*

Because getting a new heart was serious business.

Grace Armstrong had to have the best and the brightest. Had the luxury to afford the best and the brightest. And in Dr. Azor Moses Sparks, she had gotten numero uno.

Dope was winning the battle of wits with Grace's brain. Sparks's face had lost clarity, sat behind a curtain of haze, his features becoming blurry except for the eyes. They peered through the muck like high-beam headlights. She wanted to go to sleep. But Sparks's presence told her she wasn't permitted to do that . . . not just yet.

He spoke in authoritative, stentorian tones. The sounds bounced round Grace's brain, words reverberating as if uttered through a

1

malfunctioning PA system. Doctor's voice . . .

' *. . . what we have here, Grace. A team comprised of* me: *the primary surgeon:* you: *the patient: and my staff – the other fine surgeons and nurses who'll assist me in this procedure.'*

Grace liked how Dr. Sparks had emphasized his *fine staff. As if he owned New Christian Hospital.*

Maybe he did.

She closed her eyes, anxiety now replaced by the overwhelming need to go comatose. But Sparks wouldn't let up.

'Grace, open your eyes. We still have uncompleted business to finish.'

Grace opened her eyes.

'We mustn't forget someone very important,' Sparks reminded her. 'The most important *member of our team.'*

The surgeon paused.

'Do you know who that is, Grace? Do you know whose Hands really control this entire effort?'

Grace was silent. Though groggy and heavy, she felt her ailing heart fluttering too fast. He was testing her and she was flunking. She regarded Sparks through panicky eyes. The doctor smiled, gently patted her hand. The gesture reassured her immensely.

Sparks pointed upward. Grace's eyes followed the narcotic-induced flickering path of the surgeon's index finger.

Respectfully, Sparks said, 'We mustn't forget Him.'

'God?' Grace was breathless.

'Yes, Grace.' Sparks nodded. 'We mustn't forget our holy, heavenly Father.'

Grace spoke, her words barely recognizable. 'Believe me, Dr. Sparks, I've been praying nonstop.'

Sparks smiled. It lit up his face, gave warmth to his stern demeanor. 'I'm very glad to hear that. So let us pray together, Grace. Let us both ask God for His help and for His guidance.'

The surgeon went down on his knees. At that moment, Grace thought him very odd, but didn't comment. Sparks's manner suggested that the ritual wasn't subject to debate. She closed her eyes, managed to put her hands together.

'Dear heavenly Father,' Sparks began, 'be our guiding light through this time of darkness. Be a strong beacon to direct us through this upcoming storm. Show us Your mercy and Your love in its abundancy. Let Your wisdom be our wisdom, Your perfection be our perfection. Let Grace Armstrong be upmost in her fortitude. Give her strength and faith. In Your abundant love, allow me and my staff to be swift and sure-footed as we embark on another journey to heal the sick and mend the feeble.'

Grace winced inside at the word feeble.

'And now a moment of silence,' Sparks said. 'You may add your own words of prayer here, Grace.'

Her own words were: Please, let me go to sleep, wake up and have this shitty ordeal behind me.

Sparks's eyes were still closed. Grace's head felt leaden, her brain so woozy it threatened to shut down. She managed to make out Sparks's face, his lids opening. Suddenly, his eyes seemed injected with newly found vigor.

Grace liked that.

Sparks regarded his patient, swept his skilled hands over her lids, and gently closed them. 'Go to sleep, Grace. Tomorrow you'll be a new woman.'

Grace felt herself going under. No longer was her health in her hands.

It was up to Sparks.

It was up to God.

At that moment, they were one and the same.

3

1

The living room was dimly lit, the house motionless, reminding Decker of his divorced, bachelor days – days he'd be reliving soon if he didn't start making it home earlier. To wit: The dining room table had been cleared – dinner long gone – and the door to Hannah's nursery was closed, Rina nowhere in sight. Yes, she was a patient woman, but she did have limits. Decker often wondered how far she could be pushed before she'd explode on impact. Because as of yet, no one had developed a road test for wives.

He placed his briefcase on the empty table, his fingers raking through thick shocks of carrot-colored hair. Ginger came trotting in from the kitchen. Decker bent down and petted the setter's head.

'Hi, girl. Are you happy to see me?'

Ginger's tail wagged furiously.

'Well, someone's glad I'm alive. Let's go see what the crew had for dinner.'

Decker dragged himself into the kitchen, draped his jacket over an oak kitchenette chair. Rina had kept his dinner warming in the oven. He put on a quilted mitt and fished it out. Some kind of Chinese cuisine except, by now, the snow peas and broccoli were limp and khaki green, and the rice had developed a yellowish crust. At least the noodles appeared nice and crisp.

He set the dish on top of a meat place mat and took out cutlery. Washed his hands, said a quick blessing, but paused before he sat down. He noticed a light coming from under the door of his stepsons' room. To be expected. As teens, they often went to bed later than he did. Perhaps he should say hello to the boys first.

That should take all of five minutes.

Kids had been preoccupied lately, hadn't seemed to have much time for quality conversation. Maybe they were peeved at the late hours he'd been keeping. The more likely explanation was typical teenage behavior. His grown daughter, Cindy, had gone through sullen moments in her adolescent years. Now she was doing postgrad work back in Criminal Sciences. A beautiful young lady who truly enjoyed his company. Ah, the passage of time . . .

He glanced at his withered food, eyes moving to the dog. 'Don't get any ideas. I'll be right back.'

He knocked on the door to his sons' room. He heard Jake ask a testy 'What?' Decker jiggled the doorknob. It was locked.

'Someone want to open the door, please?'

Scuffling noises. Desk chair wheels sliding against the floor. The lock popped open but the door remained closed. Decker hesitated, went into the room.

Both boys were at their desks, books and papers spilling over the work surface. They mumbled a perfunctory hello. Decker returned the greeting with proper articulation, and studied his sons.

Sammy had grown tall this last year. At least five ten which, according to Rina, already made him a couple of inches taller than his late father. From the pictures Decker had seen of Yitzchak, the elder boy strongly resembled his dad – same long face, pointed chin and sandy hair. His complexion was smooth and fair, freckles dabbling the bridge of his nose. His eyes were dark and quiet in their intelligence. He was also nearsighted like Yitzchak; Sam wore wire-rimmed spectacles. Jake had been the one to inherit Rina's stunning baby blues, her 20/20 eyesight as well.

The boys were still in their school uniform – white shirt and navy slacks. The fringes of their prayer shawls – their *tzitzit* – were hanging past the hems of their untucked shirts. Jake wore a knitted yarmulke, its colors designed to look like a slice of watermelon. Sammy had on a black, leather *kippah* embossed with his Hebrew name in gold letters.

'How's it going, boys?' Decker asked. 'What're you doing?'

Sammy put down his textbook. 'A paper on the evolution of the American Ideal through the literature of Mark Twain. A real conversation stopper.' He rubbed his eyes under his glasses, peered at Decker. 'You look real tired, Dad. Maybe you should go eat something. I think Eema left you something in the oven.'

'Trying to get rid of me?'

'No, I just thought . . .' Sammy frowned. 'Jeez, try and be a *nice guy* around here. Do whatever you want.' His eyes went back to his notes. He picked up a highlighter and started underlining.

Well, that was spiffy, Deck. He shifted his weight, wondered what to do next. Jake came to his rescue. 'You have a hard day, Dad?'

'Not too bad.'

'Felons took the day off?'

'Never.'

'But no famous people accused of murdering their wives.'

'No, not today.'

'Too bad,' Jake said. 'You woulda looked cool on the witness stand.'

'Thank you, I'll pass.'

Sammy said, 'Jeez, Dad, where's your sense of adventure?'

'Adventure is for the young,' Decker said. 'I'm just a stodgy old coot.'

'You're not a coot,' Sammy said. 'What is a coot anyway?'

'A simpleton,' Decker answered.

'Nah, you're definitely not a coot.'

'As opposed to stodgy and old.'

'Well, better too stodgy than too cool.' Jake grinned. 'You read that article in the paper? 'Bout the father who was arrested for contributing to the delinquency of a minor or something like that with a stripper?'

'What's this?' Sammy's interest was piqued.

Jake guffawed as he spoke. 'A father hired a stripper to perform at his son's twelfth birthday.'

7

Sam wrinkled up his nose. 'That's gross.' His smile was wide. 'Kinda fun, I bet, but gross.'

Jake was doubled over. 'One of the kids . . . told his mother. The mother complained and they arrested the guy . . . stupid jerk. The father said he was just trying to be a "cool dad." '

Now Sam started chortling. 'Now, why can't you be a cool dad like that?'

'Your *rabbaim* would really love that,' Decker said.

'Yeah, they'd get mad,' Jake said, his eyes wet with tears. 'But only because we didn't *invite* them.'

Both boys were seized with laughter. Decker smiled and shook his head. 'How you talk about your elders.'

'A very stodgy response.' Sam got up, kissed Decker on the cheek, and patted his shoulder. 'You don't have to hire a stripper for my birthday to be cool. But I wouldn't mind a motorcycle.'

Decker gave Sam a paternal smile that said 'over my dead body.' Sam shrugged. 'No harm in asking.' He sat back down at his desk. 'Gotta get back to work. Huck Finn is calling.'

Jake looked at his homework – a tractate of incomprehensible Talmud. 'Shmueli, you learned *Baba Kama*, didn't you?'

'More like a few parts. What don't you understand?'

'I don't understand any of it.'

'You gotta do better than that, Yonkie.'

Jake squinted at the mini-print text in an oversized tome of Talmud. 'Something about if a guy's tied up in a field . . . and there's fire in the field . . . if it's murder or not?'

'It would be murder according to American law,' Decker said.

Jake bypassed Decker's bit of professional input. 'I don't know *what* Rav Yosef is talking about. This man is on another planet.'

'Why don't you ask Rav Schulman?' Decker suggested.

Jake gave him an 'are you a moron?' look. 'Dad, I don't think a big Rosh Yeshiva like him has a lot of free time for *basic* questions.' The boy sighed. 'Besides, I don't want to look stupid.'

His voice turned desperate as he spoke to Sam. 'You didn't learn this at all?'

'Sounds vaguely familiar. Read me the *passuk*.'

The conversation between the two continued. Feeling superfluous, Decker said, 'I think I am going to go eat.'

Both boys said a quick good-bye, returning their attentions to their respective academic plight.

Decker trudged back into the kitchen, Ginger still parked under his chair. She picked up her head and made a pathetic squeaking noise. Throwing her a piece of overcooked beef, he sat down and picked at his shriveled dinner.

A minute later, Rina walked into the room, her cheeks pink with warmth. She had tied her ebony hair into a long plait, and her lids were still half-closed as her eyes adjusted from the darkness of the nursery to the white glare of the kitchen's fluorescent lighting. She squinted at Peter.

'Are you a husband or a hologram?' She bent down and kissed his lips. 'I do believe you're flesh and blood.'

'Funny.'

Her eyes stopped at his dinner plate. 'Chinese doesn't appear to keep well. Let me make you something fresh.'

'Nah, don't bother.'

'How about salami and eggs?' Rina proposed. 'Easy to make and guaranteed to drive your cholesterol off the scale.'

Decker pushed the dish away. 'Actually, that sounds great. How's my baby daughter? Does she still remember me?'

'With much fondness. You look very tired, Peter.'

'As always.'

Rina began to rub his neck. 'You're very tense, Atlas. Why don't you pass the world onto someone else's shoulders?'

'I tried. No one would take it.'

Rina said nothing, continued the massage.

'Feels good,' Decker said.

'Maybe you can juggle some paperwork, put me on the

department payroll as your masseuse. Isn't that how the politicians work it?'

'Too bad I'm not a good politician.' Decker blew out air. 'I'm not a good bureaucrat, either. I'm also lousy at delegating tasks. As a result, I'm swamped with paperwork. My own doing, of course.'

'Would you like a rope for self-flagellation, or perhaps a cat-o'-nine-tails?'

Decker smiled. 'Where do you know from a cat-o'-nine-tails?'

Rina hit his shoulder, went over to the refrigerator, and took out eggs and a roll of salami. Decker looked at his wife as she sliced and diced. As tired as he was, damn, if she didn't look good enough to devour. He still marveled at how the gods had smiled on him. Seven years ago since they had met . . .

'It's not that I don't have my virtues,' Decker said. 'In fact, I have many.'

Rina pushed sizzling salami around the pan. 'That's the spirit.'

'I sometimes miss working in the field, that's all. I miss working with Marge as a partner. I've teamed her with Oliver. They work well together. But I think there's friction.'

'Big surprise. Marge is a straightshooter, Scott's a slick old goat.'

'He's in his forties. That's not old.'

'But he is slick and he is a goat.'

'True.'

'Is Marge complaining?'

'No, she's too much the professional to do that. I should talk to her, find out if she's happy. Tell the truth, I don't want to open up a can a worms. I figure if there are real problems, I'll learn about them sooner or later.'

'In other words, you're playing ostrich, burying your head in the sand.'

'More like . . . selective ostrich.' Decker smoothed his mustache. 'Sometimes, I have to look the other way. Otherwise, you spread yourself too thin.'

The phone rang.

Both of them looked at the wall, at the malevolent blinking business line. Rina poured the eggs into the pan and scrambled fiercely. 'How about doing some fancy head-interring right now, Mr. Cassowary?'

'Lieutenant Cassowary.'

Wordlessly, Rina picked up the receiver, handed it to her husband. He took it, shrugged helplessly.

'Decker.'

'It's Marge. We need you.'

'Can I finish my dinner?'

'You may not want to. Just found sixty-plus white male slumped inside an '86 Buick. Gunshot wounds to the forehead, as well as multiple stab wounds to the chest. The man had ID on him. Pete, it's *Azor Sparks*!'

It took a few moments for Decker to put flesh and bone on the name. 'The *heart* doctor?' He felt a sudden pounding in his head. Jesus! What happened?'

'What?' Rina asked.

Decker waved her off. Marge said, 'The car was found parked in the back alley behind Tracadero's. A busboy was taking out the garbage when he saw that the Buick had the driver's seat door wide open. He went over to investigate . . . Oh Christ! . . . Pete, a stray was on top of him, snout buried in his chest—'

'I'll be right over.' Decker hung up the phone.

Rina handed him his plate of salami and eggs. 'You don't have time to bolt it down?'

Decker's stomach lurched. Not the time or the inclination. 'It's bad, Rina. You don't want to know.'

'Will I hear about it on the news?'

'Probably.' Decker grimaced. 'Dr. Azor Sparks, the famous heart transplant surgeon. He was found dead in his car . . . in a back alley behind a restaurant.'

Abruptly, Rina paled, brought her hand to her throat. Decker

11

regarded his wife. As gray as ash. 'Sit down, honey.'

'I think I will.' She melted into a chair.

'You want something to drink?'

'No, I'm . . .'

The kitchen went silent. Decker studied Rina's expression.
'Rina, did you know this man?'

Slowly, she shook her head no. 'Not personally. By reputation.'

'I'm sorry you have to witness such ugliness through me.'

A baby's cry shot through the room. Rina stood on shaky legs.
'Hannah's up. It's like she has a sixth sense . . . I'd better see . . .'
She took a deep breath and let it out slowly. Smiled at her husband,
but left without a good-bye.

Decker waited a beat, then slipped on his jacket, puzzled by
Rina's strong reaction.

Odd.

But maybe not.

Homicides weren't a daily occurrence in her life.

2

Tracadero's was one of the few hoo-hah, nouvelle, chic, posh, pick-your-own-effete-adjective restaurants in the West Valley. Translation to Decker: Pay a lot for tiny portions. He had been here once. The inside had been done up to look like scaffolding. For that kind of money and atmosphere, he could have just as easily bag-lunched it at a construction site. The place was located midblock in a commercial strip of street.

A long block. As Decker fast-walked through a decently lit back alley, he noticed a pizzeria, a clothing boutique, a guitar store, a pharmacy, a hair and nail salon, and a tropical fish store. The night was foggy and cool, the glare of starlight spread behind a wall of filmy clouds. Yellow crime tape had been stretched across the alley's main entrances, two black-and-whites nose to nose at the driveways preventing pass-through traffic. As he came closer to the actual crime spot, the crowd grew dense. Uniformed and plainclothed officers swarming around a bronze Buick. The strong odor of garbage mixed with metallic stench of fresh blood and excreted bowels.

Marge and Oliver had already arrived. So had Martinez and Webster, the newest imports to Devonshire Homicide. Bert Martinez came from Van Nuys Substation, having worked *Crimes Against Persons* detail, Tom Webster was a transplant from Mississippi with ten years of gold-shield experience and a BA in music composition from Tulane. With veteran Farrell Gaynor, they would comprise the team for this case, as major homicides were usually worked in groups of five. Gaynor was on his way, his wife having reported that he had just left. The old man moved like a

13

slug, but had a microscopic eye for details and patience fo
paperwork.

Decker reached inside his jacket, slipped on a pair of late
gloves. Marge noticed him first, pushed silk blonde hair out of he
brown doe eyes and gave a wave. She was a big woman, five nin
plus, large-boned and all muscle. Unmarried as well. Not too man
guys could compete against her in either the brains or brawn
department. The others gave him nods as he approached thei
huddle.

First thing up: Clear unnecessary people. Decker said
'Martinez, Oliver, Webster, and Dunn. You stay here. How man
cruisers were sent here? Anyone know?'

'Seven,' someone answered.

'Four of them are blocking the entrances to the alley.' Decke
thought a moment. 'All right, the other three loose black-and
whites, start making passes around the area. Use extreme cautio
if you see anything suspicious. And always *call* for backup. Th
rest of you, go back to the barricades and wait for furthe
instructions. On your way out, don't touch anything, watch wher
you step. Go.'

Slowly, the crowd scattered, leaving Decker full view of the ca
The driver's door was still wide open, legs protruded out, shoe
scraped the asphalt. Good shoes. Quality black leather, mayb
Ballys or Cole-Haan. They were splattered with sticky clots c
blood. Decker advanced, peered inside the car.

An abattoir. Jackson Pollock in shades of red and brown. H
held his breath and exhaled carefully, thankful his stomach wa
empty. Stab wounds had turned the doctor's chest into a siev
bullets had pierced through the great man's head and necl
Carefully, he touched the cheek.

'Body's still warm.' Decker looked at his glove. Wet with bloo
He'd have to change it before he touched anything else. He checke
his watch. Nine-twenty. 'Anyone call up the ME?'

'Yo.' Oliver ran his hands through a mound of dark hair. H

rown eyes flitted through the scene. 'Called the coronor's office, called Forensics as well. They should be here any moment.'

'What about Captain Strapp?'

Marge said, 'I left a message for him, Pete . . . er, Loo.'

Oliver flashed Marge a white, toothy smile. She ignored it and im. Pity because Scott was well built and good-looking. He even ad moments that could be roughly defined as charming. Just too ew of them and *way* too far between.

Out of the corner of his eye, Decker saw a stoop-shouldered an wrapped in a cardigan sweater, inching toward them. Marge ollowed Decker's stare, shook her head. 'I think you woke him p from his nap.'

Decker waved Gaynor forward. The man attempted a trot but ave up. His belly was too big, his legs too spindly to carry that uch weight while running. Oliver said, 'I thought he retired. He hould be retired.'

'C'mon,' Martinez whispered impatiently. He twirled the ends f his Brillo mustache. 'Guy's an antique. Don't know why the epartment keep him on. He doesn't even help it out with ffirmative action.'

Oliver said, 'You know, this team would fail even the most beral affirmative action qualifications. Too many white males. ot enough minorities. No blacks, Indians, Asians, women—'

Marge said, 'Uh, excuse me—'

'Hispanics—'

'A-*hem*,' Martinez broke in.

'No deaf-blind paraplegics, no midget cretins, no mentally eranged or morally handicapped—'

'Look in the mirror, Scott,' Marge said.

Oliver said, 'I don't know *where* you fit in, Webster. Man, they on't make 'em any WASPier.'

'Enough, Scott,' Marge said. But he did have a point. Tom was Ir. Perma-Prest with his perfect chip of blond hair falling in front f sleepy bluebell eyes. Most detectives exuded an excitement

15

when starting a case. Webster seemed injected with ennui, as i forced to put up with another hot and humid August day in Bilox Mississippi.

Oliver went on, 'Actually you're *more* than WASP, Tommy bo You are down-home DWM.'

'Beg your pardon?' Webster drawled.

'Dead White Male,' Marge said.

'Don't hate me 'cause ahm beautiful,' Webster said dryly.

Oliver smiled, started whistling 'Here Comes Santa Claus' a Gaynor arrived, sweaty and winded.

'Hey, gentlemen.' Farrell looked at Marge. 'And ladies.'

Oliver said, 'We were all wondering why the department hasn put you to pasture since you don't help them with affirmativ action.'

Gaynor said, 'I'm elderly. Gray power.' He held his fist in th air. 'God, it smells awful.'

'It *is* awful,' Marge said.

'Take a look for yourself, Farrell,' Oliver stated. 'If your hea can take it.'

'Old ticker's stronger than you'd think.' Gaynor walked over t the car, looked inside, and winced. He slipped on glove 'Gruesome. It's definitely the primary crime scene.'

'I can see why they keep you on,' Oliver said. 'Astute powe of observation.'

Decker said, 'Sparks worked exclusively with New Christia Hospital, didn't he?'

Gaynor said, 'I know he was there a lot. Friend of mine us Sparks a couple of years ago for bypass surgery. It was done New Chris.' He smiled benignly at Oliver. 'One day you'll kno from these things.'

Oliver gave him a sick smile.

Decker said, 'He must have had his office there, right?'

Blank stares. Gaynor said, 'When I had my angiogram don it was a hospital procedure. But my doctor had a regular offic

He thought a moment. 'But he was a cardiologist not a surgeon.'

Decker said, 'Dunn, find out where Sparks saw his patients when he wasn't operating. In any event, I want you and Oliver to go over to New Chris, see if Sparks was coming from the hospital. While you're on your way, make calls and find out who Sparks's secretary is. If he kept his office at the hospital, tell the secretary to meet you there. I want to get hold of Sparks's daily planner. Hopefully, nobody lifted it.'

'Got it,' Oliver said. 'I'll interview all the nurses personally. One by one. In private.'

Decker stared into space. 'Parked in a back alley like this . . . Sparks wasn't sightseeing. So what was he doing here?'

'Parking the car for the restaurant,' Martinez suggested.

'Then why wouldn't he have used the valet up in front?'

'He was cheap,' Oliver said. 'Lots of rich people are.'

'Or was it a carjacking?' Webster added.

Decker didn't buy it. A carjacker wouldn't make his drop in back of a populated restaurant. His eyes traveled back to the car, scanned the corpse. The scene hadn't gotten any less horrifying. Could be someone lured Sparks here. Let's get a time frame for him. Try to reconstruct his day. Go back to New Chris and talk to *anyone* who saw him. Call me in a halfhour for an update. Go.'

Marge and Oliver looked at each other. Oliver said, 'You drive?'

'I'll drive.'

Oliver flipped her the keys and they left.

Decker said, 'Anyone talk to the valet yet?'

Martinez said no. 'Guy's Hispanic. Want me to do it?'

'Yes. Find out if he heard or saw anything. Also the kitchen faces the back alley. Maybe the help heard something.'

'Si, si, Señor Wences.'

Decker turned to Webster. 'You canvass the block?'

'It's all stores, Loo,' Martinez said. 'Everything's shut down at this hour.'

'How about someone working late in one of the back rooms?'

Webster said. 'Some soul mighta heard something going down.'

Decker agreed. 'Canvass the block. On your way back, Tom check all the alley Dumpsters. We've got a gunshot wound, maybe we'll find a gun. We've got multiple stab wounds, maybe someone chucked a bloody knife.'

Webster said, 'Odd, Loo. We got gunshot *and* stab wounds.'

'Very.'

'Suggestive of more than one person?'

'Indeed.' Decker looked around. 'This much blood spatter . . maybe we'll find more than one shoe print.'

Martinez said, 'Or a bloody glove.'

'Man, you jest, but somewhere there is a pile of bloody clothing begging to be tagged and filed. Be *careful*. And before you pick up anything to bag it, snap a picture. Anyone have a camera?'

'I got a thirty-five millimeter in my car,' Martinez said.

'Good,' Decker said. 'If you got enough film, Bert, take a few pictures of the body for me.'

'Will do.'

'Y'always carry a camera, Bert?' Webster asked.

'The missus keeps one in the car for spontaneous family shots,' Martinez answered. 'I think I've got half a roll left over from our Labor Day picnic.'

Webster said, 'Might be a good idea if *you* took that one in for developing, Bert. Separate the post mortems of Sparks from the family snapshots.'

'A very good idea,' Decker concurred. 'Everyone be sure to cover your butt. It plays well on prime time.'

Martinez said, 'Speaking of prime time, Loo, look who's coming our way.'

Decker's eyes strained in the darkness. Strapp with camera crews in tow.

'I'll handle it.'

'Then we're dismissed?' Webster said.

'Unless you want to talk to Strapp.'

Martinez waved good-bye. He and Webster headed down the alley, jogging away from Strapp.

Decker turned to Gaynor. 'You stay here at the scene, wait for the ME and Forensics. Make sure that no one . . . and I mean no one . . . screws up evidence. You watch them, Farrell, stand over their shoulders and direct if necessary. No screwups. Not while I'm in charge.'

'Where are you going, Loo?'

'I'm going to satisfy Strapp, and hopefully deflect the media. Get the field clear so my detectives can do their jobs. Then, I'm going to notify next of kin.'

Gaynor patted his back. 'Brave man.'

Decker felt sick inside. 'Someone has to take out the garbage.'

3

As the captain advanced with the television army, Decker held up his index finger indicating a minute. Strapp held out an open palm, telling the media troops to halt, and said something to a coiffed brunette in a blue silk pants suit. She placed her hands on her hips, and shook her head defiantly. Strapp was not impressed and shot back a response, his face hard, his shoulders stiff. The brunette looked upward, threw up her hands, then went back to her underlings. Strapp approached Decker by himself. Gaynor stood back to guard the body, happy to be out of the picture.

Because the captain was a formidable man. He was of average height – a lean man with lean features. But his eyes were knowing, intense. Strapp was a clear thinker and a good problem solver. Deliberate, almost cagy at times. Decker had trouble reading him. So far, the Cap seemed to be a man of his word.

Strapp said, 'Fill me in.'

'I just arrived around fifteen minutes ago.' Decker smoothed his mustache. 'I've sent Martinez in to interview the restaurant personnel, Webster's canvassing the block. We've got at least three additional patrol cars making passes through the area. Gaynor's waiting for the ME and Forensics. I've assigned Oliver and Dunn over to New Chris where Sparks operated and attended.'

Strapp nodded. 'So you know who Azor Sparks is . . . was.'

'Yes, sir. That's why I'm here.'

'Any murder is a blow for our community. Shit like this is an effing big, *black* eye. Whatever you need for this one. Just get it done and get it done quickly.'

'Absolutely.'

'If that means double shifts, then you work double shifts.'

'No problem.' Decker stuck his hands in his pockets, thought of Rina, made a mental note to send her flowers. Better make them roses . . . long stems.

Strapp said, 'You looked at the body?'

'Yes, sir. It's really bad.'

'Jesus, Decker, who'd want to murder someone like Sparks? He *was* New Christian Hospital. Without him, the place is going to fold. Because without him, they aren't going to get the big donors.'

Decker didn't answer. Though Strapp was thinking like the politician, his assessment was right on. Sparks had put New Chris on the map. A tiny hospital, it had become renowned, mostly because Sparks had turned it into his personal place of business. And the hospital had been a tremendous source of revenue for the West Valley, drawing in lots of philanthropists. There had been quite a bit of dollar overflow into the area, the hospital paying for extracurricular school programs, park programs, health programs, as well as extra community-based fire and *police* programs. Just six months ago, New Chris donated a dozen of its old computers to the detectives' squad room.

Strapp said, 'Anything you need to solve this sucker quickly, Decker. Whatever manpower it takes just as long as it's done textbook clean. Has anyone on your team ever had a race or sex problem?'

'Not that I know of,' Decker said. 'Scott Oliver does have a mouth. I wouldn't be surprised if he's said things.'

'Pull him off.'

'No, I don't want to do that.'

Strapp's eyes shot up to Decker's face. 'Why not?'

'Because he's a good detective. I've got him teamed with Dunn. She should keep him clean. Besides, there's nothing controversial here. Sparks was white.'

'What if his killer was black?'

'Why don't we take it one step at a time—'

'I'm just saying, I don't want some A-hole liberal legal eagle making my men out to be monsters. You tell everyone to tread carefully, like we're handling toxic waste.'

'Agreed.'

'You want to take the media, Decker?'

'Not much to tell them yet. Next of kin hasn't been notified yet, so we can't give out any names—'

'Too late. Networks already know who the stiff is.'

Decker was appalled. 'How'd that happen?'

'Obviously some jerk slipped over the scanner.'

'*Christ!*' Decker felt his teeth grind together. 'The family doesn't even know.'

'So get over there and tell them. I'll hold them off as long as I can. But you know these guys. They eat a strict no-ethics diet.'

Decker checked his watch. Nine fifty-two. 'I'm out of here.'

He sprinted back to his Volare, turned on the engine, and peeled rubber. Sparks had lived about ten minutes away from where someone had made his grave. If speed and luck were with him, he'd make it to the house before the ten o'clock news.

Decker identified himself behind a closed door. As soon as it swung open, he breathed a sign of relief. Because the expression on the young woman's face suggested apprehension mixed with ignorance.

She didn't know.

She was pretty – regular features, peaches-and-cream complexion, grass-green eyes, clean, straight, shoulder-length pecan-coloured hair. Appeared to be around twenty, looked like a co-ed with her body buried in baggy jeans and an oversized sweatshirt. Very wholesome face, wore no makeup or jewelry except for a simple cross around her neck. A disembodied voice came from behind her. 'Who's there, Maggie?'

'It's the police,' she answered.

'*Police?*'

23

Decker said, 'Is your mother home, ma'am?'

'She's rest—'

A young man suddenly appeared. Straggly dark curls falling over his forehead. Bright, nervous blue eyes peering beneath the curtain of tresses. Older than the girl, probably in his mid-twenties. He was wrapped in an argyle sweater over a button-down Oxford shirt. His pants were beige chinos, his feet tucker into loafers without socks. 'How can I help you?'

Decker's face remained flat. 'I'm Lieutenant Decker from LAPD. Actually, I came to speak with Dolores Sparks.'

The man said, 'What do you want with my mother?'

'Is she in, sir? It's an emergency.'

'Oh my God!' Maggie shrieked. 'Is it Dad?'

The young man paled. 'My father? Is he okay?'

'May I come in?'

The door opened all the way, and Decker stepped inside a three-story entry, quickly scanned the place. Living room to left, dining room to right, family room straight ahead. It held a set of French doors that opened outward. There were also lots of floor-to-ceiling windows topped with thick valances and tiebacks. Couldn't make out much of the backyard. At this time of the night, it was all fog and shadows.

Decker looked upward. A wrought-iron staircase snaked its way to the top. The house appeared enormous. But the interior, though neat and clean, had seen better days. Peeling wallpaper, scarred wood flooring, chips in the ceiling molding. And old furniture. Thirty years ago, it had been top-notch. But now the upholstery had faded, the pillows were lumpy and lopsided. A spacious house, even in this neighborhood of big homes, though it now sat in genteel neglect.

Decker focused his attention back on the young man with the curly hair and blue eyes.

'Are you Dr. Sparks's son?'

'One of them. Michael. What's this about?'

'I really need to speak to your mother.'

Michael stood his ground. 'First, tell me what's going on.' His voice turned shaky. 'It's Dad, isn't it?'

'Sir, we found a homicide victim about an hour ago. I regret to say that we have reason to believe that it's your fath—'

'Oh my God!' Maggie put her hands over her mouth. 'Oh my God, oh my God, oh my God—'

'Maggie, call Bram.'

'Oh my God! Oh my God—'

Michael grabbed his sister's shoulders. 'Maggie, *go* to the phone and call Bram *now*!'

The order shook her out of her mantra. She dashed to the phone. Decker said, 'I'm very, very sorry, sir. But I really do need to speak to your mother.'

Michael didn't move. His skin had become as transparent as onion skin. In gross contrast to his ebony curls.

A soft voice came from above. 'Michael, what is it?'

Again, Decker looked upward. A woman stood on the upstairs landing, her silver hair clipped short around a round, full face. She wore a multicolored caftan, her skin heavily flushed. Michael's knees caved in, but he recovered before he fell.

Decker put a hand on his shoulder. 'I'll handle it.' He started up the steps, but the young man dogged his heels. Before Decker could speak, Michael said, 'Mom, I think you should go back to bed.'

'Why?' The woman was tall and stolidly built. Beads of sweat covered her forehead and sprinkled the top of her upper lip. Green eyes like her daughter. Clear, focusing sharply on Decker. 'Who are you?'

'Mrs. Sparks, I'm Lieutenant Peter Decker of the Los Angeles Police—'

Michael blurted out, 'He's here about Dad—'

'Something's wrong then.' The woman looked squarely at Decker. But her eyes had already moistened. 'Is it Azor? A car

25

accident? He works late hours, doesn't get enough sleep.'

Decker trudged on. 'Ma'am, we discovered a homicide victim about an hour ago, and have reason to believe it's your husband. I'm very, very sorry.'

The eyes continued to peer into his face. Tears went down her cheeks. She shook her head vehemently. 'No, no, you're wrong, then. Very wrong—'

'Ma'am.'

'Go back and check. Because no one would want to hurt Azor. You have to be *wrong*!'

Michael said, 'Mom, maybe you should—'

Tears flowed openly over her ruddy face. 'Michael, tell this man he's wrong. Tell him he made a big mistake.'

'Mom—'

'I'll call Father right now. Prove he made a mistake.' She stepped forward, then faltered. Decker caught her, kept her upright as she leaned on his strong shoulders. No easy trick. The woman was around five ten and weighed about one seventy. 'Where's her bed?'

'I'll take her.' Michael gripped his mother soundly. He was slightly taller than her, but his hold was firm. 'Let's go back to bed.'

'Oh Michael, what *happened*?'

'I don't know—'

'Did you call Bram?'

'Right now—'

'Maybe he knows. Bram always knows.'

'Maybe, Mom—'

'Tell him to come right away!'

'I will,' Michael said. 'Come on, Mom. You've been sick—'

'Just let me phone Father. To tell this man he's wrong.'

'Mom, he isn't wrong.'

'But he *has* to be wrong! It can't be.'

She started to sob loudly as Michael pulled her into a room.

Then the door closed in Decker's face. Left him standing there, alone and useless. He could make out sounds behind the door – moans, sobs . . . no words. At these moments, he felt like a Peeping Tom, privy to private grief. Dirty and perverted. He could never understand why people watched talk shows. Why see people at their worst?

He exhaled slowly, hoping Dolores Sparks would have enough emotional and physical strength to make it through the night. He would have liked to have questioned her, asked her what her husband had been doing, parked in the back alley behind Tracadero's . . . asked her about Sparks's daily habits. But nothing would have sunk in right now because the woman was still in denial. Perhaps when the shock wasn't as overwhelming, they could talk. Tomorrow, he would try again.

No sense standing around, so he went downstairs. Maggie was shaking, a phone receiver in her right hand. She turned to Decker, her cheeks soaked with tears. 'He's not in. What should I do?'

'Why don't you sit down, Maggie? Is there a doctor I can call? Maybe a close family friend of your mother's?'

Michael came running down the stairs. 'She's asking for Bram, Mag. Is that him?'

'He's not home! I called his apartment *three times* and just got the machine!'

'You called his *apartment*?' Michael sighed. 'Maggie, you should have called the church!'

'Oh God, what's the num— auto-dial-one, right?' She held the receiver to her ear.

Michael began to pace. To Decker, he said, 'I gave her a sedative . . . to calm her down.' He rubbed his face, continued to pace.

Maggie shouted into the receiver. 'Bram, if you're there, *pick* up the phone! This is an emergen . . . Hello? It's Maggie Sparks, can you please get my broth—'

Michael grabbed the phone away from her. 'Get my brother on

27

the phone, now. This is an emergency!' To Maggie, he said, 'Go upstairs and look after Mom. And try not to be so hysterical!'

Maggie dashed up the steps.

Michael yelled into the mouthpiece. 'You've got to get over here quick! There's been a terrible . . .' Tears exploded from Michael's eyes. 'Police are here, Bram. Dad's been murdered.'

Decker could hear a voice over the line saying, 'Oh my God!'

Michael said, 'You'll come over?'

Another pause. Michael saying, 'She's in the bedroom with Maggie. I gave her a sedative . . . No . . . not yet. Can you call them? I can't . . . no . . . no . . . no . . . he said he thought it was Dad, but I'm not sure . . . Look, why don't *you* talk to him?' He shoved the phone in Decker's face, and resumed pacing.

Decker said, 'This is Lieutenant Peter Decker. To whom am I talking, please?'

A beat. Then a soft voice said, 'I'm Dr. Sparks's son, Abram. What happened?'

The voice was calm, especially when compared to the surrounding hysteria. Decker said, 'It would be better if we talked in person.'

'How's my mother?'

'Resting. Your brother gave her a sedative. Is that all right?'

'Yes, that's all right. My brother said my father was murdered. Is this true?'

'Yes, sir, that appears to be the situation. I'm very, very sorry.'

'Are you sure it's him? Has someone identified him?'

'His personal identification was on him – his license, his credit cards, his professional cards. Besides, your father is a recognizable person in this community.'

'I want to see him.'

'I'd be happy to escort you to make an identification.'

'Tell me where to go.'

'I'm sorry but I'll have to escort you. Anything I can do to help you and your family through this terrible crisis?'

Another beat. 'I'm so stunned, I don't . . . May I please talk to my brother again?'

Decker noticed he said 'may' instead of 'can'. Shaken but in control. 'Of course.' He handed the phone back to Michael.

'When are you going to get here?' Michael barked into the phone.

'I'm going down . . . to make sure it's Dad,' Bram answered. 'Someone has to call the others.'

'Can you do it? Maggie's useless and I'm . . . I can't handle Paul right now.'

'All right. I'll do it.'

'When are you going to get here? Mom's asking for you.'

'As soon as I can, Michael. Where's Maggie?'

'With Mom.'

'Mike, watch Mom like a hawk. Keep her away from the medicine cabinet.'

'Right.'

'Also, get Maggie to take her Theo-Dur—'

'She seems okay—'

'As a precaution, Mike. Her attacks are usually delayed. I can't deal with Maggie's asthma right now. Tel Mag to lie down and rest until I can get there.'

Michael nodded.

'Are you there?'

'Sorry, yes. I'll keep watch over Mom.'

'And Maggie too. Take care of *both* of them. Are you getting this down, Michael?'

'Yes, keep watch over Mom. And Maggie, too. Just get here.'

'As soon as I can. Put Decker back on.'

'Who?'

'The lieutenant.'

'Oh . . .' Again, Michael gave the phone to Decker.

'Yes?'

Bram said, 'Do you know where the Church of St. Thomas is, Lieutenant?'

'Of course.'

'How far is it from where my father . . . ?'

'I could meet you at St. Thomas's if you'd like, Mr. Sparks.'

'Thank you very much. I'd appreciate it. I need to call my other siblings. To tell them what's going on. I'll meet you outside the church in twenty minutes.'

'That's fine.'

The phone disconnected.

Michael said, 'Is he coming over?'

'No,' Decker said. 'First he wants to identify your father. I'm picking him up in front of St. Thomas's.'

'God . . .' Michael paced furiously. 'I hope he gets here quick. I don't think I can handle the others by myself!'

'Who are the others?' Decker asked. 'Your siblings?'

Maggie came running down the stairs. 'Michael, she's moaning. What should I do?'

'I'm coming.' Michael bit his nail. To Decker, he said, 'Excuse me a moment.' He started up the stairs with his sister. 'Oh, Maggie. Take your Theo-Dur. As a precaution.'

'I'm all right—'

'Just do it, Mag. Don't argue.'

Maggie seemed angry but said nothing. As they climbed up a serpentine twist of staircase, they disappeared from view, leaving Decker down below in the faded dowager of a house. He took the opportunity to nose around, went into the family room.

The walls held no artwork. Instead, they were plastered with family photos. The Sparkses appeared to have lots of children, although some of the adults could have been daughters- or sons-in-law.

The most striking photos were two fourteen-by-twenties framed in gilt. The sittings appeared almost identical. Obviously, they had been taken on the same occasion, and it had been a formal one. Dad had been decked out in a tux; Mom, in a blue sequined gown.

The men wore dark suits, the women expensive suits or cocktail dresses.

The first photograph held many more people — the parents, their children with spouses, lots of grandchildren, ranging from teens to infants. Too many people for Decker to sort out.

The second photograph was more manageable. Eight people. The parents – Azor and Dolores – with four young men and two young women, among them Michael and Maggie. Probably their children because all of them bore resemblance to their parents. Though the dress had been formal, the posing had been much more casual. All the parties seemed relaxed – no frozen smiles, no stiff postures. Everyone seemed to be having a good time.

The kids broke down into two groups: Dad's side with black, curly hair and blue eyes, and Mom's side with light brown hair and green eyes. Michael and another brother looked like Dad, the other men, Maggie and a sister favored Mom.

Decker took a closer look at the photo. One brother wore a clerical collar. St. Thomas's was a Catholic church. Perhaps brother Bram was actually Father Bram. No wonder he had been so composed over the phone. The clergy were used to dealing with crises.

A good-looking man in a pale, scholarly way. A face with regular features, and accented cheekbones. Sharp, sea-colored eyes behind the rimless glasses. Oak-brown hair and long. It fell past his shoulders.

Decker continued to examine the picture, then did a double take. Another brother standing next to Dad. Bram's face but without the academic pallor and glasses. Fleshier in the cheeks with shorter, styled hair.

Michael came down the stairway. 'She's sleeping, but it's restless.'

'Do you have a family doctor you want to call, Michael?'

'No, not really. Dad has always handled our medical care. We're generally a very healthy bunch, including Mom. Maggie's with her. She'll be okay.'

31

Decker pointed to the picture. 'You have twin brothers?'

Michael's eyes went to the photograph. 'Actually, triplets. Luke and Bram . . .' He pointed to the faces. 'These two are identical twins obviously. They look even more alike now that Luke has taken off a few pounds.'

'Bram's a priest.'

'Yeah. But we're not Catholic. Only he is.'

'Who's the other triplet?'

'Paul.' Michael's coloring had returned. 'He looks more like me than his own twins. That's genetics. Toss of the dice. This one is my older sister, Eva. She was born after the triplets. She's kind of . . . well, my mother's favorite after Bram. I think Mom was really happy to get a girl after three boys.'

'I can imagine. How old are your sibs?'

'Triplets are thirty-five, Eva's thirty.'

'And you're . . .'

'I'm twenty-five. Maggie's twenty.'

'Your mom had children every five years.'

'I guess she did.'

'When was that picture taken?'

'For my dad's sixtieth birthday . . . about two years ago. Seems like a hundred years ago.'

Michael rubbed his eyes.

'I feel like such a jerk. I'm a med student. Second year. I've been to Africa on missionary work. I've taken care of very sick people. I shouldn't be falling apart like this. I should be doing better. Dad wouldn't approve.'

'You're doing great under the circumstances, Michael.'

'I don't think so . . .'

Decker patted his back.

Dad wouldn't approve.

Said a lot about the kid. Twenty-five, a med student, and still concerned about what Dad might think. Must be hard to be a son of a legend. Hard to forge that own identity. Said something for

Michael that he chose to go into his father's field, knowing that people would always be making comparisons.

Michael said, 'It's just that it's such a shock. What happened? *How'd* it happen?'

'He was found dead in his car.'

'Where?' Michael bit his nails as he walked back and forth. 'In the hospital parking lot? I've told Dad those places aren't safe. I've told him a hundred times that he should carry Mace or pepper spray. Something. Anything.'

'It happened in a back alley of Tracadero's restaurant.'

Michael stopped walking 'What? Where?'

'In back of Tracadero's,' Decker repeated. 'Any idea what he was doing there?'

'None whatsoever.'

'Does your father eat at Tracadero's?'

'Maybe for a special occasion. Like one of our birthdays. Dad does like good food.' Michael bit his lower lip. 'Mostly, he ate at the hospital. He practically lived at the hospital.'

'Not home a lot?'

'Almost never except for Sundays.'

'Your mom is a nervous type?'

'No, not at all.' Michael became tense. 'Why do you ask that?'

'Just because you keep sedatives in the house. I get the feeling she's used to taking them.'

'Oh . . . only occasionally . . . to help her sleep. Usually she's full of energy. The woman is tireless. Dad was never home when we were growing up. She raised us all really by herself. That's why she needs sedatives . . . she's so full of energy, if she doesn't take them, she doesn't sleep.'

Nothing to do with anxiety, guy? Instead, Decker nodded sympathetically. How people deny. He checked his watch. 'I've got to leave to meet your brother. Are you going to be all right by yourselves?'

'Yes . . . I'm . . . yeah, I'm okay. Just tell Bram . . . as quick as

33

he can.' Michael looked seasick. 'I mean . . . tell him everything's under control . . . but if he could . . .'

'I'll give him the message.' Decker regarded the young med student. He was dog-paddling, barely breaking surface, in an ocean of shock and grief. 'Are you sure you'll be okay?'

'Yes,' Michael insisted. 'Yes, I can handle it. Thank you, Lieutenant. Thank you for . . . I don't know why I'm thanking you . . . I don't know what I'm doing. Please tell Bram to hurry.'

'He takes care of the family, doesn't he?'

Michael wiped tears from his eyes. 'Bram takes care of the world.'

4

Impressive in size and Gothic in style, the church of the Holy Order
of St. Thomas would have felt at home on the banks of the Thames.
It was especially noticeable because West Valley architecture was
typically confined to blocklong shopping malls, and anywhere
USA strip malls. True, there were a few magnificent million-
dollar-plus housing developments. But the vast majority of the
homes located within Devonshire Substation area were one-story
ranch houses – three bedroom, two bath – serviceable and modest.
The church's spire loomed above its residential neighbors,
overlooking its domain like a prison turret.

As Decker pulled the Volare curbside to the front steps, a thin
man dressed in jeans, a black corduroy blazer over a black shirt,
and running shoes bounded down the stairs. As he got closer,
Decker saw the clerical collar. The man peered into the window.

'Lieutenant?'

Decker nodded, opened the passenger door.

The priest slid inside, shutting the door with excess force.
Threw Decker a glance, then put on his seat belt. Decker studied
the clergyman for a moment. Streaks of gray at the temple, wavy
creases in his forehead. He was fine-featured, almost pretty.
Dressed in satin and lace, he could have walked out of a Gains-
borough. Except for the eyes – alert, too intelligent for peerage
foppery.

Decker said, 'I'm sorry to meet you under these circumstances,
Father.'

The priest nodded. 'How's my mother doing?'

'Pretty well, considering.' Decker pulled away from the church.

35

'Michael's anxious for you to be there.'

'I should be there. But I need to be here. I need a clone.'

Decker nodded. The priest had said *clone*, not *twin*.

Ergo, the twin was obviously not a clone. Not the right time to press him on that.

Bram pushed locks off his forehead. His hair wasn't quite as long as it had been in the pictures. But it still brushed his shoulders. Didn't look like the padres Decker had seen growing up in southern Florida. Modern times. Modern priests.

'I managed to reach all my siblings except for my brother Paul. My brother-in-law is trying to reach him. Is there a way I can call out?'

Decker picked up the mike, asked for the number. The priest gave him the digits. A moment later, an angry male voice came through the static of dispatch.

Calmly, Bram said, 'Hi, it's me again. Did you reach Paul yet?'

'About two seconds ago. Are you at the house?'

'No, I'm—'

'You've *got* to get over there. Eva's distraught. I don't trust her to be alone.'

'Michael's there—'

'Michael!' The voice turned sarcastic. 'Oh, that's a great comfort—'

'David—'

'I'm nervous . . . letting Eva drive by herself. You know how hysterical she can get. But she insisted. Our live-in's vacationing in El Salvador and I can't get a baby-sitter at this hour.' His voice grew louder. 'It's almost eleven. Where the hell are you, Bram?'

'With the po—'

'Paul's asking me all these questions. Like *I* have the inside dope. How the hell do *I* know what's going on? What *is* going on?'

'David, I hate to cut you off, but I'm talking on an open mike and the lieutenant can hear everything we're saying. Let's wait until we can talk in private.'

36

'Well, when are you going to the house?'

'As soon as I identify the body as my father's.'

Silence. Then the voice said, 'I'm sorry, Bram, I'm . . .'

'It's all right, David. I've got to hang up now. We'll talk later.' Bram handed the line to Decker who hung up the mike. The priest slumped in his seat.

Decker waited a beat. 'They depend on you, don't they?'

Looking out the window, Bram said, 'How far are we from the spot?'

'About ten minutes away.'

'Where was he found?'

'In his car. It was parked in a back alley behind Tracadero's.'

Bram faced Decker. 'Tracadero's?'

'Any idea why he would be there?'

'No.' He shook his head. 'None.'

'Have you ever been there with him?'

Bram exhaled aloud. 'Dad rented out the back room a couple of years ago for Mom's birthday. There are about thirty of us with all the kids and in-laws. But there was nothing going on with the family tonight.'

'He never goes there without the family?'

'I wouldn't think so. Dad rarely goes out because he's always on-call.'

'Your brother said he practically lives at the hospital.'

Again, Bram brushed hair from his eyes. 'Only thing I can think of is maybe Dad was meeting someone from the drug company for dinner.'

'Drug company?'

'My dad had developed an important surgery drug in his lab in conjunction with Fisher/Tyne Pharmaceuticals. It's currently being tested by the FDA.'

Decker took in his words. 'Your father developed a drug for Fisher/Tyne?'

'Yes. Curedon. Some kind of post surgical, anti-rejection drug.

My father's a heart transplant surgeon. I guess you know that.'

'Yes, I do.' Decker paused. 'I hate to ask you this, Father. This drug, Curedon, that your father developed. I take it there's money involved?'

Bram thought a moment. 'No doubt. Why?'

'We're at the beginning stages of this investigation. I don't have a smoking gun. I'm looking for suspects. I'm scratching for motives. Money's always a good one. How much money are we talking about? Big amounts?'

'Honestly, I don't know. You might ask Michael about it. He'd know more than I would.'

'So he often has dinner with someone from Fisher/Tyne at Tracadero's?'

'Actually, I don't know anything, Lieutenant. I'm just guessing.'

Decker smoothed his pumpkin mustache. 'So your father is a chemist on top of his other many talents?'

'By default. About fifteen years ago, he decided he didn't like what was commercially available. So he went back to UCLA and got a Ph.D. in biochemistry. The hospital – New Christian Hospital – built him a lab.' Bram clasped his hands tightly. 'Could be he went out to dinner with one of his colleagues. But that doesn't sound like my father, either.'

'Who are your father's colleagues?'

'You mean names?'

'If you don't mind.'

Bram nodded. 'Dr. Reginald Decameron, Dr. Myron Berger and . . . goodness, I'm blanking . . . the woman . . . not Heather. That's his secretary.'

'Who's his secretary?'

'Heather . . . Heather . . .' Bram looked up. 'At thirty-five, I'm going senile. Heather something. The other doctor is also a woman.'

'They all work in your dad's lab?'

'Yes.'

'So they're your father's employees?'

'I think there's a bit more parity than a typical boss-underling relationship. They're all doctors. But yes, my father did hire them.' He paused, his eyes darting behind his spectacles. 'Fulton. Elizabeth Fulton. Doctor Liz, he called her. That's the other doctor.'

'And you think your father might have gone out for dinner with one of them?'

'Maybe it was one of their birthdays. I don't know.' Bram adjusted his glasses. 'From the questions you're asking, you don't think it was a random murder, do you?'

'At this point, I'm still assessing information, Father. I'm sorry I can't be more helpful to you.'

Bram looked out the window, rubbed his eyes under his glasses 'What a nightmare!'

'I appreciate you coming down to make a positive identification. Better you than your mother.'

'That's for certain.'

'Is she a well woman?'

'Why? What happened at the house?'

'Nothing at all. It's just that . . . well, she takes sedatives.'

'And . . . ?'

'Uh, no. Nothing else. I was just curious why she took medication to help her sleep.'

'Lots of people do. It means nothing.'

'True.'

Bram said, 'You're sure it's him? The body, I mean.'

'Certain enough to call you.'

The priest looked upward. 'Are you going to perform an autopsy?'

'With homicide, it's the law.'

'So burial will be delayed?'

'Hopefully it wouldn't take too long. Several days. Maybe a week.'

'Perhaps that's better,' Bram said. 'Maybe we'll do some kind of . . . memorial service . . . for the public tomorrow. For Dad's friends and colleagues. Get the circus over with. Then, when you release the body, we can have a private burial service for just the family.' He sighed. 'I'm thinking like a priest. Step one, do this. Step two, do that.'

'Someone has to make arrangements. Your family seems to depend on you.'

Bram fell quiet.

Decker said, 'Michael told me you're not only an identical twin, but actually a triplet. Three boys.'

'Yes.'

'Is your twin a priest?'

'No.'

'What does your brother do? Your twin.'

Bram looked away, pretending not to hear. The priest was forthcoming when talking about Dad and his professional life. As soon as Decker brought up the family, Bram reverted to one-word answers.

'Does your brother work?' Decker pressed.

'What?' Bram's eyes stared at nothing. 'Pardon?'

'What does your twin brother do?'

'Luke's a drug and alcohol rehabilitation counselor.'

'Another one in the helping profession,' Decker said.

Bram was quiet.

'Where does he work?' Decker paused. 'Are my questions getting on your nerves, Father? I don't want to upset you.'

'You can call me Bram. Everyone else does.' The priest rubbed his eyes. 'I know you have to ask basic questions. I don't resent them or you. Luke works at the Bomb Shelter.'

Decker paused. The Bomb Shelter was a halfway house with a reputation for hiring former addicts and rehabilitated ex-cons as counselors. 'Does he live there?'

'No.'

40

'He's married? Single? Divorced?'

'Luke's married. Has a couple of kids.'

'Is your brother an ex-user?' Decker asked.

'Lieutenant, if you want personal information about Luke, ask Luke.'

'Fair enough. How about your brother Paul? What kind of work does he do?'

'He's a stockbroker. Married. Four kids. My sister Eva's married as well. She and her husband own a chain of clothing stores. They have four children under the age of seven. A fertile bunch. Making up for me. You've met Mike. He's in his second year of medical school, lives at home, going with a very nice girl from the church. Dad's church, not mine. I'm the only Catholic in the bunch. Magdeleine's the baby of the family. She's in her second year of college at UCLA. Psych major. She wants to be a social worker. That's the family in a nutshell.'

'I appreciate you talking to me.'

Bram sank into silence.

Decker glanced at the priest, but said nothing. Usually, people under these circumstances . . . all they needed was a prompt or two and they became fountains of verbal diarrhea. They spoke from raw-edged nerves, from gut-stinging anxiety, spitting out whatever came to mind. This one was quiet. Not uncooperative, but he spoke with measured words.

And then it dawned on Decker. Bram was a priest. Secrecy was his stock-in-trade.

They drove without speaking the rest of the way, Decker slowing as they neared the spot. 'Over to the right.'

Bram glared out the window. 'There are *television* cameras! How did *they* find out before *I* did?'

'Networks have people listening to local police scanners. A famous name like your father's pops up—'

'Oh for goodness . . .' Bram was taut and angry. 'Is there no privacy even in *grief*?'

41

Decker was quiet.

'What a crazy town,' the priest said. 'Bare your soul to the world for your ten minutes of fame.'

'Don't worry. I'll get you through. You might want to duck just in case someone gets pushy.'

Bram slid down into his seat. Quickly, Decker drove up to the barricades, flashed ID to the uniforms who kept watch over the scene. Before Decker could roll up the window, a microphone was jammed into his face. Holding it was a woman crowned with an over-sprayed hive of blonde hair. Decker pressed the accelerator to the floor, almost taking the mike with him as the Volare thrust forward. In the distance, he could hear the blonde swearing.

Bram sat back up, his complexion wan. 'It's not that I haven't seen bodies . . . or haven't seen people die as a matter of fact.'

'It's different when it's your own.'

The priest said nothing. As they closed in on the Buick, a gasp escaped from his lips. In stark view was the meat wagon. Bold letters holding nothing back—

LOS ANGELES COUNTY MORGUE.

Bram looked at his lap. Decker felt for him. *Welcome to hell, buddy. How long will you be staying?*

Two white-coated lab assistants gleamed like headlights under the back alley illumination. They were hunched over, peering inside the Buick, one of them holding the body bag. Next to them was the police photographer who was making lightning with her Nikon. Jay Craine's car was parked a few stores down. Decker couldn't see the Medical Examiner. Probably kneeling, examining the body.

Decker shut the motor. Bram started to open the door, but Decker held his arm. 'Wait here.'

The priest had turned gray.

Decker said, 'Do you feel sick?'

'Just the stench,' Bram said. 'It's okay. I'll get used to it.'

'Give me a moment, Father, to clear things. You're sure you're not sick?'

'I'll survive.'

Decker got out of the car. Farrell Gaynor was in front of the Buick's grille.

'Sparks is still in the car?' Decker asked.

'Yep. Craine's just about done. Ready to load him on the wagon.' Gaynor scratched his nose. 'Who you got in the car?'

'Sparks's son. One of his sons. He's a priest.'

'So the son is actually the father?'

Despite the grimness, Decker smiled. 'I don't want him to see his father sprawled out like that. We'll bag him first, put him on a stretcher. Then I'll bring the son over to make the ID.'

'Will do.'

Decker went over to the car. Craine stood up from his knees, took a step back when he saw Decker, and brought a hand to his chest. 'Do you always sneak up on people, Lieutenant?'

'Sorry, Jay. What do you have?'

Craine appeared pensive. 'Body's still warm, no rigor evident. The homicide's quite recent. But you don't need me to tell you that.'

Gaynor said, 'Yeah, Loo, I meant to tell you. Scott Oliver called while you were gone. Sparks was at the hospital today. Last anyone remembers, he finished up a meeting with a bunch of doctors around eight. Nobody seems to know what Sparks was doing here. At Tracadero's, that is. Because he had dinner at the hospital. At least, that's what his secretary said. Her name is Heather Manley.'

'Is she still at the hospital?'

'I don't know where Scotty talked to her. On the phone or at the hospital.'

'So the great man was last seen about eight.' Craine snapped up his black bag. 'It's now quarter to eleven. You have an accurate time frame. Better than the one that science could provide.'

'Did you know him, Jay?'

'I knew of him, Lieutenant. Everyone knew about Dr. Sparks.' Craine turned away. 'This is very difficult. Seeing such a man as he ... butchered like this.'

'Tell me about the murder.'

'Shots to the head and neck. Severed his brain stem. Most likely that was the primary cause of death. The other savagery ... the chest wounds. I'd say they were postmortem. Someone was very strong and very angry. To crack the sternum and rib cage and expose his heart. A long knife with a big blade. I found some pulverized bone matter. Anything might have been used to smash the chest cavity. A crowbar, a baseball bat. A hammer or a mallet.'

'Things easily found in any car or toolbox or kitchen,' Decker said.

'Yes,' Craine agreed. 'Whoever did this was a strong person.'

'Male then?'

'I would think. Even a strong woman ... to do this much damage ...' Craine furrowed his brown in concentration. 'If I were you, I'd be looking for someone with a penis.'

Gaynor held back a smile. 'Smashing up the chest and exposing the heart. Sounds like someone was making a statement.'

'Indubitably.' Craine took off his gloves. 'We'll take him to the morgue now. Autopsy will be done first thing tomorrow.'

Decker said, 'I have one of Dr. Sparks's sons in the car. He's come down to make the ID.'

'It's Azor,' Craine said. 'I'll state it formally, if you'd like. Save the man some agony.'

'I think he knows it's his father. I think he just wants to see it for himself.'

'Good gracious why?'

'He's a priest,' Gaynor said. 'Maybe he wants to perform last rites on him.'

'Can you do last rites on someone who's deceased?' Decker asked. 'Besides, Azor Sparks wasn't Catholic.'

'He was very religious,' Craine said. 'Everyone knew about

44

Azor Sparks, his Fundamentalist beliefs, and his commitment to God.' The ME paused. 'Perhaps he did have a hot line to the Supreme Being. He certainly saved a lot of lives.'

Decker said, 'I'll bring the priest over as soon as your men put him in the bag and on to the stretcher. I don't want him to see the crime scene.'

'Very considerate of you, Lieutenant,' Craine muttered. 'Very considerate. Copious amounts of spatter. The image is haunting even for the most professional of us. Goodnight.'

Gaynor watched as Craine got into his car and drove away. 'He seemed upset. Well, maybe not upset. More like . . . affected.'

'Aren't we all.' Decker shook his head. 'Where're Webster and Martinez?'

'On Dumpster patrol.' Gaynor pointed into the darkness. 'See those blips of light?'

'I don't see anything.'

'Good thing about getting old,' Gaynor said. 'You become very farsighted. I see the flashlights. Maybe they're about a block and a half, two blocks down. Want me to get them on the walkie-talkie?'

Decker peered down the empty space, trying to make out light. 'No, I'll talk to them later. Let me get the identification over with.' He turned his eyes back to the scene. They had loaded Sparks onto a stretcher. 'Clear the decks for me, Farrell. Give the son some breathing room.'

Decker walked back to the Volare, opened the passenger door. Bram got out, balancing his weight on the car before he stood up.

'You need help?'

'No.'

'Over here.' Decker led the priest to the stretcher, the body encased in a vinyl bag. He nodded to an attendant who unzipped a portion of the plastic sheath.

The priest glanced downward, quickly averted his eyes, then stepped backward. '*Dear God!*'

Decker peeked. Dead eyes stared upward at the foggy moon. He took the priest's arm, but Bram shook him off.

'I'm all right.' He covered his mouth, then let his hands drop. 'I'm all right. I want to see him again.'

Decker stared at him.

'Please,' Bram said quietly. 'Please, I need to see him again. Have them unzip the bag.'

Decker nodded to the attendants. Again, they opened the vinyl casket. The priest came forward, forced his eyes downward. Without warning, he dropped to his knees and crossed himself. Closed his eyes and clasped his hands. He brought his fists to his forehead and prayed, his mouth incanting a slurry of what sounded like Latin. Decker crooked his finger, beckoning the lab men away from the stretcher.

Give the man his illusion of privacy.

5

The last registered event in Dr. Azor Sparks's daily calendar was an in-house dinner meeting with three people: Reg, Myron, and Liz. It took only a quick call to Sparks's secretary – Heather Manley – for Oliver to find out that Reg was Dr. Reginald Decameron, Myron was Dr. Myron Berger, and Liz was Dr. Elizabeth Fulton. This entry was one of many that had appeared in Sparks's business book – a semiweekly research meeting of some sort, according to the secretary, Heather. And the dinner meetings were always held in Sparks's conference room, not at Tracadero's. That was all he could glean before Heather's hysteria broke through.

Oliver's eyes moved off the pages of Sparks's daily planner and scanned the office. Place was twice as big as his apartment. A hell of a lot nicer, too. Wood-paneled walls, plush hunter green carpeting, surround-sound stereo speakers, wet bar, and fridge – all this plus a canyon view of the nearby mountains. True, there was no booze in the bar, only fruit juices, but that could be remedied. He cast his gaze on the ceiling-mounted television set. To Marge, he said, 'Maybe we should turn on the TV.'

Marge shut Sparks's top desk drawer. Nothing of substance in it. She tried the file drawers in his walnut desk, then the ones in his credenza. Locked, of course. 'Think you're outta luck, Scotty. He probably doesn't subscribe to *Adam and Eve*.'

'How kind of you to sum me up as a horndog.' Oliver began putting stickums on Sparks's planner. 'I just wanted to see if the murder hit the networks yet. Because as soon as it gets out, hospital's going to be thrown into a panic. Just like his secretary.

Where the hell is she? She said she only lives fifteen minutes away. It's not exactly rush hour.'

Marge investigated a wall of built-in bookshelves, her finger moving over the spines of thick medical tomes. 'Didn't she say she was going to call up his co-workers?'

'Three doctors. How long does it take to call up three doctors?' Marge shrugged. 'Sure, turn on the set.'

Oliver stretched and flipped the power on the ceiling-mounted TV. The monitor filled with a dark image – the climax of some series cop show. He watched an actress in a police uniform chase a bad guy, her breasts jiggling and heaving as she followed him to an alley. Her pants were skintight, showed off a well-formed ass as she peeked around a garbage can. Oliver's eyes crept over to Marge. She was dressed in a baggy pantsuit and had gunboats on her feet.

'See anything interesting in his book?' Marge asked.

'Nothing that means anything to me.' Oliver paged through his notes. 'Patient names, procedures, surgeries, staff meetings, reminders for birthdays and anniversaries . . . quite a few of those. Maybe he owned stock in a greeting card company.'

Marge glanced at the wood paneling. Interspersed with numerous diplomas and certificates were family photographs. 'Looks like Sparks had lots of children and grandchildren. What a shame!'

Zing went the bullet against the trash can on TV. The heavy-breasted actress jumped back. Her makeup was still perfect, not a drop of sweat sullied her brow. Man, if that had been him, he'd be browning his jockeys. Oliver said, 'Sparks had lots of meetings with various companies.'

'Which ones?'

'Biolab, Meditech, Genident, Bloodcell, Armadonics, Fisher/ Tyne – that name came up on a regular basis. About once a month. Isn't that a drug company?'

'Yeah.' Marge scratched her head. 'My God, he was a busy bee.

Wrote two medical textbooks, co-authored another four, and was an editor of a dozen others. Where did he find time to do all this?'

Oliver's eyes went back to the TV. The big-boobed cop was now draped in a filmy nightie. She lay in bed, nestled in the arms of a stud with a deep voice and a cleft chin. As she talked, Mr. Cleft looked at the babe with the expression 'Jesus, I'm an earnest guy' stamped across his puss. Okay, so he wasn't humping her bones. Which would have been the real picture if this was real life. Okay. So maybe they had just humped, and he was older and had a long refractory period. Oliver could *maybe* buy that. What he couldn't buy was the fact that he was *listening* to her. In real life, the guy would be completely zoned out, thinking about tax dodges or rotary baseball.

Marge checked her watch. 'Manley does seem to be taking her time.'

'Lucky the janitor had a key,' Oliver said. 'What'd you think about her reaction to the news?'

'After I got my hearing back?'

'Yeah, I could hear her scream across the room. Most people, upon hearing news that their boss was popped, are stunned. They don't say anything.'

'Heather's obviously the hysterical type.'

'All women are the hysterical type,' Oliver pronounced. 'But Manley letting go with a wallop like that . . . weird. My head's still ringing.'

Marge smiled, continued going over the books in Sparks's shelves. 'Heather reacted as if she was more to Sparks than just a secretary.'

'I have no trouble believing that,' Oliver said. 'According to his daily calendar, he spent most of his waking hours at the hospital. And Heather is a nice piece of pie.'

'How do you know what she looks like?'

'Pictures on her desk.'

'She keeps pictures of herself on her desk?'

'Nah, pictures of her and some guy. But you know how it is. Secretaries and their bosses. Especially someone like Sparks. Power is the ultimate lady-killer. How else do you explain ugly, old guys getting laid by nymphets?'

'Well, if Sparks was boffing her, he's your typical religious fanatic hypocrite.'

'Don't let Decker hear you say that.' Oliver paused. 'Why do you say that?'

'Because he's got three bookshelves filled with religious material – Christian newspapers and magazines, lots of prayer-books and numerous Bibles.' Marge shrugged. 'Maybe Sparks and Heather read Bible together.'

Oliver laughed. 'Well, I have no trouble believing that sweet Heather was on her knees.'

The door pushed open. A female voice screaming, 'Just *what* do you think you're doing!'

Marge brought her index finger to her right ear and rubbed it against the skinflap. Oliver held out ID.

The young woman was in her late twenties with big, big hair. Lots of it spilling down her shoulders and back. She was slim, wore a red knit dress that showed off curves. She whacked Oliver's shield away. 'I don't care *who* you are! You have no right to invade my boss's *privacy*!'

The news came on the TV. Sure enough, Sparks's death had made the headlines. The young woman burst into a crescendo of wails. 'I can't believe it. I *can't* believe it!'

'Ms. Manley,' Oliver said tentatively, 'why don't you sit down?'

She pulled on her overteased tresses, her saucer eyes spilling tears as she yanked. 'Who would hurt the doctor? He was the gentlest person on the face of the earth! Why would anyone *hurt* him?'

'Ms. Manley, why don't you sit down?' Marge mouthed to Oliver, 'Turn the damn thing off!'

Oliver cut off the newscaster midsentence. Heather was still moaning. He said, 'Why don't you sit, Ms. Manley?'

She continued to pace.

Oliver said, 'Sit down, ma'am . . . as in *sit* down in a chair.'

The secretary stopped treading, stared at Oliver. He pulled out the chair. 'Please?'

She sat, the hem of her dress resting midthigh over smooth, white legs. Oliver did a rapid once-over, then said, 'We need your help, ma'am. Did you get hold of any of the doctors that were at Sparks's six o'clock meeting?'

Heather sniffed loudly. 'Dr. Decameron said he's on his way over here. Dr. Fulton . . . she can't come down because she can't get a baby-sitter. And her husband isn't home yet. The dirty rat is *never* home. He's a real jerk, suffers from a Peter Pan complex.'

Marge took out her notepad. 'Now this Dr. Fulton is one of Dr. Sparks's co-workers?'

'Yes.' Heather pulled a Kleenex out of her purse, blew her nose and dried her eyes. 'She works with Dr. Sparks on Curedon. They all do.'

'Who's all?' Oliver was having trouble following Heather's train of thought.

'Dr. Decameron, Dr. Fulton and Dr. Berger. They work with Dr. Sparks, testing his drug, Curedon.'

Oliver perked up. 'Dr. Sparks discovered a new drug?'

'He didn't *discover* a new drug,' Heather corrected. 'He *developed* one. After years of research in his laboratory. Curedon is an antirejection drug. Fisher/Tyne bought it.'

'What do you mean, bought it?' Marge asked.

Heather sighed. 'I'm not sure. You'll have to ask Dr. Decameron and hope for the best.'

'Hope for the best?' Oliver asked.

'Reggie is a jerk. Try getting any answers out of him. I don't know why Dr. Sparks puts up with him.' Heather wiped her eyes again. 'Actually, I do know why. The doctor was the best boss I've ever had. The most honest, sincere, nicest, gentlemanly . . . not that he didn't have his moments. But once you understood his genius . . .' She exploded into a new wave of sobs.

'How long had you worked for him, Ms. Manley?' Oliver asked.

'Five years,' she cried.

'You were close to him?' asked Marge.

'I *loved* him!' she wailed.

Marge and Oliver exchanged glances. Heather caught it. 'Not in the way you think. I loved him as in "*hopelessly* in love" with him. He never laid a finger on me.'

Maybe not a finger, Oliver thought.

Heather said, 'He was a gentleman in every way. Completely devoted to his wife and family. He wouldn't ever think of touching another woman, much less have an affair. He was deeply religious.'

Again, Marge and Oliver looked at each other. Oliver said, 'You sound like you're pretty sure about that.'

'I'm positive!'

'You know, Heather, if you're trying to lead us down the wrong path—'

'I'm not—'

'I'm not saying you are,' Oliver said. 'All I'm saying is that if something was kinky with Sparks, it's going to come out.'

'Nothing . . . and I mean *nothing* . . . was ever kinky with Dr. Sparks! The only thing he ever got into trouble for was being *too* good.'

'How's that?' Marge asked.

'Like I said, he was deeply religious. He had tremendous faith in God and didn't understand those who didn't—'

'Oh *please*, Heather, spare them the Jesus on the cross routine!' A forty-plus man stuck out his hand to Marge. 'Reginald Decameron. This is just horrible! It's already made the news! I heard it coming over. Someone want to tell me what's going on?'

Marge regarded the doctor. Slender, well-coiffed, well-dressed. Thin features, piercing dark eyes. Self-assured to the point of haughtiness. He wore white shirt, grey slacks, and a blue cashmere blazer. Pocket handkerchief in the blazer, hand-painted silk jacquard around his neck. She took the proffered hand. 'Thank you for coming down.'

'How could I *not* come down?' He turned to Heather. 'Where are Dr. Berger and Dr. Fulton?'

'They can't make it—'

'*What?*' Decameron was outraged. 'Azor is . . . *murdered*, and they can't see fit to talk to the police?'

'Dr. Fulton couldn't get a baby-sitter, Dr. Decameron. Her husband wasn't home when I called.'

'And what was Myron's excuse?' Decameron raised his brow. 'Bad hair day?'

Heather glared at him. 'How can you be so awful at a time like this?'

'What better time?' Decameron snapped back. He hugged himself, looked Oliver up and down. 'This is truly horrid. What in the world happened?'

Oliver squirmed under Decameron's intense but rapid scrutiny. Overt, sexual overtones. The man was gay. 'That's what we're trying to figure out, Dr. Decameron.'

Marge stepped in. 'As we understand it, Dr. Decameron, you, Dr. Berger and Dr. Fulton last saw Dr. Sparks at a dinner meeting.'

'Yes, one of our weekly staff get-togethers. Started around six, ended around eight.'

'Anything unusual happen at the meeting?'

It was Decameron's turn to squirm. 'Well, I might as well fess up. Myron's going to jump at the opportunity to tell you this. It might as well come from me.'

The room fell silent.

'Azor was miffed at me,' Decameron admitted.

'What happened?' Oliver asked.

'Well, our research meetings are ostensibly an open forum to exchange ideas. Sometimes I get a little aggressive in my opinions offending our great Grand Imperial Wizard.'

'That's not what *I* heard,' Heather piped in.

'I'm getting to that, child. Hold your hair, for goodness sakes.' Decameron turned to Marge. 'Azor became miffed at me. I peeked at some of the great doctor's data on his fax machine before he had a chance to see it. Not a terrible thing. But not courteous, either.' He paused. 'Azor was angry. After the meeting . . . after Myron and Liz had left . . . I smoothed things over with him. Of course, they weren't around to witness it. But I am telling you the truth.'

'What time was this, Dr. Decameron?'

'A little before eight. I remember it distinctly because we ended earlier than usual. Azor had received a call from one of his sons and cut the meeting short.'

'Okay.' Marge wrote furiously. 'Does this son have a name?'

'Paul.'

'Was Dr. Sparks planning to meet Paul somewhere?'

'I haven't the faintest idea. His sons call often. They're always hitting him up for money.'

'That's ridiculous,' Heather interjected.

Decameron paused. 'Okay. Paul and Luke are always hitting him up for money. True or false?'

Heather snapped her lips together, folded her arms across her chest.

'How many sons does Dr. Sparks have?' Oliver asked.

'Four.' Decameron said, 'The youngest one, Michael, he's what we call a legacy med student. Someone who gets in because of . . . connections. I call them capons.'

'Michael's not bright?' Oliver asked.

'Neon, he's not,' Decameron replied. 'But he is young. He could season if he'd cut the strings. He still lives at home, so the little snot gets whatever he wants—'

'You don't like his kids, do you?' Oliver said.

'I don't like anyone, so don't go by me.' Decameron sighed. 'No, I don't like his children. They're all suck-ups. Except the priest. He's independent so far as I can tell. And a good man.'

'Who's he?' Oliver asked.

Heather said, 'Father Bram.'

Decameron said, 'Azor was livid when Bram took his orders. First, Bram had the nerve to convert from Azor's strict fundamentalist Church to Catholicism without asking Daddy's permission. And then when he became a priest . . . well, what can I say? The truth hurts.'

'What truth?' Heather asked.

'Darling, what do you think?' Decameron's eyes roved between Oliver and Marge. 'Bram is clearly gay—'

'What are you *talking* about?' Heather asked.

'The whole family's in heavy denial. Because to Azor, et al, homosexuality is still an abomination before the Lord. He couldn't deal with it – his beloved son being a faggot.'

'Dr. Decameron, there's no reason to use pejoratives,' Marge said.

'Oh come, come. Surely you can tell I'm talking from personal experience? Yes, Azor can deal with gays like me on a professional level. Just like he can deal with Jews like Myron Berger. But between me and these walls, I'm sure he thought of both of us as hopeless sinners.'

'I think you're wrong!' Heather exclaimed. 'And what does it have to do with poor Dr. Sparks being murdered?'

'I'm just giving them background, Heather.'

'When did he receive this call from Paul?' Oliver asked.

'About seven-thirty.'

'Was he upset when he came back to the meeting?'

'Well, he was upset with *me*. But he didn't seem upset by the call.'

'What's this project you're working on?' Oliver asked. 'This Curedon?'

'So you know about Curedon?' Decameron squinted at Heather. 'We've been talking, haven't we?'

Marge said, 'Dr. Decameron—'

'All right, all right. What do you know about Curedon?'

Oliver said, 'It's an antirejection drug, whatever that means.'

'You know what Azor Sparks is noted for, don't you?'

'Heart transplants,' Marge said.

'Yes.' Decameron looked upward. 'Heart transplants. The man is . . . was one of the greatest surgeons ever to land on our fair planet. Even I can't joke away his genius.' He gazed at Marge. 'Because Azor was a genius in every sense of the word. Terrible. For someone to cut him down . . . and with his death, dies all his skill and knowledge. Too bad Azor didn't live long enough to set up a protocol for a brain transplant.'

Decameron cocked a hip.

'Now that might have been interesting. His brain in my body.'

'That would have been obscene!' Heather muttered.

Decameron rolled his eyes. 'Curedon was just one of Azor's many contributions to medical science. One in which I was privileged enough to participate. May I sit?'

Marge pointed to an empty upholstered chair. 'Please.'

Decameron sat. 'How to explain this.' He thought. 'Whenever a transplant of any kind is effected, the human body has a natural tendency to reject it.'

Oliver said, 'I'm lost.'

'Our bodies are amazing inventions. It almost makes you believe in God.' Decameron paused. 'Almost. We have a wonderful invention called the immune system. It recognizes the Huns out there, the invaders of our bodies, and wipes them out. Any foreign substance – a virus, a bacterium, a cancer cell – will eventually be discovered as an interloper and destroyed if one has a properly functioning immune system. A very good thing. Without it, we'd all take the route of AIDS patients.'

Decameron looked at Oliver.

'Okay, so far,' Oliver said. 'Go on.'

'Well, sometimes you can have too much of a good thing. Sometimes the immune system is overactive. For most of us, if

ve get an irritant up our noses or get a bee bite, we might sneeze
a bit . . . or swell up locally. But eventually everything settles
own. A few unlucky souls have immune systems that overreact
and send out droves of histamines to fight off a little interference.
Cellular walls break down, fluid is poured into the tissues, and the
body swells up.'

'An allergic reaction,' Marge said.

'Exactly,' Decameron said. 'The most dangerous sequela of an
allergic reaction is in the lungs. The breathing apparatus can
become so inflamed that often air can't pass through.'

'So what does this have to do with Curedon?' Marge asked. 'It
prevents an allergic reaction?'

Decameron nodded. 'In a sense, that's what it does. When a
heart is transplanted into a body, the body's in-place immune
system doesn't recognize the heart as a necessary part of the body.
It sees it as a foreign substance, and sends out white cells to destroy
it.'

Oliver asked, 'So it's like the patient has an allergic reaction
to his or her new heart?'

'Essentially, yes,' Decameron said. 'Without proper medication,
the immune system would eventually eat the heart away.'

Marge said, 'I thought that transplant patients are tested to
make sure there's a fit between the new heart and the old body?'

'Of course, we type-match, Detective. We do the best we can.
But often it isn't enough. There's a sad shortage of hearts and lots
of people with heart disease. We have to make do. That being the
case, we have to work around the immune system. We have to
undermine it. Hence, the class of drugs known as immunosuppres-
ants. Cortisone for example.'

'You give heart transplant patients cortisone?'

'No, but surgeons give them related immunosuppressants. Like
prednisone. The most commonly used drugs are Imuran and
cyclosporin. With severely compromised renal patients, surgeons
often use the more experimental class of immunosuppressants –

Orthoclone or OKT3 – and the other Ks like FK506. Sorry to bore you with details, but it will help you understand the importance of Curedon.'

The room fell quiet. Marge wrote as fast as she could.

'Curedon has a completely different chemical structure from the other immunosuppressants. The way it binds and interacts with T-cells through the production of interleukin 2 . . . Curedon seems to subdue the immune system without suppressing it. What that means is, we see far less unwarranted side effects. This is very very important. Because transplant patients are on immunosuppressants for *life*.'

'Forever?' Oliver asked.

'Ever and ever,' Decameron said. 'We put them on as minimal a dose as possible. But even so, there are side effects.'

Marge asked, 'Such as?'

Decameron ticked off his fingers. 'Pulmonary edema, ulcer from mucosal sluffing, chills, nausea, fever, dyspnea.' He shook his head. 'It's a long road for these patients, and our goal, as members of the healing arts, is to make them as comfortable as possible. Curedon is as close to any miracle drug as I've ever seen in my twenty years as a physician and researcher. Azor had worked years on it. I learned more about 2.2 resolutions and X-ray crystallography than I'd ever wanted to.'

Decameron fell quiet.

'But I did learn.' His eyes became moist. 'I did *learn*. And it was an honor for me to be part of something so cutting edge.'

'What's going to happen with Curedon now that Dr. Sparks is gone?' Oliver asked.

'Not much probably. The initial trials of Curedon have been quite successful in general.' Decameron's smile was tight. 'Although we have had a few ups and downs lately. That's why was so pleased when I saw Azor's data coming through his fax. just couldn't wait for him to come out of surgery. But it was wrong An invasion of his privacy.'

58

Marge tapped her pencil against her pad. 'What do you mean "ups and downs"?'

Decameron looked pained. 'A small rise in the mortality rate—'

'That's death rate in common folk language?' Marge interrupted.

Decameron smiled. 'Yes. Death rate.'

'With Curedon?'

'Yes, with Curedon.' Decameron looked at Marge pointedly. 'The patients aren't dying from the drug, they're dying from heart and renal failure. The sharp rise is puzzling, but kinks aren't uncommon. Ah, the glamorous life of a research physician. Probably data error. Or a transcription error . . . or, alas, it could actually be a problem with the drug.'

'And if it is a problem with the drug?' Oliver asked.

'We'll work it out. Curedon's been a marvel. Too good to be true. Some bumps are inevitable. But mark my words. The drug will come on the market within the next five years.'

He paused.

'For Azor not to see the fruits of his labors . . . that is a tragedy of Greek proportions.'

Oliver asked, 'Who do you do the trials on?'

'Actually, our team doesn't run the trials. The FDA – Food and Drug Administration – analyzes the numbers in conjunction with Fisher/Tyne, who actually run the trials.'

'Wait a minute.' Marge turned to Heather. 'I thought you said Fisher/Tyne bought the drug from Sparks?'

'They did buy it from Sparks,' Decameron stated. 'I don't know how much they paid for it. But I do know Sparks received a huge initial cash deposit and was promised a percentage of the profits after the drug hit the marketplace.'

'Who will get Sparks's percentage now that he's dead?' Marge asked.

'I don't know,' Decameron said. 'Certainly not me. Effectively, Fisher/Tyne own the rights to produce and market Curedon. Those rights were sold to them by the cash deposit.'

Oliver looked over his notes. 'I'm confused about something.'

'Sorry. Teaching isn't my forte.'

Oliver asked, 'What do you mean when you say that the FDA is testing the drug in *conjunction* with Fisher/Tyne?'

'Fisher/Tyne, under our guidance and protocol, are running the lab tests for Curedon. The FDA gets copies of the results and analyzes them. At the moment, I'm the liaison between Fisher/ Tyne, Dr. Sparks, and the FDA.'

'Fisher/Tyne are running the FDA tests for a drug they *own*?' Marge was taken aback. 'Isn't that a conflict of interest?'

'Happens all the time, my dear,' Decameron said. 'Who do you think ran the tests for Prozac? Eli Lilly, of course. The FDA doesn't have the skill, manpower or knowledge to test all the *thousands* of drugs that get put on the market. The FDA is the drug police. It determines policy and safety, but in general, it does *not* test. It relies heavily on the drug companies for their results.'

Oliver and Marge traded looks.

'That's incredible!' Marge shook head. 'Who protects the consumer?'

'The integrity of the drug company.'

'We're in big trouble,' Oliver stated.

'Actually, it's not as bad as you think,' Decameron said. 'It's not that drug companies are the bastion of honesty. But they are practical animals. An unsafe drug goes on the market, it spells L-A-W-S-U-I-T-S. They have a vested interest in making sure the drug is safe.'

'How about safe and *effective*?' Oliver asked.

'Effective?' Decameron raised his brow. 'Of course, the drug must be effective.' He paused. '*How* effective? Well, that's another issue entirely.'

6

The accusing voice hit Decker's face like a bucket of ice.

'What the *hell* is going on!' it boomed.

Bram said, 'Can you please let the man walk through the door first?' He stepped aside, allowing Decker to enter.

A sea of eyes upon him. With a sweeping glance, Decker took them all in. By now, he could tell who was who. Luke appeared older than his twin, his face fleshier and heavily lined, his eyes weary and cushioned with deep pouches. He was dressed in jeans and a sweater, his feet housed in sandals and socks. Unlike his twin, he wasn't wearing glasses. Could be he had on contacts.

Mr. Booming Voice was Paul, the odd man of the trio. Handsome, though, with fiery blue eyes that held a nervous twitch. He blinked often and hard. He wore the standard gray business suit, but the tie was off, the white shirt was open at the collar.

Maggie and Michael sat on the sofa, eyes on Bram's face. The remaining sister, Eva, was off to the side, staring into space. Her complexion was as smooth as alabaster, her features fine and delicate. Her hair was pulled back, gold earrings clamped to her lobes. Garbed in a pale pink silk pantsuit, she was very striking in an unapproachable way.

Michael got up, took Bram's coat. 'You're white,' he said. 'Let me get you some tea.' He turned to Decker. 'Would you like some tea, Lieutenant?'

Decker shook his head.

Maggie stood. 'I'll brew a pot, Michael.'

'Sure?'

'Sure.'

Bram kissed his sister's cheek. 'Thanks, Mag. Did you take your med—'

'Yes.' The young woman's face crumpled. She ran off, disappearing down a hallway.

Paul blinked rapidly. 'Can I talk now or do I have to raise my hand?'

Bram gave him a tired glance. 'Why don't we all sit down?'

'I don't feel like sitting,' Paul said.

'Fine, Paul. *You* stand. *I'll* sit.' Bram went into the living room and sank into the floral-faded overstuffed couch. Paul continued to pace, Eva remained leaning against the gold flocked-paper wall of the entry hall, staring upward at the dusty chandelier. Some of the brass fittings had been corroded rusty red.

Decker surveyed the room once again. The worn sofa took up most of the space. It was a three-piece sectional and faced two lumpy overstuffed chairs. A distressed-wood coffee table stood amid the seating. It held a half-dozen garden magazines and the King James Bible. In the far corner was a black grand piano, the sound box lid shut tight. Again, Decker was struck by the absence of any art on the walls. Just montage after montage of family photographs. He sat in one of the chairs.

Bram asked, 'How's Mom doing?'

'She's sleeping.' Michael tugged at his sweater. 'I gave her tea to keep her fluids up. She drank a little. Main thing is to keep her quiet—'

'I believe you used the word *medicated*,' Luke said.

'If absolutely necessary,' Michael answered.

Bram asked, 'Did you give her something else?'

'Nothing since we last spoke.'

'Good.' Bram said. 'One should last her through the night.'

'Which is good.' Paul paced the carpet, his lids twitching as he talked. 'Because the news is on TV. Shots of the car. I don't think she could stand it.'

'Phone's been ringing nonstop,' Michael said. 'I've unplugged here, but you can hear it from the kitchen.'

'Machine on?' Bram asked.

'Yeah, but it's running out of tape pretty quickly,' Michael said.

Bram said, 'Why don't you do this? Make another announce-ment tape. Uh ... something like ... "Sparks family wishes to thank all of you for your concerns and sympathies. If you wish to pay your personal respects to Dr. Azor Moses Sparks, there will be a preburial, memorial service for him at ..."' He looked around the room. 'What time, guys?'

Paul said, '*You're* doing the service?'

'Don't worry, it won't be Catholic,' Bram said. 'Or you can do it, if you want.'

Paul didn't answer, continued to pace, eyes moving like shutters.

Bram asked, 'What time?'

'Two?' Luke asked.

Michael said, 'What about Uncle Caleb? He's going to want to be here.'

'You're right,' Bram said. 'I'll call him. How about three? That would give him enough time to get out here.'

Nods all around.

Bram turned back to Michael. '"A memorial service at three P.M., First Church of the Christ Child. In lieu of flowers, the family requests that donations be made in Dr. Sparks's name to local charities." Sound okay?'

The room fell silent.

Bram spoke to Michael: 'Go make the message, Mike, then call Dad's service and let them know the plan.'

'I should get this cleared with Pastor Collins,' Michael said.

'Fine. Call him up. I'm sure you won't have any problems.'

Without protest, Michael left the room.

Bram looked at Decker. 'My father was a very prominent man. I'm sure he'll get a big crowd. Any way the police can help us direct traffic so we can make this thing as orderly as possible?'

'I'll take care of it,' Decker said.

'Thank you,' Bram said. 'Who wants to pick up Uncle Cale~~l~~ from the airport?'

'I'll do it,' Paul said. 'Just get me the information.'

Again, nobody spoke.

'How'd the news get out so fast?' Paul demanded of Decker.

'Newspeople have lots of contacts.' Decker took out a notebook 'Somebody had a big mouth and leaked it. I'm sorry.'

Maggie came back in with the tea, handed it to the priest. H~~e~~ said, 'You should lie down. You're pale.'

'I'm fine,' she said weakly.

Bram said, 'Then come sit with me.'

Maggie nestled deep into her brother's arms.

Paul sat down, blinking hard. 'Can someone tell me what' going on?'

Decker took out a pad. 'Your father's car was discovered by ~~a~~ busboy in the alley behind Tracadero's around . . . eight-thirt~~y~~ tonight.' Decker said, 'The Buick was parked at an off-angle. H~~e~~ peeked inside and saw a homicide victim—'

'How . . .' Paul asked. 'How did it—'

'I don't know about the rest of you,' Maggie interrupted, 'bu~~t~~ I *don't* want to hear details.'

'I don't, either.' Luke turned to his twin. 'It was bad?'

Bram just shook his head. Decker's eyes moved between th~~e~~ twins. They not only looked alike, but sounded *exactly* alike. Sof~~t~~ deep voices, similar inflections.

To Paul, Decker said, 'If you'd like, Mr. Sparks, I can tell yo~~u~~ more privately. But first, let me say this. We haven't got a suspec~~t~~ or a motive right now. I've got men at the scene—'

'Does anyone know what Dad was doing at Tracadero's?' Luk~~e~~ asked.

Bram said, 'Lieutenant Decker and I were talking about that. ~~I~~ don't have the faintest idea.'

'Me, either,' Michael said, reentering the room.

Paul stood, stared at the ceiling. It seemed to calm his tic. 'Maybe it was somebody's birthday. Somebody at the hospital.'

'Your brother Bram mentioned that as a possibility,' Decker said. 'But I just found out that Dr. Sparks had dinner at the hospital.'

'That sounds like Dad.' Michael turned to Decker. 'You should be questioning people at the hospital.'

Decker said, 'I've got detectives at New Chris right now. We will be questioning hospital personnel extensively. Tonight, tomorrow, the day after tomorrow . . . as long as it takes until we're satisfied.

'After I leave here, I'm going back to the crime scene. Right now, I have men canvassing the area, going door to door, questioning everyone around the area. All the necessary forensic professionals have been called in. I'm investigating every angle of this case. Which means . . .' Decker tapped a pencil on his notebook. 'I'm afraid I'm going to have to ask all of you some questions.'

'Now?' Paul asked. 'It's after eleven.'

'I know it's late, Mr. Sparks. But these things tend to get solved quickly once we get leads. Best time to get leads is within twenty-four hours of the onset of the case. Information that you may think is trivial could turn out to be vital to us. I hope I won't take up too much of your time. But we're pushing hard on this. Help us out.'

'No objections,' Luke said.

Paul batted his eyes. 'Me, either.'

'Eva, are you with us?' Bram asked.

She turned her head, eyes red and angry. Bram said, 'Sit next to me.'

She did, sitting on his left side, her spine ramrod straight. Bram put his arm around her. She collapsed under his touch and leaned against him. It relaxed her coiled features.

Decker said, 'My questions might upset you. I'm sorry if they do, but I have to ask them.' He turned to Paul. 'Can I start with you?'

'Me?' Paul blinked furiously. 'Why?'

'Because I also found out from my people that you called your father around seven-thirty. Can I ask you what it was about?'

Paul became crimson, his eyes a series of spasms. 'It was private. Why is this important?'

Decker didn't answer.

Paul said, 'It has nothing to do with my father's death. I don't have to answer it.'

The room was quiet. Luke said, 'Must be money.'

Paul shot his brother a deadly glance.

Luke said, 'It's no big deal, Paul. So you borrowed money from Dad. We all did from time to time.'

Nobody spoke.

Decker looked at Paul.

Paul's eyes worked like strobe lights. 'I called to ask him for a small loan—'

Michael let out a small laugh. Bram threw him a razor-sharp glance that shut him up.

Paul said, 'Anything else?'

Decker said, 'You asked him for money. What did he say?'

'He said, yes, of course. My father was a generous man.'

'Did you make the call from home?' Decker asked.

'From work. I work at Levy, Critchen, and Goldberg. I'm a stockbroker.'

'You were at work the entire evening, then?'

Paul's eyes worked furiously. 'No.' A meaningful pause. 'After I made the call, I took a ride . . . by myself.'

'Must have been a long ride,' Decker said. 'You made the call at seven-thirty. Your brother-in-law didn't get hold of you until around ten-thirty.'

Silence.

Paul looked upward again. 'Well, there goes any semblance of my privacy.'

'If you'd like, Mr. Sparks, I can ask you these questions one on one.'

Paul was quiet, his hand mowing through his pile of black curls. 'Oh what the hell!' His smile was bitter. 'I had words with my wife over asking my father for money. I was angry and didn't feel like going home.'

More silence.

Paul said, 'I had just asked my father for money about four months before. I didn't feel like hitting on him again. My wife didn't understand that.'

'What was the last loan about?' Decker asked.

Paul glared at Bram. 'Why don't you tell him? I know Dad tells you everything.'

Bram's face was flat.

Paul blinked hard. 'I had a margin call and didn't have enough cash to cover it. Dad footed me a loan, one that I'm currently in the process of paying back rapidly because my stocks have since shot up. Tonight's phone call had to do with the kids' tuitions. You have no idea how expensive private schools can be. I didn't want to do it, but my wife practically accused me of being a negligent and rotten father if I didn't.'

Paul fell into the empty overstuffed chair.

'So those were my last words to my father. Asking him for money.' He dammed back tears. 'Wonderful.'

Again, the house turned quiet.

Eva said, 'Well, while we're on the subject of loans, I guess you're going to find out anyway. We borrowed . . . my husband and I . . . borrowed money about a year ago. My dad co-signed the loan. We're also in the process of paying it back.'

Paul threw his sister a grateful look.

'Can I ask what the loan was for?' Decker asked.

'My husband owns a chain of discount clothing stores.' Eva pronounced the word *discount* with disdain. 'He took over the family business, thank you very much. Retail apparel took a dip.

He had to close up some of the smaller boutiques and with the leases and mismanagement, he accrued some debt.' Her face grew tense as she talked. '*I* didn't want to ask him. But my husband put me in a bind. Because he got caught in an interest crunch and had already taken out a second loan on the house to expand two years before. Rather than get stuck with exorbitant rates, David asked Dad to co-sign a secured loan based on *his* assets.'

'Which are many,' Luke added.

'It seemed easier at the time,' Eva said. 'And it hasn't cost Dad a *penny*. David's paying it back.'

'Where were you this evening?' Decker asked Eva.

'At home until I heard . . .' She looked down and turned away. Decker's eyes went to Luke.

'I was at work,' he said. 'I finished up with a client around eight and was in my office doing paperwork until Bram called me.'

'You work at the Bomb Shelter?' Decker asked.

Luke rolled his eyes. 'Yes, I work at the Bomb Shelter. Yes, I was an addict. Yes, I no doubt ingested thousands of dollars up my nose. Yes, I am now flat broke. Yes, I am now also sober. Yes, I've been sober for three years. Yes, I was alone for two hours in my office. No, nobody saw me. And no, I didn't kill my father.'

Bram stifled a smile. Luke caught it and smiled back. Paul said, 'I'm glad you two can find humor at a time like this.'

Luke said, 'My dad is . . . was a wealthy man, Lieutenant. He and my mom hardly spent a dime. They, unlike me, are simple, modest people. I also went to him when I needed something especially in my glorious drug days. We all borrowed from Dad . . . well, not Bram. He's the Golden Boy—'

Paul said, 'Guy made a vow of poverty, and he's the only one of us with money in the bank.'

'Church gives him everything,' Luke said to Decker.

Quietly Bram said, 'Can we change the subject?'

Luke said, 'All I know is you've upward of fifty grand—'

'*Luke!*' Maggie said.

68

'What would you like me to do with my stipend, Lucas?' Bram asked.

'Give it to me,' Luke said.

'Speaking of money,' Bram said, 'did Dad have a will?'

No one answered.

Michael said, 'I know Dad has a lawyer. The guy from the church.'

'Which guy, Michael?' Luke asked. 'There are lots of guys—'

Michael glared at Luke. 'With the white hair and the veiny, red nose.'

Luke said, 'Well, that narrows it to about three thousand—'

'He's an elder on the council,' Michael tried again. 'He lost his wife a couple of years ago. Gosh, I can't think of his name!'

'I know who you mean,' Maggie said. 'Waterman.'

'Waterson,' Luke and Paul said simultaneously.

'William Waterson,' Bram said. 'Paul, you take care of the funeral arrangements so Mom doesn't have to be bothered with them.'

Paul's eyelids twitched. 'You expect *me* to pay?'

Bram was patient. 'No. If need be, *I'll* pay. But if Dad had a will and left us anything, maybe we can borrow against some of the funds to pay for the funeral. Save Mom some unnecessary heartache. And since you know about finance, it makes the *most* sense for *you* to call up Waterson and ask the questions.'

Paul's voice was tight. 'I have no problem with that, Abram. I just didn't know what you meant.'

'So, now you know,' Bram said. 'I'll handle the service tomorrow. I'll do as much of the calling as I can tonight, then I'll finish up in the morning. I'm not going to sleep anyway. Any objections?'

No one spoke.

'If it's all the same to you, I'd like to get started. Dad had lots of friends and admirers, and it's going to take me a while.' Bram turned to Decker. 'Can you drive me back to St. Thomas's?'

'I'd be happy to,' Decker said. 'I just need a little bit more information.' He turned to Eva. 'Can I get your last name, ma'am?'

'Shapiro.'

Decker's pause was fractional before he wrote it down. Suddenly, Eva burst into tears. 'It was all so stupid!' She looked at Bram with wet eyes. 'Why is life so *stupid*?'

'I don't know why.' Bram turned to Paul. 'Maybe you should take her home.'

'Everything is so meaningless!' Eva opened a Gucci bag, pulled out a silk handkerchief, and dabbed her eyes. 'I didn't even have a chance to say good-bye. Or to say I love you. And just when we were starting to get along!'

Maggie broke down into heavy sobs. Bram said, 'Michael, could you check on Mom? It's been a while.'

Wordlessly, Michael went up the stairs.

Eva faced Decker. 'My parents and I haven't been on very good terms for some time.'

Bram said, 'You don't need to get into this, Eva.'

'He's going to find out anyway,' Eva said. 'It's actually my husband and my father. *They* don't get along. *I'm* caught in the middle.'

Bram said, 'Eva, honey, maybe we should save this—'

'You see, my parents are very devout people,' Eva continued. 'Religious, *good* people. But . . .'

'But your husband's Jewish,' Decker said. 'It's created some problems.'

Eva stared at him, dumbfounded.

Bram rubbed his eyes. 'Last name, Eva. It's a giveaway.'

Decker said, 'I can understand how intermarriage might cause conflict.'

'It isn't that David's religious,' Eva said. 'Quite the contrary, he isn't religious at all. Neither are his parents. David never grew up with any kind of religious training. And from the start, he's had no objection to me raising the kids as Christians. They've been baptized and confirmed. The kids and I attend church regularly. David doesn't care. But for some stubborn reason, he refuses to convert! Jews are very stubborn peo—'

'Eva,' Bram chided.

'Bram, you can't deny that it says right in the Bible that they're stiff-necked—'

'Eva, enough.'

'It *doesn't* say that in the Bible?'

'You're quoting Bible to me?'

Eva stood up from the couch, fire in her eyes. 'I'm *telling* you what it says right in the holy book.' She picked up the Bible from the coffee table. 'Would you like me to find the passage?'

'Exodus thirty-two, nine,' he said wearily. 'You're being literal—'

'And you're being condescending.'

'Eva, can we save the biblical exegesis—'

'You know, Bram, maybe I don't know Hebrew like you do. But I do know Jews—'

'Fine, Eva, you're a *mavin* on contemporary Jewish Zeitgeist. Can we move on?'

'What in the world is a Zeitgeist?' Paul asked. 'Sounds like something from a fifties horror flick.'

'Honestly, Bram, I think you pull these words out of a hat!' Eva exclaimed.

'Isn't it a sociology term?' Maggie asked.

Bram said, 'It's the intellectual, moral, and cultural state of a people in a given era.'

'Sure, I knew that,' Luke said.

'What's a *mavin*?' Paul asked.

'Expert,' Bram said. 'Comes from the Hebrew word *lehaveen* – to understand.'

'So why didn't you just say "so you're an expert on Jews"?' Eva crossed her arms and tapped her foot. 'You're just infuriating sometimes. Always *complicating* everything. Just like David. He

71

couldn't make things easy on me and the family and just convert. No, he had to be spiteful—'

'Maybe the poor guy was just trying to assert himself,' Paul said. 'Dad can be very intimidating.'

'The word is bossy,' Luke said.

'How can you talk about him like that after what happened to him!' Eva yelled out.

'You know, Eva, you don't have a monopoly on grief,' Luke said. 'I'm just as devastated as you are.'

Eva went on. 'If David really cared about his family, he could have converted. Of course, now it's too *late*!'

'Cold nights ahead for David,' Luke muttered.

Paul stifled a smile. A beeper went off. The priest looked at his belt, checked the number, then stood up. 'Excuse me for a moment.'

After Bram left the room, Eva turned her ire to Paul. 'You know when Spencer was sick, David sure didn't mind Dad handling all the surgeries and the medical expenses. Suddenly, Dad's take-charge attitude didn't bother him a bit!'

'What was wrong with Spencer?' Decker asked.

'He was born with a cleft palate,' Eva said. 'It was a very difficult labor. Afterward, I ran a high fever and started hemorrhaging. David was completely useless. Couldn't deal with it. He just went off and buried himself in his work. Left me to fend for myself—'

'He was very upset, Eva,' Paul said. 'He just didn't know what to do.'

'Well, he might have stuck around instead of bolting.' Eva looked at Decker. 'My father had to step in – not only for me but for Spencer. My mom took over the care of my other children while David *composed* himself. And you know what, Lieutenant? My father never lorded it over my husband—'

Luke interrupted, 'Well, that's not quite true—'

'*Excuse* me, Lieutenant,' Eva said forcefully. '*I'd* like to check on my mother now. Any other questions I can answer?'

Decker kept his face flat, shook his head.

Eva turned on her heels and trotted upstairs.

The woman had her opinions. Then Decker remembered her position in the family. The little girl after three boys. No doubt Eva had been indulged.

Luke said, 'I loved my father dearly, Lieutenant. But it wasn't that simple.'

Maggie said, 'It's Eva's business.'

'I just don't want the lieutenant here thinking that David's a total jerk.'

Maggie said, 'He was a total jerk—'

'Dad emasculated him—'

'He did not!' Maggie broke in. 'So he berated David. David deserved it. Deserting Eva like he did.'

Paul said, 'No offense, Mag, but you don't understand how wives can be.'

'Amen,' Luke said.

'I don't believe this,' Maggie said. 'Another stupid boys against the girls argument.'

Michael came back down. 'Where's Bram?'

'He had to use the phone.' Paul turned to Decker. 'Do you really need to hear all this?'

Decker stood, folded his notepad. 'No, I think I have all the information I need right now. I'll leave as soon as Bram gets off the phone.'

Luke said, 'We're bickering like when we were children. It's all the stress.'

Michael said, 'We all loved Dad very much. I think I speak for everyone when I say, anything you need from us to find whoever . . .'

'Absolutely,' Maggie said.

'Anything,' Paul said. 'Just find the bastard and bring him to me. I'll handle the son of a bitch!'

Decker said, 'Let the police handle it, please.'

'Fucking asshole—'

'Paul, please!' Maggie said.

'Probably some bastard carjacker.' Luke began to pace. 'Crime's unbelievable in this city.'

Paul looked pointedly at Decker. 'That's what happens when the police handle it.'

Decker said, 'Sir, I know—'

'Dad didn't drive an expensive car,' Michael butted in. 'Why would anyone carjack a Buick?'

'They use the car for crime,' Paul said. 'They see an old guy, they think easy target. Knowing Dad, he probably resisted.' To Decker, he said, 'My father was tough. He wouldn't give up without a fight, I could tell you that much.'

Bram came back in.

'Emergency?' Michael asked.

'No, somebody from my church just using my emergency line. I have a feeling I'm going to get a lot of that tonight. Where's Eva?'

Paul pointed up.

Bram sighed, looked at Decker. 'Can I go make peace with my sister? We are all kind of fragile right now.'

Decker nodded. Bram left the room. Luke said, 'Eva's marriage is . . .' He splayed his hand and rocked his wrist back and forth.

'It's not any of his business,' Michael said.

'But it does explain her behavior,' Luke said.

Bram came down a moment later, hugging Eva who was sobbing in his arms. The priest said, 'Maggie, can you take Eva into the kitchen and make her a cup of tea?'

Maggie swooped her sister into her arms. As they headed for the kitchen, Maggie began to cry.

Luke said, 'I think the reality of what happened is finally dawning on us.'

Bram closed and opened his eyes. 'Who's staying with Mom?'

'Nobody has to stay,' Michael said. 'I can take care of Mom.'

'You're going home, Paul?' Luke asked.

'No, I don't want to go home tonight. I just can't face . . .' Paul stopped talking, sighed. 'Maybe I'll take a drive.'

'Be careful, bro,' Bram said.

'Yeah.'

'I mean that.'

'I know you do, Golden Boy.'

A moment passed. Then Paul and Bram embraced.

'Get some sleep,' Bram told his brother.

'A nice thought, but not likely.' Paul left, gently closing the front door behind him.

To Luke, Bram said, 'What about you?'

'Think I'll stick around.' Luke averted his eyes. 'Can you do me a favor, Golden Boy?'

'What?'

'Call Dana for me.'

'Lucas—'

'Abram, I can't deal . . .' Water seeped from Luke's eyes. He squeezed them shut, tears rolling down his cheeks. He made a quick swipe at them, then headed for the kitchen.

'Everybody's falling *apart*!' Michael threw up his hands and paced. 'Of course, everyone's falling apart. What did I expect!'

Bram said, 'Why don't you go into the kitchen, Mike? Go drink some tea.'

Michael opened his mouth to speak, but instead just shook his head and left the room.

Decker placed his hand on the priest's shoulder. 'Ready?'

Bram nodded. On the way out, he said, 'Thank you for helping me through that terrible ordeal earlier in the evening.'

'Are you all right?'

Bram shook his head. 'I don't know. I had to see him . . . to make sure. But heavens, it was . . . painful . . .'

'I hope I can give you all some resolution quickly.' Decker

opened the passenger door to the Volare. 'I'll get you a traffic cop for tomorrow's service.'

'Thanks.'

Decker got in and started the car.

Bram said, 'You handled my family well. Low-key works well with us.'

'They depend on you a lot, don't they?'

Bram looked out the window. 'I wouldn't say that.'

Decker waited for more. Nothing came. The priest had shut down.

'Do me a favor, will you, Father?'

'How can I help you?'

'Watch your brother Paul. I don't need a vigilante for homespun justice.'

'He's just talking.'

'He's agitated.'

'We're all agitated. Right now, I think we're all too dazed to do anything.'

'Sometimes that's when people lash out.'

Bram sat back in his seat. 'Violent city we live in. No regard for human life. It's terrible.'

'Often these things do get solved if you're persistent and patient,' Decker said. 'I try to be optimistic. But I don't want to get anyone's hopes up too high.'

Bram laughed, a sad sound. 'I fervently believe in God, Lieutenant. But I've given up believing in miracles.'

7

Cradling the phone in the crook of his neck, Scott Oliver flipped through his notes. The machine must have had a hands-off feature, but Oliver couldn't figure out how to use it. To Decker, he said, 'The secretary claims she left the hospital around eight. Decameron says he left with Sparks about a quarter to. They walked out to the doctors' lot together. Decameron had pissed Sparks off and was trying to smooth things over.'

'Which means Decameron was probably the last person at the hospital to see Sparks alive.' Marge spoke from the extension in Heather Manley's office.

'How'd Decameron anger Sparks?' Decker asked.

'Apparently Decameron read some of Dr. Sparks's data without his permission. A big no-no.'

'I can see that,' Decker said. 'I hate snoops.'

Marge said, 'He wasn't snooping really, just excited about some positive data concerning Sparks's pet research project.'

Oliver said, 'Decameron said he apologized and Sparks accepted it. End of story.'

'Up front with it,' Marge said. 'Told us about it right away.'

Decker said, 'When Sparks left the hospital, did Decameron notice if his boss seemed in a hurry?'

'We asked him that.' Oliver transferred the phone to his other ear. 'Decameron didn't notice anything special. But he added that it wasn't Sparks's style to rush. Even when he was under pressure, he appeared calm, completely in control.'

Decker said, 'Any idea if he was meeting someone?'

Marge said, 'We asked that, too. Sparks didn't say. But if he was meeting anyone, both Decameron and Manley thought it was probably his son Paul.'

'Because Sparks cut the meeting short after he received Paul's call,' Oliver added. 'Did you meet Paul, Loo?'

'I met all of Sparks's children. These aren't TAC lines, so I'll talk about it later. Where are Decameron and Manley now?'

Oliver said, 'The night staff have called an emergency meeting. Decameron is briefing them on how to proceed with Sparks's cases. It's a mess here – a very nervous hospital filled with panicky patients.'

Marge said, 'Sparks did all sorts of cardiac procedures, not only transplants. The great majority of the hospital are his heart patients. Everyone is anxious.'

Decker asked, 'Is Decameron a practitioner as well as a researcher?'

Marge said, 'He's trained as a cardiac surgeon, but he doesn't have many clinical patients any more. His energies are directed to transplant research. He did say – albeit grudgingly – that Myron Berger, one of their colleagues, is a very good surgeon, capable of filling in for Sparks.'

'Grudgingly with a capital G,' Oliver added. 'Decameron works with Berger, but he hates him. Course, Reggie boy doesn't seem to like anyone. He's also a flounce.'

'Flamingly gay,' Marge said. 'Proud of it.'

'You gotta kind of admire him for that,' Oliver said. 'And he's *real* smart. Clever as well as academic.'

Decker paused. 'I wonder if Decameron's gayness created tension between him and a Fundamentalist like Sparks?'

'Not according to Decameron,' Marge said. 'He said Sparks could work with anyone on a professional level.'

'He also mentioned that Sparks had a gay son who was a priest,' Oliver said. 'Maybe that made Sparks more tolerant.'

Decker thought for a moment. Bram didn't seem overtly gay. But that didn't mean anything. 'What about Dr. Berger? Anyone talk to him yet?'

'Can't get hold of him,' Marge said. 'We've left a half-dozen messages—'

'I don't like that at all.'

Oliver said, 'We didn't either, Loo. Sent a cruiser by there a half hour ago. House is dark, but nothing appears out of order. Just looks like no one's home.'

'So where is he?' Decker asked. 'If Berger's a surgeon with clinical patients, he *must* have a pager.'

'Yeah, we tried his beeper,' Oliver said. 'His answering service said he wasn't on-call tonight. A resident named Kenner is covering for him. I guess Berger shuts down when he's off.'

Unlike Sparks who basically lived at the hospital. Decker said, 'Sparks also worked with a woman named Elizabeth Fulton. What do you know about her?'

Marge said, 'Now we did reach Fulton. She can't come to the hospital at the moment, because she can't swing a baby-sitter.' She was silent for a moment. 'Isn't that weird? A doctor of her stature not having twenty-four-hour help?'

'But she's not a practitioner,' Oliver said. 'Strictly research.'

Marge said, 'Still, she's a busy woman. You'd think she'd have a live-in.'

Oliver said, 'Anyway, she's more than willing to talk to us if we want to come to her place.'

Decker checked his watch. Almost midnight. 'Call her up. Tell her you'll be down there tonight. Did you check out the rest of the hospital staff?'

'Not yet,' Oliver said.

'We're going to do that now,' Marge said. 'Unless you want us to see Fulton first.'

Decker said, 'Webster and Martinez are just about done over here at the crime scene. I'll send them over to the hospital. You go interview this Dr. Fulton. What happened to the secretary, Heather Manley? She still around or did she go home?'

'Went home,' Marge said.

'No reason to keep her.' Oliver felt his lips arc upward in a grin. 'Well, I've got a reason to keep her, but it doesn't have anything to do with the case.'

'Good-looking?'

'Very nice, Loo.'

'Affair material?'

'Definitely,' Marge said. 'But Heather claims no. Sparks was way too close to Jesus to do something like that.'

'What do you think, Scott?'

Oliver brushed the lapel of his Armani blazer. Got this baby used from a secondhand shop, but it was in perfect condition. Wonderful fabric, the wool was lightweight but warm. 'What do I think? Sure I think it's a possibility despite what Manley says.'

'He doesn't sound like the kind to me, Pete.' To Oliver, Marge said, 'You know, there are some men who don't do it, Scotty.'

'Two classes of men, Marge,' Oliver said. 'Those who cheat and those who're going to cheat. Only thing that separates them is timing.'

Decker said, 'Who's taking over Sparks's patients right now?'

'Residents,' Oliver said. 'As soon as Dr. Berger is reached, Decameron is sure that he'll fill in. There have also been lots of surgeons from other places volunteering to help out. Everyone speaks highly of Sparks.'

Decker said, 'Okay. Go interview Dr. Fulton. By the way, did Decameron mention a drug called Curedon to you?'

'Did he mention Curedon?' Oliver laughed. 'Marge and I have doctorates in immunosuppressants.' He brought Decker up to date on Sparks's research.

'See, that's why Decameron swiped the data from Sparks's fax machine,' Marge said. 'It was good news. Lately, Curedon has undergone some problems in its death rate. This particular batch of data was positive. Decameron said he just didn't want to wait until Sparks handed him the sheets.'

'And that was the only thing that pissed off Sparks?' Decker sked. 'Sure there wasn't more to the argument?'

'Not according to him,' Oliver said. 'Of course, one of the other doctors might offer a different version.'

Decker said, 'Why should Decameron care so much if it's Sparks's drug? He doesn't make money off it, does he?'

'Decameron says no,' Oliver said. 'But—'

Marge said, 'He told us that as of right now, he is the liaison between Fisher/Tyne, the FDA, and Sparks's lab.' She paused. 'I know this may sound corny. But I really get the feeling that Decameron takes his job seriously, has a great deal of pride in his work. He had a personal stake in Curedon's success if not a financial one.'

'Hmmmm,' Decker said.

'You know differently?' Oliver asked.

'Nah, just my normal suspicious nature,' Decker said. 'Someone should go talk to people at Fisher/Tyne ASAP. Find out if the company did pay Sparks a hefty sum for the right to manufacture the drug. Because where there's money, there's motive for murder.'

Oliver said, 'We don't even know where Fisher/Tyne are located, Loo.'

'Ask Decameron,' Decker said.

Marge said, 'What if they're out of state?'

'If necessary, we'll send you there.'

Oliver smiled. 'Let's hope for Florida.'

'There's gators in Florida,' Marge said.

Oliver said, 'There're gators everywhere, Margie. Most of them're just two-legged.'

Decker took a final sip of coffee, hung up the mike, then heaved his body out of the Volare. He lurched forward into the cold mist, checked his watch again.

Midnight.

Most normal people were retiring for bed.

Bed was a very nice thought.

Bert Martinez walked over to him. Decker offered the detective some coffee from his thermos.

'No thanks,' Martinez answered. 'Wife packed me a jug full of Mexican coffee. Strong stuff. Spicy. Want a cup?'

'Where were you ten minutes ago . . . before I tanked up on this swill?'

Martinez smiled.

Decker stuck his hands in his pockets. Rocked on his feet to give them circulation. Man, it was cold out here, fog attacking the skin with tiny, icy needles. Standing in a back alley perfumed by rotting food, cold asphalt seeping into the soles of his shoes.

He said, 'Take it there's nothing to report? Otherwise we wouldn't be talking about coffee.'

Martinez closed the zipper on his windbreaker, streaks of silvered-black hair plastered to his sweaty brow. He blew on his hands, then stuck them in his pockets. He was more squat than tall, but his muscles could pack a wallop.

'The problem is that the restaurant's dishwashing area faces the back alley.'

Even with the kitchen door closed, Decker could hear the hum of machinery combined with the rhythmic blare of trumpets. Someone had the radio on.

'You think the noise is bad out here,' Martinez said, 'nothing like it is inside. Dishwashers running full tilt, the help have cranked up the music to earsplitting level. Besides, there's lots of noise coming from the front portion of the kitchen. Appliances running, pots and pans clattering, and the chef screaming at everyone.'

'No one heard anything?' Decker asked.

'That's the consistent story,' Martinez said. 'Believe me, I interviewed everyone in the back *en español* so no one can say they didn't understand my questions. Between the whoops of the salsa music and the whir of the dishwashers, you can't hear yourself think. Besides, you know Latinos. Especially the green-card holders. Close mouthed when it comes to the police. Half of hem think we're in cahoots with INS. Hard to get their confidence, ard to get them to talk. *Especially* the men. It's a macho thing, a vay they can play one up on us.'

Decker smoothed his mustache. 'So Sparks was shot and carved nd, supposedly, no one heard a thing?'

'It could be the truth. Maybe the guy used a silencer. Maybe e worked fast.'

'The more likely explanation is we're working with more than ne person.'

'Because of the dual MO.'

'Exactly,' Decker said. 'Was there any cash in his wallet?'

'Few bucks in cash and his credit cards were still there. Either t was an incomplete mugging, maybe someone spooked the nuggers. Or robbery wasn't the motive.'

'Shit,' Decker muttered. 'Be nice if we could have traced credit ards or *something*!' He cursed again. 'What about the valets, 3ert? Did they hear anything?'

'They park the cars in front of the restaurant, not in back.'

'Sound travels at night,' Decker said.

'The street's a main thoroughfare at eight-thirty. Lots of cars vith loud radios, backfires, and revved-up motors.'

Webster sauntered over to them, wearing a set of earphones. Ie removed them, stowed them in his pocket.

'What are you listening to?' Martinez asked.

'Selections from Saint-Saens. Specifically, *Danse Macabre*. Cerily apropos.' He kicked a clod of broken asphalt with his shoe. Not much in the way of trash, Loo-tenant. Y'all want me to search gain, I reckon I have the time. Still got a *Samson and Delilah* CD to listen to.'

'Got another assignment for you two,' Decker said. 'I'm sending ou both out to New Chris to interview the staff there.'

Martinez said, 'You want us to talk to everyone or just the eople who Sparks worked with on a regular basis?'

Decker said, 'Talk to everyone.'

'I see you don't b'lieve in sleep,' Webster said.

'I'm not sleeping, buddy, you're not sleeping.' Decker's brain was buzzing. Too much coffee. 'We have a gruesome murder and so far the only remote motive we've pulled out was an academic tiff between Sparks and one of his colleagues. That's not much.'

Webster said, 'It's a start.'

'It ain't enough,' Decker said emphatically. 'I'm not saying we've got to solve this within the twenty-four-hour cutoff. But we got to do better than this. Sparks was known as a rich man. Could be some hospital worker intended to tail him and rob him. Find out who called in absent today.'

'Anybody know what he was doing here?' Martinez asked. 'In back of Tracadero's specifically.'

'No,' Decker said. 'Call me in an hour to brief me on your progress.'

Tom nodded. 'You want to drive, Bert?'

'No problem. You want some coffee?'

'You got coffee?'

'A whole jug of Mexican stuff – strong and spicy. I also got some pasteles and fried tortillas with powdered sugar. Wife's a good cook.' Martinez patted his gut. 'Too good.'

'Y'all don't have to eat it.'

'If it's in front of me, I eat it.'

Decker watched them disappear in a swirling snowstorm of street-lit mist. He folded his arms over his chest, let out a fog-visible sigh. Farrell Gaynor was still poking around the scene. Decker walked over to the Buick.

'Impound should be here momentarily, Loo.' Gaynor was half in, half out of the car, legs dangling from the interior. Finally, he began to push his body out. It looked like the Buick was giving birth to a breech baby. He straightened his spine, handed some paper to Decker. 'Couple of gas credit slips. He kept his car real neat. Not surprising considering what he does.'

'Yeah, think you would want your heart surgeon to be the compulsive type.'

'Now, this is more interesting, Loo.' Gaynor offered Decker a white business card.

'Wait, let me put my gloves on.' He slipped on latex, then took the piece of paper.

The background was imprinted with the Harley-Davidson logo – wings attached to a big H. Bold Gothic letters were overlaid across the center of the card.

Everyone needs an Ace In The Hole.
Because Sparks fly hard and hot.
Born to be Wild.

No address, no phone number on the front. Decker flipped the card over. Nothing on the back, either.

Gaynor said, 'What do you make of it?'

'Where'd you find it?'

'In the glove compartment,' Gaynor answered. 'Stuck between the pages of a Thomas guide. Only other thing in the compartment was the owner's manual.'

'Ace In The Hole? Sparks fly . . . ?' Decker laughed. 'Azor Sparks. Ace Sparks?'

'Maybe the good doctor is a secret Hell's Angel.'

'Yeah, he's really a kingpin crank supplier who's been manufacturing meth out of his hospital lab,' Decker said.

'Can't you see it in the headlines?' Gaynor said. 'Head doctor is secret head.' Suddenly, he grew pensive. 'You know, Loo, the case does have the look of a drug retaliation hit.'

Decker laughed. 'You can't be serious.'

'Lots of brutality. You yourself said it looks like a gang hit. I know it sounds lunatic. But maybe it's worth checking out.'

'It's absurd.'

'So is finding that card in Sparks's car.'

'Unless it isn't his. Could belong to one of his kids.'

'Ace sounds like Azor to me.'

85

Decker rolled his tongue in his mouth. As of this moment, he didn't have squat. What would it hurt to look at this through every possible lens? He pocketed the business card. 'I'll look into it.'

'It's stupid, but what the hey.' Gaynor rubbed his shoulders, massaged his neck. 'Cold out here.'

'Call it a night, Farrell.' Decker took off the gloves and blew on his hands. 'I'll wait for impound. You go back to the station house and finish up the paperwork. Tomorrow, start the paper train on Sparks. His bank accounts, his credit cards, brokerage accounts if he has any. And I'm sure he does because his kid is a stockbroker.'

'That doesn't mean he invested with him.'

'Find out. If he didn't, that says something. Tomorrow, you also begin a paper trail on his children, starting with son Paul. He owed his dad some bucks. And so did Sparks's daughter, Eva Shapiro. Those are the only two who fessed up to being in arrears with Dad. But I want you to check *all* of them out.'

'You going home after impound, Loo?'

'No, I'm going by Myron Berger's house. Something's way off with that.'

'Be careful.'

'Always am.'

'See you, Loo.'

'See you.' Decker rubbed his hands, then his arms, watching Gaynor totter back to his car. The man had two more years before he'd be forced to hang up his shield. Forty-five years of police service; thirty-five of them as a detective third grade, fifteen of those as a homicide detective in brutal gang territory. And yet the guy was always neat, clean, punctual. As dependable as Big Ben and still had a bounce in his step at twelve-thirty in the morning.

Way to go, Farrell.

8

omething Marge could never understand: why someone would
uy a house abutting the foothills. A bad month of rain and, lo
nd behold, a thousand-pound avalanche of mud occupied space
nat once was the living room. Yet, Pete's house sat at the edge of
ne mountain. So did the home belonging to Dr. Elizabeth Fulton.
or her domicile, she had chosen a sprawling one-story ranch thing
nade out of wood siding. A big piece of property. At least a couple
f acres separated her from her nearest neighbor.

Unlatching the metal gate, Oliver said, 'Guess the doctor isn't
bug on landscaping.'

Marge nodded. The lot was fenced with chain-link, the lawn a
cratch pad of scrub grass. No flowers, no shrubs, no bushes, no
lants that hadn't come from airborne seeds. In the background,
ehind the house, Marge could see several rows of tall citrus. She
ould smell them too, blossoms giving off a tart, sweet scent. They
alked up to the front entrance. The doctor answered the door
efore they knocked, her complexion mottled gray and dappled
vith perspiration.

No wonder, Marge thought. The doctor was wearing sweats *and*
sweater. Internal chill. Her face appeared childlike, probably
ecause of her eyes. The size of beach balls, they seemed to take
p half her face. Big, brown irises, red-rimmed at the moment.
etween the orbs sat a button nose spangled with freckles. Her
nouth was wide with lush lips. Woolly henna hair was pulled back
nto a ponytail. At a quick glance, she looked to be barely twenty.
ut with smile lines apparent and ripples in her neck, Marge
gured her age closer to forty.

'Dr. Fulton?' Oliver took out his badge and ID.

Fulton gave it a cursory glance, then motioned them across the doorway. 'Please, come in.'

The living room had been decorated pseudo-country. Cheerful floral prints covered a traditional sofa and two matching chairs. A wall-sized bay window was topped with a pleated valance and the tiebacks were sewn from the same flowered fabric. The actual window curtains were drawn, made from lace that allowed light to pass through. At one in the morning, the outside view was of a screen of still shadows. In the middle of the bay stood a polished pine rocker resting on bleached oak flooring that had been pegged and grooved. The fireplace was going full blast. It was *hot* and Marge could feel wet circles under her armpits. The hearth was masoned from bouquet canyon stone, the plaster mantel hosted a half-dozen photographs of a chubby toddler boy.

'Sit wherever you'd like,' Fulton whispered.

Oliver chose a chair, Marge took the sofa. The doctor stood next to the fireplace screen and rubbed her hands together. 'I shouldn't be here. I should be there . . . at the hospital . . . helping.' She brought her hands to her face and cried into them.

'Are you sure you wouldn't like to sit?' Oliver asked.

'No.' She wiped her eyes with her fingers, folded her arms across her chest. 'What *happened*?'

'That's what we're trying to find out,' Marge said.

'Was he kidnapped? Carjacked? I mean no one would have hurt him if they had known who he was, right?'

Oliver took out his notepad. 'You sure you don't want to sit, Doctor?'

'Positive.' She shook her head. 'I mean . . . *why*?'

Oliver said, 'If you could help us with the why, you'd be doing everyone a service. When was the last time you saw him, Doctor?'

'Last night. At our research meeting.'

'The Curedon meeting,' Oliver clarified.

'Yes. How did you— You've spoken to Dr. Decameron, then?'

'Yes.' Marge took out her pad. 'You have regularly scheduled meetings?'

'Yes and no. Dr. Sparks sends us a memo when we're to meet. It works out to about once or twice a week.'

'You don't mind that?' Marge asked.

'Mind what?'

'That he sends you a memo at his . . . discretion?'

Fulton threw Marge an impatient look. 'He's a very busy man. Of course, we work around his schedule.'

'When was the last time you actually saw him?' Oliver repeated.

'Oh gosh! He cut our research meeting short. It must have ended around seven-thirty, maybe quarter to eight.'

'Why did he cut the meeting short?' Marge asked.

Fulton said, 'Well, he really didn't cut it short, per se. He just summed things up rather quickly after he took the phone call from his son. He gave no reason for hurrying things along.'

'Did he seem upset after the phone call?'

'He was upset when he took the call. He was angry at—' She stopped short.

Oliver said, 'Dr. Decameron told us he had an argument with Dr. Sparks.'

'It wasn't an *argument*. Dr. Sparks just became a little irritated shall we say.'

'Irritated at Decameron?'

'Yes.'

'Why?'

Her eyes grew suspicious. 'Dr. Decameron didn't tell you?'

'We'd like your opinion,' Marge said.

She stared at Marge, appeared to be weighing her words.

'Dr. Decameron read some of Dr. Sparks's faxes. The latest Curedon trial results. Of course, Reggie apologized right away. He was just excited about the data. You see, there had been some slowdown of Curedon's efficacy rate. The newest numbers however were very encouraging.'

'Yeah, Dr. Decameron told us something about that,' Oliver said. 'How you've been getting a lot more deaths lately.'

She bristled. 'Not a lot. Just some . . . Dr. Decameron seems to feel it might be a lab or computer processing error.'

Oliver said, 'Maybe he's making excuses because he's anxious to bring Curedon to market.'

Marge said, 'Big boost in his career as an academician, right?'

'Yes, but—'

'Maybe he's even been promised a piece of the profits?' Oliver suggested.

'No, no, no,' Liz protested. 'That's entirely false. The only one who would gain anything monetarily is . . . was Azor. You're way off base.'

'You're sure about that?' Marge said.

'Sure, I'm . . . at least to my knowledge.'

'Let's go back to the meeting,' Marge said. 'It ended around seven-thirty, maybe quarter to eight?'

'About that time, yes. Then Dr. Sparks and Dr. Decameron walked out together. Maybe that was ten minutes later.'

'Did Dr. Sparks seem in a hurry?'

'Well, he did push the meeting. But no . . . he didn't seem as if he was rushing to get somewhere. Of course, that wasn't Dr. Sparks's manner . . . to hurry things.'

Marge said, 'Did Dr. Decameron and Dr. Sparks often have arguments?'

Fulton gave a mysterious mile. 'One doesn't argue with Azor— With Dr. Sparks. Yes, we do have some academic exchange of ideas. But you try not to displease him. If you do, then you figure out what you've done and make amends. You either play his game or you're not on the team.'

'That doesn't make you feel . . . hemmed in?' Oliver asked.

'Hemmed in?' Fulton gave him an incredulous look. 'Sir, that's just a given when you work with someone of his stature. That's how it is with medical academia. Dr. Sparks owns *everything* that comes from his lab, even if he's only worked tangentially on the project.'

'That doesn't seem fair,' Marge stated.

'That's research science,' Liz said. 'Get on Azor's good side, you might get some credit. And you need credit if you want to advance. You must publish the right material under the right people. Someone with *clout*. For that privilege, you have to eat . . . you know.'

'Sparks make you eat a lot of . . . you know?' Marge asked.

'Well, he was graceful about it. He could afford to be because he knew who he was. I've worked for him for the last four years. It's nice to have a boss who's a benevolent tyrant. Because I've worked under the other kind, too.'

'Benevolent tyrant,' Marge repeated.

'Tyrant is too strong a word.'

'Dictator?' Oliver tried.

'Put it this way. After a while, you know when to suggest something and when to keep your mouth shut.'

'Does Decameron know the rules as well?'

'Reggie is an individualist. More forceful than I am, certainly. More than once at our meetings, he played devil's advocate. But he knew when to stop. The man is no fool.'

'Dr. Sparks was deeply religious,' Marge said.

'Yes.'

'How'd he feel about Dr. Decameron being homosexual?'

'I don't know. It never came up in any of our conversations.'

'Never talked about "those" kinds of people?' Oliver asked.

'Not to me.'

'A passing derogatory phrase never slipped from his lips?'

Fulton smiled. 'Nothing *slips* from Dr. Sparks's lips. If he "utters" something, it's for a reason.'

'Dr. Decameron said that one of Sparks's sons is gay. You know anything about that?'

'Which one?'

'The priest.'

She waved Oliver off. 'That's ridiculous. I mean I don't know if Bram is or isn't. But I don't know why Dr. Decameron would know, either. Unless he's indulging in wishful thinking. Bram's a nice-looking man.'

Marge asked, 'I take it you never detected Sparks having a problem with Dr. Myron Berger being Jewish?'

'Dr. Berger and Dr. Sparks have known each other for thirty-plus years. They attended Harvard Medical School together.'

'So, they're . . . peers?'

'Yes,' Fulton said.

'Being his peer,' Oliver said, 'is Dr. Berger just as . . . respectful of Dr. Sparks's rules? Or does he have more independence than either you or Dr. Decameron?'

'We all had *independence*,' Fulton said testily. 'We aren't chattel.'

Oliver said, 'You know what I'm getting at.'

'Frankly I don't, Fulton said.

'Was Sparks Berger's boss?' Marge asked.

'Of course.'

'And that didn't create resentment?' Marge asked. 'Two of them going to medical school together, and now Sparks is above him?'

Fulton rubbed her shoulder. 'If Dr. Berger felt resentful, he certainly had the skills, the experience, and the publications to move on. Being as he hadn't, I'm assuming he's comfortable with the relationship he has . . . had with Azor . . . with Dr. Sparks.'

'What kind of relationship did Dr. Sparks have with his family?' Marge asked.

'They adored him.'

'Did they ask him for money?' Oliver said.

'I don't know,' Fulton said. 'He didn't divulge things like that.'

'Ever?'

'No.'

'Dr. Decameron seemed sure that his children asked him for

money. Where did he get his information from?'

'I don't know where Reggie digs up his gossip.'

'His son Paul called Dr. Sparks tonight,' Marge said. 'Is that correct?'

'Yes.'

'Do you know what it was about?'

'No.'

'Did Dr. Sparks say he was cutting the meeting short to meet his son?'

'No. He didn't say anything.'

'Did his kids call him often?'

'I didn't monitor his calls. Ask Heather.'

'From your perception, Doctor,' Oliver said. 'Did they call him often?'

'I can't tell you yes or no because I don't know how you're defining often. Yes, they called him. Yes, his wife, Dolly, called him, too.'

'In the middle of meetings?'

'Sometimes. And if they did, the doctor usually interrupted himself to take their calls. He loved his family. And they loved him.'

Marge asked, 'Did his wife or any of them ever visit Dr. Sparks at work at the hospital?'

Oliver said, 'Maybe they'd drop in to say hello or have a cup of coffee with Dad?'

'You don't *drop in* on someone like Dr. Sparks.'

'Did you ever meet his wife and children?'

'Occasionally, I would see one of his kids visiting with him at the hospital.'

'What about his wife?'

Liz thought a moment. 'She'd come to the holiday parties.'

'What's she like?' Marge asked.

'Reserved, religious like him. But very, very proud of her husband and family. Beams when she talks about them. An old-fashioned woman. Her family is her life.'

Oliver said, 'And you observed all this by her presence at a Christmas party?'

Liz shook her head no. 'Once Azor was gracious enough to invite us to the house for Sunday dinner. Dolly . . . Mrs. Sparks must have spent most of the time in the kitchen, serving the food, happy to do it . . . to play hostess. We told her to sit, but she just laughed. Said she only sat for dinner on her birthday. What a feast! A mound of food. All of Azor's children and grandchildren were there. Sunday was a big day in his life. Like I said, Azor was very religious.'

'And everyone seemed to get along.'

'To my eyes, yes.'

'No tensions?' Marge asked.

'Not when I was there.' Fulton rubbed her eyes. 'My husband and I used to joke they were a Norman Rockwell poster from a bygone era. Especially when you compared them to us—' She stopped talking.

'Compared to you, how?' Marge pressed.

'My personal life isn't relevant.'

As if on cue, a rumbling motor belched loudly then suddenly stopped, leaving in its wake an uneasy silence. The door opened and a man stumbled in – long-limbed and *skinny*! A marionet of bones wearing a leather vest, torn jeans, and scarred black leather boots. His facial features were hidden behind several days of beard growth, unruly blond curls of hair hovering around his shoulder blades. He was sweating Scotch . . . could smell it as soon as he came flying past the doorpost. He looked at his wife, looked at the company with bleary eyes. 'What's goin' on?'

Fulton's face had become red, a portrait of anger. 'I'm going back to the hospital, Drew. An emergency.' Her eyes filled with tears.

Drew looked confused. 'Huh? What time is it?'

'A quarter past one.'

'Why're you goin' to the hospital?'

94

'Because Dr. Sparks has been murdered—'

'*What?*'

'The hospital needs help, Drew. I have to go. Excuse me.' Covering her face, Fulton flew out of the room

'Mur . . .' Drew was dazed, slumped in the pine rocker and looked at Oliver. 'No shit?'

'No shit.'

'God . . . that's . . .' Drew scratched his cheek, rubbed watery blue eyes floating in seas of pink. 'Think she'll lose her job?'

Marge stared at him. 'I don't know.'

'What happened?'

Oliver walked over to the door and opened it. Anything to air the place out. Maybe the jerk would take the hint and leave. He didn't. 'That's what we're trying to figure out.'

'You're the police?'

'Yes.'

'God, this is serious stuff, huh.'

Marge asked, 'What is your full name, sir?'

'My name?'

'Yes, your name.'

'Drew McFadden. I'm not under suspicion or anything?'

Marge and Oliver traded looks. Oliver walked over to him, leaned against the bay, looked down on Drew. 'Why do you think you're under suspicion?'

Drew looked up, puzzled, had no answer. 'Is Liz under suspicion?'

'Should she be?' Marge asked.

'I don't think so.' Drew laughed. 'But I don't know much.'

A good insight, Marge thought. 'She and her boss were close?'

'Real close. I often—' He stopped talking. His wife had returned.

She had changed into a white shirt, black pants, and a white lab coat, ID tag with her name and picture resting on its lapel. To the police, she said, 'If you need any further information, I'll be

95

at the hospital.' She glanced at her husband. 'Henry's bottle is in the fridge. In case I don't get back, Marta is due in at seven.'

'I'll take care of it, Liz.'

'Right.'

'That's too bad about Dr Sparks, Liz. I'm sorry.'

Fulton's face softened. 'Thank you, Drew. Go get some sleep.' To Oliver and Marge, she said, 'Can I walk you out?'

'Like to use the phone first, if I could,' Oliver said.

'Help yourself,' Fulton said. 'Good night.'

The door closed softly. Drew stared at the cops. 'You can use the phone in the kitchen.'

Marge said, 'You were saying that your wife and Dr. Sparks were very close.'

'Yeah. Yeah, they were.'

'In what way?' Oliver asked.

'What way?' He wrinkled his nose. 'Are you asking me if they were fooling around? I don't think so. Liz isn't the type. She's like . . .' He sliced the air. 'Straight arrow. At least, I think she is. But hell, I don't read women too well. She could be messin' with my head and I wouldn't know it.'

'Are you a straight arrow, sir?' Marge asked.

'Huh?'

Oliver's smile was oily. 'She means do you get around?'

Drew smiled back, but said nothing.

Oliver place his hand on Drew's bony shoulder. 'I mean she is gone all the time.' He winked. 'I know how it is.'

Drew started rocking, gave Oliver a conspiracy grin. 'Liz gets pissed at me. But hell, it wasn't my idea to get married.'

'No, I imagine it wasn't,' Marge mumbled.

Oliver shot her a dirty look. He said, 'How'd she talk you into it?'

Drew smiled enigmatically.

'You knocked her up. She gave you an ultimatum.'

'Hey, I didn't mind. I like Liz. *Love* the kid. Man, he's a cute

96

little sucker. You know, I think that's what gets to her. I'm home a lot with the kid. We're like real tight. Then she waltzes in on the weekends and the kid doesn't want to go to her. 'Cause he's used to me, unnerstan'?'

'I understand,' Oliver said.

'Pisses her off. I keep telling her it's only because I'm home so much. She shouldn't worry. Once Henry figures out what a jerk his old man is, he won't want nothing to do with me. So . . . I'm enjoying him while I'm still something in his eyes.'

Drew shook his head, smelled his armpits. 'I really stink. I'm sorry.'

Oliver smiled. It was sincere. 'You weren't expecting company.'

'No, that's for sure.'

'Are you a musician?' Marge asked.

'Yeah. Bass player. I'm part of the house band at Smokey's. Regular gig. Steady income. Not much income, but it's steady. I mean, what does Liz expect? You know, you start out in this business, thinking you're gonna be the next Eddie Vedder or Axl Rose. Hell, I'm thirty-four, man. Not too many people break it big at thirty-four. I'm real grateful to Liz. I mean real grateful. Rest of the band's living in shit, and I got this nice house, a decent car. It's not a Porsche but it's no broken-down Honda, either.'

Oliver glanced out the window, at the driveway. A red Miata convertible. 'Nice set of wheels.'

'Thanks. Liz bought it for me after Henry was born. Bought herself a baby Benz. I say, right on. She deserves it. She works hard.' His eyes clouded. 'Man, I hope she doesn't lose her job.'

'Was she in danger of losing her job?' Marge asked.

'If she was, she didn't tell me. She don't tell me much about work.' Drew smelled himself again. 'You want me to take a shower or something?'

Yes, screamed Marge's brain. Instead, she said, 'Nah, we'll be leaving in a few minutes. Did she ever mention anything about her job being in jeopardy?'

'Jeopardy? Isn't that a game show?'

'About her job being cut,' Oliver said.

Drew scrunched up his forehead. 'Well, she always used to say she was the last person on Sparks's project. If he was gonna bump anyone, I guess it would be Liz. But I met the old guy couple of times. He seemed to like her. After we ate dinner at his house, I told her that. I told her I thought he liked her. I told her not to worry.'

Marge said, 'If you don't mind my asking, when you ate dinner over there . . . how did Dr. Sparks react to you?'

'You mean 'cause of the way I look?' Drew rocked in the chair. 'Oh, I fixed myself up. I wore a suit and tie, put my hair in a ponytail. I wouldn't want to do anything that might make Liz lose her job. He was real polite to both of us.'

Drew stopped a moment.

'You know, he was an okay guy. We brought Henry of course. Dr. Sparks said something about how good I was with the little guy. I told him I loved kids. Sparks had a bunch of grandchildren. They started getting antsy at the table, you know, running around like kids do. I just got up and started playing with them. Felt a lot more comfortable with the kids than I did with the grown-ups. Especially when they started arguin'.'

Oliver's eyes met Marge's. 'Who was arguing?'

'I don't know. I left the table.'

'Think, Drew,' Marge prodded. 'Was it Dr. Sparks and one of his children, Dr. Sparks and his wife—?'

'No, it wasn't the wife. She and him barely spoke. She was busy serving all this food. Man, I never seen so much food in my life. Turkey and ham and roast beef and mashed potatoes—'

'So if it wasn't Dr. Sparks and his wife, it was . . . ?'

Drew held his finger in the air. 'The priest. Dr. Sparks and the priest. Actually, I think the whole family was arguin' with the priest.'

Oliver paused. 'About what?'

98

'Stuff about God. Stuff I didn't understand.'

Marge asked, 'You don't remember any of it?'

'No.'

'You remember enough to recall them arguing,' Oliver said. 'Doesn't anything stick in your mind?'

Drew paused again. 'Something about evil thoughts being evil or whatever. I remember that because I remember thinking: Drew, you're in trouble. 'Cause you have *lots* of evil thoughts. Liz could tell you better.'

Marge asked, 'Did she participate in the argument?'

'I don't know. If she did, it was probably on Dr. Sparks's side. She wouldn't do anything to piss him off.'

Oliver asked, 'Was the priest angry?'

Drew stopped rocking, folded his arms across his chest. 'You know, everyone was dumping on him. His name was Bram.' He smiled. 'Guess I do remember some things.'

'Go on,' Marge said.

'I remember thinking, "If I was getting dumped on, like he was, I'd either blow or go." He just sat there, real calm, just taking it. Never raised his voice.'

'Why were they dumping on him?' Marge asked.

'I don't know. I guess they didn't like what he was sayin'.'

'What was he saying?'

'I don't know. I just felt for the guy, wondered why everyone was dumping on him. But maybe he was used to it. 'Cause when the missus called the kids for dessert, conversation went back to being polite. And the priest acted like nothing happened. Smiling with the kids. Playing magic tricks . . . you know, making nickels disappear and reshowin' up behind their ears. I like that one. I do it all the time with Henry. The priest has a twin brother, you know.'

'Luke,' Marge said. 'Was he dumping on him, too?'

'They all were—' Drew paused. 'No, you're right. How about that. You're real good.'

Marge said, 'Good about what?'

'The twin. A few minutes after they started arguin', the twin got up and started playing with the kids, just like me. Must be another one who hates conflict.'

'You hate conflict?'

'Boy, yeah, I hate it. Bad Karma. When Liz starts to yell, man, I'm outta here. If I don't leave, I blow.'

'I hear you,' Oliver stated.

'Maybe the twin was like that. 'Cause he just got up from the table and started making a building with Legos. He's got two cute ones – boy and a girl. Twins just like he is. He's actually a triplet, can you believe that? I wouldn't have minded Liz having twins. But I think three would have been too much for me.'

Marge asked, 'So the priest wasn't angry at his father?'

'Not to my eyes. Just ate his dessert and played magic tricks with his nieces and nephews.'

'Now about Dr. Sparks? Was he angry with his son?'

'He didn't appear pissed. He ate his dessert, too. It was pie. She's baked like a hunnerd pies. I had two pieces – blueberry and peach. Man, that woman could cook. I told my wife afterward that I'd put on a tie any old day of the week, if they want to have us again.'

'What did your wife say about that?'

'She patted my head, said not to count on another invite for a while. Not because I blew it or anything. Just that Dr. Sparks doesn't invite people to his house a lot.'

'Especially if there was tension in the family,' Marge added.

'I wouldn't say tension. But they did have an argument.'

'Drew, maybe it was just an intellectual discussion, instead of an argument,' Marge said.

'Ma'am, I don't know too much about intellectual discussions,' Drew said. 'But I do know a whole lot about arguments. Take my word for it. It was an argument.'

9

'Berger's here, Loo. At New Chris.' Webster checked his watch. 'Arrived 'bout ten minutes ago. He said that he and his wife went to a dinner theater in Tustin—'

'*Tustin?*' Decker interrupted.

'Yeah, a little off the beaten path.'

'I'll say.' Decker spoke into the Volare's mike, turned down the fan to the heater so he could hear Webster over the radio receiver. 'It's about a two-hour drive from New Chris.'

'Anyway, Berger said he and the wife saw *My Fair Lady*, had no idea what was roaring until he heard it on the radio. If he's to be b'lieved.'

'You have reason to doubt him, Tom?'

'Nope. He came straight to New Chris from the theater. Wife dropped him off directly, didn't even change. And he did come in wearing a suit and tie. Croc Ballys on the feet. The kind y'all wear only when you're goin' out.'

'Where is he now?'

'In a private meeting.'

'So you haven't really interviewed him?'

'Not yet. He's holed up with a bunch of 'em, consulting with one n'other – Dr. Berger, Dr. Fulton, Dr Decameron. Now there's a piece of work.'

'In what way?'

'Ya haven't met him yet?'

'I haven't. I heard he's opinioned and open about his gayness.'

'Yes, sir, he is very decisive and very gay. I think the word is flamboyant. But I'll tell y'all something. He's real good with the

101

staff. Nurses come up to him, he isn't afraid to hug 'em or kiss 'em or let 'em cry. And ya know he isn't doin' it to make time. What do you want Bert and me to do with Dr. Berger? I think it would be bad form right now to pull him out of an important meeting.'

'Agreed,' Decker said. 'How is the staff interviewing going?'

'Bert and I talked to most of the night staff. Nothing that I think will impact heavily on the case, but a few interesting personal tidbits.'

'Like what?'

'Oh, things like how the doctor used a thermometer to make sure his coffee was the right temperature. He was so particular 'bout things, he once got mad because they changed the brand of surgical sponges. Claimed he could tell the difference.'

'Maybe he could.'

'I could tell you more, but I'd have to go over my notes carefully. And right now, they're not in real good shape . . . my handwriting at this hour isn't swift. I gotta go back and type everything neat like.'

'It can wait until morning.'

'Thank you, sir.'

Decker said, 'We'll talk in the morning. Both of you, go to the station house and finish the paperwork. I'll see you tomorrow.'

'What about Dr. Berger? You don't want me to wait to interview him more completely?'

'I'll do him. I've got a brief stop to make. Probably by the time I'm done, he'll be out of his meeting.'

'You sure you don't want us to wait for him?'

'No, it's all right. I'll do it.'

'Thanks, Loo. I was hoping you'd be insistent.'

'See you later.'

Decker hung up the mike, sat back in the driver's seat, and turned up the fan to the heat. It was almost two in the morning. Most homicides were solved within twenty-four to forty-eight hours. At this moment, he had nothing. No motives and no suspects with the scarlet K for Killer branded on their forehead. He hoped this wasn't random. If so, he was going to have a hard time.

He looked at the evidence bags on the passenger seat. A single business card.

Ace Sparks . . . born to be wild.

A glimpse at another side of Sparks. Out of context with the religious, stern, exacting physician, the common portrait drawn by people who knew him.

Ace Sparks.

Born to be wild.

What the hell. One more stop wouldn't kill him.

He turned on the motor to the Volare.

After five years of being a practicing Jew, Decker felt strange entering a church. As he walked up the steps to St. Thomas's he wondered if he'd feel any emotional tug when he passed the chapel. Probably not. Much to Ida Decker's consternation, he hadn't ever been much of a churchgoer as a youngster.

He walked up the stairs, gave the double wooden doors a tug, and found them locked. He knocked, though he suspected it was a useless gesture. The doors were so thick and the building was so big, in order to be heard someone would have to be near by happenstance.

No response, of course.

He thought about trying the side doors when he saw the white button by the side of the entry. *Now there's a novel thought, Deck.* A doorbell. He depressed the button and a harsh buzz screamed out. Waited a minute, pushed the bell again. Several minutes later, he finally heard footsteps. The door unlocked, a pair of eyes peeking through a crack.

'Yes?'

Decker took out ID. 'Lieutenant Peter Decker. I'm here to see Father Abram Sparks. Is he in?'

The eyes moved frantically. 'Can you come around to the rectory?'

'Where?'

'The side area. You'll see a door there. Okay?'

'Okay.'

The door closed. Decker climbed down the stairs and walked around to the side. He followed a well-lit, stepping-stone pathway that hugged a wall; behind it looked to be a courtyard. About five hundred yards down was a two-story stucco building. The door was open when he got there.

The eyes belonged to a kid . . . twenty if that. His chin and forehead were still dotted with acne. He wore jeans and T-shirt and blocked the doorway. 'Father Sparks is . . . his door is closed.'

'Why don't you knock on it?'

A voice in the background asked who it was.

'Police,' Decker shouted out.

Sparks came out, draped his arm around his young charge. 'Thank you, Jim, you can go back upstairs now.'

'I didn't want to disturb—'

'It's fine, Jim.'

'Are you sure, Father?'

'Positive.' Bram smiled. Weary. Edgy. 'Bye.'

Jim stared at Decker, then turned and walked up a staircase.

'Come in,' Sparks said.

The place was halfway between an office suite and a residence. A living room at one side, a receptionist's office on the other. Once it might have been a dining room.

'This way.'

Sparks led Decker past a small kitchen into a den area. A few beat-up sofas populated the room. He unlocked a pair of french doors and took Decker outside into a courtyard illuminated by low-voltage spots. It was thickly planted with flowers and foliage. A three-tiered fountain sat in the center of the landscape, spilling out glittery drops in the white light. Cool out here. Peaceful, too. They walked down a colonnade into a separate one-story bungalow marked CHANCELLERY.

Sparks opened the door.

'Welcome to my mess.' He quickly crossed himself. 'Watch your step. I've got material on the floor, too.'

Mess was an understatement. Sparks's entire office was crammed with junk. Enough papers and books to replenish a tropical rain forest. Piles upon piles of notes on his desk – his desks. There were three of them. Walls of bookshelves, all of them overflowing with reading matter. As Decker looked around, there was some loose logic to the categories. Books inscribed in Greek were all placed together in one case, matter written in Russian or some other obscure Cyrillic language occupied another case. The Latin and English tomes comprised the biggest portion of his collection, taking up the entire back wall.

But Decker's eyes were transfixed by other things. The texts written in Hebrew and Aramaic. Specifically, a Hebrew Bible, a *Chumash*, along with a complete set of Talmud that took up two shelves.

The holy book of his newfound faith.

There were other Hebrew books as well, but Decker couldn't understand the titles. For just a moment, he wished Rina were here. Then he scratched that thought. Because he could only imagine how uncomfortable she would feel in this library. Because Orthodox Jews feel antsy about anyone outside the faith dissecting their *sepharim* – their holy books. Yet here was a slew of holy books that Rina kissed because God's name was written inside them – sitting in bookshelves, handled by a priest in an office that also held an enormous wall crucifix of Jesus.

Fighting fatigue and a pinch of uneasiness, he forced himself into his professional mode. A man had been brutally murdered. He had a job to do.

Next to the wall crucifix were several framed photographs. The first was a candid – Bram in a cassock, sitting at a table, his head resting on his open palm, reading a tome in Latin. The other two were posed shots. Bram with old men dressed in ornate religious vestments. In the last photo, Decker recognized all the parties. Bram with the Pope.

Sparks said, 'Rome and I get along.'

'I can see.'

The priest took a pile of papers off a chair and placed it on the floor. 'Please. Have a seat.'

Decker sat. 'I came around through the front. Pity that churches have to lock their doors.'

Sparks took a seat behind one of his three desks, unplugging the phone and answering machine. 'When someone controls the vandalism, I'll keep the door unlocked.'

'Fair enough.' Decker took out a notepad. 'The rectory. You have residential quarters there?'

'Yes.'

'So you live at the church?'

'Basically, yes. I've been the resident priest here for seven years. But I've always maintained a one-bedroom apartment off grounds. Growing up in a large family, once in a blue moon, I have a fierce need for privacy.'

'Who's Jim?'

'The young man who answered the door?'

'Yes.'

'He's one of my many pass-through seminarians. Currently, I've got two. They're doing field training here. They send them down from St. John's in Camarillo. That's where the Los Angeles diocese runs its seminary.'

'You're the church's sole priest?'

'Sole *resident* priest. If I'm out of town, Loyola/Marymount will send over some guys to do Mass for my congregants.'

'Do you teach?'

'Currently, I'm conducting six different classes here – basic bible, faith in the face of adversity, the true meaning of Christmas, current events and religion . . . things like that.' Sparks looked at

Decker. 'I have brochures. But I suspect that's not why you're here.'

Decker smiled. 'Maybe another time.'

'Of course.'

'Do you teach at the University as well?'

'Occasionally. But academic teaching is time consuming. I've got a parish to run.'

Decker's eyes swept over the room which was more of a library. 'You seem like the . . . academic type.'

Bram smiled. 'Should I take that as a compliment?'

'A simple statement. The chancellery's full of books.'

'I do some independent work for Rome, mostly translating ancient papers and documents. I was a Classics language major in college. I've got a natural feel for words. But it's the church that owns my heart. It's my family.'

'You have *lots* of family, then.'

'Yes, sometimes it's too much of a good thing. But I've no complaints . . .' Sparks shook his head. 'Until tonight . . .'

'How are you doing, Father?'

'Call me Bram. I'm doing lousy. But thanks for asking.'

'I hope I didn't wake you.'

'Not at all. I was up . . . trying to make sense . . . driving myself crazy actually. Asking myself, *why him?*'

'I have no answer for you.'

Bram sighed. 'I'm a purveyor of faith. I'm used to ambiguities, believing without seeing. I try to see God's will in everything. But this . . .' He threw up his hands. 'Maybe it's a test of some sort. If it is, I think I'm flunking.'

'You're allowed to grieve, Father.'

'I suppose. Hard being on the other end. Receiving comfort instead of giving it.'

Bram grew quiet . . . pensive. Decker studied the priest. Calm, but not because he lacked emotions. Just not overtly effusive. Well suited for the clergy. 'I meant to ask you this at the house. Does your father have living parents?'

107

'No. My paternal grandparents are dead. Dad has a brother. He lives in Indiana. He's coming out for the memorial service tomorrow.'

'Uncle Caleb.'

'Ah, you have a memory.'

'No, but I take good notes,' Decker said. 'Is he a doctor also?'

'A pastor.'

'Runs in the family.'

'According to my dad, that's the way it was in the Midwest back then. Oldest son goes into the profession to support the younger son who goes into the ministry.'

'You did it backward in your family.'

'Pardon?'

'You're the priest and your brother Mike is the doctor.'

Sparks rubbed his eyes under his glasses. 'Becoming a priest wasn't part of the play. What can I do for you, Lieutenant, at . . .' He checked his watch. 'At two-fifteen in the morning? You keep going this long, we can say morning prayers together.'

I don't think so. Decker asked, 'Do you have patience for a few quick questions?'

'Certainly. We're both after the same thing.'

Suddenly, the priest let out a small laugh.

'What?' Decker asked.

'Nothing. Inside joke. How can I help you?'

Decker pulled Azor Sparks's Harley card from his pocket and handed it to Bram. 'Any idea what this is about?'

A smile rose to the priest's lips – genuine. 'Son of a gun.' He shook his head. 'Can I keep this?'

'Not at the moment. I found it in the car, so it's evidence. What is it?'

'My father . . .' Sparks chuckled. 'Believe it or not, my father rode with a club.'

'A motorcycle club?'

'Your basic weekend warrior.' Bram sat back in his chair, stared at the card. 'My brother Luke and I went with him to buy his first bike. We begged him to take us along. Because some people see an older man . . . they take advantage. I don't know about you, Lieutenant, but when I go out to buy something specialized, my knowledge of the acquisition is usually pretty bad. I remember when I had to buy some computers for the church. The salesperson started talking about megabytes and RAMs and ROMs and CD-ROM for virtual reality. I didn't have a clue.

'My father goes to buy a motorcycle. The salesman takes him over to a bike.'

Bram laughed softly, his eyes watching a distant memory.

'Dad starts launching into this lecture of what's wrong with the motorcycle. The cam chain tensioner isn't calibrated to exact zero. The front hydraulic fork isn't welded properly to the brake caliper. The rear drive sprocket . . .' He smiled. 'All these years of education and I still don't know what a sprocket is.'

'It's the teeth in a gear that fit into a wheel,' Decker said.

'Good for you. I can see why—' He stopped midsentence. 'Anyway, Dad blew the salesman away. They became instant friends. He's been riding with this hard-case leather pack for a couple of years now. They called him Granddaddy Sparks.'

Bram looked at the card, handed it back to Decker.

'Apparently he enjoyed it a lot more than he let on. Which was typical of my father. He kept it close to the heart. It's nice to know my father indulged in fantasies.'

'Did you call them to come to the service tomorrow?'

'You mean his motorcycle friends?'

'Yes.'

'No, tonight I only called the relatives and Dad's church friends. I wouldn't even know how to get hold of these guys.'

He thought a moment.

'I suppose I could call the dealership tomorrow.' Again, the priest smiled. 'Now that would be something to see. Dad's biker buddies sitting next to the church ladies.' His eyes suddenly moistened. 'So needless. What a horrible, *horrible* . . . tragedy. As much as I try to fight it, say it was in God's hands . . . because we're all in God's hands . . . I keep asking myself why *my* father? Why Azor Moses Sparks? Who did so much good. Just a colossal . . . *waste*!'

'I'm sorry.' Decker waited a beat, then said, 'If you're up to it, I've one more question.'

'Sure.'

'I was comparing notes with a few of my detectives. Did you often eat Sunday dinner with your family?'

Bram looked at Decker. 'Why do you ask?'

'Please, Father. Just bear with me.'

'If I had no church obligations, I would eat Sunday dinner with my family. Why?'

'Ever any tension at the dinner table?'

Sparks gave Decker a quizzical look. 'Lots of opinionated people under one roof. Sure, there was occasional friction. In general, the dinners were remarkably polite. You can't judge us by the way we were this evening.'

'I realize that.'

'No, it goes even further than the fact that we were all in terrible shock. My siblings and I have an enormous respect for our parents. We keep the conflict to a minimum when they're around.'

'Always?'

Again, Sparks stared at Decker. 'What do you want to ask me, Lieutenant?'

'Your father once had a colleague of his and her husband over for dinner.'

'A colleague of his and *her* husband.' Bram brushed long hair out of his eyes. 'Dr. Fulton. Her husband's name was Drew. Drew McFadden. Funny. I couldn't remember her name earlier this evening. But her husband's a man I met maybe two times . . . remembered his name in a snap. What would Freud say about that?'

Decker said nothing.

Sparks said, 'Maybe he left a bigger impression on me than she did. Anyway, what about the evening?'

Decker looked the priest in the eyes. 'He said you got into a big argument with your father. Something about evil thoughts.'

Sparks maintained eye contact. 'I don't argue with my father, Lieutenant.'

Decker said, 'Maybe I should say your father was arguing with you?'

Again, Sparks pushed hair from his face. 'I don't know a thing about Mr. McFadden or his wife, Dr. Fulton, or their relationship with each other. Not a thing, all right?'

'Fine.'

'So this digression is theoretical, okay?'

'Go on.'

'Suppose Mr. McFadden is a passive type of person. A guy who might be happy to stand back and let his wife support him, take care of him. So he can do his own thing. A person like that, who lets others run his life, might choose to avoid confrontation. In that person's misguided perception, it is possible for him to misinterpret a theological discussion as an argument.'

'A *heated* theological discussion?'

'Not heated. Nothing much more than what you witnessed earlier this evening with my sister, Eva. Would you call that heated?'

'She was aggravated.'

'She was stunned over her father's untimely death.'

'So Mr. McFadden was wrong? There was no argument?'

'No argument. There was a discussion.'

'Funny, because he told us that it was very much an argument. As a matter of fact, he told me it wasn't just your father. He said everyone was dumping on you. And you just took it.'

'Why is this important? Are you trying to establish a year-old animated discussion between my father and me as a motive for murder?'

111

Decker raised his brow. *Maybe.* Because at the moment, he was grasping at straws. He said, 'I'm merely asking a question, Father.'

Sparks exhaled, rubbed his eyes. 'I remember the discussion. We were talking about the different religious perceptions of evil thought versus evil action. Were the two equivalent? Not in a judicial sense. No one was debating the difference between evil thought and action in American jurisprudence. We were talking theology. Before the eyes of God, are evil thoughts indeed evil actions?'

Bram looked at Decker, gauging him. 'Yes, it's weird. But it beats "how 'bout them Dodgers?"'

Decker said, 'I understand what it's like to live in a religiously driven home.'

'Thank you.'

'Go on.'

Sparks said, 'Evil thought as a moral trespass is a Christian concept – a very *Catholic* concept as well. Evil thoughts require confession, penance and absolution just like evil action. Why? Because if evil thoughts aren't dealt with . . . atoned for and expunged from the idiorepertoire of our mental workings, they will lead to evil action.'

'Okay.'

'Two schools of thought. Evil ruminations grow into monsters unto themselves until the individual is forced to act upon them. Or my philosophy, which certainly isn't original, that with ninety-nine percent of us, evil thoughts are pressure valves. A way to release our frustrations or lusts or anger. Ergo, are penance and atonement *really* necessary for evil thoughts or immoral fantasies? Furthermore, are religious representatives – such as myself – doing a disservice to their flocks by convincing them to drive away these thoughts? Cutting off an avenue of escape from tension. suggested this kind of narrow-minded repression might even be potentially harmful. My family – especially my father – took exception. Said a clean mind was tantamount to a clean soul.

112

Words that my mother agreed with wholeheartedly.'

'How'd you respond?'

'I didn't. I backed down. And that, my friend, is it.'

Decker rolled his tongue in his cheek. 'Why'd you back down?'

'My, you're inquisitive.'

'I'm a detective. It's my job to find things out. Not unlike yours, Father.'

'Hardly, but why go into that now?' Sparks looked down, then up. 'I don't argue with my father because we don't have *parity*. As religious and learned as he is, he is at a distinct disadvantage simply because I've had more theological education. I can pull rabbits out of my hat. He can't. As far as my sibs go . . . Lord, I'm tired.'

Decker waited.

'I backed down with my sibs because I didn't want to come on too strong in front of our parents. Religion is my field, my calling, my *life*. If I make a brilliant analysis using theological exegesis, in their eyes, I'm not Bram, the learned priest. On the contrary, I'm Bram, the Golden Boy, scoring brownie points with my parents. Uh-uh, I'm not going to play that game.'

'You're all adults.'

'You're right. It's absurd to have to think about these things at thirty-five. But old habits are hard to break.' Bram grew pensive. 'And there's a history behind it. They grew up with a brother to whom being right was the eleventh commandment.'

His eyes grew far away.

'I used to love to debate . . . argue. I could always use words to drive someone into the ground. A big power lust for me.'

His eyes refocused, zeroed in on Decker's.

'I had a cherished friend once. A man who could use words better than I. We used to spend hours together, arguing about God. I loved him like a brother. Then one day he started seeing double. He took sick. Ten months later, he was dead.'

He swallowed hard.

'All of a sudden being right wasn't important any more.'

His eyes were wet, and hot. Decker kept his gaze steady, his face impassive. Then abruptly, Sparks's face went slack, a candle sculpture melting into exhaustion. 'So let them dump on me. I can take it.'

He checked his watch.

'It's late. Don't you have a wife and kids at home?'

Decker was quiet.

'That was rude. I apologize. What else do you need?'

'Nothing at the moment.' Decker stood. 'Thank you for your time.'

'Something else pops into your head, feel free to call, drop in.' The priest plugged the phone back in. 'Because it's a certain fact that I'm *not* going anywhere.'

Turning on the lamp. More of a symbolic gesture than anything else. Because Rina had given up on sleep a long time ago. Her eyes took a minute to adjust to the harsh light. She checked the clock.

Half past two.

Peter said it was going to be a long night.

A very long night.

Her fingers brushed over the phone. The name of the place escaped her. A vague recollection, but nothing clear came into view.

With determination, she hoisted herself out of bed and retrieved the Yellow Pages. Plopped back into bed and began looking under C for churches. It took her just a moment to find The Holy Order of St. Thomas's.

That was it.

Was a church ever open twenty-four hours a day? Synagogues weren't. But pulpit rabbis often had emergency beeper numbers. In case there was a crisis with one of their members.

She dialed. Two rings, three rings. The machine kicked in. An anonymous female voice . . .

She had reached the Holy Order of Saint Thomas's Church. 'Please leave a message at the sound of the beep. For emergency

114

counseling and immediate consultation with Father Abram Sparks, please dial . . .'

Rina waited patiently while a series of numbers and instructions were recited. Finally, she heard the beep.

It took a moment for Rina to find her voice. Then she said, 'Yes, this is Rina . . .' A beat. 'This is Rina Lazarus . . . Decker placing a call to Father Abram Sparks. I just wanted to—'

'Hello?'

Bram's voice cut through the line. And with a single sound a thousand memories flooded her mind. She couldn't talk. Dead silence between them.

Bram said, 'Phone's been ringing off the hook. I put the machine on because I haven't had the stomach to talk to anyone. But you . . .' His voice cracked. 'I can't tell you what this means to me.'

'Bram, I'm so sorry, I'm . . .'

'I know.'

Nobody spoke.

Rina said, 'Is there anything I can do for you?'

'You calling is enough.' He paused. 'Your husband just left my office. Actually, he came to the house about three, four hours ago.'

Rina didn't respond.

'Asked us some questions,' Bram said. 'He treated everyone with sensitivity. He's a good man, Rina. I'm sure Yitzy would have liked him.'

Rina felt her throat constrict as ghosts talked to her from the grave. 'Your father was a very important man. I'm sure Peter has every available man . . . oh dear, that sounds so . . .'

Bram didn't answer.

'Can't I do *anything* for you?' Rina pleaded.

Bram said, 'We're holding a service tomorrow for my dad at his church. Not a funeral . . . body is still in autopsy . . . but it's a remembrance more than anything. Three P.M. Be nice if you came.'

'Of course, I'll be there. Where is it?'

'It's going to be mobbed, Rina. My father was a respected man with many admirers. I won't see you if you come on your own. Let me pick you up—'

'Bram—'

'I'll meet you in front of the Yeshivat Ohavei Torah at two tomorrow. I'm going to see Rav Schulman in the morning anyway.'

'He called you?' Rina paused. 'Of course, he'd call you.'

'Five minutes after the news broke. He wanted to come to the service, too. But he told me he's not feeling too well lately. What does that mean?'

'He had a minor stroke about a year ago. He's as alert as always. But it's hard for him to walk.'

'I'm sorry to hear that. It's been a while since I've visited him. Anyway, I'm going out there. I'm giving the eulogy tomorrow. I've found a couple of verses of *Tehillim* that I think are particularly appropriate for my father.'

Rina noticed that Bram said *Tehillim* instead of Psalms.

'I want to go over them with Rav Schulman,' Bram continued. 'I'm sure he'll give me a fresh insight. The man is a wellspring of knowledge.'

Rina mumbled a 'yes' as the word *Tehillim* bounced around her brain. *Tehillim.* Prayers that spoke of God's many praises. How many times had she uttered them as her first husband, Yitzy, lay dying? They were prayers for the dying. Prayers for the dead.

Rina said, 'Two o'clock in front of the yeshiva. I'll be there.'

Bram hesitated. 'Have you told your husband? That you know me . . . through Yitzy?'

'I haven't spoken to him since he got the initial phone call. He's been gone all night. Besides, it's not really relevant, is it?'

'No, it's not relevant. But it is a good idea. To tell him we're . . . well acquainted. He is investigating my father's murder. It's best to keep everything in the open. If he finds out we know each other through a third party, like Rav Schulman for instance, he might get upset.'

Rina said, 'I'll tell him tomorrow after the service.'

'Rina, he'll probably *be* at the service.'

'If he is, I'll handle him, Bram. I can handle my own husband.'

'I won't say another word.'

Rina bit her lip. 'I'm an idiot, jumping on you—'

'It doesn't matter—'

'Bram, every time I mention Yitzy, it unnerves him.'

'I can understand his feelings.'

'I do understand them. That's why I want to tread lightly. But you're right. I'll tell him first thing tomorrow morning. He should know we're friends. Certainly from a professional standpoint. I don't want anything hidden that might interfere with your father's investigation.' She sighed. 'Even if it means opening past wounds.'

'Rina, if it's too painful for you, I can pretend this phone call never happened.'

'Absolutely not, Abram. I wouldn't hear of it.' She cleared her throat. 'I'll meet you . . . tomorrow at two.'

'Thanks for calling, Rina. It means the world to me.'

She hesitated, then said, 'You knew I'd call, Abram.'

'Yes, Rina,' he answered. '*This* time I knew you'd call.'

Sadness washed over Rina. She said nothing.

Bram said, 'Good grief, that was stupid!'

'It was a well-deserved rebuke, Abram. I was wrong.'

'So was I.'

Rina said, soothingly, 'Just goes to show you. Sometimes two wrongs do make a right.'

10

The third floor of New Chris was taken up by the Cardiac Care unit – six divisions, each with its own central nursing station surrounded by a dozen private suites. The rooms, radiating from the center like spokes on a wheel, reminded Decker of biblical leper caves – isolated, dark, quiet, ominous. No human noises, just the occasional electronic whine of high-tech equipment at work.

Decker leaned against the wall, watching it all, fascinated by the sci-fi medicine. Someone tapped his shoulder. He straightened and turned around.

A heavyset nurse with muscular forearms. Young and well scrubbed. In another life, she might have been a milkmaid. She whispered, 'Dr. Berger will be with you in a moment. Would you like more coffee?

'No thank you,' Decker said softly. The nurse's ID tag told him her name was Tara. 'I'm pretty much coffeed-out. What exactly is Dr. Berger doing?'

'Pardon?'

Decker cleared his throat. 'It's almost three in the morning. Aren't most of the patients asleep?'

Tara said, 'He's just finishing off two o'clock vitals check. Normally, we nurses record the numbers, dispense the necessary medicines according to the doctor's orders. But Dr. Berger wanted to familiarize himself with Dr. Sparks's patients. It will help ease the transition . . . as much as that's possible.' She swallowed hard. 'Dreadful!'

'Horrible.'

'Who would do such a terrible thing?'

119

'I don't know, ma'am.' Decker leaned in close. 'You wouldn't have any thoughts about it, would you?'

'Why no!' Tara looked down. 'Well, I have thoughts. But they don't mean anything.'

'Tell them to me anyway.'

She started to talk, stopped, then bunched her facial muscles in concentration. 'Well . . . to me, it sounds like . . . maybe he picked up the wrong person.'

Decker looked around the room. 'What do you mean by "picked up"?'

'Like a motorist who he thought needed help. But the motorist was really a robber. Isn't that a possibility?'

Decker slipped out his notebook. 'Have you ever known Dr. Sparks to pick up people?'

'Not hitchhikers. But he was a take-charge kind of man. And he was a *doctor*.'

'Meaning?'

Tara dropped her voice even further. 'Let's say he thought he saw an accident. I'm sure he would have pulled the car over to help, no?'

The woman was making sense. Decker said, 'Go on.'

'But suppose it wasn't a real accident? Suppose it was a dodge . . . to entrap some poor unsuspecting motorist. And of course, Dr. Sparks would pull over. And when he did, he was carjacked. Robbed. Taken to a dark place . . .' She shivered. 'It's awful to think about it.'

'Do you know if Dr. Sparks ever did that before? Stopped at the scene of auto accidents?'

'Once. The driver had had a heart attack and had crashed into the sidewalk.' She paused. 'Everyone was talking about it the next day . . . it became a joke.'

'A joke?'

'Yeah, the bad news is you had a heart attack at the wheel of your car. The good news is Dr. Sparks was in the neighborhood.

And it's true. The accident victim *was* lucky. She wouldn't have made it if Dr. Sparks hadn't stopped.' Tara thought a moment. 'You know that wasn't the only joke going around.'

'Tell me.'

'Everyone used to josh that Dr. Sparks secretly carried a paramedics' scanner.'

Decker wrote sloppily, his tired brain trying to decipher what she was saying. 'Why?'

'I'm not sure why. Maybe to hear if there were any auto accidents near to where he was. So he could help out. One of his many famous lectures dealt with the importance of the first few minutes when treating the victim of a cardiac infarct. Or it could be the joke came about because of Dr. Sparks's incredible dedication to saving people's lives. If someone needed help, he was there – oh, there's Dr. Berger. Excuse me.'

Tara scuttled away.

Round but compact, Berger moved quickly toward Decker. But his carriage belied his energy level. Of medium height, he appeared to be in his sixties with fleshy features – a bulbous nose and thick lips. His lids drooped, puffy pillows under his eyes, cheeks sagging with wan flesh. A face that had been dragged under the wheels of exhaustion. The dome of his head was pink, shiny skin dotted with sweat. A small gray ring of hair clothed the bottom and sides of his cranium. His clothes were stylish but in need of a pressing. In fact, his whole body seemed wrinkled with fatigue.

'I really am very busy, Lieutenant.'

'I know you are, Dr. Berger. All I need is just a few minutes of your time.'

Berger nodded. 'Step out into the hallway.' On his way out, he said, 'Tara, what the hell is going on in 4D?'

Tara looked up from behind the nurse's desk. 'Pardon, Dr. Berger?'

'Where is Mrs. Gooden?'

'She was moved to 6B yesterday.'

121

'Who moved her? Dr. Sparks?'

'Yes, sir.'

'Well, move her back here. I want all *my* patients in one wing, okay?'

Tara paused. 'You want me to move Mrs. Gooden *now*?'

Berger barked, 'By eight o'clock tomorrow. Unless she's fibrillating. Then you can leave her until she stabilizes. You might think I'd be allowed to have one division to myself since Dr. Sparks has the other five.'

Tara blinked rapidly. 'Yes, sir.'

Berger glanced back at Decker, a blush rising to his cheeks. 'This way.'

Decker followed Berger into the hallway.

Berger said, 'It may seem petty to you, but it makes my life a hell of a lot easier . . . to have all my patients together.'

Decker didn't answer.

Berger rubbed his eyes. 'What do you need from me? I told the other detective, Wooster or Werber—'

'Webster.'

'That's it. Mr. Southern Boy. I told him that my wife and I were at a dinner theater in Tustin. As soon as I heard the news, I came rushing back. What else do you need from me?'

'I'm just trying to get a timetable for Dr. Sparks—'

'I saw Dr. Sparks leave with Dr. Decameron around a quarter to eight. Which means these questions are best directed to Dr. Decameron. Now, if you'll excuse me, I have a hospital to run.'

He started to walk away. Decker said, 'Lucky for New Chris that they found someone to fill Dr. Sparks's shoes. And so fast.'

Berger stopped, pivoted around. 'Are you being snide?'

'No.' Decker's face was flat. 'Just that everyone keeps saying Sparks is a one-of-a-kind. It's fortunate that he had you on his team to take over in this crisis.'

Berger's cheeks turned crimson. 'I'm not saying I'm Dr. Sparks, sir. I'm just saying there are patients here and *someone* has to take care of them.'

'Absolutely,' Decker agreed 'Dr. Decameron said you were a fine surgeon.'

Berger stared at him. 'He said that, did he?'

'He did.'

'Well, I'll have to thank him for the vote of confidence. Now, if you'll excuse—'

'Will you also take over the FDA trials of Curedon, Dr. Berger?'

Berger pursed his lips. 'I don't know. I haven't thought that far in advance.'

'I was just wondering if Curedon was more Dr. Decameron's bailiwick.'

'Not at all—'

'Being as Dr. Decameron . . . and Dr. Fulton for that matter . . . are primarily researchers. And you're primarily a practicing surgeon.'

'You can stop right here, Lieutenant.' Berger held out his palm. 'You've got some facts turned around and right now, I don't have time to correct your wrong impressions.'

'When will you have time?' Decker asked. 'Don't want to go around with a wrong impression. Might cause me to jump to wrong conclusions.'

Berger tossed Decker a mean smile. 'I've got work to do. If you come back . . . say a half hour before my six o'clock rounds, I'll talk to you.'

Decker looked at his watch. Three-fifteen A.M. Berger wasn't the only one with work to do. 'Five-thirty, it is.' He slipped on his jacket, bade the doctor a good night.

Bunking down at Devonshire made infinitely more sense than waking up Rina. At his desk, Decker left a message on their answering machine, telling his wife that he loved her and that he'd call in the morning.

He went inside the squad room – empty except for Homicide. The team was filling out thick stacks of forms, mowing through paperwork. Though there were a half-dozen open computer stations, much of the pencil pushing was still done by hand. They needed a break. Decker put on a fresh pot of decaf and called a meeting.

The detectives' squad room was wide-open space, the perimeter outlined by filing cabinets and shelving units containing hundreds of blue case notebooks. Taped onto the walls were an assignment board, a preprinted poster of procedure rules, lots of Gary Larson pig cartoons, and a dozen street maps of the division's territory, one of them overlaid with a dartboard outline. The different details – GTA, CAPS, SEX, JUVENILE, BURGLARY – were demarcated by placards hanging from the ceiling. Narcotics and Vice sat upstairs. Homicide took up the back area, cordoned off from the others by a filing cabinet barrier. Like other LAPD units, the detectives' desks in Devonshire were set up in a capital I-configuration. After pouring coffee for everyone, Decker took a seat at the crosshatch. He opened his notebook.

'We'll start with the basics. Random or not random. Pros. Cons. Marge, you go first.'

She pushed wilted dishwater hair from her tired eyes. 'Could be random carjacking, the drop point being the back alley. Why else would Sparks's car be there? If he had come to Tracadero's willingly, I think he would have used the parking valets in the front.'

'Maybe he was cheap.' Martinez chewed on his mustache. 'Or maybe he didn't trust the valet to drive his wheels.'

'How about a gang robbery thing?' Webster said. 'Tracadero's attracts rich blood. Not a bad place to hang out if you want to hit someone with cash.'

Martinez said, 'He had cash on him, Tom.'

'Maybe something scared off the muggers,' Webster retorted. 'Maybe Sparks fought back, they killed him and left.'

'Awful lot of damage for panic-stricken muggers,' Marge said.

'Maybe Sparks made the muggers mad.'

Decker said, 'Either way, carjacking or robbery, has to be at least a two-person attack.'

'The shooting *and* stabbing,' Marge said. 'Unusual that one perp would use two methods.'

The detectives agreed.

'I had an interesting conversation with one of New Chris's nurses, maybe a half hour ago.' Decker downed coffee. 'Seems that Sparks had a reputation for being a good Samaritan with auto accidents.' He told the group Nurse Tara's theories.

Marge said, 'That supports a carjacking over a restaurant robbery.'

'Weird.' Oliver pulled out a comb and ran it through thick, black hair. 'He can't break out of his doctor mold even when riding home in his own car.'

'I know several *lawyers* who do that kind of stuff,' Gaynor stated. 'Use scanners. But it isn't for altruistic purposes.'

Webster drawled, 'I once arrested a sucker that did that – chased calls from ambulance scanners. Stopped at the accident sites and pretended he was a doctor. Eventually, we did arrest him. But let me tell you, he did a right fine job of patching people.'

'A hero's complex,' Marge stated. 'What some people won't do to be the star of the show.'

'You'd think Sparks would get enough of that in the operating room.' Oliver pocketed his comb.

Gaynor said, 'I guess it's hard for some people to come down to planet earth.'

'If I were a big shot like Sparks, I wouldn't be anxious to come down to earth,' Oliver said. 'It's nice getting all that reverence. Having people bow down to you.'

'Like his secretary,' Marge said. 'She thought he was God.'

'Exactly.' Oliver turned to Decker. 'What about his kids? How'd they view their old man?'

Decker thought for a moment. 'The younger ones seemed very upset. The others weren't overly emotional about the death. Probably they were *all* in shock.'

'It's hard for kids to live with God as a father,' Oliver said. 'No one made a Freudian slip about Dad?'

Decker flipped through his notes. 'Two of the brothers – Lucas and Paul – talked about Dad being intimidating . . . bossy . . . emasculating—'

'They used *that* word?' Marge asked.

'Uh . . . no, they said Dad emasculated his son-in-law.'

'Veddy interesting,' Oliver said, rubbing his hands together.

Decker said, 'I think they rebelled against him in their own ways. Two of his children have money problems, another was a former drug addict, another became a Catholic priest instead of a minister of Sparks's Fundamentalist church, the older sister married a Jew—'

Marge broke in, 'How did *that* come up?'

'It came up,' Decker said.

'Did she convert?' Marge asked.

'No, she didn't. She still belongs to her father's church. And so do her children. Nonetheless, she still married a man who refused to convert to her faith. She's unhappy about it *now*. But way back when, when she originally married the man, you have to think she was telling her Fundamentalist Christian Daddy to go screw himself.'

'Sounds like they all got their digs in,' Martinez said.

Oliver said, 'Makes me feel better.'

'What about the wife?'

'Dolores Sparks,' Decker said. 'Didn't talk to her much. Upon hearing the news, she immediately started denying he was dead.'

'Did she ask how?'

'Uh, she did ask if it was a car accident. When I told her no, it was a homicide, she immediately went into denial. He can't be dead. That kind of thing.'

Marge said, 'So it's okay if he dies from a car accident but not from a homicide?'

Decker paused. 'Never thought of her reaction like that, but . . . I guess murder was too hard for her to digest. Her son gave her a sleeping pill, so she was out when I interviewed the kids. I'll take another crack at her tomorrow.' He sat back in his seat. 'So is this random or not?'

Shrugs all around.

Decker said, 'Okay. Let's assume that Sparks was carjacked or lured to the spot by *someone he knew*. Give me a list of suspects.'

Marge scanned her notes. 'Decameron pissed off Sparks. That's a given, right?'

The team nodded.

'They walked out to the parking lot together. Now Decameron said he smoothed things over. But what if he didn't? Maybe Sparks threatened to fire him. Then one thing led to another—'

'Then Sparks would have been offed in the hospital parking lot,' Martinez said.

Marge continued. 'So listen to this. Maybe Decameron offered to make amends by taking Sparks out to Tracadero's. The ride started out okay, but something went awry and Decameron went for the jugular.'

'More like the heart,' Webster said. 'That was a nasty chest wound. Your scenario precludes premeditation.'

'So it wasn't premeditated?' she said.

'I've never seen Decameron,' Decker said. 'Does he look like the kind of guy who could take Sparks down?'

'Loo, the scene was full of blood spatter,' Oliver said. 'Knife wounds, gunshot wounds. You should see how Decameron dresses. He's a fop. He'd never do something that sloppy.'

'So he hired out,' Marge suggested.

'Then that negates the fight as the precipitating event to the murder,' Decker said. 'If Decameron hired out, it had to be premeditated.'

127

Webster said, 'Maybe Decameron picked a fight on purpose, did something he knew would piss his boss off. Then lured him to the spot where a waiting gang jumped him.' He paused. 'I'm not saying it happened like that. I'm just following through the scenario that y'all are talking about.'

'What do you think, Farrell?' Decker asked.

Gaynor said, 'Dr. Azor Sparks had an alter ego – Leather Boy Ace Sparks. Maybe bikers did him in.'

'*Bikers?*' Martinez asked.

Decker filled them in on the card with the Harley logo – Sparks's weekend entertainment.

'I like bikers as the bad guys,' Marge said.

'But why would they do that?' Decker asked.

''Cause they're bikers,' Oliver said. 'They're assholes.'

'Now I know this is far-fetched,' Gaynor said, pointing as he talked. 'But suppose Sparks was operating a speed lab—'

The other detectives groaned. Gaynor said, 'Can you hear me out?'

'Shoot, Farrell,' Decker said.

'Maybe he decided to shut it down,' Gaynor said. 'His speed lab, that is. And maybe the bikers didn't like it.'

No one spoke.

'It's not likely, granted. But we're just throwing out ideas. Why not that?'

'Sparks as a *speed* supplier?' Webster shook his head.

Oliver smiled. 'A world-famous surgeon, a renowned researcher and chemist, a deeply religious man, and a meth pusher. Which one *doesn't* belong?'

'We all like bikers as bad guys because they fit our notions of villains,' Decker said. 'But that takes our concentration away from other possibilities.'

'So who do *you* see as the bad guy, Pete?' Marge asked.

'Like I said before, a couple of the kids have money problems. As a matter of fact, son Paul called Daddy up during the research meeting, specifically asking to borrow money. According to Paul, his dad agreed to help. But what if he was lying? What if this time, Sparks refused to come through with the money?'

'*In*-surance!' Oliver stated, sounding like a blackjack dealer.

'You got it!' Decker said.

'What about his will?' Marge added.

'Good,' Decker said. 'We're back to basics now. Who has the most to gain from Sparks's death?'

'More paperwork for me to do tomorrow,' Gaynor said. 'Bank accounts, insurance, policies, wills and codicils. I'm in heaven.'

'Sparks's estate lawyer is a man named William Waterson. He belongs to Sparks's church.' Decker felt his stomach grumble. Hungry but too queasy to eat. 'Farrell, give him a call. Not that he'll tell you anything. But sound him out anyway.' To Marge, he said, 'You tell me Sparks had a lot to gain with the production of this drug he developed?'

'Curedon,' Oliver said.

'I'm wondering what happens to Curedon now that Sparks is gone.' Decker rubbed his eyes. 'Ever find out where Fisher/Tyne are located?'

'The corporate office is in Delaware, some of the labs are in Virginia. But there's a regional office with labs here, too ... in an industrial park in Irvine.' Marge turned to Oliver. 'It ain't Florida, Scotty. But then again, there're no gators in the waters.'

'There's *nothing* in their waters,' Oliver groused. 'I hate those spanking new corporate developments with their pseudo-Hawaiian palm tree landscaping and their oh-so-clean manmade waterfalls. Everything's so theme-park plastic. Makes me want to puke.'

'I'd rather work there than a dump in the inner city,' Gaynor said.

'Ah God, bury me if I ever feel that way—'

'Scotty,' Marge chided.

'No, it's okay,' Gaynor said. 'I understand what Scott's saying. And once, I even felt like that, too. But then you age and your perspective changes—'

'No, no!' Oliver made a cross with his two index fingers, held it up to Gaynor. 'Shoo! I ate garlic! Go away!'

Decker said, 'Be on the road by ten.'

'Will do,' Marge said.

Decker said, 'Bert and Tom, tomorrow you do alibi check. I want a timetable for all the major players. Where they were before, during, and after Sparks's murder.'

'Got it.'

'And I get the paperwork, right?' Gaynor said.

'It's all yours, Farrell.'

'Can I use the computer in your office?'

'Farrell, we've got six computers sitting idle in the squad room.'

Gaynor replied, 'Yours is hooked up to more information data banks.'

Decker said, 'Okay, Gaynor, when I leave, you can use the computer in my office.'

'What are you going to do, Loo?'

'I've got an interview scheduled with Myron Berger in an hour. Maybe I'll snag a few hours between Berger, my paperwork, and Azor Sparks's memorial service.'

'They're doing a memorial service *before* the viewing, the rosary, and funeral?' Martinez questioned.

'It's not a Catholic service, Bert. It's a Fundamentalist service. The doctor's church.'

Martinez said, 'Still, they didn't want to wait until the body was released and do a funeral?'

'Apparently not.'

'When's the memorial service?'

'Three P.M.'

'That should be interesting,' Marge said. 'Everyone crammed together in one spot. See how they all react with one another.'

Decker said, 'That's why I'm going.'

11

At first, he thought the noise was his brain bouncing against his cranium. Then he realized that someone was at the door. Bram lifted his head from his folded arms, blinked back nausea. He had fallen asleep at his desk.

His mouth felt like sandpaper, his limbs ached, his body a plexus of raw synapses. Fingers crawling like spider legs, he felt around the desktop for his glasses. Found them and slipped them on. Immediately, everything came too clearly into focus. He stood on unstable legs, went to open the door.

Luke. Still had on the same sloppy sweater and jeans. By now, he smelled pretty rank. They both did.

'Sorry, did I wake you?'

Bram looked at his watch. 'I had to get up for six o'clock Mass anyway. I need a shower something awful. I can't believe I fell asleep. You want some tea, bro?'

'Sure, bro.' Luke skipped around a floor covered with books and papers as Bram trudged over to the water machine.

The priest took out a couple of tea bags, dropped them into Styrofoam cups, and doused them with hot water. 'Sit. What's going on at home?'

Luke parked himself on a folding chair. 'Eva left around two. Mag and Mike went to sleep about a half hour later. Me? I've just been driving around and around and around and around . . .'

After handing his brother his tea, Bram sat at his desk. 'You might try going home.'

'I've got a great idea, Abram. Why don't *I* put on your collar and conduct Mass? And you go home to Dana—'

'Lucas—'

'What did she say when you called her?'

'What do you think? She's worried sick about you—'

'Betcha she invited you over—'

'Don't start—'

'She *didn't* ask you to come over?'

Bram said nothing. Luke clapped his hands, pointed to his brother. 'Gotcha. Did you go?'

'No, I didn't *go*! It wasn't my place, and I certainly wasn't in the mood to wax pastoral.' Bram's face hardened. 'You should have called her. *You*. Not *me*. You should go home and be with her right now.'

'You be with her. After all, she was your girlfriend.'

Bram closed his eyes, dropped his head in his hands. Then he looked up. 'That was almost two decades ago. Things *change* in twenty years. For instance, I wasn't a priest in high school—'

'Just calm her down for me, bro.'

'I'm tired of calming her down, Luke. Truth be told, I've had it up to here with Dana.' Bram brushed his forehead with his hand. 'I'm sick to death of being your go-between. *You* married her. Not me. *Deal* with it.'

'All right, all right, I'll go home.' Luke squirmed in his seat, but gave no indication of rising. He sipped tea, eyed his brother through swollen eyes. 'Who the hell would murder Dad?'

Bram shook his head. 'I don't know.'

'I mean I'm so dumbfounded, I don't even know how to ask the right questions.'

'Don't ask questions,' Bram said. 'As a matter of fact, don't think. It'll drive you crazy. Let the police think. Let the police ask the questions.'

'I just wished the lieutenant would have talked more. Told us more. Not the gory details. But *some* details. Some theories. And I sat there like a turnip or worse, being a wiseass.' His eyes became wet. 'He should have told us more.'

'He came to my office a little while ago.'

'What did he want?'

'He asked about Dad and his weekend warriors.'

'How'd he find out about *that*?'

'Dad had cards printed up. A Harley logo with the name ACE SPARKS printed on it, can you believe that?'

'You're kidding.' Luke settled back in his chair. 'Old Azor had a fantasy life?'

'Looks that way.'

'That's wild.' Luke smiled. 'Maybe he had some busty biker mama on the side.'

'You're obscene.'

'Don't they say that the biggest sinners always pray the loudest?'

Bram started to rebuke his brother, but instead laughed softly. Then he grew serious. 'What a crazy world we live in . . . where some animal could wipe out such a great man.'

'You think it was a random act of violence, then?'

'Yes, of course.' Bram paused. 'Don't you?'

'I don't know what to think.'

The room went quiet.

Luke said, 'Paul got hold of William Waterson, by the way. He stopped by to express his *deepest* sympathies.'

'That was nice of him.'

'Waterson said he'd take care of the funeral . . . pay the expenses out of Dad's estate . . . which of course all goes to Mom.'

'That makes sense.'

'It's a real *big* estate, bro. We couldn't get the exact figures out of him, but it was clear that Dad was worth a *lot* of money. More than we . . .'

Bram said, 'Mom's going to need lots of help and support now. It's good she won't have to worry about money.'

'I'm just wondering if Mom's up to it?'

The priest waited for his twin to continue.

'Mom isn't Dad,' Luke stated. 'A fortune suddenly drops in her lap, she isn't used to dealing with that kind of balance sheet . . . I don't want people to rip her off, that's all.'

'She's not helpless without Dad—'

'I didn't say she was—'

'She handled all the household finances—'

'That's *not* the same thing as investing and maintaining a seven-figure bank account. Dad's always taken care of her, Golden. I'm suggesting we keep a watch over her.'

'Fine. We'll keep a watch over her.'

Luke scratched his head. 'Waterson mentioned something about an insurance policy also.'

'Good.'

'Six million bucks, to be exact.'

'*Whoa!*' Slowly, Bram sat back in his chair. 'Man, that is a *lot* of money.'

'A proverbial shitload.'

'I don't recall the word *shitload* in the Book of Proverbs, but yes, that's a tremendous haul.' Bram paused. 'That is a *large* insurance policy. The premiums must have been enormous. I wonder why Dad did that when he had so much in the bank? I love Mom, but she doesn't spend on anything except food. What in the world is she going to do with six million dollars?'

'Mom's not the beneficiary.'

Bram stared at his brother.

'Six million . . . six kids.' Luke shrugged carelessly. 'Dad was always an even-handed guy.'

Bram opened, then closed his mouth. 'You're *kidding.*'

'You should have been there when Waterson told us. Paul's eyelids were beating so fast, he just about flew away.'

Again, the office went quiet.

Luke said, 'A rather fortunate windfall for him—'

'Luke—'

'The man is in deep debt.'

'David and Eva aren't doing so hot, either.'

'Nothing like Paul. He's *drowning* in red ink.'

'Your insinuations are ugly.'

'So you're better than me. We already know that.'

Bram stared at his brother, then rubbed his eyes. 'You want some advice?'

'Can I stop you?'

'Truth be told, Lucas, even I, the saint of St. Thomas's, entertained the same thought as you about Paul. But I'm smart enough not to verbalize it. Because once you talk, you can't take it back. Do you ever think before you speak?'

'Nah, you do enough of that for the both of us.'

'You say things, Luke. I know what you mean. But no else does—'

'Mind you, I really don't think Paul killed Dad for money. But hey, a lot stranger things have happened.'

Bram looked at the crucifix on his wall. 'Why do I bother?'

Again, the room went silent.

Luke looked at his hands. 'So what are you going to do with the money?'

'What?'

'The *money*, Bram. What are you going to do with it?'

'I don't want to talk about money.'

'Well, it's better than talking about death!' Suddenly, Luke sprang up and leaned against the back wall, burying his face in his hands.

Sluggishly, Bram sighed, checked his watch. Half hour until Mass. He rose from his desk, went over to his brother, and placed his hand on his shoulder.

'Lucas, I know you're hurting. I know that wisecracks are your way of dealing with pain.'

Luke turned around, wiped his eyes. 'How much do I owe you, Herr Doktor?'

The priest looked his twin in the eye, seeing his own tired reflection. 'Bro, listen to me. Lieutenant Decker is nobody's fool.

He is a very, very . . . very, very *smart* man. You keep talking about money, throwing stuff around about Paul, trying to joke your way out of your pain, you're going to tweak his antenna.'

'What do I care? I didn't do anything.'

'Of course, you didn't *do* anything. But look at it from his perspective. A weird homicide like Dad's. First thing police will do is scrutinize the family. You add to that an . . . an outrageous insurance policy that makes us all rich—'

'Millionaires to be exact.'

Bram hit his forehead. 'Am I getting through at all?'

'Not much.'

'Lucas, the police can get very nasty. I don't need the hassle. And you certainly don't need it.'

Bram paused, organized his thoughts.

'I realize you're stressed. And I know what stress does to you. But we're all in this together. So instead of pulling away from each other, let's deal with it as a unit. Deal with it constructively—'

'Does that mean heroin is out?'

Bram kept his voice calm, tried again. 'Luke, you've come so *far*. Nothing's worth the setback. Not even a million dollars.'

'I don't know about that, Golden Boy. For a million bucks, I think I could *well* afford a couple of setbacks.'

Bram pulled away, knocked his head against the wall. Useless arguing with Luke when he was in one of these moods. Completely irrational. For a moment, he wondered if his twin hadn't already had a major setback. His eyes were glazed . . . unfocused. But that could easily be from confusion, grief, and lack of sleep.

'So, bro . . .' Luke ambled over to the water machine and made himself another cup of tea. 'What are you going to do with your share of the money? Start a food bank? Open a mission? Buy a new church? Just what the fuck does a priest *do* with a million dollars?'

Bram gave up, started making preparations for the six A.M. Mass. 'I've got to shower.'

Luke drank tea, squashed the cup and two-pointed it into the waste can. 'I'm going to buy a house. That should keep Dana happy for a while, don't you think?'

'Whatever.'

'Think Dad would approve of me using the money for a house?'

Bram was silent.

Luke shrugged. 'I think he would. Much better than shooting it in my veins.'

Softly, Bram asked, 'Are you high, Lucas?'

'No, Abram, I am not. But sincerely, I wish I was.'

The priest walked over to his brother, embraced him tightly. To his surprise, Luke fell into his arms and wept bitterly. And also to his surprise, Bram felt his own eyes overflow. For several moments, he couldn't tell who was actually crying. Holding his twin. It was as if he was holding himself.

Berger wasn't happy, but he was resigned to the inevitable. He motioned Decker to follow. Together, without speaking, they took the elevator down to the second floor. Berger moved swiftly, cornering the series of corridors like a four-wheel drive on a mountain. He stopped short, unlocked a door, and let Decker inside his office.

Small and neat. A tiny anteroom, the open door showing about a hundred and twenty square feet of dawn-lit space. Berger flipped on the lights. He had a desk, a matching credenza, a couple of worn patient chairs and bookshelves. Not much else. Not much else would fit. The doctor hung up his white coat on a brass rack and sat down in front of his desk. Decker pulled up a chair, positioning it directly across from Berger. He took out a notepad.

Berger checked his watch. 'I don't know what I could possibly tell you. But go ahead.'

'You've worked with Dr. Sparks for a long time?'

'Yes.'

'You went through medical school with him?'

137

'Harvard. Although I'm sure you know that already.'

'Yes, I do. Have you always worked with Dr. Sparks?'

'You mean are we joined at the hip? The answer is no.'

'So you've had positions other than your current one with Sparks?'

'I don't see the point of this line of questioning.'

'All right, I'll be direct. You've got a great reputation as being a surgeon in your own right. But with Sparks, you were always the number two man. Did that ever lead to resentment?'

Berger looked Decker in the eye. 'Yes.'

Decker was quiet.

'Surprised?' Berger asked.

'Surprised that you admitted it.'

'Yes, at times, I was resentful . . . very resentful. We'd walk in a room together, Azor would get the accolades, I'd be standing there, nodding my head like some carnival kewpie doll. Of course, I was resentful. But I didn't murder the man.' Berger's voice went harsh. 'If that was your reason for questioning me, you're going about this investigation all wrong. I think you'd better reevaluate.'

Decker was silent, wondering why the man was so *hostile*. Berger was finally in the medical spotlight. Maybe he had a bad case of stage fright and was covering it with bravado.

Again, Berger checked his watch. 'I've got rounds—'

'What position did you hold before you hooked up with Dr. Sparks?'

'I don't see where that's any of your business.'

'Dr. Berger, I can look up your professional background in a snap—'

'So do it.'

'You're not going to make this easy on me?'

'I didn't kill the man, period. That's all you have to know.'

Decker smoothed his mustache, trying to figure out how to work around the man's anger. Attempt a different approach. Suddenly, something dawned on him. He said, 'Do you have a past, sir?'

Berger seemed poised for another attack. Abruptly, he wilted. Silence thickened between them.

'Why don't you just go away?' Berger whispered.

Mildly, Decker said, 'I'm ready whenever you are.'

Berger looked at the ceiling, said nothing.

'I'm going to find it all out. Might be better if it came from you.'

Berger kneaded his hands, slowly began his recitation. 'My father was a good man. Worked hard . . . was very proud of me.'

'I'm sure.'

'A good man,' Berger repeated, 'but a gambler. At the age of fifty-one, he dropped dead from a heart attack and left my mother helpless and penniless. I was a senior resident at the time . . . away from home. Of course, when I heard the news I rushed back to my mother's side, took over the many responsibilities that she couldn't handle. Squared her away.'

'Big burden,' Decker said.

'It was because my father had left big debts. But we took care of them. I stayed long enough to get her on the right footing, then I left home once again to continue on with my studies . . . with my life. I came back just in time to take my specialty boards. Needless to say, I was a wreck. Flustered and disoriented. Still reeling from grief, overrun with worry. I hadn't had a moment to study. I was caught cheating.'

No one spoke.

Decker said, 'Obviously, you've overcome the mishaps.'

'After pleading and begging, yes, I was allowed to retake my exams. And I passed. But no hospital would permit me to attend because of my black eye. They didn't come right out and say that my cheating was the reason for denying attendance privileges. But after applying to fifty-plus institutions, you see the writing on the wall. If you're a surgeon, Lieutenant, you need hospitals.'

'What did you do?'

'I worked as a general practitioner for a while. Lebanon, Indiana. Did quite well.'

'But you were frustrated.'

'That is an understatement, sir. I was miserable. In my eyes, not only was I a failure, but a dishonest one at that.'

'So along comes your old friend Azor Sparks, a man with a renowned international reputation, who took a chance.'

'And we all lived happily ever after.'

Again, no one spoke.

Decker said, 'You must have been very grateful.'

'I just about wept at his feet, I was so thankful.' Berger blew air into his hands, rubbed them together. 'My first assignment was assisting him. Like any other resident surgeon, I'd been out of practice for a while . . .'

He tapped his hands on the desk.

'The next time out, he handed me the scalpel. A routine bypass that evolved into a complex situation. I was sweating buckets. I kept waiting for Azor to step in. But he didn't. Yes, he watched, but never said a word. The upshot? I handled it masterfully.'

'Congratulations.'

Berger smiled. 'Thank you. And that was it. We've been working together ever since. As colleagues, side by side. Having said that . . . I always knew his position. And I always knew mine. Yes, occasionally, I suffered a bruised ego. But better a bruised ego than none at all.'

Decker wrote as he spoke. 'Let me ask you this, Dr. Berger. If you applied to other programs and institutions now, how do you think you'd be received?'

'After working with Azor for twenty-five years, I could write my own ticket.'

'So your past wouldn't follow you?'

'Perhaps . . . if the position was a very big one like the head of NIH or the dean of Harvard Medical School . . . it might come out that I took my boards twice. But I strongly doubt the reason would be exposed. Unless someone was determined to unbury this oddity in order to *ruin* me.'

'Who would that be?'

'No one,' Berger snapped. 'Even Reggie Decameron doesn't hold that kind of animosity toward me. It would only come up if someone purposely launched an *extensive* probe.' He looked pointedly at Decker. 'Someone like the police.'

Decker kept his expression neutral, wondering why the doctor spilled so easily if his past had truly been that well interred. Maybe Berger confessed to cheating in order to hide something more nefarious. Decker said, 'Well, not much point in my looking into your past now.'

'Which is the reason why I told you. Better to head you off at the pass, so to speak.'

'So few people know about your ordeal?'

'The generation that knew my plight way back when has practically died out.'

'A theoretical question,' Decker said. 'What would happen to you if your past was suddenly made public?'

Berger's eyes turned stony. 'I can't answer that because it wouldn't happen. The only one of my current colleagues who was aware of it was Azor. And he never said anything to anyone.'

'As far as you know.'

'I do know.' Berger glanced at the clock on his wall and stood. 'I really must tend to my business. We have very sick people here who have just lost their doctor . . . a person they view as saving their lives. They're distressed. They need care. They need comfort. Please?'

'Of course.' Decker got up. 'Some other time, maybe we can talk about Curedon.'

'I'd be happy to, except . . .' He tapped his watch. 'I'm swamped at the moment.'

'Thank you for your time, Dr. Berger.'

'I can't say that I enjoyed it. But I have been completely honest with you. I shouldn't have to say this, but I'll say it anyway. I expect complete confidentiality with my thirty-year-old secret. It's nobody's business but mine.'

Decker nodded. His secret wasn't anyone's business.

Unless it became a reason for murder.

12

Oliver tightened his grip on the wheel of an unmarked Matador. 'If I see one more shopping mall, I'm gonna throw up.'

Marge sipped coffee from a thermos, stared out the window at an endless stretch of freeway. The asphalt bisected hillocks covered with untrimmed crabgrass, California orange poppies, mustard wildflowers, and royal purple statice. 'Not much to do here. Shop, eat, sleep. Maybe have an affair.'

'Last option sounds like a winner, especially if I was female. Doesn't cost anything and it burns off calories.'

Marge glanced at him, then returned her eyes to the front windshield. Oliver drummed his fingers on the wheel. 'What's the contact's name again?'

'Gordon Shockley.'

'Dr. Shockley, right?'

'Right.'

Silence except for the staccatoed communications between the radio dispatchers and the patrol officers. Oliver started to whistle – tuneless, formless. Marge was about to say something, but changed her mind. The tweetie noises were annoying, but so was the quiet.

Forty-five minutes into the ride, and Marge was going nuts. Probably, Scott wasn't doing much better. The first twenty minutes had been passable because they had talked shop, gossiped a little. Now they had run out of small talk. Desperation time, because neither wanted to open the door marked *personal*.

Oliver said, 'Mind-numbing out here.' He paused. 'Not that I do so much at home . . .'

'But you have the option,' Marge filled in.

'Yeah. Exactly.'

A long pause.

'Any more coffee?' Oliver asked.

'Sure.' Marge handed him the thermos. 'You want me to take a shift, Scott?'

'Nah, I'm fine.' He swigged some java. 'I'm not looking forward to this.'

'Why?'

'I hate talking to these kinds of guys. Especially because we have to ask technical questions. Which means we'll get technical answers. Makes me feel like I should have stayed longer in college.'

'You and me both.'

'How many years did you go?'

'BA in sociology.' Marge laughed. 'Like that's really going to help.'

'You finished, then.'

Marge looked at him, smiled. 'Are you impressed?'

'Yeah, kinda.'

'It's only State.'

'But you're still a college grad. Me? I majored in pool and beer.'

'Bet you got straight As in that.'

'You'd better believe it, sister, I'm a card-carrying member of the Sigma Beta Tau. We threw the best parties west of the Mississippi, east of the Ohio, and anywhere else in between.'

'That's everywhere.'

'That's right! No one gave parties like Sigma Beta Tau.'

The car grew silent as Oliver fell into a blue funk. Finally, he said, 'Yeah, we had parties. Unfortunately, chucking your cookies in rhythm to "Stayin' Alive" didn't turn out to be a marketable skill.'

Marge smiled. 'Did you actually attend any classes?'

'A few.' Oliver ran tapered fingers through thick, black hair. 'I think I even took a sociology course. Something like *Group Thinking*.'

'That sounds like sociology.'

'Yeah, I thought it was.'

'I think I had the same course,' Marge said. 'Only we called it *Group Analysis*. At the onset, the class was given a number of questions and asked to find solutions. First, we were told to solve the problems by ourselves. Then we divided up into teams, and were told to seek resolutions to the same problems.'

'Then compare the results?'

'Exactly. I told you it was the same class.'

'God, this brings back some Kodaks. The minute we started up in teams, everything got bogged down—'

'All these slow people dragging their asses—'

'Stupid *people*,' Oliver said. 'Got so mired in procedure—'

'Future LAPD brass,' Marge said.

They both laughed.

'Everyone had to have a turn,' Oliver expounded. 'Whether they had something to say or not. Especially these touchy-feely broads.'

'Yeah, we had a couple of those,' Marge said. 'I kept saying, fuck the feelings and let's get on with the tasks. I made this one girl cry. Her friend chewed me out, said . . . get this . . . "You don't have to be so *brutal*!"'

Oliver gave a Marge a wide grin. 'I love it when women are brutal.'

Marge dropped her smile, then looked away.

They rode the next few minutes without conversation.

Oliver muttered, 'Talk about touchy-feely.'

Marge didn't answer.

'Jesus Christ, Dunn, I was just making a joke.'

'I know.'

'So what are you getting so pissed about?'

'I'm not pissed.'

'Dunn, I know when a woman is pissed. And you're *pissed*.'

'Oliver, I want a partner I don't have to worry about, okay?'

'You don't have to worry about a thing, lady. It's the farthest thing from my mind.'

'Good.'

'Just trying to stroke your ego—'

'My ego doesn't need stroking.'

'Funny. Everyone else's does.'

Marge stared at him. 'You want to stroke my ego, tell me I'm a good cop.'

Oliver spoke quietly. 'You're a good cop.'

Marge paused. 'Thank you.' Again, she hesitated. 'So are you.'

Oliver brushed hair off his forehead. 'Thanks.'

He started whistling again. This time Marge recognized the tune – the refrain of 'Stayin' Alive'. His mouth-puckering sounds came out as sharp, shrill stabs. Over and over and over and over.

After five minutes, Marge said, 'Can you cool it with the bird songs?'

Oliver quit whistling. 'What?'

'You sound like an avian mating call. I half expect some mesmerized, horny robin to fly into the car and start showing you her tail feathers.'

'Dunn, you talk that way, you get me hot—'

'I don't believe you, Oliver. You're doing it *again*.'

'Lady, you started it, talking about horny robins and tail feathers. What's an old goat to think?'

Marge was about to speak, but laughed instead. She did kind of set him up. Besides, she got her point across. No sense belaboring it.

The industrial park was blocks long, set on acres of rolling, manicured lawn that sported a variety of specimen willows and elms. The commercial buildings ranged in size, but each was fashioned from brick, and landscaped with shocking pink impatiens, pastel pink azaleas, and emerald ferns, giving the development uniformity. In the middle of the complex was a rock waterfall that emptied into a pond complete with goldfish and koi.

Fisher/Tyne's entry faced the waterscape. It was a two-storied structure with double doors. The lobby was masoned with white marble, the furniture sleek – suede couches, glass tables, and chrome lamps. Oversized unframed canvases hung on the walls, the artwork being modern and stark. A couple of trim, blonde, blue-eyed receptionists wearing headsets sat behind a glass window. Marge glanced at her partner, wondering if Oliver would be distracted by the view. His eyes revealed nothing.

He took out ID and showed it to one of the cuties in the seethrough cage. 'We're here to see Dr. Gordon Shockley.'

The cutie stared at the ID, spoke into a mike. 'It's about Dr. Sparks, right?'

Oliver pocketed his badge. 'Is Dr. Shockley in, ma'am?'

'I'll check.' She punched a couple of buttons, spoke into the headset that encircled her face. To Oliver, she said, 'He'll be down in just a few minutes. Would you like some coffee?'

Oliver turned to Marge.

'Pass.'

'Maybe later,' Oliver said.

'Just have a seat, then.'

Marge parked herself on the sofa. It had all the give of a park bench. Oliver sat next to her. The lobby held several windows that looked out to the pond.

Marge said, 'Nice view.'

'Plastic.' Oliver lowered his voice. 'Or do you mean the ones in the cage?'

'Talk about plastic.'

He grinned. 'Polymers have their place, Dunn.'

'Polymers is right,' she whispered. 'All of them made out of the same mold—'

'Hey, you get a winner, stick with it.'

Marge turned to him. 'Are you talking for my benefit only or are you really this shallow?'

'No, I'm really this shallow, Dunn. Get used to it.'

Marge laughed and so did he. A moment later, a man walked through a door marked PERSONNEL ONLY, a mellow voice introducing himself as Gordon Shockley. He shook Marge's hand first, then Oliver's.

Midforties. About six two, and well built. Curly, bronzed hair streaked with gray and thinning at the top. Deep brown eyes, aquiline nose, thin lips, and the smooth, almost wet-looking skin that comes from a very close shave. He wore a custom-made suit, the last button on the sleeve left undone to prove the point. Navy wool crepe. Oliver eyed it enviously. It spoke Italian. It said, '*I'm Expensissimo.*'

'This way, please,' Shockley led. 'Were the directions adequate?'

'They were fine,' Marge answered.

They followed Shockley back through the PERSONNEL ONLY door to the elevator, and went up a flight. His office was a corner suite. Marge noticed another young cutie secretary as they passed through the receptionist's office into Shockley's chamber. Obviously, the same designer had done up the entire building. Same marble, same dark suede furniture and glass tables, and the same talentless art. Shockley's desk looked to be eight feet long, constructed out of a single piece of black granite. Had as much warmth as a sarcophagus. The saving grace of the place were two walls of view. Green hills covered with wildflowers bleeding into a silvery-blue blade of ye olde Pacific. A whispery sky crowned the scene.

'Please, have a seat,' Shockley stated. 'Can I get you some coffee?'

'Nothing, thanks,' Marge said.

'Detective?' Shockley looked at Oliver.

'Right now, I'm fine, thanks.'

'Easy customers.' Shockley's expression turned grave. 'Terrible thing about Dr. Sparks. I'm stunned.'

Oliver slipped out his notepad. 'Did you know him well?'

'I knew him on a professional level. A very brilliant man.'

'Seems to be the general consensus,' Marge said, also taking notes.

'His genius is absolutely undebatable.'

'I heard he was also very exacting. Did you get along with him?'

Shockley eyed Marge. 'Of course he was exacting. With that high an intellect, I wouldn't expect anything less.'

Oliver repeated, 'Did you get along with him?'

'Yes.' Shockley smiled. 'We're both exacting people.'

Ergo, both of you are of high intellect. Marge said, 'No conflict?'

'What kind of conflict, Detective?'

'You were doing business with him, Doctor,' Oliver said. 'There's always negotiation in business.'

'We weren't trading rugs, Detective.'

'No, you were trading millions of dollars.'

Shockley folded his hands and placed them on the desk. 'I'm not sure why you people have decided to come out here. But let me clue you in on something. Fisher/Tyne is a major corporation in this country. We are public. Information about us is available to you through various K-forms and prospectuses. All very up and up. If you want to find out more about us, help yourself.'

Marge and Oliver traded glances. She said, 'Doctor, what is your official position at Fisher/Tyne?'

'West Coast Vice President in charge of Research and Development. I also act as a liaison between the West Coast labs and our labs in D.C. Virginia.'

'I'm really ignorant on how all this works,' Marge said. 'For instance, how did you come to buy Curedon? Who made that decision?'

'How'd you even find out about it?' Oliver asked.

Shockley continued to sit with his fingers interlocked. 'Why would this interest the police?'

Oliver said, 'A man was murdered. We're looking for reasons.'

'And what reasons did you hope to find here?'

'Money,' Marge said. 'Lots of money.'

'Always a good reason for a homicide,' Oliver said.

'Like for instance, we all know that Dr. Sparks was paid a handsome up-front fee for Curedon,' Marge said. 'And we all know he was promised part of the percentage of the profits if the drug came to market.'

'Now that he's gone,' Oliver said, 'we were wondering what happens to the percentage. Is it passed on like the rest of his estate?'

Shockley smiled. 'And you expect me to divulge private information just because you're the police?'

Marge said, 'Maybe we can talk in general terms. Like if you promised Gentleman X a percentage of profits from drug B that you bought from him—'

'A percentage of profits *if* drug B comes to market,' Oliver added.

'And if Gentleman X happened to be murdered,' Marge went on, 'who would inherit the percentage promised to him?'

Oliver smiled. 'She's just talking theoretical.'

Shockley's face remained flat. But if his neck muscles grew any tighter, they'd pop his collar pin. 'Who have you been talking to?'

Marge said, 'Lots of people.'

'Everyone says the same thing.'

'But no one knows the exact numbers,' Marge said. 'Not that we're asking for exact numbers—'

'That's good, Detective,' Shockley said. 'Because the numbers are none of your business.'

Oliver frowned. ''Fraid you were going to say that. Let me ask you this, Doctor. By the way, are you a heart doctor like Dr. Sparks?'

A slight smile appeared on Shockley's lips. 'I've got a Ph.D. in both pharmacology and chemistry.'

Oliver said. 'You answered that question real easily. We'll try another. I understand that Fisher/Tyne were testing Curedon for the FDA. Just how does that work?'

Shockley said, 'I don't know what you're asking.'

Marge said, 'You are testing the drug for the FDA, correct?'

'Correct.'

'To test the drug, you need patients.'

'Correct.'

'Where do you get the patients from?'

'That's confidential information.'

'We're not asking for names and locations,' Oliver said. 'We just want to know how you get the patients. Do you have your own hospital somewhere? Or do you talk doctors at hospitals into trying out the drug?'

'We don't talk doctors into anything.'

'We're just wondering how you get patients to participate?' Marge said.

'That's also none of your business.'

Oliver blew out air, sank back into the hard sofa. 'You're not being forthcoming.'

'You're asking internal policy questions. I've neither the position nor the inclination to answer them.'

Marge turned to Oliver. 'Maybe we should save these questions for Dr. Decameron? Betcha he'd know all about this.'

Shockley snorted.

Oliver said, 'Ah, so you've met Dr. Decameron? Which means you've obviously worked with him. In what capacity?'

Shockley said, 'If Dr. Decameron is so forthcoming with the police, why don't you ask him?'

'You want us to go by his statement only,' Oliver said. 'Fine with us.'

'Just what does *that* mean?'

151

Marge said, 'That means, Doctor, if you and he have had any disagreements, you might want to tell us *your* side.'

'We've had no disagreements.' Shockley squirmed.

'No conflicts at all?'

'No business conflicts,' Shockley said. 'Perhaps some personality conflicts.'

'I see.' Oliver smoothed his hair. 'You don't like gays.'

Marge's eyes widened. Shockley winced. 'I didn't say—'

'Fine, you didn't say,' Oliver said. 'Let's drop the PC crap, Doctor. He's overtly gay and he's *proud* of it.'

'Nothing wrong with that,' Marge said.

'Absolutely not. You are what you are and we all know what Decameron is.' Leaning in close, Oliver said, 'Reggie boy made me do a little squirmy-wormy when I was around him. Might make me squirm a *lot* if I had dealings with him. Did you have dealings with him, Doctor?'

Oliver sat back in his seat and waited, giving Shockley a chance to size him up. Hoping he caught the bastard by playing on his fears and weaknesses. Because men like Shockley were public image, never dared to admit prejudice until they were safely ensconced within the paneled walls of their clubs.

Shockley eyed Oliver. Unsure how to proceed.

Marge stepped in, playing good cop, giving Shockley the needed escape. 'Did you have professional dealings with Dr. Decameron, Dr. Shockley?'

Shockley waited a beat. 'Some.'

'What kind of dealings?'

Shockley weighed his options . . . to talk or not to talk. 'Next to Dr. Sparks, Dr. Decameron is the most actively involved in our trials of Curedon.'

Oliver said, 'Does he work out of Dr. Sparks's lab or your labs in Virginia?'

'Both.'

'How'd that work? Does he fly in and out?'

'Yes.'

'Lots of back-and-forth travel?'

'Yes,' Shockley answered. 'Lots of back-and-forth travel. As a matter of fact, the travel was the main reason we started working with Dr. Decameron in the first place. The flying became prohibitively time-consuming for Dr. Sparks's hectic schedule. After the initial negotiations for Curedon were in place, Dr. Sparks handed the task of overseeing Curedon trials to Dr. Decameron.'

He paused.

'Actually, he first gave the assignment to Dr. Berger, then to Dr. Decameron.'

Marge asked, 'Why the switch?'

'I don't know why,' he said quickly. 'I do know that Dr. Berger is also a practicing cardiac surgeon. Perhaps he was also scheduled too tightly for the travel. Actually, I was glad about the switch. Despite what you've implied, I have *nothing* against homosexuals.'

'Why were you glad about the change?' Oliver asked.

'Because . . .' Shockley tried again. 'Once I . . . understood Dr. Decameron, I found him easier to deal with.'

'Easier than Dr. Berger,' Marge clarified.

'Yes.'

'How's that?'

'A better team player. Quicker. Faster. Cutting edge. More willing to try unorthodox approaches if conventional ones weren't working. I found Dr. Berger to be a very, very cautious man. Which is always a good thing when you're testing out a new drug. But he was cautious to the point of being mulish. Had it been up to him, I'm sure Curedon would still be relegated to Sparks's homespun lab. You know, if you're going to do good for humankind, eventually you have to take the drug out to the market and test it on humans. There's only so much you can infer by testing the drugs on primates.'

'Berger didn't feel the drug was ready to be tested on humans?'

'He never actually espoused that opinion, no,' Shockley said.

'Because Sparks always called the shots, of course. But the DC labs were frustrated by Berger's pickiness.'

'Maybe some would call that exacting,' Oliver said.

Shockley's smile was mean. 'There's being exacting . . . and there's being ridiculous.'

'Ah,' Oliver said. 'I guess it takes a person of very high intellect to know the difference.'

Marge shot Oliver a look, and he backed off. He asked, 'Did you express your lab's frustration with Dr. Berger directly to Dr. Sparks?'

'Of course not. We had complete confidence in anyone who represented Dr. Sparks. And I don't want to imply that we were unhappy with Dr. Berger. We just felt that Dr. Decameron was . . .'

Oliver said, 'More with the program?'

Shockley's smile was condescending. 'Better suited to the job.'

'Dr Decameron told us the initial trials of Curedon looked promising.'

'Yes.'

'He's also told us that some of the latest data was not so promising.'

Shockley said, 'There are always wrinkles. That's why we have trials before the drug is presented to the public, my friends.'

'Would you have the latest results?'

'Not at my fingertips.'

'Could you get them for us?'

'No. They aren't your business.'

Marge said, 'We can get them from Dr. Decameron.'

'So do that.' Shockley's smile was smug. 'You know, I am trying to help you out. But you can't expect the company to just open up its data banks for you. First, it would serve no purpose. Second, it's confidential information. For all I know, you two might be industrial spies.'

Oliver couldn't help it. He broke out laughing, swinging a look Marge's way. 'My Ph.D. in chemistry must be showing.'

Shockley frowned. 'Are you putting me on, Detective?'

Oliver said, 'Yes, sir, I am putting you on. I apologize.'

Shockley glared at him. Oliver flashed him the peace sign. 'No disrespect meant.'

Mollified, Shockley folded his hands and said, 'Besides, you wouldn't get a thing out of the trial data. Just a bunch of numbers and figures. Impossible to interpret unless you're intimately involved in the trials.'

Meaning you dumbshits couldn't understand them anyway. Marge said, 'What do you think about Sparks's other colleague, Elizabeth Fulton?'

'I never dealt with her.'

'Never?' Oliver asked.

'Yes, I believe I did say never, Detective.'

Oliver said, 'You spent lots of money developing and refining a drug like Curedon, right?'

'Researching and refining,' Shockley corrected.

'Yes, you're right, of course. Sparks developed the drug.'

'Yes, he did.'

Oliver said, 'Say you spend lots of money researching and *refining* a drug, and it turns out to be a bust. What happens?'

'We move on.'

'You take a huge loss just like that?' Oliver asked.

'We move on,' Shockley repeated.

'Then how do you stay in business?'

'Our profits exceed our losses.'

Marge thought of something that Decameron had brushed upon. 'How about this, Doctor? We all know there're a million different names for the same aspirin tablet out there, right?'

'I've never analyzed all the different acetylsalicylic compounds. I can't answer that yes or no.'

'You're being picky, doctor,' Oliver said.

'I'm being exacting.'

Marge was not about to be put off. 'What if a drug proved to be safe and effective? But not much more effective than what's available on the shelves.'

'Or what's in the pharmacies,' Oliver stated.

Marge asked, 'Do you still market the drug?'

'I can't answer that, Detective.'

'Not even evasively?' Marge asked.

Shockley smiled, but said nothing.

Marge said, 'I mean why would drug companies spend all this money to put something on the market when it's not a big improvement over what's already out there?'

'Like we have a million types of cold medicines,' Oliver said. 'Or a million types of toothpastes.'

'Or a million types of cola sodas, Detective.' Shockley made quote signs with his fingers when he stated the word *million*. 'Or all the different brands of cigarettes, coffee, orange juice, yogurt, et cetera, et cetera.'

'Different strokes for different folks,' Oliver said.

'I couldn't have phrased it better,' Shockley said.

'Is Curedon more effective than what's out there?' Oliver asked.

'Detective, we're back to where we started.'

'Are the trials going to continue now that Dr. Sparks is gone?'

'I don't know for certain,' Shockley said. 'But I can't see why they shouldn't continue.'

'And you'd still be working with Dr. Decameron?'

'I'm not sure of anything at the moment.' Shockley stood. 'Your police business has caught us all off guard.'

'Our police business?' Marge said. 'Is that your way of saying Dr. Sparks's murder?'

'Yes, Detective. Exactly.' Shockley walked over to the door. 'I do have business to tend to. If you both don't mind, it's getting late. Do call if you have further questions. If I'm not available, you can always leave them with my secretary.'

Marge and Oliver exchanged glances. They were being unceremoniously dismissed. Oliver shrugged. They both got up and thanked Shockley for his time.

'You drive or I drive?' Marge asked.

Oliver flipped her the keys. 'We didn't learn too much, did we?'

Marge opened the door, slid in the drivers's seat, and reached over to unlock the passenger door. Once Oliver was belted in, she started the motor. 'We learned that Decameron replaced Berger in the Curedon trials. If Shockley's to be believed . . . that he didn't complain to Sparks about Berger . . . I'd like to know why Sparks yanked Berger from the trials.'

'Yeah, that's something.'

Marge pulled the Matador out of the vast parking lot chock full of Japanese subcompacts. She turned left, onto the lone boulevard leading to the freeway. 'I wonder how Berger felt about it . . . being cut from Curedon?'

'Maybe it was Berger's decision.'

'Nah, Sparks made all the decisions regarding Curedon. The rest just followed orders.'

'And Berger resented Sparks for making the switch.'

'Possibly.'

'And that's a motivation for *murder*?'

'What if money was involved? Whoever worked with Sparks got a piece of the profit?'

A good point, and Marge told him so. She took the on-ramp to the 405 north. 'You know, Scott, you put money together with some big *egos* . . . you get a powder keg.'

'Man, ain't that so. I've never seen people so full of themselves.'

'Guess you play the part of God long enough, you begin to believe your own method acting.' Marge switched over to the left-hand lane. 'We also found out that Shockley preferred Decameron over Berger. That says a lot.'

'You're right. Berger must have been a real obstacle for Gordon

157

Shockley to prefer a gay blade like Decameron.'

'Yeah, Scotty,' Marge fidgeted. 'I want to talk to you about that. You think it was wise, bringing up the gay thing?'

Oliver grinned. 'Made Shockley feel *real* uncomfortable. You know, Marge, sometimes you just gotta go for it. I had to get to the prick, and I did. He began to talk a little after that. Plus, he lost that smug smile of his.'

'What if it gets back to Decameron?'

'So what?' Oliver picked up the old thermos and took a swig of lukewarm coffee. 'But if you want me to tell Decameron what went down, I'll do it. I'm not the least bit embarrassed. I'd call him a queer to his face. He'd probably love it.'

'I don't know about that.' She paused. 'Does anything embarrass you, Scotty?'

'A lot embarrasses me, Margie. But I'm not gonna tell you about it.'

Marge smiled. 'Too embarrassed?'

Oliver smiled back. 'Too embarrassed.'

13

He was waiting when Rina swung the Volvo into the parking lot. She pulled alongside his ten-year-old Toyota, paused before she opened the door. Clad in a somber brown knit dress that fell below the knee, her hair pinned and covered with a chocolate tam, she thought she looked appropriate. Her face was clean, but without a drop of makeup. Let him see all the wrinkles and worry lines.

She got out, straightened up, and brushed imaginary lint from her skirt. She tried not to stare, but did anyway.

He had aged a bit, but wore it well. Overtones of white mixed into his chestnut-colored hair, and silvering at his temples. He still kept it the same way – one length and long, the ends nipping his shoulders. His green eyes were as sharp as ever, lying calmly behind hexagonal frameless glasses. His face was a bit bonier, but his shoulders had widened, his build was more mature and mannish. Even with the stress stamped across his face, Abram Matthew Sparks cut a handsome figure.

He leaned against the car, looked upward, stuck his hands in his pockets. 'Thanks for coming.'

Her eyes went moist. 'I'm sorry, Bram.'

'So am I.'

Such *pain* in his voice.

He looked at her face, then at the ground. 'You look exquisite as always. Married life has been good for you. How long has it been since you've tied the knot? Five years?'

'Five years exactly.'

'So it's been what . . . around six years since we've last seen each other? Where has the time gone? You haven't aged a whit.'

159

'Tell me what I can do for you.'

'Nothing, unfortunately.' Bram walked over and opened the passenger door. 'Nothing at all.'

Rina blinked back tears. 'It's agonizing to see you in such misery.'

His eyes went to hers, then he looked away. 'Better me than you.'

She knew his words were heartfelt which made the pathos that much stronger. Longed to hug him, to comfort him as he had done for her. But she quelled the thought. It wouldn't suit either of them. Instead, she took his hand, his fingers tapered and smooth, his palm uncalloused. A scholar's hand. She gave it a gentle squeeze. Abruptly, he pulled her to his chest, hugged her hard, burrowing his face in her tam. He was trying to control his tears, but she still felt warm droplets on the back of her neck. Embracing her as if she were his life raft as he sputtered to stay afloat.

Hastily, he broke it off and walked away. 'Dear God, I'm losing it.'

'Stop being so hard on your—'

'I know, I know.'

Rina was quiet. He was red-faced, embarrassed. The car door was still open. She slipped inside the Toyota's front seat, burying her hands into the soft folds of dress fabric. Piled in the back were stacks of university library books written in ancient exotic languages. Among them, at the bottom of one of the heaps, was an oversized tome of Talmud. Tractate Sanhedrin, Volume One. Sanhedrin dealt with the laws of the Jewish court. Without thinking, Rina removed the book and set it on top. Holy work shouldn't ever rest under secular ones.

Bram wiped his eyes, moved into the driver's seat. 'Sorry, forgot who I'm dealing with . . . with whom I'm dealing.'

Rina blushed. 'Force of habit.'

'It's fine. *Anything* you do is fine. Anything at all. Anything, anything. I don't know why I even mentioned it.' He tapped his fingers against the steering wheel. 'I'm rambling, aren't I?'

'You're perfectly coherent.'

'My, you're kind.'

'You're using Steinsaltz?'

'So much for purism.' He rolled his eyes. 'What a firebrand I was back then.'

'Enthusiastic.'

'You mean obnoxious. Which I was. Yes, I'm using Steinsaltz. Besides being a remarkably clear thinker, he believes in readable print and punctuation. My eyes are going.'

Rina regarded his face. 'Did you get any rest at all, Abram?'

'Actually, yes.' He pulled a crucifix out from under his shirt, kissed it gently. 'I grabbed around four hours between six A.M. and noon Mass. I feel okay.'

With that, he started the car, jamming the gear into first. Speeded up as he drove through the winding mountainous road. Bram had always been a fast driver. Occasionally, the Toyota seemed to lose its grip on the asphalt. Rina clutched the door rest and hoped for the best.

She stole a quick glance his way. He was dressed in the requisite black suit and black clerical shirt. His nails had been bitten to the quick. She looked away, eyes peering out the window.

'Considerate of you,' she said. 'Wearing your cross inside your shirt when you were with Rav Schulman. Especially considerate to be thinking of him at this time in your life.'

'Yes, I've grown up.' He was reflective. 'I don't know why Rav Schulman put up with me way back when. Such a cocky kid. Cocky, abrasive, argumentative, rude, irritating ... a veritable thesaurus of unpleasantness.'

'You're turning your grief inward,' Rina stated. 'Don't. It doesn't help.'

Bram was silent. Then he said, 'Thanks for calling last night.'

'I wouldn't think of doing otherwise. After everything you did for...' Rina's eyes started to water. She hid her face in her hands. 'I'm sorry.'

Bram gave her a packet of tissues. Rina dabbed away tears, tried to compose herself. 'Was Rav Schulman helpful?'

'Always. The man's a stone genius.' The priest pushed the Toyota into fourth gear. 'I wish he had known my dad well enough to eulogize him. I wish he were speaking instead of me.'

'I'm sure your father wouldn't have wanted anyone else but you.'

'Flaws and all.' Bram's voice held a bitter tinge. 'I suppose you're right. At least it will be from the heart. You've been okay, Rina?'

'Very well. I had a baby three years ago – a daughter.'

Bram's happiness seemed genuine. 'That's wonderful! You got your little girl. And what a lucky little girl she is to have a mother like you. I hope she looks like you.' He let out a gentle laugh. 'No offense to your husband.'

'None taken. And you've been well?'

'Chugging along. I can't believe I've lasted this long as a parish priest. But it's a good place. We've grown tremendously. At the moment, we're just about five hundred families.'

'Big congregation.'

'Very. Goes in cycles. Right now, church is in.'

'As if you've had nothing to do with it.'

'Not much. We're practically the only Catholic show in town.' Bram turned onto Foothill Boulevard and headed toward the freeway. 'I know several guys from Loyola. Went to seminary with them in the States. They're great about picking up slack during my absences.'

'Then you're still traveling to Rome?'

'Yes, the Pontiff and I are very tight.'

'It's a simple statement. You're allowed to impress me without doing penance.'

Bram smiled. 'The Vatican needs people fluent in ancient languages. It's for their twenty-first century synod.'

'What are you doing?'

'Comparing the simultaneous writings of various ancient accounts and events – holy or otherwise. I'm attempting to date some recently discovered texts that have shown up over the last ten-plus years. Most of the works are in Aramaic, Hebrew or Latin. Some are in Greek . . . Phoenician.'

He paused.

'I think several were in Ugaritic.'

'What?'

'Ugaritic. A Canaanite cousin to biblical Hebrew. As opposed to Ugric . . . which is related to Hungarian. Something you'd know more about than I would. Anyway, by using syntax and colloquial phrases, I can put a century on most of the ancient manuscripts. Then I analyze them to see if the writings fall within the prescribed dogma of the church. If they do, I determine how the See can best use them to its benefit.'

'Very interesting.'

'Pretty esoteric, huh?'

'I feel like I'm back with Yitzy. No wonder you two got along so well. You both spoke the same intellectual language. Left us mere mortals in the dust.'

'Hardly. Whenever you chose to grace us with your presence during one of our many long-winded diatribes, I recall you holding your own quite nicely. That is whenever we piggish males allowed you to get a word in edgewise.'

'You're pushing seventy-five on the speedometer, Father. Can you please slow down?'

The priest hit the brakes, became somber. 'Yitzy was a great teacher, Rina. Better for me than Rabbi Schulman because I wasn't inhibited with him. I could make mistakes without feeling dumb. And, I did make mistakes. Here I was, a classic language major with a minor in biblical languages, and I couldn't hold a candle to a high school yeshiva boy.'

'There's nothing like learning a language as a child.'

'I found that out. Yitzy and I were about a year apart in age.

163

His fluency in the Hebraic texts astounded me. I was humbled rather quickly. It was a pleasure to learn with him.'

'You know, Bram. I've always wondered why you became a parish priest as opposed to an academic. I always figured you'd wind up teaching at Notre Dame or some other university. You've got a professor's mentality.'

The priest was quiet. Then he said, 'I think Yitzy's death knocked the intellectual fire out of me. Afterward, I wanted to do some actual good in the world, make a difference on a human level. Be a *real* priest.'

He smiled, but his eyes had misted.

'This sudden, terrible loss . . . meeting your new husband . . . seeing you . . . it has evoked all sorts of old feelings. I miss Yitzchak, Rina.' He paused. 'I miss you.'

A long pause. Silence except for the car's elderly straining gears. Rina said, 'I'm not dead.'

Bram smiled. 'Thank God.'

'You could call. I do have a phone.'

'It would be awkward.'

Rina knew that was true enough. She didn't answer. He tapped the wheel. 'What am I doing . . . running off at the mouth about Yitzchak because I can't deal with my own father's death? I'm sorry.'

'Please don't apologize. Would talking about it help?'

'I don't know. Right now, I'm so confused, I don't know what I'm doing.'

A strand of hair was tickling his cheek. Rina would have liked to tuck it behind his ear but didn't dare do it. The gesture would have been way too intimate. 'You're pale, Bram. Would you like me to drive?'

'No, I'm . . .' He sighed. 'Why would anyone want to hurt my dad? He didn't have an enemy in the world.' He tried to bite his nails. Nothing left to gnaw on. 'My mom's acting stoic. I'm worried.'

'Maybe it's her way of grieving.'

'No. Being a priest, I've dealt with grief umpteen times. But this doesn't seem normal. She's too . . . detached.' He paused. 'In truth, she's acting stoned. Could be the sedatives we gave her last night. She had been hooked on them in our early years. You knew that.'

'Actually, no, I didn't.'

'I didn't tell you?'

'Never.'

'Must have slipped past me. Maybe it didn't come up because she was off them when we knew each other.' Bram rubbed his eyes. 'When we were growing up, my dad was never home. And I mean *never* except for Sunday morning church. Then we'd go to the afternoon picnics, and he'd go back to the hospit— Now I know you've heard all this before.'

'It's been a while. Refresh my memory.'

'Nothing to say except, basically, she raised six kids by herself – three boys at one sitting. It was too much for her. She needed help. With her fundamentalist beliefs, secular therapy was out. And back then, they didn't have Christian counselors.'

'What about her church pastor?'

'No, she would never embarrass Dad like that. How could the wife of Doctor *Azor Moses Sparks* possibly have any problems? To the outside world, she was the model mother. Strong, solid, a firm churchgoing woman. And most of the time, while I was growing up, I viewed her that way, too. Like most mothers, she was our family anchor.'

Wasn't that the truth. Rina nodded.

'But she had another side,' Bram continued. 'Scared, frightened. Left alone in an empty bed most of the night. She had a hard time falling asleep. She turned to pills. Barbiturates. You know how they work. At first, they knock you out so you do sleep. Then, your body acclimatizes. You either take them or you bounce off walls. And with six of us, she did her fair share of bouncing. On the outside, she could maintain. But there were times . . . her mood swings . . . they were sometimes very hard to deal with.'

'Why didn't her doctor wean her off the medication?'

'What doctor? She got the pills from my father.'

Rina held back surprise.

'Actually, Dad gave them to me, told his Golden Boy to keep a watch on her, especially after Magdeleine was born. He was worried about postpartum depression, which she had with Michael. At the grown-up age of fifteen, I was in charge of dispensing Class Two narcotics to my mother.'

Rina remained silent.

'Anyway, she did wean herself off by the time we finished high school. I hope and pray she can handle my father's death without a major relapse.'

'You still have siblings at home, don't you?'

'My youngest brother and sister. But they never knew her as an addict, thank God. None of my siblings knew. Later on, Luke figured it out. Could interpret her odd behavior for what it was. Probably because of his own illicit drug use.'

'Is he still an addict?'

'Thank God, no. He's been clean for three years. But I'm concerned about him, too. He's fragile. His marriage is unstable. My sister-in-law is a very difficult person.'

'Dana.'

'You've got a good memory.'

'The girl who broke your heart.'

'A very good memory.' He kissed his cross again. '*Te amo, Jesu Cristo*. There are things worse than celibacy.'

Rina smiled and so did he. Then he turned grave. 'I know we're all our brothers' keepers. We *are* responsible for each other's welfare. But sometimes I wonder if I'm strong enough.' He rolled his eyes again. 'Now I'm whining.'

'You're talking.'

'I'm rambling actually.'

Rina looked down. 'It's good for you to talk. Bram, I really do have a phone number.'

'I appreciate it, Rina Miriam, but it wouldn't work, with your being married . . . I'd feel . . . he'd feel . . .' He waited a beat. 'Did you tell your husband about us?'

'I haven't been able to get hold of him, Bram. He slept at the station house last night. I've left him messages to call me. But we keep missing each other.'

The car was silent.

Rina said, 'I'll tell him. I know it could be a problem with your father's investigation. Not that you're a suspect—'

'He's going to be looking into me . . . into all of us as soon as my father's will is read. Because I just found out, we all inherited a lot of money.'

Rina was silent.

Bram said, 'You're not involved in his professional life, correct?'

'Generally, no.'

'That's good. Because things could get dicey. Some of my sibs are in deep debt. Deeper than he's aware of at the moment. But I'm sure he'll find out. He's going to start doing background checks, asking us lots of personal questions. The past could come up. That's why you've *got* to tell him you know me.'

'If I see him at the service, I'll tell him on the spot.' Rina tried to rein in her sick stomach. 'You're not in trouble, are you?'

'*Me?*' Bram let out a soft laugh. 'No, my life is an open book. But that doesn't mean there won't be friction.' Traffic started to slow. 'We're getting close.'

A thunderous roar from a motorcycle brigade came zooming past. A deafening noise. Rina held her ears and looked quizzically at Bram.

'My father loved motorcycles,' he said. 'Rode with a club on weekends. I'm assuming that caravan was his riding buddies.'

'Your father rode *motorcycles*?'

'Faithfully for about the last two years.' Bram downshifted. 'Saturdays. Not Sundays, of course. This hobby of his came on really quickly and soon became a passion. He got hooked up with kind of a hard-core bunch. I met them a few times. Like everyone else, they were in awe of him, of course. But it was a *strange* association.'

'I'll say.'

'He even gave money to some of their causes . . . much to my mother's chagrin.'

'What kinds of *causes* could bikers possibly have? Save the local methedrine lab?'

'Yeah, declare it a landmark so no one can touch it.' Bram shrugged ignorance. 'My father, with all his education and knowledge, wasn't very worldly. Flatter him a little and he was an easy mark. If someone needed a handout, he was there with open pockets.'

'A handout is one thing. But giving money to outlaws?'

The priest shrugged. '"For just as by the one man's disobedience, the many were made sinners, so by one man's obedience, the many will be made righteous."'

Roma smiled. 'I don't know the text.'

'No, you wouldn't. Romans five, nineteen. It refers to the redemption of mankind from original sin by Jesus's grace. Maybe Dad thought himself on a mission. Because he was really *into* this club.'

Bram thought a moment.

'Or maybe the reason was much more plebeian. Maybe they made him feel young and irresponsible – a word that's not normally in my father's vocabulary. They had him all hepped up on some kind of environmental freedom petition. To my jaded eye, it looked like a scam. To Dad, it was his version of Save the Whales. How're the boys, Rina?'

'Big.'

'They get along well with . . . him?'

'You may call him Peter.'

'I will call him *Lieutenant*.'

Rina smiled, looked away. 'They were very young when Yitzchak died . . . especially Jacob. Peter is the only father he's really ever known. He adores them both. And they love him as well.'

'That's good to hear.'

'Abram, one doesn't replace the other.'

'But life goes on.'

'Yes, it does.'

Bram waited a beat, then said, 'I'm really happy for you, Rina. Sincerely. It's taken me a while to get to this place. But I've arrived nonetheless.'

'Thank you, I . . . are you happy, Abram?'

'Yes, I am— I mean I'm not happy at this moment. But I feel I made the right decision.'

'That's wonderful.' Rina began wringing her hands. Softly, the priest put his palm over her tightened fists.

'What's on your mind, Rina?'

She relaxed her hands. 'Nothing.'

Bram pulled his hand away and waited.

Rina said, 'What did you mean when you said there might be friction? Did you mean friction between you and Peter?'

'Maybe.'

'What *kind* of friction?'

The priest sighed.

Rina said, 'Forget I said anything.'

'No, I'll answer you.' He paused. 'You know we've told each other private things. Not officially under the sacramental seal . . . but things in confidence. Have you thought about what you'll do if he starts asking questions about me?'

'Why should he? Our past has no bearing on this case.'

'But what if he thinks it does?'

No one spoke. The car ground to a halt as they reached the

grounds of the church. Rina looked out the window . . . mobbed with people.

'I've got to get out of this lane.' He jerked the car to the left, then made a sharp right until he was riding on the grass. An attendant flagged him down, then saw who it was.

'Father Sparks, I'm very sorry for your loss.' He looked down. 'Everyone's loss.'

'Thank you for your sympathy, Ralph.'

'You didn't ride in the hearse with the others?'

'No, I was tied up with other things. Where should I park?'

'Just go straight over the grass.' Ralph pointed out toward the field. 'All the way in front of the line. I'll radio Tim that you're on your way.'

'Thank you.' Bram jammed the car into second gear, the tires stalling in the soft dirt. He downshifted back to first and tried again. The Toyota bucked forward.

'Another long day.' His eyes watered. 'There's going to be lots of them. What a nightmare! My heart's coming out of my chest.'

'You'll get through it.' Rina spoke assuredly. 'Everything's a blur now . . . time is endless . . . but the day will end, I promise you. And you'll survive.'

'You should know.'

'Believe me, I do.' But Rina wasn't as certain as her words. Trying to keep her stomach from coming through her throat. Seeing the hearse, seeing him dressed in black. Too many memories.

'Rina, about what I said—'

'He won't interrogate me, Bram. He's not like that.'

'I phrased it badly. I didn't mean to imply anything.'

Rina buried her head in her hands. 'You didn't imply anything. I'm acting defensive. I'm sorry.'

'Rina, just let me get this thought out, okay? Because I don't know when – if ever – we'll be alone again.'

'Go ahead.'

'Rina, without a doubt, your loyalties lie with your husband. But mine lie with my family. *If* push should come to shove, I bind with my kind, no matter what. Your husband may ask me questions that I may not answer. That could anger him, frustrate him. Maybe . . . just maybe, he'll come to you for personal information about me.'

'I don't think Peter would do that.'

'Then I'm worrying for nothing. I'm just mentioning it because I don't want you to feel divided in your loyalties. If it should happen . . . you have my permission to tell him whatever you feel comfortable with. The *last* thing I want is to create conflict between the two of you.'

'It won't happen.'

'Good.'

'Divided loyalties,' she whispered. 'I detect a pattern.'

Bram raised his brow. 'You said it, Rina Miriam, not I.'

14

Stifling hot from a houseful of packed flesh, yet the men still wore jackets. Decker wiped his brow, reaching a compromise. He'd leave the jacket on, but loosen the tie and undo the top button of his white shirt. Good that he was tall. Standing on the landing steps of the Sparks's home, he could see over the human yardage. Even from this vantage point, with so many people, he couldn't keep a definitive watch over the siblings. Kept scattering from place to place like little black ants. Especially the twins, both of them wearing almost identical black suits and *glasses*. True, the priest had longer hair and wore a collar. But without putting the two side by side, Decker was easily confused.

The widow, Dolores – known as Dolly to her friends – was holding court in the back of the living room. At present, she was mobbed by well-wishers offering her solace, surrounding her, patting her hand, stroking her shoulder, wiping her wet cheeks. It would have been inopportune for Decker to intrude upon her grief. Yet, he knew he was going to have to question her.

Because her husband was murdered in the back of a fancy restaurant.

Which could mean a paramour.

Which could mean a jealous husband or boyfriend.

Or, dare he say it, even a jealous wife.

Because as of yet, Decker still lacked a damn motive.

Some of the guests were eating, popping things into their mouths, or drinking something unnaturally red out of plastic glasses. Obviously, there must be food somewhere. Holding his breath, Decker dove into the pool of humanity. He intended to pay

173

his respects to the widow. But first he'd take a look around.

The family room held the bulk of the people. To its immediate left was an enormous dining room, windows facing the front lawn. It was also packed. A giant flower arrangement sat in the middle of a long table; around it were plates of assorted cookies, finger-sized danish, bite-sized muffins, sugared ladyfingers, and bowls of candies. On the buffet was a coffee urn with cream and sugar and hot cups. A sideboard held a filled punch bowl with cold cups. Put the scene in another context, add a little music, and it was party time.

Decker squeezed his body out of the dining room, back to the main drag. Yet he wasn't quite ready to introduce himself to Dolly Sparks. He noticed that off the dining room was a swinging door. Decker pushed it open, found himself staring down an empty hallway. And since no one was telling him it was off-limits to foot traffic . . .

Glancing over his shoulder, he ventured down the foyer. Opened a few doors. A bathroom, an office with a computer, a butler's pantry. At the end was another closed swinging door.

What the heck. He'd gone this far.

Decker leaned on it, allowing him entrance to a massive kitchen/breakfast nook area. At least a thousand square feet. An oversized refrigerator, an eight-burner stove. Walls and walls of cabinets – white, scalloped frames surrounding lemon-yellow panels hand-painted with flowers and scrolls. But they were old, the designs being chipped, faded, or missing altogether. Paper goods and boxes of pastries had been strewn over the counter. Hand-painted tile. Though the grout was clean, it had grayed with age. Several uniformed housekeepers scurried about: setting up cookie platters, bringing in empty plates, taking out pitchers of punch, or making more coffee.

Decker suddenly noticed that except for the help, he was alone. Nice. He could breathe. But it looked funny.

A maid carrying two platters of cookies winked at him as she passed by.

Decker held back a laugh.

The swing door opened. Immediately, Decker's eyes grew in diameter.

'I thought I might find you here skulking about,' Rina said. 'I've got to talk to you.'

Involuntarily, he felt his anger rise. He was working on a big murder case, his attention focused on *business*. Rina's presence was not only a supreme distraction, but a problem. Personal digressions could screw up his credibility. 'What are you *doing* here?'

'Can you keep your voice down to a civil level?'

Decker looked around. The hired help was staring at him. He took a deep breath. 'Sorry.' He leaned over, kissed her forehead. 'Sorry, I just didn't expect—'

'I know. You're working on a case. I'm interrupting your concentration. But I couldn't help it.' Rina began kneading her hands. 'I know Dr. Sparks's son Abram. He asked me to come.'

Decker paused, weighed his words because he didn't want to say the wrong thing. 'He *asked* you to come?'

'Yes.'

'He *called* you?'

'No, I called him. Last night.'

'You called him.' Decker smoothed his mustache. 'Okay. That must mean you know him well.'

'Bram had been a dear friend to Yitzchak. At one point, I knew him very well. I know I should have said something as soon as you told me about the murder. But frankly, I was in shock. I have been trying to reach you all day.'

Decker softened. 'I know you have, honey. And I got the messages. They told me it wasn't an emergency.'

'It wasn't.'

'Is this what you wanted to tell me?'

'Yes.' Her face crumpled. 'This has been a very stressful day for me. At best, I don't do well with these kinds of things. And

175

seeing Bram brought back all these memories and I . . .'

She erupted into tears. Decker pulled her into his arms. 'Oh, sweetheart, don't cry. It's fine . . . no big deal.'

It was a very *big deal.*

Decker kissed his wife's hat. 'Honey, it was nice that you came. But you shouldn't have to go through this. It might be better if you just went home. We'll talk later.'

She dried her tears with a tissue. 'I came with Bram. Can you take me back to the yeshiva? The Volvo's there.'

'Bram *drove* you here?'

'Yes.'

Decker was silent. For a woman as religious as Rina to be alone with a man – even a priest – implied a close relationship. 'Just the two of you?'

She pulled away. 'Yes, Peter, just the two of us. We met at the yeshiva at his request. Because he had business with Rav Schulman. Then we drove together to the service. Afterward, he asked me if I wouldn't mind coming back to the house. He wanted to spend a little time with his family before he drove me back.'

Decker looked at her, said nothing.

Rina said, 'Is my acquaintance with Bram going to mess up your investigation?'

'It's going to have to be dealt with. How'd you come to know him so well?'

Rina stared at him, not angry, just weary. 'He just about moved in after Yitzchak fell ill. He read to him when Yitzy's sight failed, he carried him from room to room when he couldn't walk, he fed him . . . bathed him . . . put on Yitzy's *tephillin*, oh God—'

She looked away, attempting to hold back tears.

'Towards the end, Yitzy became a *twenty-four-hour job*. I had two small children who didn't know what was flying . . . only that their father . . . Bram took care of Yitzchak so I could take care of them. So I could catch my *breath*! There were times . . . if Bram hadn't been there . . . I think I might have gone insane.'

No one spoke.

Decker threw up his hands. 'Where were his Jewish friends? Where were your parents, where were *his* parents, for godsakes?'

Rina wiped her eyes. 'They all came to visit . . . his friends, the *rabbaim*. All of them. And lots of them. Faithfully. But eventually they all went home. Because they had families, Peter. They had lives.'

'Bram didn't have a life?'

'He was unattached. I think he had just graduated seminary or was about to graduate. He hadn't taken his orders yet, that much I remember.'

'At loose ends?'

'I suppose. I never questioned his motivation. They had been friends before Yitzchak fell ill. Two scholars on the opposite sides of the fence. Looking back, I now realize how much Yitzy enjoyed those intellectual debates. Brought fire to his eyes . . . Bram's too.'

Then Decker remembered something the priest had told him about an old friend. The passion in his voice.

We used to spend hours together, arguing about God. I loved him like a brother. Then one day he took sick. Ten months later, he was dead.

One of those once-in-a-lifetime relationships, forged from something that defied rational explanation. Just as he'd had with his old war buddy, Abel.

Rina clutched her hands, looked at her husband. 'As far as my parents lending me a hand . . . they were more work than help. They couldn't deal with the situation. Neither could Yitzy's parents. Something we both recognized at the onset of his illness . . . Not that I blamed any of them . . . four concentration camp survivors . . . it was too much. So Yitzy made a decision to keep his parents in New York because he couldn't stand to see the suffering in their faces.'

Her lower lip trembled.

'We kept them at bay, telling them things were better than they were . . . until the final weeks . . . when we couldn't lie anymore.'

Spontaneously, Decker brought his wife to his chest and hugged her tightly. She embraced him back, swayed to his rocking, allowing herself comfort from the man she loved.

The swing door opened again. Rina broke away, dabbed her cheeks.

Bram's eyes rested on Rina's face, then moved on to Decker's. Something had passed between them – a glance that bespoke of deeper things. An evaluation of his worth as Yitzchak's replacement? A longing for what might have been? Or maybe exhaustion and irritability were pushing his imagination into overdrive.

Decker maintained eye contact with the priest. 'You spoke beautifully, Father. A very eloquent eulogy.'

'Thank you.' Bram nodded somberly. 'Even though words fail to express what's in your heart, you try your best. Thank you for coming.'

The door opened again. The maid returning with empty plates. She saw Bram. '*¿Usted quere comida, Padre?*'

'*Nada, Bonita. Gracias. No tengo hambre ahora.*'

'*¿Señor?*' She looked at Decker.

'*Nada, gracias.*'

The maid shrugged, her eyes saying, I can't give the stuff away. She went back to the counter and reloaded the platter.

Bram pushed hair off his face. 'The man who sold my father his first motorcycle is here. His name is . . . no joke . . . Grease Pit. He and his leathered entourage just walked through the door.'

'Are they creating problems?' Decker asked.

'Not at all. I was just wondering if you'd like an introduction.'

'Yes, thank you.' Decker swallowed the wrong way and began to cough. 'And . . . can . . . you introduce . . .'

He broke into a spasm of hacking. Rina banged his back. 'Are you okay?'

'*S'cuse* . . .' The two maids were holding large platters of cookies. Coughing, Decker moved out of their way.

'*Gracias*.' They walked out of the kitchen.

Decker coughed, held up a finger. 'Your . . . mother . . .'

'I'd be happy to introduce you to her,' Bram said. 'Let me get you something to drink.' He walked over to the counter and began to pour punch into glasses. The kitchen door opened yet another time, reminding Decker of the old Ernie Kovacs skit . . . person after person coming out from the bathtub.

It was Paul and he was fuming, eyes going a mile a minute. So focused on his ire, he didn't notice Decker or Rina, just headed straight for his brother.

To Bram's back, he shouted, 'He's *drunk*! He's saying *vicious* things! And I'm about to lose my cool! Rein him in *now*, Bram!'

Eva barged in. 'Bram, you've *got* to do something about Luke. He's upsetting Mother!'

Pink-cheeked, Bram said, 'We've got company, people.'

Paul pivoted, eyelids fluttering like wings when he spotted Decker. Eva's pale face had reddened. Bram walked back to Decker, handed him a glass of punch. 'Can you excuse us for a moment?'

'Of course.' It came out a hoarse whisper. Decker drank and cleared his throat. 'I'll just wait outside.'

'Thank you.'

Decker smiled, took Rina's arm, and led her back into the living room. He cleared his throat again. 'Well, that was pretty ugly.'

Rina said nothing.

Decker's eyes scanned the room. Casually, he said, 'Do you know the family, too?'

'No, just Bram.'

'Never met any of his siblings . . . his parents?'

'Once.' Rina hugged herself. 'Before Yitzchak became ill, Bram invited us to his twenty-fifth birthday party – he and his two brothers, Luke and Paul. You know he's a triplet?'

'Yes.'

179

'He's also an identical twin with Luke.'

'Yes, I know that as well.'

The one who's drunk and is saying vicious things and *is upsetting Mom.*

Decker prodded. 'What was it like? The birthday party.'

'I don't remember too much. I do recall sticking out rather pointedly among all the church ladies. I didn't talk much.'

'Where was Yitzchak?'

'Talking to the men. Not that there was a formal *mechitza*. But there was an invisible one.'

'The sexes were separated?'

'Informally, yes.'

Offhandedly, he asked, 'You recall any of his siblings? Surely he introduced you to them.'

'I'm sure he did. But I don't remember anyone too well except Bram . . . and Luke. And that's only because he looked like Bram.'

'Did you meet the doctor?'

Rina thought. 'Yes, I remember his father. A very . . . dignified-looking man. Very regal. But stiff.'

'Goyishe?'

'You said it, not me.' Rina looked up. 'I owe him big, though. When Yitzchak fell ill, he gave us referrals. I never spoke to him directly. It was all through Bram.'

'Bram set up the appointments?'

'No, I set up the appointments, but Bram gave me the numbers. Looking back, Dr. Sparks must have made some prior phone calls. Because we got red carpet treatment.'

'What about Bram's mother. Did you meet her?'

'I suppose I did although I don't have a clear memory of her. I believe she, like most women, spent most of the time in the kitchen, supervising the food and help. There was a ton of food, none of which we could eat. Too bad because it looked good. And it was also a topic of conversation. "You're not eating, dear? Are you feeling all right, dear?"' Rina smiled. 'They all thought I was pregnant.'

Decker smiled back. 'Everyone seem to get along?'

'I wasn't paying any attention. Too busy being painfully uncomfortable. Can we stop talking about the past?'

Decker was quiet. 'I'm treading on sensitive ground here.'

'Yes. It brings back memories that I'd just as soon forget.'

'I'm sorry, Rina. Inconsiderate of me.' Decker rubbed his neck. 'Although I am curious how a *yeshiva bocher* like Yitzchak hooked up with a Catholic priest.'

Rina pretended not to hear, spotted Bram, his eyes searching the room. Once they found their target, Bram moved swiftly through the crowd, stopped at his twin's side.

Decker straightened up, observing. Neither he nor Rina spoke.

Bram threw his arm around Luke's shoulder, began to steer him toward the kitchen. Luke staggered as he walked, got sidetracked with people, giving them overstated hugs and big loopy smiles. But otherwise he made no attempt to break away from his brother.

'The roping of tranquilized steer,' Decker said. 'Rein him in, he did.'

Rina said nothing.

'Guy has a bad chemical problem, doesn't he?'

Rina shrugged ignorance.

Decker tried to appear casual. 'Yesterday, Luke admitted having a past problem. Yesterday, he also claimed he'd been sober for three years. Obviously, that doesn't appear to be the case. Wonder what else he's been lying about?'

'Maybe the stress brought about a relapse.'

Decker rolled his tongue in his cheek. 'Did Bram tell you that?'

Rina's eyes met her husband's. 'No. Any more questions, Lieutenant?'

Decker held up his palms. 'Okay, I'm pumping you. I'm just trying to get some insider background.'

'Peter, I wish I could help you solve this. I wish I could tell you more about the family's dynamics. But honestly, I didn't know them. Just Bram. And since he's not a suspect, I don't see how I'm of any use.'

Decker was quiet.

Rina said, 'He's not a suspect, right?'

'Right now I have no suspect. So everyone's a suspect.'

'C'mon—'

'I'm serious—'

'That's ridiculous.'

'Rina, you're entitled to your privacy. I won't put you in the middle. But if something should happen, and your friend suddenly finds himself involved in this case, I don't want you interfering on his behalf.'

'Bram can take care of himself.'

'No matter what, Rina. I've got a job to do. Which means I don't want you talking to him until the case is resolved. Otherwise, my investigation will be tainted.'

'You're right. I understand.'

Decker paused. 'You do?'

'Yes.'

Decker was in awe. 'You're being so reasonable.'

'It happens. But don't get too used to it.'

'Nah, don't want to spoil myself.'

Rina smiled, hugged his arm again. Bram was trying to come their way, but kept getting waylaid by grim ladies in gray suits embracing him. If he was annoyed by the interruptions, his face didn't reveal it. He had almost made it over when an attractive but anorexic blonde woman with a severe haircut grabbed his arm, yanked him to her. Rina couldn't tell what she was saying, but she was giving him an earful. His expression grew impatient . . . drained. The woman, dressed in black, seemed vaguely familiar.

Dana?

They looked funny together. Probably because his hair was so long and hers was so short. Within minutes, she broke down, wept on Bram's shoulder. He held her, but wasn't happy about it.

'Who's that?' Decker asked.

'I thought you weren't going to put me in the middle.'

'Simple identification question,' he scoffed.

'Peter, you're being bad. But I'll answer you anyway. I think she's Luke's wife, Dana. But I'm not positive.'

Bram was trying to direct the woman away from the crowd, but he was less successful with her than he had been with Luke. Feet rooted to the floor, she kept clinging to him, sobbing and talking at the same time.

Decker said, 'He's uncomfortable with her. Animosity, or is he like that with women?'

Rina stroked her husband's cheek. 'Do I look like Freud?'

Decker laughed. Rina hit his good shoulder and smiled.

But it was an astute observation.

Bram had always been reserved with women, including herself. He had only opened up after misfortune and grief had thrown them together. Rina had always chalked it off to his disastrous relationship with Dana. Her eyes moved away from Bram and landed on a well-dressed man talking expressively with his hands. Way too showy to be a member of the Sparks's Fundamentalist Church.

She said, 'Do you know who that man is?'

'Which man?'

'All the way back and to the left. The one in the three-piece, pinstriped suit.'

Decker's eyes skied across the room. 'You know, I bet that's . . . excuse me, darlin'.'

Decker walked away, leaving Rina alone. Her eyes went back to Bram and Dana. Amid the adult bodies, a little boy of around three pushed through everyone, ran up to Abram shouting, 'Uncle Bram, Uncle Bram!'

The woman turned fierce, screamed loudly, 'Can't you see that I'm *talking*?'

People around them stopped conversing, stared at the woman. The boy's face broke. Red-faced, Bram scooped the child into his arms, comforting him, patting his back as the boy snuggled into his uncle's chest. The woman started crying again. This time, Bram was more forceful. Without grace, he grasped her arm and led her straight to the kitchen.

Five minutes later, the priest reemerged, still holding the child. He spotted Rina, came over. Rina smiled at the boy, brushed hair out of bright green eyes.

'Luke's son?'

'Yep.'

'He looks *exactly* like you.' Rina laughed. 'I mean your brother.'

'I've got a great setup. The kid looks like me. I get all the fun and none of the responsibilities.'

'Does Uncle Bram babysit a lot?'

'Uncle Bram does babysit on occasion. But Uncle Bram has his own life. Where's your husband?'

'Talking to that man over there.' Rina pointed. 'Who is he?'

Bram's eyes followed her extended finger. 'Reginald Decameron. One of my father's colleagues.'

'Snappy dresser.'

'Indeed, especially in this conservative crowd.' He spoke to his nephew. 'You okay, Pooch?'

The little boy nodded.

'This is Peter. Peter the Pooch. As opposed to Peter the lieutenant. We call him Pooch because no one can bark like Peter. You want to show Mrs. Laza— show Mrs. Decker your bark, Pooch?'

The boy shook his head, nestled deeper into the priest's chest. Bram shifted the boy's weight in his arms.

Rina mouthed, 'How's Luke?'

Bram's face fell, shook his head. 'How about getting Uncle Bram a cookie, Peter? A chocolate cookie. Think you can do that?'

He set the child down, kneeled to talk to him.

'Here's a dime. You get me a big chocolate cookie, I'll turn this dime into two dimes. You know I can do that, right?'

Pooch nodded somberly. Bram kissed his cheek. 'Go.'

The boy didn't move.

'Come on. I'll *time* you.' Bram looked at his watch and said, 'Ready, set . . . go.'

The boy scooted off. Bram stood up. 'Works every time.'

Rina hugged herself. 'I'm sorry about Luke.'

'If he's that selfish, getting drunk at a time like this, I'm not going to waste my energies on him. I've got my mother to think about.'

'How's she doing?'

'Thanks for asking. Actually, she seems better. At least, she's crying. I find that healthy.'

No one spoke.

Bram said, 'These things are good for her.'

'What things?'

'People . . . gatherings. Keeps her occupied. When we were growing up, she was very involved with the church. She held some sway being Dr. Sparks's wife. But she used her position to get people motivated. Raised money by doing bakeoffs and yard sales. She spent a lot of time visiting the sick, comforting the bereaved. I've always admired her charitable nature. She'd cringe to hear me say this, because she's not fond of Catholics, but I owe who I am to her.'

'Why doesn't she like Catholics?'

Bram smiled. 'She thinks we're a bunch of foppish, over-indulged idol-worshipers whose rituals border on paganism. And compared to the spare Fundamentalist service I grew up with, she has a point. I see Catholic tradition as beautiful, she sees it as theatrical. And of course, Protestants don't recognize the Pope as the supreme head of the Christian faith.'

Rina laughed softly.

'What?'

'I never thought about dissension among Christians.'

'No, to our shame, we are not a unified bunch. Just look at the Reformation, Martin Luther seducing nuns from the convent. He married one, as a matter of fact.'

'That lout.'

'Indeed. Even closer to home, Rina, look at your own religious denominations, look at your Orthodox Jewish sects. Didn't you used to tell me how the Satmar Chassidim hated the Lubavitch Chassidim who fought with the Misnagdim—'

'You have a very good memory.'

'For some things.' He grew distant. 'That was a long time ago. Yet, at this moment, the conversation is fresh in my mind. Funny how that works.'

Rina bit her nail. 'Peter doesn't want me talking to you until the case is resolved. You understand his position.'

Bram sighed. 'Unfortunately, I do. And it's a very good idea. Besides, we've both got our own lives now . . . separate lives . . . best to keep it that way.'

Rina nodded. 'As sad as it was . . . as hard as it was, it was wonderful to see you again, Abram. May God be a source of solace for you and your family. May He shine His eternal light your way. I wish you and your family only the best.'

Bram regarded her eyes, his own warm and moist. 'Thanks for coming down, Rina Miriam. You know you own a special place in my heart.'

'The sentiment runs both ways.' Rina rubbed her arms. 'I'm going to leave now. Could you please tell Peter I took a taxi back to the yeshiva?'

'Of course.' Bram stuck his hands in his pants pockets, leaned against the wall. 'Take care, Mrs. Decker. I'd hug you if I could. But as someone once told me, people talk.'

'Yes, they do.' Rina smiled at him. 'Besides, Father, we have our proprieties.'

186

'Absolutely.' Bram regarded her with warm, loving eyes. 'Consider yourself hugged anyway.'

'Ditto,' Rina smiled back, then walked away.

15

Decameron said, 'This man is Lieutenant Decker, Liz. He's in charge of Azor's investigation. Lieutenant, Dr. Elizabeth Fulton.'

Decker shook her hand noticing long, slender fingers. Her face was grave, but childlike – waifish with big brown eyes. Her hair was auburn and bushy. Little Orphan Annie had grown up to be a doctor. She wore a trim black wool suit, the short skirt showing long, shapely legs.

'I don't suppose you've found out anything,' Liz said.

Decameron said, 'Darling, even Sherlock needed a couple of days before he pronounced.'

Liz said, 'Don't they say most homicides are solved within forty-eight hours?'

'Then the man still has thirty to go,' Decameron stated. 'No smoking gun?'

'Wish it were so.'

'Keep digging, Lieutenant. Everyone has a past.' Decameron smiled. 'Would you like to hear about mine?'

'I'm listening, Doctor.'

'Reggie, don't be tasteless.'

'Two charges of solicitation, both over eighteen,' Decameron said. 'I'm not a baby raper, I detest NAMBLA and its perverts, disavow anything that harms children. I'm simply queer—'

'Reggie—'

'One charge was thrown out, the other stuck. Azor just about boxed me when he found out. But I ate shit and he relented.' Decameron looked away. 'For all his rigidity and fanaticism, Azor was a soft touch.'

189

'Court put you on probation, Dr. Decameron?'

'Six months plus one hundred hours of community service.' Decameron grinned. 'I worked in Boys Town.' He grew serious. 'It wasn't bad actually. The critters grew fond of me. This was back . . . maybe two and half years ago. I still pop in about once a month. How's that for being Joe Q Citizen?'

'You read them alternative bedtime stories, Reggie?' Liz asked.

'Hansel and Hans.' Decameron cocked his hip. 'Actually, I do bona fide patient care. You'd be proud of me, Liz. I'm very doctorly.'

She looked at him. 'That's nice, Reg.'

'What do you do?' Decker asked.

'Not much. Most runaways are in deplorable health. Their bodies are battered from drug abuse, sexual abuse, physical abuse, malnutrition *plus* adolescent hormones. Basically, I put band-aids on surgical wounds. Give them medicine for the obvious infections and dispense words of Welbyan advice. Tell them there's a better way, tell them there's a life out there, tell them to be more cautious. It's like telling me to be straight. One ear and out the other. *C'est la vie.* You can't save the world. Speaking of miscreants, how's your husband, Elizabeth?' He turned to Decker. 'Have you met *Drew*?'

Liz glared at Decameron. 'Thank God you're back to normal. For a moment, I almost liked you.'

'Where is the little puppy?'

'Reggie, knock it off.'

'What about Myron Berger, Lieutenant?' Decameron asked. 'Have you met the last of Azor's three stooges?'

'This morning.'

'I suppose he brought up my tiff with Azor.'

'I brought it up, Reg,' Liz said.

Decameron's eyes widened. '*Et tu*, Judas?'

'You're mixing your metaphors.' Liz paused. 'As a matter of fact, the police brought it up to me. They said *you* told them about it.'

'I did indeed . . . to head Myron off.' To Decker, Decameron said, 'And what did Dr. Berger tell you? I was spouting smoke through my nostrils, ready to kill Azor for dressing me down in public?'

Decker said, 'Actually, he spoke temperately.'

'That's not temperance, Lieutenant, that's fear of an opinion. But don't take my word for it about Myron. Just ask around. Ah, the word of God cometh . . . and in such a pretty package.' Decameron waited a beat, then stuck out his hand. 'Hello, Father Bram. How's your mother holding up? I'd ask her myself, but she doesn't like me.'

Bram shook Decameron's hand. 'Coping. Thanks for asking. How's the hospital?'

'Myron's doing a superb job calming the patients,' Liz said. 'But your father is . . . missed. I sure do miss him.' She dabbed her eyes with a tissue, grabbed Bram's hand. 'You spoke wonderfully today.'

'Not a dry eye in the house, Padre,' Decameron commented. 'You're quite the orator. Maybe I'll show up one Sunday Mass.'

'You'd always be welcome.'

'Isn't he *wonderful*!' Decameron said. 'How's the rest of the family doing?'

'Managing.'

'What can we do for you, Bram?' Liz asked.

'Nothing at the moment.' Skillfully the priest liberated his hand from Liz's grip. 'But if I need anything, I won't hesitate. You've all been introduced?'

'More or less.' Decameron looked at his watch. 'As interesting as it's been, I should be getting back to the hospital. Do you need anything specific from me, Lieutenant?'

'Yes, I do need something if you don't mind.'

'What?'

Decker looked around, dropped his voice. 'I believe you met Detectives Dunn and Oliver last night?'

'That I did.'

'They went out to Fisher/Tyne this morning and interviewed a Dr. Gordon Shockley—'

'Oh *God*!' Decameron clucked his tongue. 'Forgive me, Father. Sin number three of the Decalogue. Am I absolved?'

'Absolutely, as long as you refrain from doing it again.' Bram smiled. 'At least in my presence.'

To Decker, Decameron said, 'Gordon's a toad. Did he give them a hard time?'

'Well, let's say he played it pretty close to the bone.'

'What do you need?'

'They were wondering if you have the data from the Fisher/Tyne–FDA trials of Curedon?'

'Yes, of course. Why do they want it?'

'Because Shockley refused to divulge it.'

'Some people are very anal retentive.' Decameron thought a moment. 'Tell them to call my secretary. We'll do lunch tomorrow. I think I know where Azor kept the Curedon data. I'm assuming you just want the latest printouts. Otherwise, I'd need a truck to carry all the computer paper.'

'The latest figures would be fine.'

'I'll go through Azor's files, look for the data. Which won't mean *drek* to them. But if they're willing to slosh through the statistical muck, I'd be happy to explain what I can to them.'

'Thank you, Doctor. I appreciate that.'

'Unless you want to do it, Liz.'

'It's more your baby, Reg.' To Decker, she said, 'Dr. Decameron is our liaison between Dr Sparks's lab, Fisher/Tyne, and the FDA. Mostly I do all the internal lab work.'

'Dr. Fulton worked extensively with Dr. Sparks in formulating Curedon's animal trials,' Decameron said. 'She was in charge of research design.'

'Don't I sound impressive?'

'It was impressive.'

Liz was quiet.

Decameron said, 'You're supposed to say thank you.'

Liz smiled. 'Thank you.'

Decameron looked at his watch again. His eyes went to the priest. He embraced him. 'From the heart, I'm very sorry, Abram. Honestly, I am.'

'I know you are, Reggie.'

'Your father will be sorely missed. I'm not sure we can go on without him. But for now, we have no choice.'

'That's what he'd want you to do.'

'You take care of yourself.' Decameron pulled away. To Liz, he said, 'Do you need a ride back to New Chris?'

'No, Drew will drive me back.' Liz looked around the room. 'Where is Drew?'

Decameron said, 'Last I saw, he was playing jacks with the children. He was up to threesies.'

'Reg, stop it!'

'I believe he's in the dining room, Liz.'

'Thank you, Bram.' She clasped him tightly to her breast. 'Call if you need anything.'

'I will.'

Decker saw Bram stiffen as she hugged him. Second time today he noticed how uncomfortable the priest became when touched by a woman.

Liz touched his cheek. 'Take care of your family. They need you now more than ever.'

'Elizabeth, that is a cursed thing to say!' Decameron chided. 'Take care of *yourself*.'

'I'll do both. How's that for a compromise?'

The two doctors waved, then walked off. Bram laughed softly when they were out of earshot. 'What a pair.'

'You seem to get along with them.'

'In a very limited scope.'

'Both of them seem quite fond of you.'

Bram eyed Decker. 'Everyone loves a priest. Rina took a cab

back home. Would you like to meet Grease Pit?'

'Yes, I would.' Decker paused. 'He wasn't at all what I expected.'

'What do you mean?'

'When you said your father was a weekend warrior, I thought you meant a doctor/lawyer dress-up club.'

'No, these guys are the real thing.' Bram pushed hair out of his eyes. 'I don't know why my father hooked up with such a motley crew. Unless he was trying to reform them.'

'Did your father try to reform people?'

'My family is Fundamentalist, Lieutenant. Saving souls is an integral part of the doctrine. All we kids have done missionary work as teenagers. My mother chose to act out her life's mission through her church, and my father saved souls through his work. But even with all the medical miracles he performed, he was still vocal about being a personal missionary as well as a professional one. He used to pray with his patients before the surgeries.'

Decker paused. 'It didn't create a conflict with non-Fundamentalist patients?'

'He showed sensitivity if the patient wasn't Christian. Spoke exclusively of God instead of Jesus. Sometimes, he'd even use the common parlance of a Higher Being.'

'What if the patient was an atheist?'

The priest shrugged. 'I would imagine everyone recognizes his or her own mortality before major transplant surgery. I don't think Dad's invocation caused a problem. If it did, I never heard about it.'

Decker looked around. Again, he spoke softly. 'Obviously, his Fundamentalist beliefs didn't influence his choice of colleagues.'

'You mean Dr. Decameron? Reggie's a brilliant man. My father wouldn't have kept him on if he wasn't.'

'He didn't find his overt homosexuality a slap in the face of his religion?'

The priest's eyes darted about. 'You don't turn your back on sinners.'

'But you don't have to hire them on. Nor do you have to *keep* them once they've been convicted of morals charges.'

Bram said, 'Take a walk with me.'

Decker followed the priest back into the kitchen. To his surprise, it was empty, leaving Decker to wonder where Bram had stowed his twin, Luke. The priest leaned against the kitchen counter, eyes on Decker's face. 'Did Dr. Decameron tell you about the arrest or did you dig that up?'

'Decameron told me.'

'It made the local throwaway papers here in a big way. You can picture the byline: RENOWNED HEART DOCTOR BUSTED CRUISING SANTA MONICA. It caused a mini-scandal not only in the hospital, but in Father's church. Dad got a lot of flak. Not to his face of course, but there were whisperings that were painful for my mother. Even so, Dad was a man of integrity. He stood behind Decameron and eventually everything died down. I called you in here because I'm asking you to *please* refrain from mentioning the incident around my mother.'

'She doesn't like Dr. Decameron.'

'No, she doesn't.'

'Because of the scandal or because he's gay?'

'Because of the scandal and because he's *overtly* gay.' The priest fingered his cross. 'She's old fashioned. Thinks that if gays really wanted to change, they could. To her, homosexuality isn't an innate, hard-wired sexual preference. To her, it's being stubborn.'

'And it's being a sinner.'

'That, too.' Bram waited a beat. 'Actually, it's the homosexual act that's the sin, not the homosexual. Though the distinction makes little difference to a woman like my mother or to a man like Reginald, it would make a great difference to someone like my father who took the Bible literally.'

'Meaning?'

'He'd have nothing against homosexuals as long as they abstained from engaging in homosexuality.'

195

Decker paused. 'So your father wouldn't discriminate against gays as long as they remained celibate?'

'Exactly.'

'Hard to do.'

'It can be done.'

Decker said nothing. The priest's face was neutral.

Bram said, 'Either celibate or sublimated in a legitimate heterosexual union.'

'But neither is the case with Decameron.'

'No.'

'And yet your father kept him on.'

'Yes.'

'Ever get an indication that your father was trying to save Decameron's soul?'

A small smile played upon Bram's lips. As if the thought was too absurd for words. 'No, I never did see any indication of that. But perhaps it was an agenda of my father's.' He looked around. 'I've got to get back to the crowd.'

'Of course,' Decker said. 'Out of curiosity, is punishing the act but not the desire how the Catholic Church views gays?'

'Our philosophy is to deal compassionately with everyone. Anybody – and I do mean anybody – is welcome in my church. Theologically speaking, confession and penance are required for all immoral thoughts regardless toward whom they're directed.'

'Although personally you think immoral thoughts could be construed as healthy outlets for tension.'

Bram stared at him. 'Ah, our discussion last night. I should be more temperate in my speech. I didn't quite mean that, Lieutenant. As an agent of the Roman Catholic faith, I feel it's not only commendable but very wise to keep the mind as spiritually focused as possible. I had just been musing for my father's benefit. He expected theological interchange whenever I was around. I tried not to disappoint.'

Decker nodded, wondering what kind of fantasies had ever danced in the priest's mind.

Bram said, 'By the way, Lieutenant, I want to apologize for my sister's comments yesterday. Eva isn't anti-Semitic. But she is having a hard time with her Jewish husband. She's another one who has trouble making distinctions.'

'How'd your parents feel about Eva marrying a Jew?'

The priest's voice leaked exhaustion. 'I'd appreciate it if you didn't bring that up with my mother as well.'

'I'm not bringing it up with her. I'm bringing it up with you.'

'We've all made peace with our differences.' He looked up, engaged Decker's eyes. 'We've run far afield.'

'I'll take that introduction to Grease Pit, Father. Sorry to have monopolized your time.'

'Actually, you did a mitzvah . . . distracted me from these unreal circumstances for a short time. Isn't that what *shivah* is all about?'

Decker said, 'You know Hebrew?'

'Yes, I do.'

Guy was probably more fluent than he was. Seems the world was more fluent than he.

Decker pushed aside his jealousy and thought about what the priest was saying. There were some similarities between this gathering and *shivah*, the required seven days of Jewish mourning. The grieving family of course, the somber dress, visitors offering words of comfort to the bereaved, even the ample supply of finger food.

But there were also distinct differences. Namely the lack of *religious* rituals. Jewish law requires that the mourners wear torn clothing, sit on low stools or the floor instead of chairs, and refrain from greeting visitors. They were not permitted to leave the house – even to pray at synagogue. Which meant a *minyan* – ten adult men needed for public prayer – was usually brought to the mourners' house. Bathing was prohibited during *shivah*. So was shaving. All mirrors were covered, usually with taped-to-the-wall sheets. And of course, the official mourning period was intense for seven days, followed by thirty lesser days, followed by eleven months of reciting the mourner's *Kaddish* in a *minyan*.

Bram said, 'Actually, the one thing I wished we would have incorporated into our memorial service was a recitation of *Kaddish*. It's a very beautiful prayer.'

'I didn't realize that priests studied Jewish liturgy.'

'In general, we don't give it more than a superficial glance.'

Decker met the priest's eyes. 'Perhaps you learned it at the *shivah* of an old friend?'

'Perhaps.' Bram cleared his throat. 'From the sublime to the ridiculous. Let's go find Grease Pit.'

The man was pushing three hundred pounds with an enormous gut and a face as large and round as a globe. Tanned skin with noticeable pores and a sweeping black mustache that topped his lip like a boa. His hair was straight and black, and fell halfway down his back. Tall sucker, too. Almost Decker's height. He had on a black shirt, too-tight black jeans that exposed a crescent of hairy belly, and scuffed riding boots. He held a spangled leather jacket. He pumped Decker's hand.

'Manny Sanchez, Lieutenant. Call me Grease Pit. Or call me Manny. I don' care. Good to meet you, good to meet you. I wanna tell you somethin' right off the bat, right off the bat, know what I'm sayin'?'

'I know what you're saying.'

Bram said, 'If you two would please excuse me, my attention is needed elsewhere.'

'You bet, Father.' Sanchez grabbed the priest's hand and shook it vigorously. 'You take care of your family, take care of your mother, you know what I'm sayin'.'

'Yes. Thanks for coming down and giving us your support.'

'For Granddaddy, you bet I came. That was one hell of a man, your daddy. Now you go and take care of your mamma. 'Cause that's what family's for, know what I'm sayin'. To take care of each other.'

'Absolutely.' Bram extricated his hand. 'Lieutenant.'

'Father.'

After Bram left, Sanchez hitched up his pants and said, 'One hell of a guy, that Father Bram. Granddaddy loved him, I can tell you that. Loved his boy, loved his kids. But it's good that he left. 'Cause what I gotta say isn't for God's ears, know what I'm sayin'?'

'Tell me.'

Sanchez jabbed the air with his index finger as he spoke. 'Because I'm talkin' to you right now. Man to man. Know what I'm sayin'? Man to man, not pussy to pussy. And I'm tellin' you this. Asshole who did this to Granddaddy should be stringed up by the *cojones*, you know what I'm sayin'.'

'I know what you're saying, Mr. Sanchez. But that isn't how we operate under American law.'

'Fuck American law.' Sanchez realized he was talking too loud. 'Fuck American law,' he repeated softer. 'I mean, not *fuck* it . . . but you know, like . . . fuck it. I mean like you gotta job to do. And I can unnerstan' that. And I don't want to fuck you up—'

'That's very wise, sir.'

'But sometimes it just don't work the way it should. You know what I'm sayin'.' Again his finger started poking air. 'Now, I'm not sayin' I'm gonna break the law or anything—'

'That's very good thinking. Because breaking the law can get you into serious trouble.'

'I'm just sayin' that if you can't get it done, then I can get it done. Now I'm talkin' man to man, unnerstan'? You get it done. Or I get it done.'

Decker said, 'Mr. Sanchez, do you have any idea who might have done this?'

'An asshole.' Sanchez tugged up on his waistband. 'That's what you gotta look for. An asshole. A punk. Someone who rips for the fun of rippin'. And that means an asshole. Probably one of these gang-bangers. Did you look at the gang-bangers?'

'We're looking into everything and everybody.'

'That's good. Hey, Sidewinder!' Sanchez shouted out. 'Sidewinder, come on over here.'

Sidewinder was slightly smaller than Sanchez – but more bottom heavy. His face, eroded by acne, held a weak chin and a mouth of crooked front teeth. He had dishwater hair tied up into a ponytail. His garb was almost identical to Grease Pit's – black T-shirt over black jeans. His boots held tips and spurs – great accoutrements for kicking recalcitrant motorcycles.

'Sidewinder Polinski, this is . . .'

'Lieutenant Decker.' He proffered his hand. Polinski turned it into a high-five handshake.

Sanchez said, 'Sidewinder, this guy here, he's in charge of Granddaddy's bump. We gotta cooperate with him. Find the asshole who did this.'

'Absolutely,' Polinski said. 'Anything we can do to help. Not just me, any one of us. We all loved Granddaddy.'

Sanchez said, 'One hell of a guy. I was just tellin' . . . tellin' . . .'

'Decker.'

'Yeah, the lieutenant here that either he finds the asshole. Or we find the asshole. Don't make no difference to me. Just so long as *someone* finds the asshole.'

'Sir, it does make a difference to the law.'

'Aw, fuck the law—'

'I know, Mr. Sanchez. We've had this conversation before.'

'Grease Pit's just frustrated,' Polinski said. 'We all are. I mean look at it from our point of view. The tax dollars *wasted* on OJ's trial. And then the Menendez mistrial . . . more tax dollars wasted. Then the retrial. More tax dollars. That's a lot of money. So you see what he's saying about taking the law into his own hands? I mean it's wrong. But it's efficient.'

'It will land you in jail.'

'More tax dollars wasted,' Polinski said. 'But that's what

this society has come to. Lots of waste.'

Decker stared at the biker, took out his notepad. 'Any idea who might have bumped Granddaddy, Sidewinder?'

'Me?' Polinski scratched his head. 'No. No ideas.'

'Nah, we don't know assholes who do this shit,' Sanchez said. 'We don't believe in random violence.'

Decker managed to keep his face expressionless.

Sanchez said, 'You shoulda seen Granddaddy on a bike, Lieutenant. Man, he was somethin'. Burnin' the tar, smoking dirt through his tailpipes. And he put his money where his mouth was. Came through when it counted.'

'How so?'

'In the cause, man.'

'What cause?'

'He means,' Polinski said, 'that Granddaddy came through when you needed him.'

'Fucking A-right!'

'What cause?' Decker repeated.

'Like when Benny got wrecked.' Polinski scratched his head again. Flakes snowed from his scalp. 'Man, did he get *wrecked*!'

Sanchez said, 'Yeah, man, that was somethin'. He really got wrecked, man.'

Decker asked, 'What happened to Benny?'

'Asshole was skunk drunk.' Sanchez adjusted his pants. 'Went flyin' head first into the ground. Blood squirtin' all over the fuckin' place. Granddaddy sprung into action. Man, it was somethin' to see that guy in action when Benny got wrecked. Old guy like him.' He snapped his fingers. 'Moved like that.'

Polinski said, 'He had him bandaged up and ready to go way before the medics came tooling by. It was something to watch him. We were all in awe.'

'What happened to Benny?' Decker asked.

Sanchez said, 'He died, stupid fuck. Massive brain injuries.'

'Not that he had much brains to start with.'

Decker said, 'He wasn't wearing a helmet?'

Sanchez sneered. 'He was playin' around in the desert. You don't expect to get wrecked playin' around in the desert. Besides, helmets are for pussies.'

Too bad Benny wasn't around to offer a rebuttal. Decker said, 'How did Dr. Sparks come to join your group and ride with you?'

'I asked him,' Sanchez said. 'I fell in love with the old guy, know what I'm sayin'. He comes into the lot with his sons, I thought: Shit, another stupid fuck. Turns out the guy wasn't a stupid fuck. Knew what he wanted, knew what he was talkin' about. I asked him . . . I said . . . hey, Granddaddy, want to ride with us on Saturday? I kinda threw it out like a joke. But he said, Yeah, I'll come ride with you on Saturday. And you know what? He came and rode with us.'

'He was good.' Polinski ran his tongue over equine frontal incisors. 'Could have used a little polishing when taking the curves. But for an old guy, he had great balance.'

Decker said, 'Either of you have any theories about his murder?'

'Yeah,' Sanchez said. 'It was some asshole.'

Polinski said, 'It's absurd. Someone murdering Granddaddy. For what reason? Grease Pit's right. It had to be some hyped asshole.'

Sanchez hit Polinski's shoulder, pointed to someone in the crowd. 'Who's that guy, Sidewinder? Don't he look familler?'

Decker looked to where Sanchez was pointing. Muscular build, curly black hair, blue eyes. 'That's Paul Sparks. One of the doctor's sons.'

Sanchez pulled up his pants. 'Who's he talking to?'

Decker regarded Paul's companion. A ruddy man who appeared to be in his sixties, around six feet with a sizable spread about his middle. Soft features – thick lips and a thick, veiny nose. White hair cut short and blunt. Dressed in a gray double-breasted suit, white shirt, red tie.

From Decker's viewpoint, the old guy seemed to be lecturing about something important. Because Paul was listening carefully, nodding at frequent intervals, his eyelids calm and steady.

'Don't he look familler?' Sanchez repeated.

'Yes, he does,' Polinski agreed. 'He's obviously a friend of Granddaddy's. But I don't remember him ever riding with us.'

'No, he didn't ride with us.'

The two bikers continued to stare.

'Didn't Granddaddy brought him into the store once?' Sanchez asked. 'When he looked at the Harley Bagger.'

'Granddaddy bought a Bagger?'

'I knowed he looked at one,' Sanchez said. 'A thirtieth anniversary Ultra Bagger. But I don't think he buyed it.' To Decker, he said, 'That is one mean mother bike – 1340 ccs at 5000 rpm, 78 pounds of torque, and fuel-injected. Tops out 'bout ninety which ain't bad considering all the shit it got on it. I remember Granddaddy was looking at a Victory Red.'

'Cool,' Decker said.

Polinski continued staring at the man.

Sanchez said, 'Think we should go over and say somethin' to him?'

'Like what?'

'I dunno,' Sanchez said. 'Like hi or somethin'.'

Again, Polinski tongued his front teeth. 'I don't even remember his name.'

'I don't either.'

Polinski said, 'Nah, I don't want to talk to him.'

'Me, neither,' Sanchez said. 'I was just thinkin' that we should be . . . you know . . . like payin' our respects.'

'We showed up and signed into the book,' Polinski said. 'That's enough. You know what? *I've* had enough. Let's get the hell outta here.'

'Yeah, good idea.' Sanchez turned back to Decker. 'You remember what I told you, right?'

'If you remember what I told you.'

'What did I miss?' Polinski asked.

'I was just informing Mr. Sanchez that lynch mobs are against the law.'

Polinski waved Decker off. 'He's just frustrated. We all are. Too much tax dollars wasted on psychos. Too many laws restricting freedom of choice. The government should be catching criminals . . . real criminals. Not passing meaningless shit that the cops can't enforce. I mean the drug czar, for instance. What a waste of tax dollars. I'm not saying drugs are good. I'm just saying the drug czar was a waste of money. No wonder people get mad and blow things up.'

'Because it's meaningless,' Sanchez said.

'Exactly.'

Decker said, 'You're entitled to think a law is meaningless. Just as long as you obey it.'

Polinski said, 'If the law told you to jump off a cliff, would you do it?'

'You're speaking in absurdities, Mr. Polinski,' Decker said.

'That's the point,' Polinski said. 'The law's absurd.'

Decker said, 'Let's talk bottom line, gentlemen. I don't want any trouble with you, I don't want you getting in my face. Do we have an understanding?'

'Hey, you do your job,' Sanchez said. 'You get no trouble from us.'

Polinski hit Sanchez's shoulder. 'Let's get out of here.'

'Before you two go, can I get your full names and addresses?'

Polinski said, 'Stanslav Polinski, aka Sidewinder. He's Emmanuel Sanchez, aka Grease Pit.'

'Addresses?'

'Right now we got a trailer in Canyon Country,' Sanchez said. 'But that don't mean nothing'. 'Cause we're always on the move.'

'Where is Canyon Country?'

'Somewhere,' Sanchez answered.

Sidewinder said, 'No sense giving you a place 'cause we move around a lot.'

'What about the shop?' Sanchez asked.

'What about it?' Decker asked.

'I work at a used-bike dealership Thursday through Saturday. You can call me anytime.' Sanchez moved in and smiled. 'Give you a great deal on the bike of your choice. Specially if you got trade-in.'

'I'll bet,' Decker said. 'What's the address of the dealership?'

Sanchez gave it to him. 'Good meetin' you.' Sanchez grabbed Decker's hand with a leathery palm, shook it hard. 'You're gonna find this asshole, right?'

'I'm going to do my best.'

'Come on.' Polinski gave Sanchez a slight nudge. To Decker, he said, 'Ciao.'

'Ciao.' Decker watched them go, swaggering and jingling, with Sanchez tugging his pants upward to hide his butt crack. Grease Pit talked a good case of avenging Granddaddy, but he was probably more smoke than fire. Still, one never knew. They both merited further investigation.

Decker made some final scratches in his pad, notes reminding him to check out certain things. He finished his scribblings, tucked the pad into his jacket. Then he looked up and scanned the crowd. Paul was conversing with a bunch of white-haired church ladies. And the man with the thick lips and veiny nose had disappeared from sight.

16

The captain was in. Phone in hand, he pointed to a seat and continued talking into the receiver. Decker sat and waited. Strapp's office wasn't much bigger than his lieutenant's cubicle, wasn't any better decorated, either. Standard-issue desk and chairs, file cabinets, a separate work station with the computer. He had a phone, a fax machine, and a slotted paper holder overflowing with multicolored police forms. The desk held the pictures of the wife and kids, the walls were hung with photographs of the professional man. A smiling Strapp showing lots of teeth standing next to the mayor, Strapp with the Guv, Strapp in uniform between the president and first lady. Other snapshots, among them a photo of the captain standing next to a little girl holding a teddy bear. The man who stood at her other side wore a white coat.

Dr. Sparks.

Decker remembered the four-year-old headline. The girl had been given a new heart and life from the tragedy of another child's untimely death.

Strapp hung up the phone, folded his hands on his desk. He was about to speak, then noticed where Decker had focused his attention.

'Patty Harrison. Cute little thing, isn't she?'

'Adorable. Do you know how she's doing?'

'No, I don't.' Strapp grew tense. 'I hope they're coping with the news of Sparks's death. This could be devastating. How's the investigation going?'

'Still gathering information. Dr. Craine should be getting back with an initial autopsy report, Farrell Gaynor's been doing paper trail for the last eight hours, the others are asking questions, sorting through physical evidence. The investigation's proceeding nicely, sir. But *I've* got a problem.'

'What?'

'My wife knows one of Dr. Sparks's sons. The priest, Abram Sparks.'

Strapp pondered the words. Slowly, he asked, 'Does she know him well?'

'Well enough to be at Azor Sparks's memorial service.'

'She went at the priest's behest?'

'Yes, although they haven't been in contact for years. At one time, they were good friends.'

'Romantically involved?'

Decker started to smile because the thought struck him as ludicrous. An Orthodox woman like Rina with *anyone*, let alone a priest. Instead, he thought a moment and decided to frown instead. There had been an intimacy between them – that swift glance. Decker knew a strong bond had been forged because Bram had moved into her life at a very crucial time. But *how* strong?

A good-looking man selflessly nursing his dying friend through the terminal stages of his illness, comforting the friend's beautiful wife with perfect words: about how there were reasons for everything and having faith in God . . .

An adulterous relationship was out of the question. Rina would never have permitted it no matter what the circumstances might have been. But what had happened between them after Yitzchak had died . . . well, Decker wasn't as certain as he should have been. Because gentile or no gentile, passionate feelings often superseded convention. His memory tape did an instant rewind as he thought about how willingly Rina had accepted the raised eyebrows in her own community when she had dated and married him.

Which was probably why Decker had reacted so strongly to Rina at the Sparks's reception. Yes, his wife's involvement could mess up his case. But equally as upsetting to Decker was his lack of knowledge about Rina's relationship with the priest. The whole thing made him feel squeamish.

He said, 'I don't think so. But I don't know.'

'Did you ask her?'

'No.'

'Are you going to ask her?'

'No.' Decker glanced at a smiling Azor Sparks, then returned his eyes to Strapp. 'As much as I want to continue on this case, I do have my priorities. I'm not about to create tension in my marriage. There are rumors that the priest might be gay. I don't know if that's true, either. That's all irrelevant right now. What is important is simply . . . there was a personal connection between my wife and Sparks's son. What do you want me to do?'

Strapp sighed heavily. 'Is he a suspect?'

'Not yet.'

'Any indication that he'd make a good suspect?'

'None so far.'

Strapp rested his elbows on the desk, made a teepee with his hands. 'You're a lieutenant one acting as a two. Your role in this homicide as with all your Dees is supervisory.'

'Yes. But occasionally I do get involved. Usually in the beginning when cases aren't cut-and-dried.'

'Like this one.'

'Yes.'

'But once the case starts gathering its own momentum, you back off.'

'I leave the nuts and bolts to my detectives unless they have a specific problem, yes.'

Strapp considered the problem in silence. Then he said, 'At the moment, I see no reason to yank you off. Tell you what. You make sure to run everything by me. And I'll back you up if this should become an issue.'

'Sounds fair.'

'Also, we should set up regular meetings so something will be on the books. Let's try to talk on a daily basis sometime in the afternoon.'

'Fine.'

'It's good you told me.'

'Absolutely.'

'Anything else?'

'No.'

'Call me with updates then.' Strapp picked up the phone. 'We'll talk later.'

The exit line. Decker stood up and left.

'Paul was in debt,' Gaynor said. 'I'm not talking a home mortgage or car payments. I'm referring to debt from personal bank loans.'

Decker ran his hand through perspiration-soaked red hair. Man, he was tired, his iron will demanding that his eyes stay open and his mind stay alert. But he knew he only had a few hours left before the brain shut down. Though it was only six in the evening, it felt two in the morning. 'How deep was he in?'

'Three hundred fifty-thou give or take a few bucks.'

Oliver shot back in his seat and whistled. 'My oh my!' He wiped his forehead with a handkerchief. 'Is it my imagination or is it suddenly hot in here?'

'No, it's hot.' Decker leaned back in his desk chair. 'We're a little cramped. Tom, you want to turn down the thermostat?'

Closest to the dials, Webster adjusted the temperature. A blast of cold air shot through Decker's office. He leaned against the wall, slapped his notepad against his palm. 'I wouldn't even know how to start spending that kind of money.'

'Oh, I would,' Oliver said. 'Spending is never the problem. It's getting it. How'd Paul weasel a heavy bank loan like that?'

Gaynor shuffled through his stack of computer printouts. 'One guess.'

Marge shifted her rear on a hard seat of plastic. 'Dad co-signed.'

'Right.'

'How long has Paul had the loan?'

'Two years. At this point, it's more like a revolving line of credit.'

'Secured loan?' Decker asked.

'Unsecured,' Gaynor said. 'Higher interest but neither had to put up any collateral. Sparks's credit and word were good enough.'

Martinez fanned himself with his notepad. 'What's the doctor worth?'

Gaynor consulted his papers. 'He had over six accounts – three money markets with three different brokerage houses, one saving account, two checking accounts. By the rises and falls in the balances, the savings account is probably for household expenses. Balance around ten grand. Checking accounts . . . uh, first one looks like household expenses again. A balance of about two grand. Then he has one for business with a balance of around twenty grand.'

'That's an awfully high balance for a checking account,' Marge commented.

'Yeah, I asked about that,' Gaynor stated. 'Apparently, it's not unusual. Doctors have high expenses.'

Martinez said, 'Except New Chris was paying for everything. It's not like Doc had equipment to buy or a payroll to meet.'

'Or even malpractice insurance.' Webster stood in front of the air-conditioning vent. 'I b'lieve New Chris even paid for that.'

Gaynor shrugged. 'I'm just giving you the facts.'

'What about the money markets?' Decker asked.

'With Levy, Critchen, and Goldberg . . . uh . . .' Gaynor shifted through reams of paper while all of them waited wordlessly. 'Uh . . . here we go. He had around a half-mil in stocks, bonds, mutual funds, and cash.'

Decker said, 'Levy et al. is Paul Sparks's firm.'

'So he did banking with his son,' Marge said. 'There must have been some kind of trust.'

'Up to a point,' Gaynor said. 'Because with Kenner, Carson,

Thomas, he kept more. About two and a half mil in assets, not counting his pension, which has another three million.'

Oliver said, 'Shit, that man was *rich*!'

Marge said, 'Emphasis on the *was*, Scotty.'

Oliver made a face. 'Yeah, won't do him much good now. Tom, stop hogging the vent. We're dying here.'

Webster stepped away from the grille. 'Sorry.'

'Doesn't the money automatically go to the wife?' Martinez asked.

Gaynor stated, 'I know his pension money does because I got hold of the beneficiary papers – don't ask me how.'

Oliver said, 'Isn't half of the old man's assets automatically owned by wifey because of community property?'

'There's a lot of factors going on here,' Gaynor stated. 'First, I think marital inheritance is exempted for estate taxes if the money was put inside a family trust . . . which it was. Which means there has to be a will somewhere. Because with trusts, there are always wills. And if there's a will—'

'There's a way,' Oliver blurted out.

Everyone laughed. Decker told Gaynor to go ahead.

Farrell said, 'Since Sparks probably had a will, he might have made specific provisions. You know, like giving money to people other than his wife. Now all of this has nothing to do with his pension's three mil. Because that was outside the trust's assets—'

'I'm lost,' Webster said.

'Unfortunately, I'm not,' Decker said. Again, he wiped his brow. Six months of doing wills and estates for his ex-father-in-law – Jack Cohen, Esq. So mind-numbing, even the substantial salary couldn't keep him in the field of estate law. With unusual resolution, Decker had defied his ex-wife and returned to his former occupation of police work. It had created a scene. Back then, everything with Jan had created scenes.

Decker said, 'Sparks had two basic but separate financial holdings – the family trust and his pension plan, correct?'

'Correct.'

'Which means everything Sparks owned – outside his pension plan – was in the trust.'

'Not quite.'

Decker paused. 'He owned other things outright?'

'Joint tenancy.'

'His house.'

'No, that's in the trust.'

'Farrell, this isn't twenty questions,' Decker snapped. '*What?*'

Gaynor smiled. 'Sparks co-owned some of his children's houses.'

'Why didn't I have a dad like this?' Oliver asked. 'Buy me a house, co-sign my loans.'

Webster drawled, 'Sounds great except nothin's for free. You want Daddy holding a string tied to your balls?'

'Maybe it wasn't like that,' Marge suggested. 'The guy worked all the time. Maybe he bought off the kids with money.'

'Except he didn't *give* them anything, Dunn. He co-signed. Kept the knot nice and tight.'

Decker asked, 'How many houses did Sparks co-own?'

'Paul's house – a three-fifty mortgage on that. He also co-owned several retail shops along with his daughter Eva and her husband, David, as well as their Palm Springs condo—'

'Now there's a really moneymaker,' Decker said.

Gaynor smiled. 'I never claimed he invested wisely. Just that he owned property in joint tenancy. And since those properties are not in the trust, he probably made specific provisions about them in his will.'

Decker asked, 'How about Luke? Did he buy him anything?'

'Nothing outright. But that doesn't mean Doc never gave them anything. Four years ago, they'd been on a monthly payback plan with a medical collection agency. They had racked up huge outpatient bills.'

'Drug rehab?' Decker asked.

213

Gaynor looked surprised. 'No. A fertility clinic.'

Decker paused. 'Luke has kids. Twins.'

'How old?'

'Around three.'

'Then I guess the treatments were successful.'

Marge asked, 'Did Doc pay off the clinic?'

'Halfway through the payments, the clinic canceled the balance, citing professional courtesy. Since then, no financial entanglements between Luke and Doc. Luke lives in a rented apartment.'

'How much money does he have?'

'He and his wife have about two hundred bucks in their checking account.'

'Savings?'

'Nothing I could find.'

'That's Generation X for you,' Oliver said. 'Can't save a penny without spending a dime.'

'Luke wasn't kidding when he said he was broke,' Decker said. 'How about Bram, the priest?'

'Now he has money. Sixty-seven grand to be exact.'

Oliver whistled. 'Sounds like he's got a bad case of sticky fingers with the Eucharist plate.'

Martinez said, 'My uncle's a priest. Priests don't make that kind of money. All they get are small stipends.'

'Maybe Daddy gave him money to even things out?' Marge suggested.

Oliver said, 'Sixty-seven grand worth?'

Gaynor said, 'If Doc gave him the maximum allowed tax-free gift of ten grand per year, he could easily accumulate sixty grand. And I do think that's part of it. But he also reports income from book royalties.'

Decker said, 'Bram wrote a book?'

'*Messianic Teachings from the Old Testament.*'

'Oh, now that's a real best-seller,' Oliver joked.

'*He* wrote that?' Martinez asked.

Oliver's eyes grew. 'You've *heard* of it?'

'My kids go to Catholic school,' Martinez said. 'Next to the Catechism, it's their most used standard text.'

'Theirs and about twenty-five hundred other Catholic schools around the country,' Gaynor said. 'I called up the publisher. Some small Christian religious house. I got the feeling the book keeps them in business.'

Decker asked, 'How long has the book been in print?'

'Seven years,' Gaynor said.

'Bram's only thirty-five.'

'Then he wrote it when he was young. Because he's been collecting royalties for a while.'

'And he *keeps* the money?' Martinez asked.

'According to the last five years' worth of tax returns, he's donated seventy-five percent of his royalties to the church. Another ten percent, he gives away to other charities. The remaining fifteen, he pockets.'

'Don't priests take vows of poverty?' Marge asked.

'Banking fifteen percent of your royalties isn't exactly chasing the buck,' Decker said.

'Especially when you consider he's built sixty-seven grand by pocketing only fifteen percent of his earnings,' Marge added. 'That means he's given away a hell of a lot of money.'

Webster said, 'Wonder why he gave it to the church when his biological brothers were in need?'

Marge said, 'Yeah, doesn't the Bible say something about being your brother's keeper?'

'As a priest, it's his obligation to give his worldly possessions to the church,' Martinez said. 'Keep the clergy honest.'

Oliver said, 'Besides, he probably knows his brothers'll just piss it away.'

Decker said, 'Farrell, does Bram spend money on anything interesting?'

'Only thing unusual is he rents a one-bedroom apartment even

215

though his official residence is listed at St. Thomas's. He has itemized it as an outside office, been leasing it for the last nine years—'

'Office my ass,' Oliver scoffed. 'Betcha the goat brings women up there.' He grinned. 'What a priest can't do with rosary beads.'

'That's truly disgusting,' Martinez said.

Oliver laughed. 'Yeah, I'm a goner, going to hell on a bullet train.'

Nine years. Right around the time Yitzchak died. Decker quelled the thought.

'Maybe he brings men up instead of women,' Marge said. 'Didn't Decameron say he was gay?'

'This is all beside the point,' Decker said. 'All we're interested in is whether he's a suspect or not. For the time being, he looks pretty clean.'

'Yeah, if you're going to choose a family member, I vote for Paul,' Gaynor said. 'He's the one deepest in debt.'

'So why should he pop his father when the old man was supporting him?' Oliver asked.

'Maybe Doc threatened to withdraw support,' Marge said.

Gaynor said, 'More likely, it's the insurance policy.'

Oliver said, 'I love how you drop these little tidbits on us, Farrell. What *insurance* policy?'

'Sparks has a whole life policy on himself with death benefits totaling six million.'

Collective gasps.

Oliver said, 'You know, I think I'll pay a condolence call on the widow Sparks.'

Gaynor said, 'The beneficiaries are the children. Don't ask me how I found that out, either.'

Decker said, 'A million per kid?'

'Right on the nailhead.'

Marge said, 'So now we have six suspects. Christ, maybe they were all in it together.'

Decker asked, 'How long has Sparks carried the policy, Farrell?'

'He took it out five years ago.'

'So if the kids popped him, why did they wait so long?'

'Biding their time,' Oliver said. 'Looks more natural that way.'

Martinez said, 'We should rank them in order of who's most suspicious. Lowest would be the priest. Not because he's a priest, just because he has money in the bank.'

'Agreed,' Gaynor said. 'Next on the list would be the two kids at home. Neither has any debt or expenses. Then the older sister, Eva. Her clothes shopping alone accounts for five grand a month—'

Marge said, 'I thought she *owns* clothing stores.'

'Yeah, but according to her credit cards, she buys the good stuff – Chanel, Armani, Christian La Croix, Cesucci, Yves St.-Laurent, Hermès, Gucci—'

'Criminy,' Marge said. 'And to think I feel guilty every time I go to Mervyn's.'

'Are they in deep debt?' Decker asked.

'No. But with the second co-owned with Daddy, they have *no* room for flexibility.'

'Finally, we conclude with Paul,' Decker said. 'Okay, that takes care of the family.'

'Except Mom,' Marge pointed out.

'Very good,' Decker said.

Gaynor said, 'Yes, the widow is now a wealthy woman.'

'Did you meet her, Pete . . . er, Loo?' Marge asked.

'Miss Dolly.' Decker smiled. 'No, I didn't meet her. She was fatigued, whisked away before I had a chance to talk to her. I'll try to arrange something for tomorrow morning. Let's move away from the family for a moment.'

Gaynor said, 'Even though the financial aspect of this case does focus attention on the kids.'

'Yes, it does,' Decker admitted. 'But let's not get tunnel vision. Farrell, did you find out any information about Sparks's financial arrangement with Fisher/Tyne?'

Gaynor shook his head. 'Nothing. It's one thing to dig up bank accounts, pension beneficiary papers, credit card slips, and tax statements. It's another to unveil personal business contracts.'

Decker looked at Marge. 'Speaking of which, Decameron said for you to call him. He's willing to meet with you and Scotty tomorrow for lunch. He's going to bring you the Fisher/Tyne–FDA data.'

'He has the numbers?' Oliver asked.

'He thinks he knows where Azor kept them and he's willing to share.' Decker wiped his brow with the back of his hand. 'He thinks Gordon Shockley is a toad.'

Oliver dabbed sweat from his brow. 'You know, the more I know Reggie, the better I like him.'

To Webster and Martinez, Decker said, 'I got a fun assignment for you two.'

'What's that?'

'Tomorrow morning, I want you to visit some motorcyclists.' He told the group about Sanchez and Polinski. 'Apparently, they're living in a trailer in Canyon Country. I'd like you two to find Sanchez . . . he calls himself Grease Pit . . . and try to talk to him alone – without Polinski. Now, I don't know where this trailer is located. But Sanchez works here.' Decker gave them the address of the dealership. 'See if you can pump out information from one of the other guys at his work location.'

'What does Polinski call himself?' Marge asked.

'Sidewinder.'

Marge grinned. 'Oh those cute little boys with their cute little superhero names.'

Decker said, 'Grease Pit mentioned something about a biker's cause. I couldn't get it out of him because Sidewinder kept steering him away from it.'

'The cause,' Gaynor said. 'I wonder if it has anything to do with the three tax-deductible environmental checks that Sparks wrote out?'

218

Decker said, 'Farrell, you do have a way of springing things. *What* environmental checks?'

'Sparks wrote three ten-thousand-dollar checks to something called the *Peoples for Environment Freedoms Act.*'

'What act is that?' Martinez asked.

'I don't know,' Gaynor said. 'I just saw the checks itemized along with all his other charity deductions. Most of them were to the church or to medical causes. These freedoms act ones stood out, not because they were so large—'

'Excuse my small southern-town perspective, but I think ten grand is a very large sum of money,' Webster remarked.

'To me too, Tom,' Gaynor said. 'But Sparks wrote a lot of five-figure charity checks. Last year, he gave a hundred thousand to his church alone.'

'No wonder the kids had the run of the place for the memorial service,' Decker said.

'I remember these three ten-thousand-dollar checks because the charity was so different from his other donations.'

Decker looked at Webster and Martinez. 'So now you have a name for the cause. Find Sanchez and ask him about the cause.'

Martinez grinned. 'Do you want us to go as cops or as parties interested in investing?'

'I've got nothing against you two acting real friendly. But don't do anything that strains the limit of credibility.' Decker sat back. 'We're all okay then?'

Nods all around.

'Okay,' Decker said. 'It's about half-past six. Finish up your case notes, leave them on my desk, and we'll meet again tomorrow.'

'One more thing, Lieutenant,' Gaynor said.

Oliver said, 'That's TV dialogue, Farrell.'

Gaynor smiled. 'Too bad I can't name the murderer. But I do have the name of the executor of the estate. William Waterson. He's also Sparks's lawyer.'

Decker wrote it down, nodded. 'Yeah, his son Michael mentioned him.'

'Did you meet him, Loo?' Marge asked.

'No I—' Decker paused. 'No . . . not yet.'

Indeed, Decker hadn't met him. But most likely, he had seen him. Because it just dawned on him that Waterson was probably the man with white hair and veiny nose, the one who had been deep in conversation with Paul Sparks.

220

17

To his amazement, Decker made it home during dinnertime. The boys looked up, greeting him with a couple of tepid 'Hi, Dads.' But the dog barked excitedly, and the baby squealed with delight, jumping into his arms. Wordlessly, Rina heaped pot roast, mashed potatoes, and peas onto his plate. After washing, he sat down with Hannah in his lap, and threw Ginger a piece of fat. He picked up a forkful of food and shoved it into his mouth.

'Delicious,' he said, after swallowing. 'Ginger, stop begging.'

'I'm glad you like it.'

'Reminds me of my mother's cooking.'

'Yes, it is a rather goyishe meal.' Rina turned red. 'Oh my goodness, I didn't mean it like that.'

Decker grinned, threw Ginger another piece of fat. 'You meant it. You just didn't mean to say it.'

'I'm sorry.'

'No need to apologize. You must be in a goyishe mood.'

Rina didn't answer. Hannah started throwing peas. Decker said, 'Young lady, we eat peas. We don't use them for target practice.' He offered her a legume. 'Eat.'

Hannah took it and threw it.

'She's totally spoiled,' Jake said. 'No discipline.'

'You threw peas, too,' Rina said. 'Once, you put one up your nose . . . or maybe that was Sammy.'

Sam made a face. 'Do we really have to talk about this?'

Hannah threw another pea. It landed on Jake's shirt. 'Eema, c'mon. Do something.'

Decker pushed the plate beyond his daughter's reach. Hannah

started squawking. 'Are you going to behave?'

'I behave.'

'No throwing peas?'

'I no throw peas.'

'All right then.' Decker kissed her forehead and pulled his plate within her grasp. She reached for one, but stopped herself.

'I no throw peas.'

'Very good, Hannah Rosie. You're a very good girl.'

Within minutes, Decker's plate was empty. Rina gave him seconds. 'It's nice that you're home with us. Right, boys?'

Sammy smiled. 'Thrilling.'

'That was very disrespectful,' Rina chided.

'It was a joke, Eema.'

Decker said, 'It's okay, Rina—'

'No, it's not okay. Apologize, Shmuel. Right now.'

'I'm sorry.'

Decker said, 'It's fine.'

Sammy said, 'What's got *into* you?'

'Nothing got *into* me,' Rina snapped. 'Look how you talk to me. You're *makbid* on everything except the fifth commandment.'

The baby scooped a handful of peas and tossed them at Jacob. He jerked his chair back. 'She is so disgusting.'

'Can you just have a little patience?' Rina yelled. 'What is wrong with you two today? I spend thousands of dollars giving you both yeshiva educations and you both have the *derech eretz* of animals.'

Jacob sat back in his chair, opening his arms in protest. 'What am I doing? I'm sitting here and she's throwing food at me. Talk about *derech eretz* of animals.'

'She's two and a half, Yaakov. You're fourteen—'

'I don't like food thrown in my face, do you mind?'

'Yes, I mind when you say she's disgusting. I mind that a lot. She's a *baby*, for goodness' sake.'

Jacob sighed. 'She's not disgusting. She's very cute.' He leaned over and gave his sister a kiss on the forehead. 'You're very cute.'

'I'm a good girl,' Hannah said proudly.

Jacob smiled. 'Yes, you are a good girl. But you still shouldn't throw peas.' He pushed his chair back and stood. 'I've got homework. Thank you, Eema. Thank you, Dad. Excuse me.'

He walked away. Hannah threw a pea at him. Rina said, 'Hannah, enough.'

Decker stood. 'How about we set you up with a video, sweetheart?'

'Silly Songs.'

'Fine.'

'I'll do it.' Rina relieved Decker of the baby. As soon as Rina turned her back, Sammy gave Decker a questioning look. Decker put his finger to his lips. A few minutes later, Rina returned, sat down and started eating.

Sammy asked, 'Are you all right, Eema?'

Rina looked up. 'I just wish you kids would act more respectful. What would your—' She shoveled mashed potatoes into her mouth, then abruptly got up and went into the kitchen.

Decker said, 'She's had a hard day.'

'Obviously.' Sammy looked at his dirty plate. 'Why is she thinking about Abba? It's not his *yahrtzeit*.'

Decker blew out air. Why did he get all the fun jobs? 'She went to a funeral of a friend of his.'

'A friend of Abba's died?'

'No, no.' Decker shook his head. Talk about Freudian slips. 'His father died. The friend's name is Abram Sparks.'

Sammy thought a moment, shook his head. 'Don't remember him.'

'He's a priest.'

'Oh . . .' Sammy sat up. 'You must mean Bram. I remember Bram. He was a real nice guy.'

'Who was?' Rina said.

'Abba's friend, Bram.'

Rina glared at Decker. He said, 'You want to be mad, be mad. I think he's entitled to know what's going on, okay.'

Rina barked, 'Why don't you just—. . . have some more pot roast.'

Decker stifled a smile. 'Thank you, I think I will.'

Rina smiled and sat down. 'Fine! So will I!'

'You two are so strange sometimes,' Sammy said. 'I know, I know. Honoring your parents. *Kibud av v'aim*. I'll work on it. So Bram's father died. That's too bad. Should I send him a card or something?'

Rina stared at her son as if he had uttered Greek. 'That would be very nice, Shmueli. I think he'd like that very much.'

To Decker, Sammy said, 'He went with us to Disneyland for my . . . sixth birthday?'

'What a memory you have,' Rina said.

'Yeah, it was the high point of that year.' Sammy's voice cracked. 'You know, I always meant to ask you this, Eema. I remember having a fit because you wouldn't let me have a hot dog.'

'Yes, I remember that well.'

'I mean, I really had a fit.'

'Yes, you had a very big one.'

'Then . . . like a couple hours later . . . after I forgot all about it . . . You got me and Yonkie . . . like a dozen hot dogs. Where'd they come from?'

Rina's eyes turned soft. 'Bram went back into town and got them at the kosher deli.'

Sammy said, 'He went from Anaheim to LA, then back again to Anaheim just for hot dogs? That's like an hour-and-a-half trip.'

'Closer to two and a half hours with traffic,' Rina said. 'It was your birthday. He wanted you to be happy. If he had told me his plan, I would have said no. But he didn't tell me. Just took the car and said he'd be back later.'

She smiled.

'I was furious with him for disappearing. I was left alone for over two hours with two very cranky boys. Demanding this and whining about that—'

'We weren't that bad,' Sammy said.

'It wasn't your fault. I was cranky, too. By that time, I was so exhausted, I just wanted to go home. Lunch had been long eaten and we were all *starving*. Bram was nowhere in sight. Then all of a sudden . . .'

Rina let out a small laugh.

'I see this guy walking toward us, wearing a cassock.'

She laughed again.

'You're not allowed to bring food into Disneyland. Bram had changed into a cassock so he could conceal the hot dogs under his skirt. He figured no one would stop and frisk a priest. Even though he had grown an enormous stomach and was reeking of garlic.'

'That's right . . .' Sammy squinted, trying to recall the image. 'That's right. He was wearing normal clothes when we started out.'

'I was ready to kill him,' Rina said. 'But the sight of him walking toward us with this pregnant belly was so comical. He brought me into a corner, pulled out the hot dogs . . . like he was selling me drugs.' She paused. 'I almost forgot to wash, that's how hungry we all were. We ate and ate and ate and ate. Plus, we got real A-one treatment after that. The ride lines parted for us like the Red Sea. The boys were thrilled.'

Decker said, 'Respect for the clergy.'

'Now I know why people impersonate police officers or priests. One woman there . . .' Rina laughed again. 'She pulled Bram aside, told him she needed to make an on-the-spot confession. Nothing could dissuade her. Since Bram hadn't taken his orders, he wasn't allowed to hear confession. He didn't know what to do.'

'What'd he do?' Sammy asked.

'I told him to hear her confession,' Rina said. 'Then he should confess the sin later on at his own confession. He thought that was a good solution. Ah well . . .' Rina began clearing the table.

Sammy said, 'It was a fun day . . . you bought us Mickey Mouse pajamas.'

'I'm impressed, Shmueli! Yes, I bought you Mickey Mouse pajamas. We stayed until the park closed. I hadn't anticipated being there that late. Had to get you into something you could fall asleep in.'

'Yeah, it was fun.' Sammy got up from the table. Kissed his parents. 'Thank you, Eema, for dinner. I've got homework. Can I be excused?'

Rina nodded, kissed him back. 'You're a good boy, Shmuel. I'm sorry I jumped on you.'

'S'right.' Sammy kissed her cheek, then left the table.

Decker took Rina's arm. 'Sit, honey. I'll clear later.'

'You want any more food?'

'Goyishe food?'

'Peter, I'm sorry.'

He smiled, spooned mashed potatoes onto his plate. 'Next thing I know you'll be making creamed chicken on toast points and lime Jell-O.'

Rina scrunched her nose. 'You really didn't eat things like that, did you?'

'Every church social had creamed chicken and lime Jell-O. I half expected to see that kind of food at the Sparks' house. Being there, even under those circumstances, reminded me of home.'

Rina paused. 'Do you ever miss it?'

'Miss creamed chicken and lime Jell-O?'

'No, Decker. Miss what you left behind.'

'I was very alienated from my church by the time you met me. Don't forget, you weren't my first Jewish wife.'

'Why were you so alienated?'

'I don't know . . . independent spirit. Maybe I just didn't like the attitude: that man was born a sinner. I could never accept the dogma that newborn babies were sinners. Then, after I found out about my Jewish roots, I became even more estranged. I find the

Jewish concept much more livable despite the restrictions. That man was put here, not just to worship God in order to be saved but to do *good* deeds. It subscribes to the philosophy that man is basically good. Which is what I believe.'

'After everything you've seen, that's quite an endorsement of mankind.'

'I've seen the worst. But I've also seen the best.'

Decker smiled at his wife. 'It was nice that you talked to Sammy about Disneyland. His memories are very important.'

Rina nodded.

'Sounds like you had a good time.'

'Relatively speaking,' Rina said. 'We stayed until the park closed, watching the electric light parade at midnight. I remember thinking how wonderful it was . . . how *normal* I felt.'

She hesitated, her eyes watching a distant videotape. She returned her focus to the present.

'Normal in a relative sense. Because there I was, a *frum* woman with two little boys wearing *kipot* and *tzitzit*, standing next to a priest in full religious regalia. Meanwhile, I had a husband dying at home. Rav Schulman had agreed to care for Yitzchak so I could take Sammy to Disneyland for his birthday. He actually asked Bram to go with me because he didn't think I should be alone. You can imagine how bad off I was if Rav Schulman sent a *goy* to be my *shomer* – my guard.'

Decker said, 'Can I ask you how he and Yitzchak became friends?'

Rina stared at her half-eaten dinner. 'Bram was writing a book – interpreting the *Chumash* in a very Catholic way – which is what they do.'

'The gentiles. Or should I say Goyim?'

'Goy is not a bad word, Peter. It means nation. It's used with Jews as well.'

'It's just the way the Jews say it when they refer to gentiles. He's such a goy—'

'You're teasing me. You're only hurting yourself,' Rina chided. 'You shouldn't be interrupting me if you want to pump me.'

Decker laughed. 'Go on. Bram was writing a book on the Bible.'

Rina organized her thoughts. 'Bram was young and very brash. Apparently, he waltzed into Rav Schulman's office one day and started asking him questions about the Talmud. Bram was lucky that he had picked Rav Schulman who treats everyone with kindness.'

Decker nodded. 'More than they deserve.'

'Probably much more than Bram deserved. The Rav was patient. Rather than brushing him off – which almost anyone else would have done – the Rav struck a deal with him. There's an *eesur* – a prohibition – against teaching Talmud to gentiles. The Rav got out of it by telling Bram that he'd be happy to answer his questions just as soon as Bram had mastered *Chumash*. Of course, Bram wasn't anywhere near that level.'

'A good dodge.'

'A very good dodge.' Rina smiled. 'But Bram was clever, too. He told Rav Schulman that he couldn't possibly master *Chumash* to the Rav's specifications because he didn't know how we taught *Chumash*. So he needed a *Chumash* teacher. Rav Schulman couldn't teach him personally, but he knew Bram wouldn't give up. Bram was very persuasive, back then.'

'I could tell.'

'He was more than persuasive, he had the ability to manipulate words. The Rav recognized this right away. He decided to send Bram to one of his students, someone whose *emmunah* – whose faith – was ironclad and indisputable. So he sent him to Yitzchak.'

'They hit it off right away?'

'Not quite. Yitzy's knowledge of *Chumash* was photographic – commentaries and all. Yitzy had a photographic memory about everything. But he had also been a *ba'al koreh* – a reader of the Torah. So he knew Torah – *Chumash* – comma by comma or rather, *trupp* by *trupp*. So along came Bram. At first, they just learned a little, went over a few basics. Yitzy was feeling him out, trying to ascertain Bram's level . . . which he thought was pretty high for someone trained outside the system. Then slowly, slowly . . . I could almost see the wheels turning inside his brain . . . Bram started trying to put things over on Yitz. You know, showing off what he had learned in seminary, coming up with an obscure Jewish source, positive that Yitzy had never heard about it.'

'Wrong approach?'

'Very misguided. Yitzy would listen politely. Then he would quote the source letter perfect, and come back with more than a few of his own sources, gently showing Bram why he was misinformed, *flooding* him with information the poor guy wasn't equipped to process. By the end of a month, Yitzy had unwittingly demolished him. Then they got along great. Because then, Bram was ready to learn.'

Decker said, 'One couldn't have expected a Catholic seminary student to know as much *Chumash* as a *yeshiva bocher*. It wasn't Bram's main text.'

'You're right. I knew that. Yitzy knew that. Rav Schulman knew that. It just took Bram a little while to catch on. Anyway, they became very good friends. Even Yitzy didn't realize how good a friend Bram was until he really needed him.'

Indifferently, Decker said, 'What happened with Bram's book?'

'Oh *that*!' Rina rolled her eyes. 'He had a contract for it. Something like Messianic Teachings in the Old Testament, as they call it. Pretty offensive to a person of strong Jewish beliefs.'

'Like Yitzchak?'

'Like *me*. I read part of it. For me, it was as if he was playing exegesis games with our holy book and using it for his own purposes.'

'But isn't that what he believes?'

'Absolutely. From Bram's point of view, he was simply interpreting the Bible the way he had been taught. One thing I should make clear. Even with Yitzchak as his friend, Bram *never* wavered in his faith. Last time I saw Bram, he was just as strong a Catholic as he is today. But after learning with Yitzy, knowing him personally, knowing how the Catholic Church had persecuted Jews over the centuries, Bram had some misgivings about publishing his work.'

Rina sighed, poured herself a glass of iced tea.

'Somehow the powers in Rome got hold of the unfinished manuscript.'

'*Somehow* they got hold of it?'

Rina smiled. 'You're right. He probably sent it to them. Anyway, they thought it was very scholarly work. About three, four months after Yitzy died, Bram was invited to the Vatican to complete two different versions of the book – one for the clergy, another more simplified version for the Catholic schools. He was also promised ordination by the Pope at St. Peter's Basilica through some hotshot seminary in Rome . . . Pontifical something. He called it "New Men" for short.'

'Ah, the power of power. Bram published the book.'

'To Bram's credit, he asked me what he should do.'

'You told him to go ahead. He knew you would.'

'Probably.' Rina paused a moment. 'Yes, I told him to go ahead. I didn't want the responsibility of stifling someone's golden opportunity. Besides, as strange as this may sound, I knew the priesthood was his calling.'

'Did you ever see him after he left for Rome?'

'Yes. Apparently, he came back right after I took the family to New York for the summer. I almost stayed there permanently. Come to think of it, I never could figure out why I returned to LA. All the men were in New York.'

'Not *all* the men.'

Rina grinned. 'Obviously not *all* men, darling.'

Decker grinned back. 'So you saw Bram after he came back from Rome.'

'I did.'

'Can you tell me about it?'

'Nothing to tell. By then, he was an ordained priest. I took him to a kosher restaurant in the city. Boy, did we get stares.'

'And that was that?'

Rina squinted at her husband. 'Yes, Peter. That was that.'

'Sorry.' Decker held up his palms as if he were fending her off. 'Sorry. Polite conversation between you two?'

'Exactly.'

'Can I ask what you talked about?'

'Most, he talked about Rome, about Italy and Europe. Like a travelogue. Stilted conversation. We were uncomfortable with each other.'

Inwardly, Decker breathed a sigh of relief. 'Well, you two didn't have much in common, I guess.'

'At that point, no.' Her smile was forced. 'Anything else, dear?'

'No.' Decker held back a grin. 'Better quit while I'm ahead.'

'Good advice for gamblers.' She kissed his lips this time. 'Even better advice for curious spouses.'

Wiping the dish, Rina thought about the Jewish concept of *shalom bais*, the keeping of marital peace. So important a tenet, a person was allowed to do everything in his or her power to keep home and hearth tranquil, even if it meant slight variations on the truth.

Because 'that' wasn't exactly 'that.'

She had seen Bram one time after their stilted lunch. About a year later. Nothing had transpired between them, so why bother relating the incident to Peter. On some level, she knew it would have angered him. Needless to do such a thing ...

She stowed the dish in the cupboard, guilt gnawing at her gut as she thought back to their awkward meeting.

Running into Bram at the local supermarket. Watching him from afar. He had been with a group of men – three or four of them, all wearing collars. They had been joking around, having a good time being young and free.

231

Remembering Bram clearly, his hip cocked, his head thrown back with laughter, Rina hadn't ever recalled him looking so happy. She didn't approach him, almost walked away unnoticed. At the last minute, he spied her, excused himself, followed her one aisle over.

They exchanged pleasantries. He spoke of his successes with Rome, of the recent publication of his book, of his new assignment as a residential priest over at the local church. A big church, he had told her. Prestigious. She was thrilled that he was doing so well and told him so. Holding back her own joy and rapidly beating heart until the time was right.

Looking at him, breaking into a smile. She remembered herself speaking softly.

'Bram, I think I met someone.' She looked down at her feet. 'A policeman of all things.'

When he didn't respond right away, Rina felt her stomach drop. Finally, he said, 'A cop . . .' He smiled with closed lips. 'Doing your bit for public service?'

Red-faced, she walked away, stung by his nastiness. Of course, he followed.

Instead of lashing out, she rebuked him with guilt. 'Of all the people I know, I would have thought *you* would have been the most happy for me.'

'I'm elated,' he said flatly.

Again she walked away. But he dogged her heels, held her by the arm. 'This isn't the right place to talk.' He blushed, dropped her arm. 'Can you come by my place around eight tonight?'

She stared at his face. 'No, I can't!'

'When can you come by?'

'Never—'

'Rina—'

'For goodness' sakes, Bram, you're a priest. You know how people talk!'

'I don't care—'

'But I do. I care for myself, I care for my friend. The cop. My bit for public service—'

'Rina, I'm sorry. I loved Yitzy. It just seems so soon—'

'That's a very odd statement coming from *you*. Mr. Peptalk. Mr. You're young and need to go on with your life. Mr. Life is short so live for the moment—'

'You're damning me out of context!'

'Then let's talk about context *now*! Your friends are going to wonder about you, Father. So you'd better go. Like I said, people talk.'

Bram took off his glasses and rubbed his eyes. He looked as miserable as she felt. Pity tugged at her heart. Within minutes, her presence had turned him from a fun-loving youth into a morose, burdened old man.

He put his specs back on. Looked at her intently and whispered, 'This isn't the right way to say good-bye.'

'So I'll say it properly.' Her voice softened. 'Good-bye and good luck. I mean that, Bram.'

'Rina, please don't—'

'I've got to go. So do you.'

She walked away.

And he had called her that night, begging her over the phone machine to pick up the receiver. When she didn't, he left a long, rambling message.

Apologizing profusely for his rotten behavior.

Not realizing what had gone on at the yeshiva just a few months earlier, how some maniac had been stalking her, terrorizing her life. How this cop, this Decker had come through for her when she had needed help. Obviously he must be of fine character to put aside his own safety for her welfare. He hadn't kept up contact with Rav Schulman so no he hadn't known. He hadn't *known*. Because if he had known . . . he would have . . . he felt like an ass . . . just please, *please* pick up the damn phone.

But she didn't pick up. Instead, she lay in her bed, tears in her eyes, listening to him implore her. Please, please, *please* call him back.

But she remained stubborn, deaf to his pleas.

A year later, out of courtesy, she had sent him a wedding invitation. Bram had sent back a gift – a silver kiddush cup – along with the reply card, an X marked in the 'yes' box.

The wedding came, the wedding went.

Abraham Sparks had been one of their few no-shows.

18

They decided to take Webster's '68 metallic-blue Hemicuda – a primitive animal that rumbled and roared, requiring a firm grip on the reins. But it fit nicely with the assignment and, more important, it flew at high speeds. From the Devonshire Substation, it was a quick hop north on the 405 until it merged with the Golden State, the empty lanes on I-5 begging for pedal to the metal. The 'Cuda zipped through the north Valley, past the smooth, glassy surface of the brim-full LA reservoir, onto the Antelope Valley Freeway into Santa Clarita. Off the freeway and deep into Canyon Country.

Quarry Country. Miles upon miles of limestone mountains, rising and falling like scoops of toffee ice cream. The sky had turned endless and virginal with puffs of crystalline cloud. No man's island. The area held electrical lines, telephone lines, smooth ribbons of asphalt, and not much else. Up close, the rocky hillsides nurtured lots of life – copses of chaparral, carpets of yellow and pink flowering weeds, gnarled oak, wizened Podocarpus, and thickets of oleander, shimmering silver with its thin, poisonous leaves. A sizeable breeze rustled through the flora, blowing sand and loose gravel from recently tarred roadways.

Webster rolled up the cuffs of his Hawaiian shirt as he raced the 'Cuda through the sinuous turns. 'Y'all think I should stuff a cigarette pack in the fold of my sleeve?'

'It would be authentic,' Martinez said. 'I like the grease spots on the denims, Tom.'

'Quite the verité. From DW-40ing my daughter's tricycle.' Tom chewed briskly on a stick of gum. 'Me? I like the sunglasses

235

hanging from my pocket. Thought that was a good touch.'

'Nice shades. What are those? Porsches?'

'A knock-off. But they are UV protected.' Webster changed the car's CD from Bizet to ZZ-Top. 'Like the shitkicker music? Bought it yesterday for the assignment.'

'Fits like a glove,' Martinez said. He had donned an oversized denim work shirt and a pair of torn, saggy jeans. On his feet were black biking boots. His hair was slicked back, and he hadn't shaved that morning. 'What kind of piece are you carrying?'

'Beretta, nine millimeter. You?'

'Smith and Wesson 686.' Martinez picked up the Thomas guide. 'You know where the hell we are?'

'I was wondering that myself. Guy at the dealership where Grease Pit worked told me to stay on Placerita, but I b'lieve I took a wrong turn somewhere. What intersects Placerita?'

Martinez skimmed through the map. 'Bear Canyon, Coyote Canyon, Rabbit Canyon . . . oh, here's a good one. Cougar Canyon.' Martinez sniffed exaggeratedly and wiped his nose with the back of his arm. 'Want to hunt some cougar, boy?'

'Just let me get my rifle and dawgs.'

'What kind of dawgs you got, boy?'

'A pit bull and a Tree Walker Coonhound.'

'A *what*?'

Webster smiled. 'A Tree Walker Coonhound. From Kentucky, indigenous to the South, suh. Anything illuminating on our map as to our whereabouts?'

'First we gotta find a landmark.'

'I'd settle for a crossroad.'

'How about a canyon? We've got plenty of canyons. We got Oak Canyon, Wilson Canyon, Maple Canyon, Ant Canyon, Bee Canyon, Tick Canyon . . .' Martinez looked up from the atlas. 'Tell me something, Tommy. How do they know that the bees stay in Bee Canyon, the ants in Ant Canyon, and the ticks in Tick Canyon.'

Webster smiled. ''Cause they all zealously guard their turf.

Little bee homeboys, brandishing stingers and wearing their wings backwards, fending off the new immigrant arrivals – industrious but interloper ants who bring over millions of relatives all crammed together in a single house. They bog down our welfare system.'

'Call up the INS.'

'And don't you know that both groups are scared witless of the tick gang-bangers drooling saliva teeming with Rocky Mountain spotted fever Rickettsia. I ain't lying about this. Just check it out with any bug CRASH unit.'

'What the hell is Rocky Mountain spotted fever?'

'My uncle once got it when he was traveling up near the Great Divide. Comes from a tick bite. You get high fever, muscle aches, chronic fatigue and lots of skin shit. He weren't pretty for a long, long time.'

'The Great Divide is around a thousand miles from here, Webster.'

'Yeah, but with plane travel anything's possible. You probably shoulda worn long sleeves.'

Martinez rubbed his arms. 'Why didn't you tell me this shit?'

'How was I to know there was gonna be a tick canyon out here?' Webster looped around a hairpin curve. 'We passed Mountain Crossing. Don't I turn there?'

'Yes, I think you do.'

Immediately, Webster swerved to the right and maneuvered an unsafe U-turn, wheels squealing under the chassis. Martinez gripped the door handle with white knuckles. 'You're crazy.'

'Where's your sense of spirit?'

'It disintegrated after I married. Turn right here.'

The road snaked upward, then leveled. At the higher elevation, the winds became redolent with the scent of pine. Blackbirds cawed from above. A mile into the climb, the mountain walls abruptly fell prey to man's progress: from a vertical barricade of hard rock to terraced soil. A couple of ranch houses, still in the framing stages, sat on dirty-covered lots. Next to the bulldozed mountain was wide-open space. Within moments, the glint of chrome winked at them. Then the motorcycles came into view. Next to the bikes was a makeshift shed. A miracle that the wind didn't do a huff and a puff and blow the thing down. Several hundred yards in the distance stood a lone eighteen-wheeler semi, as out of place as Stonehenge.

'Well, well, well,' Webster said. 'Lots more up here than a couple of trailers. We got a whole private dealership, no doubt specializing in ve-hicles without pink slips.'

'Or someone is running a chop shop.'

'That was my second guess.'

Webster pulled the car into the sandy clearing, shut the ignition, and got out, wind blowing grit in his mouth. He rolled down his sleeves. Martinez slid out of the car, popped a piece of gum in his mouth. They both took their time, sauntered over to the inventory. Immediately, a fat man came out of the shed. He wore overalls but no shirt. On his head was a Dodgers baseball cap.

'Help you?'

'Looking for Grease Pit,' Martinez said.

'You found him,' Sanchez answered.

Martinez glanced around, scratched his crotch. At this point, improvisation was in order. 'Looking for a bike.'

'You come to the wrong place.'

'Don't think so,' Martinez said. 'Guy from the dealership sent me here.'

Sanchez took off his cap and wiped sweat from his forehead. 'Then he fucked up. See, we only do repairs here, only do repairs. No retail, just repairs. He fucked up, man.'

Martinez looked up again. 'He said you could get us a good deal.'

'Well, then he fucked up double,' Sanchez insisted. ''Cause we only do repairs here.'

Webster picked up the story. 'He said somethin' about the cause.

We give money to the cause, we get a good deal. You sayin' he was lyin'?'

'I'm sayin' he fucked up.' Sanchez wiped his brow with the back of his hand. 'Who sent you here?'

'Tony.'

'Yeah, Tony.' Sanchez nodded. 'He fucks up a lot. Gotta talk to him about that.'

'What about this cause thing?' Martinez said.

'If you want to give money to the cause, I'll take it. But that ain't got nothin' to do with the bikes. Nothin' for sale. I'm only doin' repairs.'

'Well, what's the cause?' Martinez said.

'To stop the fuckin' government from tellin' us how to run our lives.' Grease Pit kicked up a toeful of sand. 'Too much left-wing regulation shit being crammed down our throats. What the fuck is it their business if we want to wear helmets or not.'

'Right on,' Martinez said.

'So . . .' Grease Pit snorted. 'You want to give me money?'

'Can you make it worth something?' Martinez said.

'Depends.'

Webster started inching toward the shed. 'You got lots of good bikes here.'

'All repairs.'

'Nothin' for sale?'

'Tell you what.' Grease Pit appeared to be thinking. 'Tell you what I'm gonna do. Yes, I'm gonna do this and I'm gonna do this just for you. You give me money to the cause, then tell me what you have in mind. Just tell me what you have in mind. I take it back to the owner. Maybe it'll fly. Maybe it won't. But maybe it will. But no promises.'

Webster moved closer to the wooden lean-to. 'You ain't got nothin' for sale right now?'

'Nothin'. I tole you it was all repairs. But you give me money, I take your offer to the owner.'

'So I give you money,' Martinez said. 'You go and tell the government to fuck off? What good does that do?'

Grease Pit sneered. 'You don't know shit 'bout how the government works, do you?'

Martinez waited.

Grease Pit said, 'You buy off people, man! Get 'em in your pocket. They vote the way you want 'em to vote.'

'Like the NRA,' Martinez said. 'Yeah, that's smart.'

'Fucking-A right it's smart. Money talks, bullshit walks. So if you want to give me money for the cause, I'll take it.'

Webster said, 'I give you money, you give us a good deal?'

'I take it to the owner, that's what I said. Didn't say nothin' 'bout givin' you anything.'

'Nothin' for sale, huh?' Webster wiped sand from his eyes. 'Shit, that's too bad.' He was almost at the door of the shed. 'I really didn't feel much like wantin' to come back.'

Sanchez shifted his bulky weight, his voice turning menacing. 'Get the fuck away from my garage.'

Webster stopped, backed off, held out his palms. 'Peace, bro. Sorry.'

'What the fuck you tryin' to pull?'

'Nothin',' Webster said evenly. 'Just the guy at the shop told us we could get a real bargain here.'

'I tole you he fucked up. He fucked up bad. Now you're fucked up bad.' Sanchez picked up a tire iron from the ground. 'You give me a bad feelin'. Get the fuck outta here.'

Webster's hand went inside his shirt, finger wrapped around the butt of his Beretta. He saw that Martinez had done the same.

Sanchez waved the iron, but didn't advance. 'Get *outta* here!'

Slowly, Webster walked backward until he bumped into his 'Cuda. Once Martinez was inside, he gunned the engine. As he pulled out, a rock crashed into the passenger door. Webster spun around, brought the car to a stop. 'Stupid *shit*!' Webster screamed. 'I'll *kill* that motherfucker—'

Another rock came whizzing past, missed the trunk by millimeters.

'Let's go, Tom.'

'Fucker put a dent—'

'Let's go, Tom.' Martinez repeated. 'Down. We're going down the mountain.'

Webster cursed again and peeled rubber as he left. Martinez blew out air. 'Slow down, for chrissakes. You'll get us both killed.'

'I should report him to the local police.'

Martinez said, 'You see that semi in the distance. Sanchez probably has a crew inside. Guaranteed, they'll be outta here in less than five minutes.'

They rode the next few minutes in silence.

Martinez took a deep breath, let it out slowly. 'Sorry about your car.'

Tightly, Webster said, 'Reckon I can fix it up pretty easy.'

'I'm not doing anything special this Saturday. If you want, I'll come over and help you sand it out.'

'Thanks, Bert. That'd be great.'

Martinez patted his shoulder. 'At least, we got what we came for.'

'I didn't. I wanted to test-drive the Ultra Bagger. You see that mother? What a beaut!'

'Too much shit on it,' Martinez said. 'Slows down the speed. I like something lighter and faster.'

'You do biking?'

'Used to do lots of it before I threw my neck out.'

'How'd that happen?'

Martinez laughed. 'I rear-ended some poor harried housewife. I was driving a bunch of kids to a birthday party in my wife's Volvo and got distracted by all the commotion.'

'You get any money out of it?'

'No, it was my fault. But the woman I hit didn't do anything against me. Who's going to start up with a cop?'

241

'The perks of the job.'

'You got it.' Martinez smoothed his mustache. 'This cause that Sparks gave money to – Peoples for Environment Freedoms Act. You think Sanchez is just pocketing the money or is there actually some kind of cause?'

'He mentioned something about buying politicians. Maybe he's buying off cops to look the other way at his chop shop.'

'Why would Sparks give money to something like that?'

'Maybe the doctor didn't really know where his bucks were going,' Webster said. 'Maybe he thought he was giving money for environmental freedom.'

'Whatever that is.'

'Telling the government to piss off,' Webster said. 'Strange as this may seem, I could see an independent thinker like Sparks getting caught up in a thing like that. Y'all talk to any doctors recently, Bert? They're real upset 'bout government telling them how to run their practices. Maybe this environmental cause struck a nerve.'

'*What* cause are you talking about?'

'Getting rid of the left-wing regulation shit.'

'Meaning?'

'Grease Pit mentioned helmets,' Webster said. 'Maybe they're trying to repeal the helmet law.'

'And you see a man like Azor Sparks giving large sums of money to something like that?'

'Passions run high, Bert.' Webster shrugged. 'You saw the card he printed for himself. Maybe he fancied himself a bad actor.'

'Don't see it.'

Webster shrugged. 'I'm just throwing out possibilities.'

In the distance, a two-year-old navy Lincoln with tinted windows was inching up the mountain road. It was heavy with poor traction, fishtailing as it maneuvered the curves.

'Odd car to drive up here.' Martinez spit his gum out the window. 'Pull off, Tom.'

Webster slowed, swung the 'Cuda onto a small, rocky ledge, the tires churning up gravel. He killed the ignition. They both watched the Lincoln Pass, chugging up the mountain at unimpressive speed.

Webster said, 'Do it?'

'What the hell?'

Webster made a U-turn, keeping lots of distance between the 'Cuda and the Lincoln. Martinez wrote down the license plate, was about to call it in. Then he remembered they weren't in the unmarked.

Webster said, 'I've got a cellular in the glove compartment.'

Martinez opened the door, took out a compact phone, and pressed a couple of buttons. 'What am I doing wrong?'

'No reception?'

'Nothing.'

'We're probably too far out,' Webster said.

Martinez's face was tight in concentration. Stuck in Lodi with no radio contact. Not good.

Slowly, the 'Cuda reclimbed the mountains, bucking at the reduced speed. No one spoke. Within minutes, the graded area appeared, followed by the two skeletal remains of ranch houses. Sure enough, the Lincoln had pulled off, was heading toward the motorcycle lot.

Which was now an empty field of scrub grass. Only the shed remained.

Webster sped up and passed the dirt clearing. 'They've gone fishing.'

'Forever.' Martinez's breath was shallow. 'Turn around. Let's get out of here.'

Webster reversed the 'Cuda, and they headed down the mountain at rapid speed. When they had reached the freeway, Martinez tried the cellular again. This time it connected through. He called in the license plate to the Radio Transmitting Officer and waited.

Webster said, 'You know, if you come over Saturday, why don't you bring the wife and kids. I'll make a barbecue.'

'Sounds great. Thanks.'

'You eat red meat?'

'Yes.'

'Steak?'

'Perfect. I got a portable TV. I'll bring it and a six-pack. We'll watch the game while we work.'

'Great.'

The cellular phone rang. Martinez picked it up, wrote down the information, then pressed the end button.

Webster looked at Martinez. His face was tense. 'Who?'

'Three guesses.'

'Huey, Dewey, and Louie.'

'William Waterson – Sparks's estate lawyer.'

Nobody spoke for a moment. Webster said, 'Think we should go back up?'

'Yeah, turn around.'

Webster moved the 'Cuda into the right lane, preparing to exit at the next off-ramp and reverse directions. Martinez picked up the cordless.

Webster asked, 'Who y'all calling now?'

'Decker.'

19

'No way you two are doing a solo tail back into boony canyon—'

'Loo, it's paved—'

'Martinez, listen to me,' Decker interrupted. 'After what you told me about Sanchez, he's going to be looking. He spots the 'Cuda, you're roadkill. All he has to do is get a couple of friends to box you in – one car in front, one behind – and bump you on a hairpin turn, down a five-hundred-foot drop. I don't turn women into widows, Detective.'

'If we wait for backup, we could miss him,' Martinez countered.

'Bert, Waterson's a respected member of the community. He isn't going anywhere.'

'What about Sanchez?' Webster piped in.

Decker barely heard the question through the ambient freeway noises. 'What about Sanchez?'

Martinez said, 'Don't you want to find out what he's up to, Loo?'

'Bert, we know what he's up to. He's running a chop shop. First, even if we wanted him, he's out of our jurisdiction. Second, even if it was our jurisdiction, we're not going to find him. He's picked a perfect area for cover. Miles of isolated canyon roadway with outlets leading to God knows where. He's gone. Forget about him.'

'Semi'd be easy to spot, Loo.'

'The hills are heavily wooded. You could easily hide the truck, yeah, even an eighteen-wheeler, off-road. Only possible way to find it would be with a low-flying chopper. Not a good use of time or money right now because we don't know who we're dealing with. For all we know, Sanchez might be armed with Uzis. Send in a copter, Grease Pit might do some target practice with the pilot. Turn around and come home.'

Martinez swore silently. Webster took the phone. He said, 'How 'bout this, Loo? We wait at the mouth of the canyon for Waterson. If he should hop on the freeway, we follow. Plain and simple and very, very visible.'

'Let me reiterate, Tom. Waterson isn't going anywhere. What purpose would it serve to follow him into the city?'

'Bert and I are just a mite curious to see where he winds up after his clandestine meeting with Sanchez.'

There was a long pause over the line. Decker said, 'Pinpoint where you want to wait.'

'The Placerita on-ramp to the 14 West,' Webster said. 'It's a stone's throw from the Sierra Highway. Very well trafficked. Give us an hour, Loo. What could it hurt?'

Decker paused again. 'The cell phone you're on. Will it maintain contact up there?'

'Probably not,' Webster admitted.

Decker waited a beat, then said, 'All right. Wait at the Placerita entrance. But I'm telling you right now. If Waterson doesn't come down through Placerita, you have direct orders *not* to go looking for him in the canyon. Stay away from anything that even hints of ambush, you hear me?'

'I hear you.'

Decker said, 'If I don't hear from you after one hour, I send a posse out. If I send a posse out, you're both in deep shit. Get it?'

'Got it. Over and out.' Webster smiled. 'Now that wasn't so hard.' He gunned the engine, edging the speedometer to ninety.

'Why don't you just put wings on the sucker and get a pilot's license.' Martinez crossed himself. 'Next time, I drive.'

'I'm just hurrying things 'cause I don't want to miss Waterson.'

'Be nice if we got there in one piece.'

'You worry too much.' Webster raced onto the 14.

'You got binoculars?' Martinez asked.

'In the trunk.'

Within minutes, the 'Cuda neared the Placerita exit. Just as Webster edged the car onto the eastbound off-ramp, Martinez spotted a midnight blue Lincoln entering the westbound on-ramp in the opposite direction.

'Shit!' he said. 'The Lincoln just got on the freeway going back toward LA.'

'Fuck!' Webster depressed the accelerator and the 'Cuda thrusted forward. The off-ramp led to a near-empty intersection. Webster shot a red light with a left turn, narrowly missing an oncoming Toyota. The shaken driver let go with a long honk and a series of lost curses. Webster floored the 'Cuda, catapulting it back onto the freeway. 'See the Lincoln?'

'No.'

'Fuck!'

A Cutlass cut in front him. Webster braked hard, throwing them both backward. He rolled down the window and screamed. 'You fuckin' *asshole*! I'm gonna *kill* you!'

The Cutlass quickly moved out of the lane and dropped back into traffic. Martinez was ashen.

'That son of a bitch!' Webster muttered.

Patiently, Martinez said, 'Slow down, Tom. *Now!*'

Finally, Webster braked. Breathing hard, he said, 'Spot the Lincoln?'

'No.' Martinez's heart was pounding in his breastbone. His eyes moved like radar, scanning through the traffic in front of him. Then he looked out at the side mirror. 'Wait a minute, wait a minute.' He jerked his head around. 'It's behind us.'

'Where?' Webster said.

'Right-hand lane, about . . . six, seven car lengths behind.'

Webster's eyes went to his rearview mirror, then slowed the 'Cuda to a speed less than the flow of traffic. 'I don't see it.'

'It's there, take my word for it.'

Webster braked again. Within moments, the Lincoln came into view. He grinned. 'Gotcha, baby!'

Martinez sat back, let out a deep breath. 'You almost got us killed.'

Webster said nothing. Then he started to laugh. A moment later, so did Martinez. He hit his partner's shoulder. 'Son of a *bitch*! Drive like that again, you'll never father another child.'

The 'Cuda cruised at a safe speed, allowing the Lincoln to gain distance until they were neck-and-neck. Martinez gave Waterson a quick once-over through the luxury sedan's rolled-up window. Dark jacket, tie, and sunglasses. Stubby fingers gripped onto the wheel. Full cheeks, white hair, liver lips.

Martinez said, 'Drop back about a hundred feet. Not too quickly. Move nice and easy. We don't want him to suspect anything.'

Webster did as told. 'Why would Waterson suspect anything, let alone a tail?'

'Because guilty people always suspect something. Mark my word, Tommy. Hanging around Sanchez, Waterson's hiding something. I believe in guilt by association.'

'Hang around scum, you become scum.' Webster thought about the statement. 'Sort of a social Lamarckian concept, don't you think?'

'I don't know what the hell you're talking about.'

'Maybe he's only doing his duty as executor of Sparks's estate.'

'What duty?'

Webster said, 'Maybe Sparks left Sanchez money for the cause. Waterson could just be the delivery boy.'

'Waterson as Sanchez's *delivery boy*?' Martinez smiled. 'Remind me never to hire you as a chauffeur *or* a casting director.'

'You put it that way, it don't make much sense.' Webster paused. 'Did the family read the will yet?'

'I don't know.'

From the 5 South, Webster hooked back on the 405 South. As he tailed the Lincoln, he suddenly noticed the flash of Waterson's right-hand blinker.

Martinez said, 'He's getting off at Devonshire.'

'I see it.'

'Not so close.'

'I know, I know. Take it easy.'

'Sorry. I just don't want to mess up at this point.'

Webster laughed. 'We're proceeding 'bout as fast as the infamous white Bronco.'

'Son of a bitch should have shot himself,' Martinez groused. 'Saved us all a shitload of money. Millions of dollars flushed down the crapper and for *what*? He's turning right, Tom.'

'I see him. He's heading west.'

The Lincoln moved swiftly down the broad, pine-lined boulevard, past small, worn ranch houses resting on an area rug's worth of land. The neighborhood had hosted thousands of citrus trees with their sweet blossoms and succulent fruit. Not many had survived the transition from agriculture to suburbia. Only a couple hundred stalwarts favored the land with their aromatic perfume, sweet edibles, and delectable shade during the sweltering West Valley summers.

As the road stretched westward, the homes gave way to apartment buildings, factory showrooms, and lots of corner gas stations and strip malls. Farther west, the area once again became open space as the boulevard neared the foothills.

Martinez said, 'He's going toward the Santa Susanas.'

'From one mountain range to another.' Webster pulled out a stick of gum and popped it in his mouth. 'Maybe Waterson and Sanchez are partners in a chain of chop shops. Sanchez does the dirty work, Waterson does the finances. An interesting albeit far-fetched concept. But whoda thought Sparks would involve himself with a bunch of bikers.'

Waterson entered the West Hills area, slowed, then turned on his left-hand blinker, heading straight into a tree-lined residential area.

Martinez said, 'Pass him up.'

'Why?'

'Because the 'Cuda doesn't have enough cover in such a quiet neighborhood. Pass him up.'

Webster kept the 'Cuda going straight, watching the Lincoln turn in his rear-view mirror. 'Now what?'

'Turn left at the next opportunity.'

Webster did as told. 'Backtrack?'

'You know what? I think I know where he's headed.' Martinez punched open the glove compartment, pulled out a street map. 'We're about a mile away from Sparks's house. Go straight about . . . half a mile, then turn right on Orchard, left on Vine, then left on Alta Vista. Betcha we'll find the car there.'

Webster raised his brow. 'You sure you want to lose him at this point?'

'We're too visible to follow him, Tom. After what happened to Sparks, he may even think that someone's out to get him. Just trust me on this.'

They rode the next few minutes in tense silence. As Webster neared the Sparks house, he slowed the 'Cuda, took in the neighborhood. Large two-story homes on what seemed like big parcels of land. But the constructions was only serviceable at best. Composite wood-sided housing or thin, textured stucco jobs. All of the homes were rooted in adobe-colored Spanish tile, giving the blocks uniformity. Giant carob trees shaded the streets. Dirt sidewalks.

Fancy area for a guy like Webster. But he couldn't help wondering why a guy as rich as Sparks would have chosen this over Beverly Hills or Malibu, or at the very least, one of the million-dollar developments in Granada Hills.

Sparks's home sat by itself at the mouth of a cul-de-sac. Parked in the driveway was Waterson's Lincoln.

'Bert one, Tom zero.' Webster did a three-pointer and turned around. 'Now what?'

Martinez picked up the cell phone and called Decker.

250

'That was fast,' Decker said. 'Where are you?'

'In front of Sparks's house. Waterson's Lincoln is parked in the driveway. You want us to pay a visit?'

'No. Right now, I want you to go over to impound and start taking the Sparks's Buick apart. Good job, guys.'

'What about Waterson?'

'I'm scheduled to see the widow today at three. So I'll drop by a little early.'

Martinez glanced at the 'Cuda's clock. 'A *little* early? It's straight-up noon, Loo.'

'My oh my,' Decker said. 'My watch is running fast.'

Michael answered the door, seemed surprised by Decker's appearance. The young man wore a crewneck sweater over a vanilla shirt, khaki pants and loafers. He fiddled with his collar, looked over his shoulder as if waiting for someone to come to his rescue. 'I thought you were coming later.'

'Sorry for the inconvenience. May I come in?'

The med student was hesitant. 'My mother is kind of indisposed right now.'

Decker stood firm. 'I'm really sorry for coming at an awful time.'

Michael ran his hand through a thick nest of black curls. Uncertainty seemed to be his hallmark. 'Could you hold on a second?'

'Of course.'

The door closed, reopened a minute later. Mike had brought reinforcements in the form of older brother Paul, both of them staring at Decker with the same deep blue eyes. Strong fraternal resemblance. But the med student was slimmer, younger, and *sans* tic.

Paul said, 'Mom's resting. If it's important, I'll fetch her.'

'The sooner I talk to her, the better.'

Paul's eyes moved at shutter speed. 'So it's important?'

251

'You have a breakthrough?' Michael asked excitedly.

'Not yet, I'm afraid. May I come in?'

The door opened completely, and Decker walked inside. Sitting on the family-room couch was the man with the veiny nose. He stood when he saw Decker, regarded Paul with questioning eyes.

'This is Lieutenant Decker, principal investigator of my father's case,' Paul said. 'Lieutenant, William Waterson, my father's lawyer.'

Decker shook the attorney's hand – firm grip, but not bone-crushing. The lawyer was about four inches shorter than Decker, around six even. He held a drinker's complexion, but his eyes were strong and lucid.

Waterson said, 'Any news, Lieutenant?'

'Nothing worth reporting.' Decker remained standing and so did Waterson. 'Are you also in charge of administering Dr. Sparks's estate, sir?'

Waterson's eyes narrowed. 'Yes, as a matter of fact I am.'

Decker said, 'Then you'll be disclosing the will's contents. See, there must be a will. Because Sparks had a family trust. When you have a trust, you have a will.'

Waterson eyed the two brothers. Michael shrugged ignorance, Paul revealed nothing. The lawyer said, 'May I ask where you obtained such confidential information?'

'Just did a little poking around. No big deal.'

Paul broke in, eyes fluttering. 'Yes, Dad and Mom have a family trust and Dad had a will. Hopefully, we'll be reading it soon. The sooner the better, as far as I'm concerned. Easier for my mom. This way she'll have access to her funds.'

And you'll have access to a million bucks. As soon as insurance pays up. Which may take a long time. Decker kept his thoughts to himself. To Waterson, he said, 'Nice of you to make house calls. Just out in the area or is this truly personalized service?'

'Azor Sparks was a dear friend. I feel I owe it to him to keep an eye on Dolly.'

'She has children. Why does she need watching from you?'

Michael nodded enthusiastically. Waterson glared at him, then at Decker. He said, 'After losing my beloved wife four years ago, I can assure you it's a *trying* time for her. Anything I can do to help ease her pain.'

'That's very decent of you, sir.'

'That's why we were put on this earth, Lieutenant,' Waterson stated. 'To love God and be decent with each other.'

Decker nodded solemnly. He lied, 'I called your office about an hour ago. You weren't in.'

'No, I wasn't.'

'Can I ask where you were?'

'Why are you curious about me?'

'Please bear with me, sir.'

'I was consulting with a client,' Waterson said stiffly. 'And no, I won't tell you who. That's privileged information.'

'So you do make house calls.'

'I don't see where this should be any of your concern. Do I detect a note of antagonism from you?'

Decker looked him in the eye. 'Don't mean to be confrontational. I was just taken aback by good, old-fashioned service, Mr. Waterson.' *Charging portal-to-portal at two hundred an hour.* 'Commendable in this day and age.'

Waterson didn't know how to read the compliment. He played it straight. 'Thank you.'

'You're welcome. You're in solo practice, Mr. Waterson?'

'I have partners.'

'But it's your firm.'

'Yes.'

'Estate law?'

'Primarily, but we do everything.'

'Do you know Jack Cohen?'

Waterson's jaw tightened. 'Yes, I do. Good attorney. Where do you know him from?'

'Used to work for him way back when.'

The lawyer was puzzled. 'Doing what?'

'Estates and wills.'

Waterson absorbed Decker's words. 'You're an attorney?'

'Was many moons ago. I'm hopelessly out of practice, but I can still recall a thing or two. Things like trusts avoid probate. That's most fortunate for Mrs. Sparks. She doesn't need financial constrictions on top of all her other woes.'

'You're absolutely right. I assure you Dolly is being well cared for.'

'Certainly appears that way.'

'It *is* that way.' Waterson stuck out his hand. 'I must be going. Nice to have met you.'

Decker took the lawyer's hand. 'Thank you, Mr. Waterson. I might have other questions. Do you have a card on you?'

'Of course.' The lawyer handed him a standard 2 × 3 rectangle, then shook hands with both sons. 'Take care of your mother. I'll call upon her later.'

'Thanks for coming down,' Paul said.

'For your family, I'd do anything, Paul.'

'I appreciate it.'

After Waterson left, Michael frowned. 'Guy's a jerk. Love thy neighbor at two hundred and fifty an hour—'

'Mike—'

'Out of all the lawyers why did Dad pick him?' To Decker, Michael said, 'Dad had an affinity for oddballs—'

'Mike—'

'It's true, Paul. Not only Waterson. Just look at his staff – Decameron, Berger—'

Decker said, 'What's wrong with Dr. Decameron?'

Paul snapped, 'Nothing is wrong with Dr. Decameron.'

'Aside from the fact he's gay?' Decker said casually.

'I'm not falling into that bullshit trap,' Paul said. 'You have your beliefs, *I* have mine. No, I don't approve of his lifestyle. But if

Dr. Decameron is good enough for Dad, I'm sure he's an excellent Doctor.'

'What about Dr. Berger?' Decker asked.

Michael said, 'He's mealy-mouthed and a wimp.'

'And Jewish?' Decker said.

Paul stared at him. 'Half the doctors in America are Jewish. What are you trying to do? Paint us as a bunch of prejudiced asses just because we believe in God? Jesus loves all His creatures, sir. You, me, everyone. And that, sir, is *my* belief.'

'I didn't mean to offend you, Paul,' Decker said. 'I'm sorry.'

The room fell silent.

Paul closed his fluttering eyelids. 'I'm testy.'

'You're holding up very well.' To Michael, Decker asked, 'Why do you think Berger is a wimp?'

'Because you can't get a straight answer out of him,' Michael said. 'And he's pompous. You know if anyone had a reason to be full of himself it was my dad. But he wasn't like that at all. Yes, he demanded respect. But he wasn't a blow hole. Even Dr. Fulton's weird . . . married to that loser—'

'*Enough*, Michael!' Paul blew up. 'It's none of the lieutenant's *business*!'

'He's investigating Dad's murder, Paul. *Everything* about us is his business!'

Decker said, 'Waterson seems to care about your mother.'

Michael said, 'Cares a little *too* much if you ask me. He's practically been living here.'

Paul snapped, 'What is *wrong* with you? Waterson's been a godsend, giving Mom and us . . . financial direction. We've all been so confused. At least, *someone* knows what he's doing.'

Michael began to pace. 'Well, Paul, I guess at this point I don't trust anyone.'

'Go get Mom,' Paul said quietly.

Michael was about to speak. Instead, he said nothing, then

disappeared upstairs. Paul said, 'Can I get you something to drink, Lieutenant?'

'Nothing, thank you. How are you doing, Mr. Sparks?'

'Not great.' His eyelids shivered as his eyes watered. 'Please take Michael's words with a grain of salt. He's upset, taking it out on Waterson. Yes, the guy's a little puffed up. But that's not why Michael's angry.'

'I realize that. Did Waterson speak with your mom while he was here?'

'Yeah, for about a half-hour. Truthfully, he *has* been here a lot. But then again, he's conducting our financial business. He has questions to ask.'

'What do you know about your father and his motorcycle business?'

Paul's expression turned puzzled. 'Now there's a non sequitur.'

'You know your dad rode with bikers, don't you?'

'What about them?'

'He gave money to one of their causes. Some Environment Freedom Act. Do you know anything about that?'

'Not a clue.' The eyelids fluttered. 'What kind of Environment Freedom Act?'

'I'm not sure,' Decker said. 'It's hard to understand these guys. From what I've gleaned, it deals with repealing restrictive legislation – things like mandatory mufflers on motorcycles, throwing back the age limit for operating All Terrain Vehicles, getting rid of the helmet law, giving motorcycles more leeway on smog emissions. Any idea why your father would contribute to something like that?'

'No.' Paul sighed. 'I hate to say it, but Mike was right. Dad did surround himself with some real strange characters. Anyway, Dad didn't confide in me.'

'Who did he confide in?'

'Maybe Bram. But you won't get anything out of him. Being a priest, Bram's pretty tight-lipped about everything.'

'What about Waterson? Did your father confide in him?'

'I doubt it. Waterson's been helpful.' Paul paused. 'I'm not looking a gift horse in the mouth. But the man is painting himself like he was some old family friend. He and Dad were church friends. I know Dad helped him out when Waterson's wife was sick. But as far as I know, they weren't bosom buddies.'

'Interesting,' Decker said. 'Why do you think he's doing that?'

'I don't know. Maybe there's money in it for him as executor of Dad's estate.'

Paul thought a moment.

'Or maybe Waterson does have some empathy at our tragedy . . . my mother's plight. He was broken up after his wife died. It was a long illness. I remember my wife occasionally cooking for him. So did Mom, my sister-in-law, and the other women at the church. Rotating days to bring him casseroles, stuff like that. Couple of times my parents had him over for Sunday dinner. His wife was too sick to come.'

'How'd that go?'

'Nice and polite. Waterson didn't talk much. Dad kind of led the discussions. He seemed grateful, thanked my parents profusely for all they had done for him and Ellen . . . his wife. I also remember my parents talking about her death . . . how young she'd been . . .' Paul smiled. 'Young meaning close to their ages.'

It was time to drop the bomb. Decker said, 'Waterson paid a visit to the bikers this morning. Any idea why?'

'*Waterson?*'

'Yep.'

'Then he was lying about being with a client.'

'Unless the client was the bikers.'

Paul opened and closed his mouth. 'How'd you find that out?'

Decker sidestepped the question. 'Why would Mr. Waterson go visit your father's biker buddies?'

'I haven't the foggiest notion. This is very weird.'

'Did your father leave them money in his will?'

'I don't know. Waterson hasn't read us the will. Maybe my father did leave them something. I was under the impression that Waterson couldn't distribute any funds until the will has been formally read. Isn't that how it works?'

'Usually. Unless your father wrote a secret codicil requesting something else.'

Paul was quiet.

'How about your mother?' Decker said. 'What would she know about your father's finances?'

'From what she's told me, not much. Dad was from the old school. Hide the problems, keep the wife and family free from worry. Which meant that Mom was pretty much kept in the dark. But knowing my mother, she's more aware than she's letting on. She's a sharp woman. Perceptive in that behind-the-scenes way.'

Paul's eyes looked upward. Suddenly, his eyelids started fluttering.

'Oh Lord.'

'What?'

'Nothing.' Paul made a face. 'I didn't realize my sister-in-law was up there with her.'

Decker looked at the woman descending the staircase. The anorexic woman with short, short platinum hair who had glommed onto Bram at the memorial reception yesterday.

'Luke's wife?'

'Certainly, she's not Bram's.'

Decker smiled. 'Ask a stupid question . . .'

Paul turned around. 'I'm sorry. I didn't mean to . . .'

'It's fine. Her name is Dana?'

Paul nodded. When she came to the bottom of the stairs, Dana appraised her brother-in-law with a cool eye. 'Hello, Paul.'

'Dana. Didn't know you were here.'

'Mother and I were just reading Bible together.' Nearly colorless eyes looked at Decker. 'Who's this?'

Paul made the introductions. She offered Decker a slender hand. 'Nice to meet you.'

'Thank you. Is your husband around?'

Dana's eyes clouded. 'He's at work.'

Decker said nothing.

'Actually, that's a good thing,' Dana said. 'Don't you think that's a good thing, Paul?'

'It's an excellent thing, Dana.'

'You're being snide.'

'Not at all, Dana.' His eyes darted back and forth. 'It's a very good thing that Luke's at work . . . occupied. Where's Mom?'

'Michael is helping her freshen up.' To Decker, Dana said, 'She hasn't gotten out of bed all day. She's very depressed.'

Decker nodded.

Dana wrung her hands nervously. 'Do you know when Bram's supposed to show up? He seems to have a calming effect on her. Maybe I should call him.'

Paul blinked hard. 'I think he's pretty tied up right now, Dana.'

'Too busy to see his mother?'

'Maggie told me he was here this morning. He does have a parish to run.'

'I'm sure his parishioners would understand—'

'I'm sure, but—'

'I think I should call him.'

From above, a strong, low female voice said, 'Dana, leave him alone. He's busy.'

Dana became flushed. Through clenched teeth, she called out, 'Of course, Mother.' She checked her watch. To Decker, she said, 'I must be going.'

'Nice to have met you.'

'Same.' She turned around and scurried out the door before her mother-in-law made it down the stairs.

Dolores 'Dolly' Sparks. An imperfect name for her. Because she was anything but a plaything. Tall, large-boned, stately, stern.

A coif of gray hair framed a sturdy face. Her eyes, though red-rimmed, were hard and threatening. Decker saw none of the vulnerability and shock he had witnessed when Michael had first broken the news to her. She wore a black caftan, her feet were housed in mules.

She gave Decker a once-over. 'That girl is something else. First, she tries to seduce Bram into marrying her. By the skin of his teeth, *he* finally manages to get rid of her. So what does Luke do? He goes ahead and marries her himself. He did it for spite. Well, good for Luke. He got his spite. He also got *her*, still mooning over his twin—'

'Why don't you sit down, Mom,' Paul said.

'Why don't you stop trying to shut me up.'

No one spoke.

Dolly's lip began to tremble. 'Where is Bram?'

Michael said, 'Would you like me to call him for you, Mom?'

'Please.' She hid her face in the palm of her hand.

Paul took her arm. 'Mom, sit down.'

This time, Dolly didn't protest. Allowed herself to be led to the couch. Paul said, 'Mom, this is Lieutenant Decker. He's leading Dad's investigation.'

Dolly wiped her eyes and nodded.

Decker nodded back. 'I apologize for interrupting your rest.'

'What rest? With Dana keeping me awake, reading me Psalms . . . trying to be spiritual. She should try making it to church on time. A good start in spiritual development.'

Paul said, 'She means well, Mom.'

'I suppose.' Dolly looked at Decker. 'How can I help you, Mr. Decker?'

'It's lieutenant, Mom.'

'Whatever,' Decker said. 'You can help me by answering a few questions.'

'I don't know who'd want to harm Azor,' Dolly stated. 'Far as I know, he didn't have an enemy in the world.'

'If I could start with something even more basic. What do you think your husband was doing at Tracadero's?'

'I'm sure I don't know.'

Decker looked at Paul, then back at the widow. 'I hate to ask you this. But is it possible he could have been meeting a woman?'

Paul's eyes twitched. But Dolly's face remained placid. 'You mean Dr. Fulton?'

Decker said, 'No, I mean a paramour.'

Dolly remained unperturbed. 'No, it's *not* possible. I didn't know much about Azor's life outside the home. But I do know *that* much.'

'Okay. Then who might your husband have been meeting?'

'I don't know.'

Decker nodded. 'What do you know about your husband's weekend friends?'

Paul said, 'He means the bikers.'

'Them?' She grimaced. 'They're lowlives, of course. Azor brought them here once. Came roaring down the street, looking like a bunch of hoods. I refused to let them step foot in my house. I almost kicked them out yesterday. But I didn't . . . for Azor's sake. If they wanted to honor him, so be it.'

Michael came back. 'Bram said he'll be here in an hour. Unless you need him right away.'

Dolly thought a moment. 'An hour is fine. I'll just take a nap.' She stood. 'Anything else?'

'A few more questions, Mrs. Sparks. I'll try not to tire you.'

She sat back down and waited.

Decker said, 'Were you aware of the fact that your husband gave money to his riding buddies for a cause of theirs?'

Her mouth tightened. 'Yes. Some freedom act. Everyone should be free. You know what, Mr. Decker? Some people shouldn't be free. Some people should be locked up in jail the rest of their lives, instead of taking money from naïve do-gooders.'

Inwardly, Decker agreed. He said, 'You felt the cause was a scam.'

'Of course it was a scam,' Dolly pronounced. 'But it was Azor's money. He never left me wanting for anything. Provided well for me *and* the children. Gave to the church and to the hospital. I suppose if he wanted to squander a little excess . . . well, there are *worse* vices, believe you me.'

Decker smiled, nodded.

Dolly stood again, this time teetering on her feet. 'I really am tired, Mr. Decker.' Her eyes suddenly watered. 'Perhaps another time.'

'Thank you, Mrs. Sparks.'

'You're welcome.' She leaned over to Paul, and he kissed her cheek. 'When's the first instalment of the tuition due, Paul?'

Paul turned red. 'Three weeks, Mom.'

'We should have this will thing straightened out by then. Send me the papers. Dad made you a promise, I'll honor it.'

'Thank you very much, Mom.'

She patted his cheek. To Michael, she said, 'Walk me up to my room, pumpkin.'

'Of course.' Michael shook hands with Decker. 'Anything you need, we're here to help. Right, Mom?'

'Right.' She started walking, then her knees folded. Michael grabbed her arm. 'Lean on me, Mom.'

Decker followed them up the stairs until they disappeared. A moment later, he heard a door close.

Paul said, 'She's exhausted.'

'Can't say I blame her.' Decker smoothed his mustache. 'She seems to have an inner strength. Guess you'd have to have energy to raise six children, especially triplet boys.'

Paul nodded.

'You get along well with your brothers?'

Paul shrugged. 'Not too bad. Being as Luke and Bram are identical, it was hard to compete with that genetic bond.'

'They were close growing up?'

'Yes.'

'Competitive?'

'Not really. Luke figured out pretty early on he couldn't compete.'

'You were the outsider.'

Paul stared at Decker, his eyes still and calm. 'Why are you interested in us?'

'Like Michael said, I'm interested in all facets of your family. I find it fascinating that Luke and Bram dated the same women.'

'You mean *woman*. As far as I know, Dana was the only girl Bram ever dated.'

'What happened between them?'

Paul's eyes twitched. 'A long story . . . it's all past. They were kids . . . not even seventeen.'

'Your mother mentioned something about Dana seducing Bram. What happened? Did he get her pregnant?'

Paul didn't answer right away. Then he said, 'Not exactly. Luke got her pregnant. While she was Bram's girl.'

'Ouch.'

'Yeah, it was . . .' Paul scratched his head. 'Bram took the fall, told our parents it was his. He covered, not for Dana's sake and certainly not for Luke's, but for his own ego. He didn't want to look like a dupe.'

'How'd he find out it wasn't his kid?'

Paul laughed, but it held sadness. 'Only one way for a guy to know proof positive that the kid isn't his.'

'He never had sex with her.'

Paul said, 'After Dana got knocked up by Luke, she tried to seduce Bram . . . to nail the kid as his. You've met my brother. Things that work on normal guys don't work on him. Anyway, he figured it out pretty quickly. Dana had suddenly turned from a shy, religious thing to this raving maniac who just *had* to do it. The more she pushed, the more he knew something was off. He pressed her and she broke down. Since she absolutely refused to admit who the father was, Bram figured it was one of us. Meaning, he thought it was me.'

'He confronted you?'

'No. Bram took it like a martyr. He really does belong on the cross.'

'Did he display anger toward you?'

'Not openly.'

'So how did he find out it was Luke?'

'Must have been my guiltless attitude. Both Luke and I treated him gently during that time. Because my parents absolutely . . . *battered* him. Mostly Dad. Bram had been his golden boy until then. The son that could do no wrong. But man, did Dad change. One mistake and Doctor came that close to kicking him out of the house.' Paul pinched off a millimeter of space between his extended thumb and forefinger. 'If Bram would have given him an ounce of lip, I'm sure he would have.'

'Bram suffered in silence?'

'Yes. Then one evening at dinner . . . God, Dad was really slamming him. How he ruined his life and dishonored himself, and his family, and had spit at God. And he was going to go to hell and all this . . . this *shit*, frankly. I couldn't take it. I told Bram, "How can you let him *talk* to you like that? Say something!" Of course, I was ordered to leave the table at once.'

'Did you?'

'No. Instead, I got into a screaming match with my father who proceeded to ground me for *three* months. Actually, it was six months, later reduced to three. I had no car privileges, no allowance, wasn't allowed to go on any dates or to any parties . . . even church activities. Except chapel of course. I was ordered to go to chapel every evening and ask God's forgiveness for disobeying my father.'

'Pretty severe.'

'Extremely. In all fairness to my parents, they were very upset. Normally, they weren't that rough on us.'

'Pretty nice of you to risk your freedom for your brother.'

'If I would have known the consequences, I would have kept

my mouth shut.' He shook his head. 'I finally stalked off to our room, Bram came in a minute later, thanked me for coming to his defense. Must have been something sincere in my voice, something that told him *I* hadn't been the one. Because as soon as Luke walked in the room, Bram hauled off and decked him.'

Paul laughed.

'I was stunned! I'd never seen Bram so enraged, much less physical. Then it all came out, though my parents never knew. I couldn't believe it. Luke had always been a wiseass, spent half of high school stoned on weed. But deflowering your twin brother's girlfriend . . . that went beyond the pale.'

'Indeed.'

'Anyway, the whole thing became moot. Three weeks before Dana and Bram were due to marry, Dana went into premature labor, gave birth to a stillborn boy. It was very sad actually. Bram was decent, visited Dana in the hospital. But man, was he *relieved*! We all were. After Dana recovered, Bram stayed away from her, from girls in general.' Paul grinned. 'Big surprise that Bram became a priest.'

Decker said, 'And Dana married Luke.'

'Irony of ironies. They remet at our fifth high school reunion. Bram didn't show, but Luke and I did. Luke and Dana started talking. I guess they hit it off. They were married a few years later.'

'It didn't bother Bram?'

'You mean did he still feel something for Dana?' Paul laughed. 'The poor guy has been trying to get her off his ass for years.'

'How'd he feel toward Luke?'

'He was icy to him for a long, long time. He didn't stand up at Luke's wedding.'

Casually, Decker asked, 'What about Bram's relationship with your father?'

'From what I could see, Bram remained respectful . . . obedient . . . up to a point.'

'Meaning?'

265

'Bram wears a cross around his neck, not a stethoscope.'

'Your father wanted Bram to be a doctor?'

'Not wanted – expected.'

'Did it create tension between the two?'

'That Bram became a priest instead of a physician?'

'Yes.'

Paul thought about the question. 'I think Dad knew he'd lost Bram after the Dana affair. Certainly he knew Bram was a goner after he became Catholic.'

'How'd that happen?'

'The summer after the Dana thing, Dad sent him to Africa to cleanse his soul with missionary work. Talk about poetic justice . . .' Paul laughed. 'The nuns got hold of him. He came back, it was all over. Nothing could dissuade him. *His* rebellion at the shit my dad shoveled at him.'

He thought a moment.

'Actually, that's probably oversimplification. Bram took to Catholicism . . . the rituals . . . customs. The formality and beauty that's absent from my church. And the intellectuality. He loved poring over dusty tomes. Archaic stuff that would bore most people to death.'

'How'd your mother react to Bram's conversion?'

'She wasn't happy. Personally, I think she was *real* pissed at my dad, though she never expressed it out loud. But you could tell by her coldness. She used to mention to him that one teaches not by harshness but by love, just as Jesus did. You notice that Michael *is* in medical school. Nothing to rebel against. Because after the whole Dana mess, Dad pretty much butted out of our lives. He was still . . . Dad. But he kept a lower profile . . . left family things up to Mom.'

'Did Bram ever forgive Luke?'

'About a year after Bram became ordained, a real peace came over him. He not only forgave Luke, he's been looking after him for the last six years. It took Luke a long time to get his act in gear.

His kids helped. Luke's a great father, I'll say that much for him.'

He paused.

'I think I'm a great father, too. Funny, because neither one of us got any role modelling. Dad was never home when we grew up. Bram took over Dad's role with my younger siblings. But Luke and I were left to our own devices.'

He laughed bitterly.

'We're also the most screwed-up of the bunch.'

Paul blinked hard.

'I've tried very hard to be an involved father. Maybe I'm over-involved. Because not a day goes by that I don't think about Angela and the kids. Everything I do, I do for them. Sometimes I think I'd be better off if I were more like my old man – distant, imposing, the *boss*. 'Cause my kids sure give me crap. But then there are moments. Like when my eight-year-old hit a game-winning three-run homer at Little League. He came running up to me afterward, hugged me in front of his friends, told me he loved me. I guess I did something right.'

Decker nodded, observing a man who had just unloaded a truckload of personal baggage. The outsider in his trio, the son of a brilliant but domineering man. Paul must have been dying to prove himself. Since he couldn't be brilliant like Dad, nor the golden boy like brother Bram, maybe he could gain his self-respect and position through money.

Hence all the bad investments.

Luke, on the other hand, never even tried. Just drowned his troubles in a sea of drugs until his kids made him grow up. Yet, Lord only knew how much residual resentment the triplet sons felt toward their father.

Paul checked his watch. 'I talk too much. I do that when I'm nervous.'

'You're nervous around me?'

'My father was murdered and I don't know why. Right now, I'm nervous around everyone.'

20

'I need to talk to you, Bram. Right away!'

'Shoot.'

'Not over the phone.'

Bram paused. His brother's voice held an eerie calm trying to mask anxiety. He massaged his pounding forehead. 'No problem. Come down to the church.'

'*Not* a good idea. Be at your apartment in ten minutes.'

A long moment of silence. 'Why the urgen—'

'Not over the *phone*!'

The voice held full-fledged panic. Bram said, 'I'll be there.'

The line went dead. Bram stood, regarded the crucifix on his wall. He knelt for a moment, said the paternoster, then crossed himself and grabbed his jacket. Fishing through his pocket for his keys to lock the door to the chancellery, he was intercepted by Jim, the seminary student.

'Father, Mrs. McDougal just called. Her son Sean was just readmitted into the hospital,' Jim said. 'Apparently, the leukemia came back—'

'Oh no!' Bram locked the door, then rubbed his eyes under his glasses. 'Which hospital?'

'St. Jerome's,' Jim said. 'Here's the room number, here's the home phone number. You look busy. Do you want me to call her for you, Father?'

'No, no, I'll do it.' Bram took the slip of paper. 'If she calls again, tell her I should be there in . . . a half hour to forty-five minutes, all right?'

'Are you sure you don't want me to call Father Danner?

You've had so much on your mind . . .'

'Thank you, but no.'

'You look a little pale, Father.'

He did feel weak. Nothing that a little orange juice couldn't cure. He hadn't eaten today, was probably suffering from low blood sugar. 'I'm fine, Jim. Thank you for your concern.' He patted the young man's back, then turned and jogged away.

Farrell Gaynor sat across from Decker's desk, shifting his rear in the hard plastic seat. 'I guess what I'm really saying is I see Paul as a problem because of his debt.'

Decker said, 'But the old man had already agreed to loan Paul the money. And Dolly Sparks agreed to honor Dad's loan. I heard that with my own ears.'

'That doesn't mean she knows the truth.'

'Dad turned Paul down this time?'

'I think Dad turned Paul down a long time ago.' Gaynor shuffled through some paper. 'What if the purpose of Paul's phone call the night of the murder was to *lure* Azor to the spot, then ice him—'

Decker interrupted. 'He murdered over tuition payments?'

'Over an upcoming balloon payment coming due on his house.'

Decker looked up from his notes. 'What's this?'

'A balloon payment due in about three months. Three hundred thou.'

'Christ!' Decker started adding up the numbers in Paul's debit column. 'With that, Paul's in the hole for close to three quarters of a million.'

'And the guy doesn't have an alibi for the night of the murder, Loo.'

Decker nodded, knowing he was going to have to bring him in for questioning.

'So let's assume that Paul hired out.' Gaynor coughed into a well-worn handkerchief. 'The next question is who?'

Decker smoothed his mustache, sat back in his chair. 'I don' know. From my brief observations, Paul and William Waterson seem to be making chitchat. And just what was Waterson doing in a remote area of the mountains, meeting a lowlife like Manny Sanchez?'

'Right.' Gaynor shifted his weight again. 'Now it *could* be that Waterson was giving Sanchez money that Azor Sparks had left him for this Environment Freedoms Act cause. But if that was the case, why didn't Waterson meet Sanchez at his dealership in town? Why the clandestine spot?'

Decker said, 'Waterson paid the bikers to be triggermen for Paul. And what Webster and Martinez saw was the payoff for Azor's hit. Good logic. No evidence.'

'Things take time.'

Decker said, 'Why would Waterson get involved in something like that? Was he in debt?'

'I don't know. I'll check into his accounts. See if any big checks were coming in or going out.'

Decker's phone rang. He picked it up, listened for a few moments, then shut his eyes. A silent stream of curse words escaped his lips. He looked at Gaynor, shook his head.

'Who?' the old man asked.

'Decameron.'

It was an isolated contemporary thing nestled into the Santa Susana Mountains, with a view of the valley below. Decameron's lot was hillside, overlaid with blooms of purple ice plants, the house semiobscured by giant banana plants and frothy green palms. The building was a square barrack of white stucco veined with brilliant red bougainvillea, almost void of windows. Instead, a dozen elongated glass-covered furrows had been cut into the walls. From the inside, the grooves had widened into wedges, becoming windows that allowed a great deal of light to enter. A clever design, like arrow slits found in the old fortress castles.

The house held high ceilings and slate floors. Footsteps echoed as Decker walked through. Lots of open space, the furnishings were spare. Everything was orderly except for the crime scene.

Someone had gone crazy with a bat, smashing windows, showering everything with shards of glass. Made it hard to gather evidence without slicing tender flesh. Decameron was spread out on his tomato-red leather couch, his mouth and eyes open. A second gaping mouth had been carved across his throat. Blood had oozed downward, across his body. There were holes in his chest and in his forehead. He was fully dressed in a gray suit, his red paisley tie and white shirt browned with blood. His face was turned upward at the skylights, his feed dangled off the edge of the cushions.

Under his toes lay another head, another body. A blond man, in a conservative blue suit. His throat had also been cut, he had also sustained shots in his head and chest.

Uniformed officers buzzed around like random bees. The call came through around twenty minutes ago, someone told Decker. A nurse phoned Decameron in as a missing person to dispatch. Hospital had been calling Decameron all morning. No one had picked up.

Decker heard his name being called and turned around. Marge coming towards him, Oliver at her heels. They both looked grave.

Oliver's eyes swept over the crime scene. 'Shit,' he whispered. 'Just when I was just starting to like the guy.'

Marge said, 'We were waiting for him, Pete. He never showed.'

'What are you talking about?'

'Decameron,' Oliver said. 'He was supposed to meet us for a late lunch. Two o'clock. He never showed. Now I know why.'

Marge said, 'He was bringing us Fisher/Tyne's trial data of Curedon.'

'Oh Christ, that's *right*!' Decker said. 'Either of you call the hospital when Decameron didn't show?'

'Yes, sir,' Oliver said. 'They paged him. He didn't answer. I tried to get a location out of them, but they were close mouthed.

Thought it was just an extra security precaution.'

'When did you call?'

'About forty-five minutes ago.' Oliver shook his head. 'Who's the second stiff?'

'I don't know,' Decker said. 'I just arrived. Phone it in to the coroner's office, then clear the area of excess uniforms and we'll get to work.'

Oliver said, 'Mind if I glove and go through John Doe's pockets?'

'Go ahead,' Decker said. 'Double glove, guy. Lots of glass. Be careful.'

The broken bits crunched underneath the soles of Oliver's shoes as he walked over to the dead blond man. Carefully sifting through razor-sharp shards, he reached into the body's pants pocket.

'Damn!' Oliver pulled out his hand, a trickle of red running down the latex. He stuck it in his own coat pocket.

'Cut yourself bad?' Decker asked.

'Nah, just a poke.'

Marge said, 'You're going to fuck up evidence.'

'Thanks for the sympathy.'

With his clean gloved hand, Oliver reached into the other pants pocket. Carefully, he fished out the dead man's wallet, slowly making his way back to Decker and Marge. She gloved and took the wallet from Oliver. Her eyes zeroed in on the driver's license.

'Kenneth Leonard.' Marge's fingers sorted through the wallet. 'He's a doctor—'

'What kind of doctor?' Decker asked.

'Doesn't say. His home address is in Laguna Nigel.'

'So he's probably not from New Christ,' Oliver said. 'Too long of a commute.'

Marge said, 'Money's here . . . about a hundred bucks. So are his credit cards. Strike robbery as a motive.'

'Unless someone was interested in stealing something else,' Oliver said.

Decker looked at him. 'The Fisher/Tyne data?'

'Loo, you should have seen the squirrelly look on Shockley's face when we asked if we could see it. I think someone really didn't want Decameron showing us the numbers.'

'Decameron kept the data at his house?' Marge said.

'Why not?' Oliver said.

Decker answered, 'He said Sparks kept the latest numbers in his files.'

'So he went through Sparks's files before he left yesterday, found the data, slipped it into his briefcase and took it home with him.'

'Where's the briefcase?' Decker asked.

'Good question,' Marge said.

She continued sorting through the flotsam and jetsam of Leonard's wallet. Receipts, credit card slips, several worn business cards. Marge pulled them out, flipped through them. Her soft brown eyes grew in circumference. 'Oh man, look at this! The stiff *worked* for Fisher/Tyne.'

Decker took the card out of her hand. Across the middle in boldface type were the words FISHER/TYNE, above it an apothecary logo of a mortar and pestle. In the right-hand corner was the name DR. KENNETH LEONARD. Underneath the name was the title VICE PRESIDENT OF RESEARCH DESIGN.

'Wait till Shockley gets wind of this,' Marge said.

'Maybe he already knows about it,' Oliver said. 'Maybe he ordered the hit.'

Decker said, 'That's a strong statement. Back it up with a reason, Scotty.'

'The trial results were disappointing. Decameron was going to make the numbers public, ergo all that money Fisher/Tyne had invested in Curedon was going by way of the crapper. Shockley didn't want that. He sent Leonard down to convince him not to do it.'

Marge said, 'Decameron wouldn't go public, Scott. He was trying to *solve* the data problem.'

Decker said, 'And if Leonard was sent down to off Decameron, why are they both dead, Scotty?'

Oliver smiled. 'Haven't worked out all the bugs in the theory. Was the guy married?'

'Doesn't say on his license,' Marge said. 'Why?'

'Just wondering who to notify,' Oliver said.

Marge made a face. 'Guess we should go to his place and see if he lives with anyone.'

Oliver said, 'Better yet, why don't we pay Fisher/Tyne another visit. Break the news about Leonard, and gauge Shockley's reaction?'

Decker said, 'You can do that.'

Oliver grinned. 'How about subpoenaing the asshole if he doesn't show us the Curedon data?'

'No, Detective, you may *not* do that,' Decker said. 'Sure, you can make a little noise. But don't lean on Shockley. Because we don't know what we're dealing with.'

'Do you want me to call Webster and Martinez down to do evidence here?' Marge pointed to the murder scene.

'I can go through it myself.'

Marge stared at Decker.

'What?' Decker said, annoyed.

Oliver sensed tension, said, 'I think I'll go place that call to the coroner's office.'

When he was out of earshot, Marge said, 'Pete, you've got a squad room to run—'

'I'm well aware of my duties, Marge.'

Marge looked up at the ceiling. 'I just don't want them talking, you know?'

'Talking about what?'

'That you're giving Homicide top priority.'

'Homicide does have top priority.'

'Not to the exclusion of the other details.'

Decker glared at her. 'Are you lecturing me?'

Marge met his hostile stare. 'Yes, I am.'

Decker was quiet. Then he said, 'Are people talking?'

'A comment or two.'

'Saying?'

'You have pets.' Marge faced him. 'A big GTA ring was busted yesterday. A couple of the guys were wondering why you were at Sparks's memorial service instead of patting them on the back.'

'So remind me to set up a chart for gold stars—'

'Pete—'

'All right, all right.' He ran his hand through his hair. She was right. It was a great bust. And yes, he could have been a little more generous with the praise. He had been preoccupied . . .

Marge dropped the wallet into a plastic bag. 'Out of curiosity, why not let Webster and Martinez do the evidence collection?'

'They're doing Sparks's car.'

'So what's more important right now?'

Again, she was right. *Batting a cool thou, Dunn*. Decker said, 'I'll call them down.'

'No offense, Pete?'

'Not at all.' Decker folded his hands across his chest. 'I'll do a little poking around until they, the coroner and the lab people get here. Does that scenario meet with your approval, Detective?'

'Touchy, touchy.'

Decker said, 'What are you doing Sunday night?'

'I got a heavy date with my video store. It's two-for-one night.'

'Come for dinner.'

'People'll talk. Teacher's pet.'

Decker grinned, threw his arm around Marge. 'Let them talk.'

21

Wordlessly, Shockley slapped the lobby elevator's up button, his angry eyes moving between Oliver and Marge. When the doors opened, he stepped in first. The ride up was silent, as was the walk down the hall to his office. The doctor opened the door and walked in. As soon as Marge and Oliver were inside, he slammed it shut.

'Contrary to what you might think, I'm not the CEO of this company.' Shockley was fierce. 'I'm an employee and have a *job* to do. If I don't do it, I'll have hell to pay.'

Marge said, 'We're sorry about coming in unannounced, but—'

'Sorry? You yank me out of a very important meeting with the board of Directors after strong-arming my secretary—'

'Sir, we didn't strong-arm—'

'Scaring her to death, threatening her—'

'No one threatened any—'

'This better be important!'

'Kenneth Leonard's dead,' Oliver said unceremoniously. 'So is Reg Decameron. Both of them were murdered.'

Shockley gasped. '*What!*'

'You want to sit down, Doctor?' Marge said.

A rhetorical question. Shockley had slumped into his desk chair. He tried to speak, but his mouth formed soundless words.

Oliver said, 'Detective Dunn and I were called to the scene this afternoon. They were murdered in Decameron's house. We picked through Leonard's pocket . . . for ID. His driver's license says he's unmarried. Do you know if he has a significant other?'

'Someone we should notify?' Marge stated.

Shockley's hands were shaking. He didn't answer.

Marge walked over to a lacquered cabinet and opened the door. She took down a decanter of amber liquid and a cut-crystal glass. 'Pour you a shot?'

Shockley nodded. Marge gave him a finger's worth of booze, and the doctor bolted it down. His face took on an instant blush, but he still couldn't seem to find his vocal cords. He held out his empty glass to Marge.

She poured him another round. 'Was Dr. Leonard involved in the Curedon trials?'

Shockley drank the hooch. 'He . . .' He cleared his throat. 'He's one of our primary statisticians in our computer department.'

'Medical Doctor?' Marge asked.

'Doctor of mathematics. His field is research design.'

Oliver said, 'Then he'd be familiar with the Curedon trials numbers.'

'Yes, I'd think so.' Shockley wiped spittle off the corner of his mouth. 'Maybe he wouldn't have the numbers memorized, but he'd know how the trials were going. Ken supervised an enormous caseload. What . . . what happened?'

Marge said, 'Do you know if he has a girlfriend?'

Shockley paused, then shook his head no. 'Not that I know of. He kept to himself. Spent more time with his numbers than with people. But that's usually the case with our design experts. More at home in front of terminals than with cocktails in their hands.'

Oliver said, 'We'll need to talk to some of his co-workers.'

'I'm sorry, but I'll have to get everything cleared. Security measures. Especially now.'

Oliver and Marge exchanged glances. Oliver said, 'How about a little leeway, Doctor. Otherwise, we come back here with subpoenas and warrants and turn this place upside down.'

Shockley frowned, wiped his brow. 'I do what I have to do. You do what you have to do.'

Mentally, Oliver counted to ten. Keep the situation under control. Oliver leaned over Shockley's shoulder. 'Do you know what Leonard was doing at Decameron's house?'

Shockley paused. 'No . . .'

Marge leaned over his other shoulder. 'Sir, you're lying—'

'I'm not ly—'

'Then you're snowin' us with half-truths,' Oliver said. 'What was he doing there?'

'I swear I don't *know*!'

'Take a guess,' Marge said.

Shockley started sweating profusely. 'Maybe discussing Curedon with Decameron.'

'Why would he go to Decameron's *house* to discuss Curedon when we have inventions called telephones and fax machines?'

Again, Shockley wiped his brow. 'I haven't the faintest idea—'

'Do you know, sir,' Marge said, 'that every time you lie, the corner of your left eye twitches?'

'Why are you pressing me? I don't have *answers*!'

'Twitch, twitch,' Oliver said.

Marge said, 'Well, if you don't have answers, Dr. Shockley, maybe you have questions. Like what happened to the Curedon data that Dr. Decameron was going to show us?'

'I don't know what you're talking about—'

'Maybe we should just bring him in for questioning,' Oliver said to Marge.

'Under whose authority!' Shockley tried to bellow. Instead, it came out a bleat. 'You have no authority here!'

'Yeah, buddy, tell that to the judge.' Marge brought out a pair of cuffs.

'This is absurd!'

'Stand up!'

'I will not—'

'Ah, so you want to add a resisting arrest charge to the others?' Oliver said.

'What other charges? What am I under arrest for?'

Marge said, 'Obstruction of justice—'

'This is absurd!'

'You're repeating yourself,' Oliver said. 'Stand up.'

'But I don't know *anything*!' Shockley was dripping sweat. 'I swear to Jesus I don't know what Ken was doing with Reginald. For all I know, they could have been lovers!'

The room fell quiet.

Oliver said, 'Is that statement conjecture based on Reggie's lifestyle or do you know something definite, Doc?'

Shockley was panting, tried to slow himself down. 'Well. Ken wasn't married . . . and I don't think he had a girlfriend.'

Marge said, 'You didn't answer Detective Oliver's question, sir. Do you know that for a *fact*?'

'No.'

'So let's drop that angle and assume the murders had something to do with Fisher/Tyne. Maybe Leonard was telling Decameron something in private. What might that have been?'

'I don't—'

'Twitch, twitch, twitch,' Marge said. 'Let's try again. What would Leonard say to Decameron in person that he couldn't say over the phone?'

The room was silent. Shockley buried his head in his hands, then looked up. 'Maybe . . . maybe, he got wind of something.'

'And what might that be?' Marge said.

'That the Curedon project's being axed.'

Again, no one spoke. Oliver tried to hide his astonishment. Marge looked up for a moment, disguising her surprise.

Shockley said, 'It was supposed to be hush-hush. But sometimes it's hard to keep secrets around here. Especially since e-mail is easily retrievable if you know the right code words.'

Oliver said, 'Why are you eighty-sixing Curedon? I thought the trials were going well.'

'They were until a couple of months ago.'

'The increase rate in mortality,' Marge said.

'Yes. How'd you find out about that?'

'Decameron. He told us it was data error.'

'No . . . it is *not* data error.' Shockley took a deep breath. 'It's not that Curedon's a total bust. It still has potential. Lots of potential. But with the recent numbers and with Azor Sparks gone . . . no longer able to guide us through the bumps . . . the board has had some substantial doubts about the drug. Some want to cut the losses while they're still manageable.'

A long silence.

Marge said, 'Why would Leonard, a statistician and research designer, care if you axed Curedon?'

'I don't *know*!' Shockley looked beseechingly at Marge. 'It doesn't make sense. Because he was the one who'd been interpreting the numbers for us. As a matter of fact . . .'

Shockley turned his desk chair around to his credenza and jerked open a file drawer. With trembling hands, he went through a number of folders.

'What are you looking for, sir?' Oliver asked.

Shockley didn't answer, kept plowing through papers. Finally, he fished out a sheet.

'Oh thank you God!' He handed the paper to Marge. 'The payoff for being organized. Here. You don't believe me, take a look for yourselves.'

A personal memo from Leonard to Shockley. Dated two months ago. Regarding Curedon trials. Skimming through the statistical mumbo jumbo of correlations, variants, and r-squares, Marge read the conclusion. Mediocre results with slight but not significant differences noted between Curedon and current market medication. Leonard's signature graced the bottom of the page. Marge handed the memo to Scott.

'This is dated over sixty days ago,' Oliver said. 'Why didn't you tell us about this memo when we first came here a couple of days ago?'

'Because first of all, I had no intention of revealing internal policy to you. And second of all, which is the truth . . . at that time,

I was so stunned about Azor's death that frankly I forgot about it—'

'Doctor—'

'It's true!'

Oliver said, 'You refused to show us Curedon's data. Is this what you were hiding? The fact that the numbers weren't great?'

'I wasn't hiding anything.' Shockley sat up. 'Yes, I was aware that Curedon was going through some rough spots. But with Azor on our team, I felt confident that we could overcome our problems. Now, with him gone, the board has recommended reevaluating the project. We had Kenny run some new correlates. We didn't like the results.'

'Let's back it up,' Marge said. 'Why would Leonard go to Decameron's house? Why not just call him?'

'I don't have any notion why.'

'Maybe he was trying to warn Decameron.'

'About what?' Shockley asked.

'About not getting in Fisher/Tyne's way, because it could lead to tragedy.'

'You're speaking hogwash—'

'It didn't lead to tragedy?' Oliver asked.

'We had nothing to do with anyone's death,' Shockley protested.

Marge said, 'When can we talk to Leonard's co-workers?'

'I'll try to get clearance for you by tomorrow. After I've broken the news to them.'

'And they're too scared to talk.'

Shockley said, 'You don't have warrants, you may not trample over our rights—'

'Gettin' kinda feisty, sir,' Oliver said.

'Get out of here!'

'You're not being very civic-minded—'

'Get out of here before I have you *thrown* out by security!' Shockley reached for the phone.

Oliver grinned. 'I don't think he's bluffing, Detective Dunn.'

'Doesn't look like it.' Marge saluted him. 'Thanks for your time.'

'I don't get it.' Oliver opened the door to the unmarked. 'Fisher/Tyne is a multibillion dollar company. You're telling me that they don't honestly *know* whether or not a drug is going to work before they invest millions of bucks in it?'

'I don't know, Scott.'

'Margie, it ain't all a crapshoot.'

'No, of course not.' Marge leaned against the car. 'Maybe Curedon looked good in Azor's lab, but not in Fisher/Tyne's lab.'

Oliver frowned. 'C'mon, Marge. Curedon must have passed some test for them to buy up its rights and pay Sparks an enormous chunk of change.'

Marge shrugged. 'Maybe it was effective with animal data, but not with human beings.'

'Not according to Decameron, Fulton or Berger. It was a miracle drug with their patients.'

'Except that it had problems lately. Besides none of the doctors is an objective party, Scott. If any of them were promised a percentage of profits . . .' Marge stopped midsentence, staring at a brunette in a black suit speed-walking toward them. She saw Marge staring at her, and waved. Marge waved back.

'Who?' Oliver asked.

'Don't know.'

The brunette reached the car, breathless, her large chest heaving with each intake of oxygen. She seemed scared. She looked around, talking to them with head turned, blue eyes scanning over her shoulder. 'Are you the police?'

Oliver nodded.

'May I see some identification?'

They took out their shields. The brunette rubbed her hands as she examined their badges. 'Does your visit have anything to do with Kenneth Leonard? Has he talked to you at all?'

No one spoke.

Marge said, 'Are you friends with Dr. Leonard?'

Again, the woman kneaded her hands. 'Maybe I should take a ride with you.'

Oliver opened the door for her. She slid in the back of the unmarked, and so did Marge. Oliver started up the car and drove off the parking lot. He parked a few blocks down from Fisher/Tyne.

Nobody spoke, then brunette asked, 'Is Kenny all right?'

Marge and Oliver exchanged looks.

The brunette's eyes moistened. 'He's dead, isn't he?'

'Yes, ma'am,' Marge said. 'Do you have a name?'

The woman's lower lip quivered. 'Belinda Sands.'

'You were his girlfriend?' Oliver asked.

The woman didn't answer. It was then that Marge noticed a wedding band on her finger. She said, 'You were having an affair with him.'

Belinda jerked her head towards Marge, eyeing her in wonderment.

'Your ring,' Marge said. 'Leonard wasn't married.'

'Oh.' Belinda studied her nails. 'It's been over for a while. But we remained friends.'

'Do you also work in Research Design?' Oliver asked.

'Accounting.' Belinda hid her face in her hands, pulled them away, and wiped tears from her cheeks. 'Something was going on with him.'

Marge said, 'Tell me.'

'I hadn't spoken to Kenny in a while,' Belinda said. 'As I said, the affair was over . . . long over. It didn't even last very long. Maybe a couple of months. I swear that's all.'

Marge nodded. 'What about Kenny, Belinda?'

'About a week ago, he came to me. He asked if we could have a drink after work. I didn't want to go, but . . . frankly, he was acting strange. I thought that maybe he was going to try to blackmail me.'

The car grew quiet.

Oliver said, 'Was Leonard the blackmailing type?'

'Oh no, not at all. It's just that . . .' Belinda blinked tears. 'I love my husband. I love my children. I made a terrible mistake when I stepped out. Luckily, Kenny let me off the hook – graciously, no scene. But I admit I was very paranoid that maybe he had ulterior motives. When he asked me out, I thought he was coming back to haunt me. But that wasn't the case.'

Oliver said, 'What did he want?'

'To talk about work . . . his data. He was very upset. He found a cuckoo's egg in Curedon's data.'

'Pardon?' Marge asked.

'A security break. Another terminal had hooked into his and was running programs from it, interfering with Kenny's data. Computer people call it a cuckoo's egg. Because cuckoo birds lay their eggs in other birds' nests. Kenny told me that someone had a specific interest in altering Curedon's data and was fudging the numbers.'

'How'd they break in?'

'I have no idea. Neither did Kenny. But he suspected it was done by someone in-house who knew the passwords. Kenny changed them right after, and the terminal shut down. But the damage had already been done. Because Kenny had made recommendations based on the fraudulent numbers. He felt that someone was setting him up to fail.'

'Who?'

Belinda swallowed. 'That's what Kenny was trying to find out. Especially after Dr. Sparks was murdered.'

'He never mentioned anyone specific?' Oliver asked.

Belinda looked up. 'He felt Fisher/Tyne was behind – the data fudging. That Fisher/Tyne was trying to stop the Curedon research.'

'Why?'

'This part is speculation, but . . .' Belinda cleared her throat.

'Kenny felt Shockley was in secret cahoots with Dr. Sparks's assistant.'

Long silence.

Oliver said, 'Which one? Decameron?'

'Dr. Berger,' Belinda said. 'He was originally assigned to the Curedon project. Then, he abruptly quit. No one knew why. But then Decameron came on, seemed to be doing a good job and that was that. Until now.'

Marge said, 'Why did Leonard think Berger and Shockley were in cahoots?'

'Because he recently saw Berger and Shockley talking to each other. Here. At Fisher/Tyne. In Shockley's private office. Dr. Berger no longer had business here. What was he doing here?'

'That's hardly indictable evidence, Belinda,' Oliver said.

'That's what I told Kenny,' she answered. 'I told him that for all he knew Sparks could have sent Berger to talk to Shockley.'

'Exactly.'

'There was more, sir. Kenny traced the break-in to a terminal in Sparks's lab. By some process of elimination, Kenny had it figured out that it had to be Berger. He became frantic, very scared.'

'Obviously with good reason,' Marge said. 'Why didn't he report this to the police?'

'He said he didn't have enough concrete evidence. And if he got the police involved without enough concrete evidence, he'd lose his job. That's why he wanted to figure it out on his own.'

Belinda went quiet.

'Go on,' Marge said.

'That was it. Yesterday, he told me he wasn't coming in tomorrow . . . that's today. So I didn't think twice when he didn't show up for work.' Her eyes filled with tears. 'But as soon as I saw your car pull up . . .'

She broke into sobs.

'I'm so scared! Am I being paranoid?'

Marge said, 'Maybe you and your family should take a few days off until we have a better idea of what's going on.'

'A few days off?' Belinda hugged herself. 'And just *what* do I tell my husband? That my ex-lover was murdered because he discovered some medical fraud, and his discovery put my family in danger?'

Oliver said, 'I don't think you have to tell him that Kenny was an ex-lover.'

'Then how could I explain the reason why Kenny *confided* in me?'

Marge said, 'Mrs. Sands, I don't know how you should phrase your words to your husband. But I do know that taking a couple of days off makes sense if you care about your family's safety.'

'Oh God!' She covered her face again. 'Jesus is paying me back.'

'Nah, I don't think it's that personal,' Oliver stated.

Belinda looked up, dried her tears. 'Oh well . . .' Her voice had taken on a resolved tone. 'I'll figure something out. I've lied before, I can lie again.'

22

Sorting through piles of broken glass. Like picking brambles from a briar patch, Webster thought. Sun rays hitting the shards, shooting rainbows of light that bounced off the furniture and walls, ceiling and floors. Might have been pretty except for the ravaged bodies and the blood spatter. He clicked off his cassette player and pulled a tiny sliver out of his arm. He said, 'Think I can file for disability?'

Martinez was squatting, retrieving shards and putting them in a bag. 'Are you bleeding bad?'

'If I squeeze hard enough, I reckon I could fill up a capillary tube.'

'Go for an artery, Tom.'

Webster sighed, turned the tape back on. Berlioz's *Symphonie Fantastique*. Because this was murder scene *extraordinaire*. Trying to clear the area of debris – to find more compelling evidence *and* to allow Deputy Coroner Jay Craine access to the bodies. The pathologist was waiting outside, eating his lunch. Crime lab had sent two techs for blood sampling, dusting and collection. The two white-coated workers were amassing pieces by the bagfuls.

Webster said, 'There is so much glass, blood, and guts here, it's like wading in a deadly offal soup. I don't know how the lab's gonna blood-type on all these bitty bits.'

Martinez said, 'Guarantee you, mixed in with all this shit is blood from the perp . . . or perps. You can't do this much damage without getting scratched.'

'Wonder why someone did this much damage?' Webster shrugged. 'It serves no purpose.'

'It serves a purpose,' Martinez said. 'It makes our job a hell of a lot harder.'

Webster said, 'Someone did this to confuse us?'

Martinez said, 'Or maybe someone just likes destruction.' He looked up from his kneeling position. Decker had come back. 'Hey, Loo. How's it going?'

'Find anything?'

'Lots of glass and blood.'

'Grab a pair of gloves, Rabbi,' Martinez said. 'Get your hands dirty for old times' sake.'

Decker slipped latex over his hands. 'Anyone check the other rooms?'

'Neat and orderly if you please,' Webster said. 'Decameron was a compulsive type.'

'Where's his office?' Decker asked.

'In the back. Why?'

'Go through his papers?'

Webster said, 'Just a quick glance. But nothing appears rifled through. What are you looking for?'

'Decameron was supposed to show Oliver and Dunn the Curedon/FDA trial data. Just wondering if he had the data somewhere in the house.'

'Like I said, his office is in the back. Help yourself.'

Decker walked through a skylit hallway off which three rooms sat – a bedroom, a guest room, and Decameron's office. Webster was right – all of them appeared untouched. Decker started with the office.

Light poured into quarters – from above and from the windows. A bay oriel framed a view of Decameron's patio garden – dozens of lush potted plants along with a three-tiered tiled fountain spilling gentle sheets of water. Decameron had done his work on an eight-foot granite drawerless desk. Atop the stone were a phone, a fax, a desktop copy machine, and a blotter and pencil holder.

The walls held no artwork – just shelves and banks upon banks of file cabinets. Decker pulled out a few drawers. All of them unlocked, seemingly undisturbed.

Some were reserved for patient files, but the majority had been dedicated to research data, most of the folders having to do with Curedon. Decker scanned the topics.

Curedon – Renal complications in rhesus monkeys.

Curedon – Iatrogenic blood dyscrasia caused by phagocytic T-cell response.

Curedon – postmortem intractable acute renal rejection during application of cyclosporin versus OKT3 versus Curedon.

Decameron had laid Curedon out into neat, assessable packages. Anyone interested in pilfering scientific information would have had an easy time. Decameron, for all his sardonic wit and cynicism, had been a trusting soul.

He thought a moment. If someone had been after the data, why make a mess out there and leave the office pristine? To throw him offtrack?

Decker sighed, slipped on his glasses, and began sorting through the Curedon folders, this time looking specifically for the Fisher/Tyne–FDA trial data. Reading sentence upon sentence, paragraph after paragraph of scientific mumbo jumbo until after an hour, his eyes bugged and blurred. Medical jargon was worse than legalese.

'Loo?'

Decker spun around. Martinez looked grave. His hand held something small and shiny.

'Maybe you should take a look at this.'

Decker walked over, his head awhirl with columns of highly statistically significant numbers and the horrible medical sequelae host-graft rejection. He took off his glasses and rubbed his eyes with his bicep. He took Martinez's offering.

Small and shiny and gold.

A chain with a cross.

Decker said, 'Not Decameron's type of jewelry.'

291

Martinez said, 'You know, anyone could have been wearing this. A cross is pretty neutral.'

Decker studied the ornament, flipped it over from side to side, noticed some scratch marks only because he was wearing his reading glasses. As he brought it closer to his eyes, the etching took shape. 'It's engraved. I see a word. You tell me if I'm right.'

'Can I borrow your glasses?'

Decker gave Martinez his glasses and the cross. Bert studied the writing for a moment. 'It says Sparks.'

'Yes, it does. See any first initial?'

'Nope.'

'Neither do I.' Decker chose his words carefully. 'There are six Sparks children. But only one's a priest.'

Webster walked into the room. He held up a lone key with an ID tag, both dangling from a ring. 'I found this in Decameron's pocket. Just an address, no name. I ran it through our backward directory. It matches an apartment rented out to Abram Sparks.'

And all Decker could think about was how this would affect Rina. He didn't want her hurt, yet he knew it would be impossible to hide it from her.

It stank of a setup. But an investigation wasn't run by its smell. He said, 'Okay, we'll do it this way. Tom, you stay here with the lab people and continue to direct the search. I'll call up and get two warrants – one for the church, one for Bram's apartment. I'll do the apartment. Bert, you do St. Thomas's. You being Catholic, it'll play better if you search the church.'

'What are you putting on the search warrant?'

'The weapons, of course. Splinters and pieces of glass with brown stains on them. And clothing. We're looking for bloody clothing . . . lots of bloody clothing.'

Key in hand, Decker didn't expect anyone to be in. But he knocked on the door as a courtesy. To his surprise, the priest asked who it was. After Decker identified himself, there was a long pause. The door opened a crack, the priest came into view. His appearance was neat, but his face was pale.

'Lieutenant.' Bram stepped outside, closed the door behind him. His voice was controlled but not calm. He was garbed in black with a clerical collar. No cross. 'Can I help you?'

Decker held out the key. 'I believe this belongs to you.'

Bram eyed the key. 'Thank you.'

As he reached for it, Decker snatched it from his grasp. 'Can I come in, Father?'

Bram paused again. 'This isn't a good time. I was on my way to the hospital to visit a parishioner. A very sick boy.'

'Then this comes at a bad time for you.' Decker took out the warrant, handed it to Bram. The priest stared at the paper, but his eyes went through the words. Decker sidestepped around him and walked inside. Gave the place a quick once-over.

Oliver had mentioned in a joke that the apartment was probably Bram's secret den of iniquity. If that were the case, the priest kept his sins well hidden. First thing Decker noticed was a wall crucifix to the right of the door.

The place was so spare it could have been listed as unfurnished. Pushed against the cheap wall paneling was a worn pea-green couch that sat under the living room's sole window. The pillows and cushions were clean but sagged like half-empty balloons. The middle of the room was taken up by a folding table piled with papers, and two folding chairs. Bookshelves leaned against the wall. The kitchen was the size of a shed, but the appliances – or at least the oven – worked. The smell of chocolate and sugar permeated the air. Decker took a quick peek at the bedroom. A mattress on the floor, more books on shelves, and another wall crucifix. Luxurious quarters for a monk, but by anyone else's standards, it was bare-bones.

Decker came back into the living room. Bram had shut the door, was leaning against it. He pushed hair off his face. 'How long will this take?'

'I think it would be a good idea to assign another padre for your pastoral duties.'

Wordlessly, Bram went over to the phone, called another priest to sub for him at the hospital.

Decker started by opening the kitchen cabinets. A few stray dishes, not even enough for the standard set of four. The upper shelves were empty. 'What smells so good?'

'I baked cookies. For the boy I was to visit.'

'Nice of you.'

'Would you like one?'

'No, thank you.'

'Something to drink? I have some orange juice.'

'Nothing, thanks.' He went to the lower cabinets. A few pieces of unmatched cookware. 'How long have you rented this place?'

'Ten years.'

'You use it for an office?'

'Yes.'

'You don't have enough working space in your office at the church?'

'Sometimes I like privacy.'

'How often do you come here?'

'Depends on my mood.'

'Why are you here today?'

Bram was quiet.

Decker moved into the bedroom, starting with the closet. A few shirts hanging from the bar as well as a couple of pairs of black pants. Resting on the closet shelf were several clerical collars, socks, and underwear, and a pair of sneakers. Decker picked up the mattress and peered underneath.

Nothing.

He went into the bathroom. It was connected to both the bedroom and the living room. A few towels and washclothes stored in the lone cabinet. A single towel hanging beside the sink. On the rim of the bath was a bar of soap, a razor, and a bottle of shampoo. Boringly devoid of anything incriminating. Yet, never once did the priest ask Decker what he was looking for. And that was significant.

So much for the quick overhaul.

Now for the detailed inspection. Decker gave the walls a couple of knocks just to hear what they sounded like. Cheap paneling over thin drywall. If there was a hidden compartment, it would be hard to find.

First, he decided to look behind the bookshelves. He started with the texts in the living room, since that was the biggest wall in the apartment. Standing on a chair, he began with a top shelf. Swiftly, he pulled down religious volumes and let them drop to the floor with a thump, did this several times as the books scattered across a worn shag carpet.

Bram hurried to pick them up.

Decker regarded the priest as he collected his tomes, noticed he was wincing. Decker was unnerving him.

And that was good.

Decker purposely moved faster and with great abandon, carelessly tossing the texts about.

Bram continued to retrieve them, then stopped. 'You know, to me these are holy books.'

'Sorry about the mess.' Decker let another volume topple downward. 'I don't have time for the niceties.'

'It's called respect. Something your wife knows a great deal about.'

Decker ignored the barb and let several more books land on the floor.

'I can't believe . . .' Anger had seeped into Bram's voice. 'Can you *hand* them to me at least?'

'Sorry. It'll take too long.'

'You're not going to find anything behind the books, Lieutenant.'

Decker turned and faced him. 'And where will I find things, Father?'

Bram maintained eye contact, but didn't speak.

Decker said, 'You know, if you're hiding something, I'm going to find it. I'm going to toss every book, knock on every piece of paneling, look under every single floorboard, and rip up your mattress if necessary. So why don't you save both of us some trouble and show me what you have.'

Bram's face was a study in stoicism. Without speaking, he walked over to the wall crucifix. He genuflected, then said a silent prayer. A minute later, still in the kneeling position, he deftly removed a piece of paneling. The broken seams had blended so smoothly with the wall, Decker hadn't noticed them on visual inspection. Inside the open space was a floor safe.

Decker climbed off the chair and donned a pair of gloves. 'You want to open the safe for me?'

Bram hesitated, then started turning the combination lock. Several minutes passed.

'C'mon,' Decker said. 'Stop stalling. I'll blast the thing open if I have to.'

Red-faced, Bram looked up. Perspiration was pouring off his forehead. He wiped his face with the sleeve of his shirt. 'I'm nervous. My hands are shaking. If you want, I'll give you the combination and *you* can open it.'

Decker spoke quietly. 'You do it. I'll be patient.'

'Thank you.'

It must have been another couple of minutes. Bram continued to maneuver the lock until there was an audible click. The priest pulled down the handle and the safe door popped open. He stood, went over to the couch and sat, hands folded in his lap, eyes resting on the wall crucifix. As Decker knelt, an acrid odor tickled his nose. With gloved hands, he pulled out a folded pile of clothing. Gave them a sniff. Sweat-soaked with the distinct sweet, metallic scent of blood. He examined the cloth briefly. Splotches of fresh blood on the knee and cuff areas of the pants, on the sleeves of the shirt. Bits of reddish brown scattered throughout the rest of the fabric. Good news for Forensics. Lots of samples from which to work.

Bagging the clothing, Decker continued searching in the darkened safe. Farther back was a pair of sneakers, the soles reddened with blood, sparkling with splinters of glass. Decker distinctly remembered Martinez pointing out bloody shoe prints to Forensics at Decameron's house. Nice to have shoes, especially sneakers with their distinct rubber-sole swirls and whirls.

Decker pressed on, looking for weapons. No guns or knives. But tucked into the back, previously hidden by the clothes, was a pile of magazines. About a dozen periodicals. He pulled them out, thumbed through the first one.

A case of 'seen one, seen 'em all.' Still, there was something particularly disturbing about the pornography. Not because it was gay, but because it looked like it hurt. The bondage seemed benign enough. It was the body-piercing that caused Decker's stomach to churn. Needles, pins and hypodermics cutting through flesh – through noses, through lips, through eyelids and tongues, and through nipples, penises and scrotums. Decker tried to keep his face blank but it was hard to remain indifferent.

He got up, a magazine in hand, and walked over to Bram. He opened it to a pinup – a blond proudly displaying a variety of needles and restraints around his torso, neck, and groin. He showed the picture to the priest. Bram averted his eyes.

Decker said, 'I can see why you kept your own apartment.'

Bram was silent.

Decker sat down. 'I'm really not interested in your proclivities except if they're germane to my homicide cases. The bloody clothes and shoes in your safe are a different matter altogether. I'm going to have to arrest you.'

Bram nodded, eyes still on the crucifix.

'The clothes and shoes are going to be gathered as evidence.' Again, Decker held out the magazine. 'These are going to taken up as well.'

Gently, Bram pushed the magazine out of his line of vision. 'Do as you will.'

Decker Mirandized the priest, reading him his legal rights. Then he asked Bram all the necessary questions, including if the priest wanted to waive his rights to an attorney.

'It doesn't matter.'

Decker paused. 'At this point, I'm supposed to ask you to sign my card.'

'Where?'

'Here.' Decker gave him a pen. 'You sign here to indicate that you understand your rights as I read them to you.'

Bram signed the card, gave it and the pen back to Decker.

'This line here says that you waive your rights to an attorney.'

'Fine—'

'Which means that anything you say after you sign that line can be used against you in a court of law.'

'I understand. Give me the pen.'

'Are you sure you want to do that? You lose protection, Father.'

'It doesn't matter. I don't have anything to say with or without an attorney.'

'Eventually, you're going to have to talk to someone.'

'I talk to God.'

'I meant someone who can physically help you.'

Bram looked at him. 'If God won't help me, then so be it. If you want me to sign the card, I'll sign it.'

Decker said, 'Can I use your phone?'

'It's on the kitchen counter. Help yourself.'

Slowly, Decker got up, eyes on the priest, and called in for a transport vehicle. After he hung up, he asked, 'Anyone you want me to call for you?'

'No one.'

'No one in your family?'

'Least of all, anyone in my family.'

'I'm having a car take you to the station house where you'll be

298

fingerprinted and booked. I'll instruct the cruiser to take you around the back. But there may be some newspeople hanging around.'

'I understand.' Bram looked at Decker. 'You're being kind to me. I know it's for Rina's sake, but thank you anyway.'

'You should get yourself a lawyer.'

'If I had something to say, I would.'

'Talk to me, Father. Because right now, your silence is more damning than words.'

Bram didn't respond.

Decker said, 'I'm taking myself off this case. Because of your prior involvement with my wife. You'll be questioned of course, but by someone other than me. If *you* want to talk to a detective, there are five people assigned to this case.'

Bram nodded, walked over to the kitchen, looked out the small window.

Decker tried again. 'Jail's no place for you, Padre.'

'I'm used to cells.'

'Who are you protecting?'

Bram continued to stare out the window. Decker gave up. The priest said, 'Car's here. Are you going to handcuff me?'

'Yes.'

Bram put his hands behind his back.

Decker said, 'I'll cuff you in front.'

'It doesn't matter to me.'

'Nothing matters to you, does it?'

Bram spoke to the wall. 'Not true. There are a few people in this world who significantly matter to me.'

Starting with my wife, Decker thought. Again, the priest put his arms around his back. This time, Decker cuffed him that way.

23

Along with the other Dees, Oliver made himself comfortable in Decker's small office. Really comfortable. He put his feet on the desk and said, 'Just when I had Shockley nailed, you arrest the *priest* . . . which screams *setup*.'

Decker pushed Oliver's feet off, sat back in his chair, paged through his notes. 'So give me another scenario.'

Martinez loosened his tie. 'We just ignore Forensic evidence—'

'I'm not ignoring anything,' Oliver said. 'I'm just saying that Shockley was involved—'

'Is that clock right?' Gaynor asked out loud.

Decker looked at his wall clock, then his watch. Ten minutes to seven. Another late night. 'Yeah, it's right.'

Gaynor shook his wrist, then laid his arms across his stretched stomach. 'My watch must have stopped. I've got five-thirty.'

Oliver said, 'Anyone want to hear my take?'

'Shoot,' Decker said.

Oliver ran his hand through limp black hair. 'First off, the clothes weren't drenched with enough blood to account for the priest doing the popping. You shoot and stab two victims like that, you're gonna hit an artery. You hit an artery, you're gonna get a bath.'

Webster scratched his head, the ubiquitous headphones dangling around the nape of his neck. 'So Bram wasn't the hit man. But he was there.'

Oliver said, 'For all we know, he could have come to the scene afterwards—'

Webster asked, 'Then why would he keep silent if he didn't do anything?'

301

Marge took off her gray suit jacket and draped it over the back of her chair. 'He's protecting someone.'

Decker said, 'Who?'

'One of his family members, most likely.'

'No, no, no!' Oliver protested. 'You're moving away from Shockley!'

'Maybe the putz didn't do it,' Marge said.

Oliver said, 'Can I play this out for you?'

'Go,' Decker said.

'Okay. Somebody's been fudging the Curedon data, right?'

Webster said, 'Computer boys really have a clever way of phrasing things, calling the break-in a cuckoo's egg. I'd just say someone was messing with my shit.'

Marge smiled. 'Scott, all our information is based on Leonard's ex-mistress. Hardly an objective source.'

'Not true,' Oliver said. 'Decameron knew something was going on with the data. Because all of a sudden Curedon's success rate dropped and the death rate rose. Only now we know why. Shockley was fudging the numbers—'

'Why would he do that?' Webster asked.

'To make the data look better or worse or something. Because he's doing hanky-panky with Berger. The cuckoo's egg had been traced to somebody at New Chris. It ain't Decameron or Sparks. Who else is there?'

'How about Elizabeth Fulton?' Martinez said.

'But she wasn't seen hanging around Fisher/Tyne, talking to Shockley.' Oliver clenched his fists. 'Look, we know Berger was once a cheat. Say Shockley and Berger are doing some kind of research fraud. Azor Sparks found out. Shockley had him popped. Then Decameron and Leonard found out. Now they're gone. See a trend here, folks?'

'On a superficial level, yes, there is a connection,' Decker said. 'I do feel certain that Sparks's homicide is related to this new one. Because all the homicides involve shooting *and* stabbing . . . weird MO to have both.'

'Absolutely, they're all connected,' Oliver announced.

'Okay, so Berger was a cheat,' Webster said. 'Why would Shockley mess this job up to do hanky-panky with Berger?'

'Fisher/Tyne was in on it,' Oliver said.

'Where's your evidence?' Martinez asked.

'I don't *have* evidence,' Oliver snapped. 'If I had evidence, Shockley would be behind bars.'

Decker said, 'I don't know if this is worth anything, but it's interesting to note that Berger admitted his past errors right away. Maybe he wanted to keep us rooted in his past instead of concentrating on his present.'

'Exactly!' Oliver clapped his hands in triumph.

Marge said, 'Fisher/Tyne cut the deal with Sparks for a lot of money. With Sparks gone, maybe Shockley figured he could redo Sparks's contract and continue Curedon research with Berger at a reduced price.'

Martinez said, 'Wouldn't Sparks's contract with Fisher/Tyne still be in effect with his widow?'

Marge said, 'That's the point. It was bad enough paying Sparks, but he at least developed the drug. Who wants to give all that money to his widow, especially when she can't help the drug through its laboratory bumps? Scott's suggesting that maybe Shockley was fudging the trial numbers, making them look bad to get Sparks's Curedon contract stopped. Then maybe he and Fisher/Tyne would rewrite a new contract with Berger at a much lower fee.'

'But it's *Sparks's* drug,' Martinez countered. 'You can't steal his drug. There has to be some kind of patent law.'

Oliver's eyes lit up. 'That's why Shockley's doing funny business behind backs. He's hoping nobody'll catch on.'

'That's ridiculous,' Martinez said. 'Decameron would catch on.'

'And that's why he's dead!' Oliver said triumphantly. 'Him *and* Leonard *and* Sparks. Shockley got two in one today.'

'And he popped Leonard because the guy found the cuckoo's egg?' Martinez shook his head. 'B movie, Scotty.'

'Hey, you can't write it strange enough,' Oliver said. 'Can I finish?'

'Go on,' Decker said.

'Shockley realized that Leonard had caught on because Leonard had been acting real nervous. Then when Leonard didn't show up for work today, Shockley figured he had to be whistle-blowing. Who was Leonard going to drop a dime to first? Decameron, of course.'

Martinez said, 'So Shockley went over there and blew them both away. And that's why Decameron had Bram's apartment key in his pocket. And that's why the priest had bloody clothes and shoes in his safe.'

'So what *was* the priest doing there, hotshot?' Oliver asked.

'Homosexual love triangle,' Martinez said. 'All three of them were gay.'

'Leonard had an affair,' Marge said. 'With a woman.'

'A quick affair,' Martinez said. 'You told us that yourself.'

'That's also according to Leonard's ex-mistress,' Marge said. 'Maybe it was longer than she was letting on.'

'Or maybe it was quick because Leonard was bad in bed with women.' Martinez thought a moment. 'Okay . . . so maybe he's bi. Whatever. Suppose the priest was having an affair with Decameron—'

'Yeah, yeah,' Oliver yawned.

'Bram's key was in Decameron's pocket—'

Oliver interrupted him. 'And Azor Sparks found out about it. He threatened his son *and* was going to fire Reggie. So Bram or Reggie shot Azor. Then when Bram saw Decameron with another man, he went hog-wild and shot and stabbed them both. Then he tore the place up. Then he took his clothes, stuffed them in his safe along with pincushion porno, and baked cookies for one of his sick parishioners.'

'He did bake cookies,' Decker said. 'I'll be a witness to that.'

'The rest of it stinks,' Oliver said. 'Even assuming Bram might have had a reason to bump off Decameron . . . why would he bump his father? Wasn't he Daddy's golden boy?'

'When he behaved himself.' Decker told them the Dana story, how Azor had slammed his son mercilessly for a brief period of time.

Oliver whistled. 'God, that's the type of shit you see on the talk shows. *I fucked my twin's wife.* And the guy was still willing to *marry* her? What a dunce!'

'No wonder he became a priest,' Webster said.

'That all took place years ago,' Marge said. 'I can't see Bram holding a grudge for that long.'

Webster said, 'Wouldn't be a grudge unless y'all held it for a long time.'

'An eighteen-year-old soap opera is a weak motivation for this murder,' Oliver said. 'I still vote for Shockley.'

'I like Waterson and the bikers,' Webster said. 'You know why I like the bikers?'

'Why do you like the bikers?' Marge asked.

'Because of the weird MO – the shooting *and* the stabbing. More than one person. Bumping both Leonard and Decameron off would be too much work for one man – either Shockley or the priest.'

Decker said, 'Unless the one man just broke in and shot them both first.'

Webster stated, 'By the position of the quantity of the spatter marks, the deputy coroner told Bert and me that he thought that one of the stab wounds broke a main chest artery in Decameron.'

'Descending vena cava,' Martinez clarified. 'Big one right after the aorta.'

Webster said, 'Since it squirted that much blood that far, he reckoned that the victim had been alive when he was stabbed. Meaning someone didn't take 'em out first with a gun.'

Marge said, 'Not necessarily, Tom. Decameron's heart might still have been beating even though he'd been plugged through the head. If he'd been stabbed then – brain dead but his beating heart still sending blood through his vessels – there would have been arterial spatter marks.'

'But you're stretching,' Webster said.

'Not really—'

'But Decameron certainly could have been alive when he was stabbed.'

'Of course.'

Webster said, 'Look, I got no stake in pinning the homicides on any specific individuals. I am trying to examine this logically. And my logic says more than one bad guy. And to me that spells Sanchez and Sidewinder.'

'I'm trying to be logical, too,' Oliver said. 'What do all three victims have in common, Tom?'

'Curedon.'

'Exactly. If this was something personal with the Sparks family, why was Leonard bumped?'

'Then what's the priest doing with bloody clothes?' Webster said.

'What does the priest have to do with bikers?' Oliver said.

Webster said, 'Maybe through Waterson, Bram contracted with the bikers to blow Decameron away.'

Marge said, 'Because of an eighteen-year-old grudge?'

Webster shrugged helplessly.

'I like the idea that Leonard was whistle-blowing to Decameron,' Marge said. 'But suppose his finking wasn't the reason behind his homicide. *He* wasn't the intended victim. *Decameron* was. For Leonard, it was just bad timing. A case of wrong place at the wrong time.'

'I like that,' Decker said.

'Then where is our Curedon Fisher/Tyne–FDA data?' Oliver said. 'Decameron was going to show it to us. It isn't in his office, it isn't at his house. Where the fuck is it?'

'If someone was looking for data,' Martinez said, 'why wasn't Decameron's office trashed?'

Decker said, 'Because his files were nicely laid out, Bert. A scientific thief, knowing what he was looking for, could easily lift the proper folder without tossing the place.'

Oliver said, 'Be great if we could get that data—'

'Maybe we can,' Gaynor interrupted. 'If Mohammed won't come to the mountain, we'll just go to the mountain.'

Marge furrowed her brow. 'That's not the saying.'

'What *are* you saying, Farrell?' Decker asked.

'Can't get the data from Fisher/Tyne. But maybe I can get it from the FDA.'

They all stared at him. Decker said, 'You can do that?'

'I don't know.' Gaynor shrugged. 'But I'll give it my best shot.' He checked his watch. 'It's past eight, Eastern time. All the offices are closed. I'll try tomorrow.'

Oliver said, 'Your watch stopped, Farrell. It's past ten back east.'

'Oh yeah, that's right.' Gaynor reset his watch. 'Thanks.'

'Something's bothering me,' Marge said. 'Why would Bram keep his bloody clothing in his apartment safe. Why not just chuck the threads?'

Martinez said, 'Maybe he didn't know where to chuck it.'

'Anywhere's better than in your apartment safe—'

'Which brings to mind another question,' Martinez said. 'Safes don't come with apartments like dishwashers. What was Bram doing with a safe in his apartment?'

'Hiding porno,' Oliver said. 'Told you it was his den of iniquity.'

'You need a safe to hide porno magazines?' Marge asked. 'You stick them under a mattress.'

Everyone was silent.

Marge said, 'Sparks's cross just happens to be left at the scene of the crime, a key to his apartment just happens to be in

307

Decameron's pocket. Then Bram, who by all accounts is a smart guy, brilliantly decides to hide incriminating evidence in a safe inside his apartment with explicit, raunchy gay porno.'

'I told you it smells like a setup,' Oliver said.

'But he was there,' Webster said.

'Yeah, he was there,' Marge said. 'But in what capacity?'

Oliver laughed. 'He gave Decameron last rites.'

Again, everyone was quiet.

Oliver laughed again. 'Aw, c'mon!'

Webster said, 'If someone's setting him up, why isn't he protesting?'

Marge said, 'Because he's *protecting* someone.'

Decker thought a moment. 'Could be. Trouble is, the guy's not talking.'

Webster said, 'One of the most frustrating suckers I ever did meet. Couldn't squeeze a word out of him.'

Martinez said, 'He's a priest. Maybe by talking, he'd be violating his sacramental seal.'

'Did he claim priest confidentiality?' Oliver asked.

'No, he didn't claim anything,' Webster said. 'Just sat there, stoic-like, telling me he was sorry he couldn't help me.'

'Hate to be a broken record, but he's protecting someone,' Marge stated.

'You know, you can protect someone without deliberately screwing yourself up,' Martinez said. 'I still think it was a lover's spat. I think Bram went too far. And after he realized what he'd done, he panicked and fled, stuffed his clothes in the safe until he could figure out what to do.'

Marge poured herself a glass of water. 'You all realize that just because Bram was *looking* at porn, doesn't mean he was actually doing anything.'

Oliver smiled at her. 'Right!'

Webster said, 'The lady has a point. I've taken many a gander at hetero porn. But I don't cheat on my wife.'

'Yeah, but you fuck your wife,' Oliver said. 'The priest has no release.'

'He has his hands,' Gaynor said.

'Masturbation's a sin,' Martinez said.

'So is buggery,' Oliver stated. 'And didn't you just tell me you thought it was a lover's triangle?'

Martinez said, 'You know, for either sin, Bram as a priest was going to have to do major penance. As long as he had to atone, maybe he figured why not go all the way.'

Webster said, 'Well, I reckon I could see Decameron jumping at the occasion to bugger a priest.'

'I liked Reggie,' Oliver said.

'I have nothing against the man,' Webster stated. 'But he was unconventional. Taking risks with his job, knowing his boss is a major Fundamentalist, just to pick up a couple of hookers.'

Decker checked his watch. 'Has Bram set bail?'

'Nope,' Gaynor said. 'Bail's two hundred thou. Lot of bread. Still, given his bank account, posting a ten-percent wouldn't have been a problem for the priest.'

'But he hasn't posted,' Decker said. 'He's doing penance of some kind.'

Martinez said, 'You bet he's doing penance. Betcha he's been doing it for a long time . . . asking Jesus to forgive him for being gay, figuring if he prayed hard enough, Jesus would make him normal.'

'No, I don't agree with that,' Decker said. 'He once mentioned to me that being gay wasn't a choice, but an inborn preference. So if he's gay, maybe he doesn't feel guilty about it.'

'No way, Jose,' Martinez countered. 'We Catholics feel guilty when the weather turns bad. Intellectually, Bram may know being gay isn't his fault. But emotionally, he's doing penance for it.'

Too many questions. Decker said, 'Since you like Berger as a baddie, Scott, go over to New Chris tomorrow and feel him out.'

'Great.'

'Tom, you like Waterson and the bikers. Go see what they're up to.'

'Mah pleasure.'

'Farrell, you're doing the FDA connection.'

'I'll give it my best shot.'

'Good.' Decker turned to Martinez. 'You give Bram a try tomorrow. You're Catholic. Maybe he'll relate to you.'

'Why don't you do it, Loo?'

'I can't. Conflict of interest. My wife knows Abram Sparks from the past.'

Five pairs of eyes were suddenly upon him.

He shrugged. 'No big deal. Just don't want to give grist to the mill should this case turn nasty, say I have a personal involvement. Which I don't. But . . .' He shrugged again. 'You know how it works.'

Marge said, 'How well did she know him?'

'Pretty well at one time.'

Again, the room went dead. Martinez broke the silence. 'He isn't going to talk. He's a priest.'

Webster said, 'Not that I'm defending the guy, but if he did kill Decameron and Leonard, what's the reason?'

'You have to go with the gay angle,' Martinez said. 'The porno in the safe, the key in Decameron's pocket . . . it's the only thing that makes sense.'

'It was Shockley,' Oliver announced. '*He's* the only one that makes sense.'

'So why does the priest have bloody clothing?' Marge asked.

'We're repeating ourselves,' Decker said. 'Let's finish up the paperwork and sleep on it.' He stood up and opened his office door. 'Tomorrow's another day.'

The house was dark and quiet. Decker tiptoed into the kitchen to make himself a cup of tea. A moment later, Rina came in.

'You have the ears of a bat,' Decker said.

'It's called Husband Echolocation.' Rina kissed his cheek. 'Sit. I'll make you tea. You look tired.'

'I'm beat!' Decker took off his jacket and pulled up a chair at the kitchen table. 'How're my children?'

'Hannah's asleep, but the boys are still up.'

'Dare I see them?'

'Depends on how intact your ego is.'

'Not too great right now. Think I'll wait a bit.' He smiled at Rina. 'How are you?'

Rina leaned against the counter and looked upward. 'Not too great.'

'So you've heard the news.'

'Yes.'

'I can't talk about it.'

'I know. I had no intention of pressing you for details.'

'Thank you.' Decker loosened his collar, removed his tie. 'His parishioners are keeping a nice little vigil.'

'Bram wouldn't want that. He doesn't like attention.'

'Maybe he appreciates the support.'

Rina was silent.

'I'm sorry.' Decker waited a beat. 'If you want to talk to me, I'll listen.'

'What's the point?' Rina bit her nail. 'There's no point.'

'Are you mad at me?'

'Oh Peter, of course *not*!' She sat next to him. 'You're one of the most honest people I've ever met.'

'One of the most?'

'There are a few others.'

'Who?'

'My parents, Rav Schulman, my late husband . . . Bram.'

Decker paused. 'O-kay.'

Rina bit her nail again. 'So I won't bother telling you that you're wrong—'

'No, don't bother—'

'Or that you made a terrible mistake—'

'No, don't bother with that at all.'

Rina's eyes misted. She tried to cover it with a smile. Decker took her hand. 'I know you're hurting. And I feel lousy that I'm a part of it. It's my own damn fault. I should have removed myself as soon as you told me you knew him.'

'Why didn't you?'

'Ego and curiosity. It was stupid of me to go this far . . . to execute the warrant. Ah well.'

The water began to boil. Rina got up. 'So you've washed your hands of the case?'

'No, I'm still supervising. But I'm not doing any interviewing . . . no direct contact with any of the parties involved.'

'So who's questioning him? Marge?'

'Does it matter?'

'No.' Rina set a steaming mug on the table. 'Is he even talking?'

'No, actually, he isn't.' Decker stared at floating tea and mint leaves. 'Has he always been close mouthed?'

Rina thought a moment. The tears came back. She wiped them away. 'Bram's always been circumspect.'

'He talk to you at all while he was caring for Yitzchak?'

'Of course.'

'About what?'

Rina shrugged. 'Sometimes, we talked about religion. About how Hashem gives true believers trials to test their faith. It's a tenet of both religions. For us Jews, it's Abraham and the *Akeda*.'

'The sacrifice of Isaac.'

'Right. Apparently to Catholics, Mary is the ultimate figure of *emmunah*.' She frowned. 'That's weird. I just used a Hebrew word for a figure in Catholicism. Anyway, she's their symbol of faith. Mostly, Bram offered me lots of nondenominational words of comfort.'

Decker said, 'Did he ever talk about his family?'

'Sometimes.' Rina nodded.

'Anything illuminating?'

'Meaning?'

'Did he ever tell you anything about his personal relationships with his parents, brothers, and sisters . . . friends, male or female?'

'Occasionally.' Rina got up. 'You want some more tea?'

'I'd love some more tea.'

Nervously, Rina refilled the mug with steaming water. 'News made mention of some gay angle. Because Dr. Decameron was gay.'

Decker nodded.

Rina sighed. 'Did you find evidence of that?'

'We're still assessing information and evidence. I'm not evading your question, honey, I'm answering it truthfully.'

Rina looked upward. 'What a mess!'

Decker tried to think of a nifty response, drawing blanks instead. He stood up and said, 'It's late and I still have a couple of business calls to make. Think I can chance a couple of good nights to the boys without having my head blown off?'

'How brave do you feel?'

He kissed his wife's cheek. 'Not too brave. But a man's gotta do what a man's gotta do.'

Wiping the counter, Rina thought about possible excuses for running out at ten-thirty in the evening: a friend needed help . . . Rebbetzin Schulman wanted her opinion on some papers she had written . . . she suddenly wanted to visit her parents.

She discarded them one by one, all of them downright lame. Peter would laugh in her face.

Despite what Peter would do, she knew she was going to see Bram. That was given. But it would simply have to wait until tomorrow.

She heard Peter saying good night to the boys, heard his feet against the wooden floor of the hallway. A door was shut with a click.

Silence.

Rina glanced at the kitchen phone. The business line came alive.

He was dialing out from the bedroom.

Walking over to the wall, Rina ran a finger over the receiver.

Now or never. While the phone was still ringing. Because once someone picked up, Peter would be acutely aware of the extension kicking in.

She shouldn't.

It was unethical.

It was wrong.

But she couldn't look past the scene in her head. The pain in Bram's eyes as he eulogized his father . . . so reminiscent of her own heartbreak almost a decade ago.

He had been there for her in endless ways.

And now he was in trouble.

He would have done it for her without a second thought.

Quietly, she removed the phone from the cradle. As luck would have, Marge picked up at the same time.

Rina held her breath as her husband started talking.

She was ashamed of herself.

So be it. The feeling would have to keep.

24

Sitting at his desk, Decker sorted through the morning messages – four from Paul Sparks, three from Eva Shapiro, five from William Waterson on behalf of Dolores Sparks, and two from Michael. None from Maggie. More significant, none from Luke. Marge knocked on Decker's doorjamb. He told her to come in.

'An advantage of my being off the Sparks case.' Decker stood and handed her the stack of phone slips. 'I don't have to return calls. Have fun.'

'Lucas Sparks is outside. He barged into your office this morning, demanding to talk to you. We almost threw him out.'

'You should have.'

'I would have except that I think he has something important to say.'

'I can't talk to him.'

'He's insistent, Pete—'

'I *can't* do it, Marge. End of discussion.'

Marge pushed hair from her face. 'Look, why don't you explain to him personally why you can't talk—'

'Marge—'

'Pete, if you let him go, we may miss something big.' Marge clenched her jaw. 'How about if you talk to him while we all listen behind the one-way mirror?'

Decker considered the offer, feeling it was a mistake. But she was right. If Luke had something to say, stalling could give him cold feet. He took out a portable tape recorder from his desk drawer. 'Bring him in the interview room. Give me about ten minutes.'

'All right!'

Marge left. Decker poured himself another cup of hard black coffee and downed an Advil, hoping to stave off a thrashing headache. Carefully, he reviewed his notes, then walked across the hall into the interview room.

In just a few days, Luke had lost weight. He was almost as thin as his brother. His clothes sagged, but he was washed and shaved, his hair clean and neatly combed. He wore a plaid flannel shirt and a pair of denims. His feet were housed in knock-off Doc Martens. He stood when Decker came in.

'Mr. Sparks. Please sit.'

Luke sat. So did Decker.

'I've got a bit of a problem,' Decker started. 'I'm not on your father's case anymore.'

'Why's that?'

'Personal reasons.'

'You arrest my brother, then you chickenshit out when the heat's poured on.' Luke nodded. 'Typical of LA's finest.'

Decker said, 'Sir, there are five other—'

'*You* arrested him. You *listen* to me.'

'Okay, you can talk to me. But I want other people to hear what you have to say. Because I'm not doing solo interviewing.'

'Why were you pulled off? Incompetence?'

Decker ignored him. 'You see that over there?' He pointed to a reflective wall.

'It's a one-way mirror.'

'Right.'

'You've got other people listening in.'

'Right. Can you truck with that?'

'Fine with me. Just that you're gonna look like an asshole and I thought *you* might want a little privacy.'

Decker said, 'Mind if I turn on the tape recorder?'

'Go ahead.'

'Would you like something to drink?'

'No . . . no, thank you.'

Decker turned on the tape. 'So tell me how I'm going to look like an asshole.'

Luke rubbed his face, stared at the one-way mirror, then looked back at Decker. 'Yesterday, I got a phone call from Reggie Decameron. About seven-thirty . . . maybe eight in the morning. He sounded . . . strange. Calm but *serious*. Which is very strange for Decameron. He said he needed to talk to me about my family. When I asked him to be more specific, he said it was a private matter, too personal to talk about over the phone. We set a meeting time at ten. His house.'

Luke scratched his head.

'He was already dead when I got there. He and some other man. They were both . . . covered with blood . . . and glass.' His voice dropped to a whisper. He blinked hard. 'Lots of broken glass.'

There was a long pause.

'It was all I could do to keep my stomach down. I would have left immediately except something caught my eye. There were about a dozen magazines . . . in plain brown wrappers.' He waited a beat. 'They had my brother's name on them.'

Again, he stopped talking.

'I picked one up, took off the cover. It was homosexual pornography. Explicit . . . *revolting* shit!'

The room was silent.

'I totally freaked. I ran outside, got in my car and peeled rubber. A block later, I pulled over and threw up. I was shaking so badly, I couldn't drive.'

Sweat had formed on Luke's face, had deepened the color of his shirt under his armpits. Decker poured him a glass of water. Luke downed the contents in a few gulps.

'I must have sat there for . . . I don't know . . . ten minutes. Maybe longer, maybe shorter. I knew I had to go back.'

'Why?'

'Obviously, I couldn't leave crap like that with my brother's name on top of two dead bodies. I thought it might . . . incriminate . . . I went back and this time I took all the magazines with me. I don't know why I didn't just throw them away. I think I wanted to confront my brother. Have him deny they were his.'

'Why would Decameron have your brother's pornography?'

'I don't know.' Luke shrugged. 'I can only imagine it was because they were . . . involved.' He winced. 'God, the thought is so *disgusting*!'

'If Decameron was your brother's lover, why would he be calling you to talk about Bram?'

'I don't really know. Maybe blackmail. Because everyone thinks we've come into money with our father's death.'

'Have you?'

'Yes, as a matter of fact, I have. We have. Me and all my siblings. Dad left us insurance money. Maybe Decameron wanted a piece of the action. For all I know, I was the first one and he was going to hit on all my sibs. He knew my family, my parents' beliefs. He'd know we'd do anything to prevent this from coming out. For my mother's sake. Everyone knows Bram is her golden boy.'

'You'd do anything to prevent it from coming out?'

'Not *anything*. Certainly not murder. But I, for one, would have certainly paid the sleazeball off to keep quiet about my brother.'

'You would have paid him off?'

'Absolutely. His calling me up like that. I smelled something rotten.'

'Yet you came when Decameron called.'

'Yes, I did.' Luke poured himself another glass of water and drank it. 'And that is . . . the end of my story.'

Decker said, 'When you saw the bodies, why didn't you call the police?'

'And admit I was there? Are you crazy?'

'You're admitting you were there now . . . with a lot more dire consequences.'

'You arrested Bram. I couldn't let him take the rap for me.'

318

'The rap?'

'I met with him after I left Decameron's house. Called him up and told him to get his ass over to his apartment because we had things to talk about. I showed him a magazine, shoved it in his face actually. I wanted him to tell me it was a *mistake*, for God's sake!'

'Did he?'

'No.' Luke shook his head. 'No, he didn't. He just took my bloody clothes, my shoes, and the magazines. Told me not to worry, that he'd take care of it. At that point, I was so glad to rid myself of that shit, I just let him do it.'

Decker sat back in his chair. 'But you've suddenly come to your senses. Now you're being a man and bailing out your brother.'

Luke glared at Decker. 'I realize it's hard to believe a slime like me could be noble, but yes, it's true.'

Decker said, 'You know, if I were to believe any part of your story, I'd believe the part about your brother and Decameron. Which would mean that Bram, more than anyone, would have a reason to shut Decameron up.'

'Except Bram wasn't there. The evidence you have against him is *mine*! Sure, the bloody clothes fit him. Because we wear the same size. And yeah, the shoes fit him too. Because we have the same shoe size. Maybe you even have blood evidence, because picking up the magazines, I sliced myself several times. You don't have *his* blood, pal. You've got my blood. We're identical twins.'

Decker hoped his face was registering neutral. Inside, he could feel his heart taking flight in his chest. He waited a beat, then said, 'We have other things.'

'You found my cross, then.'

Decker couldn't hide his astonishment. He was silent for a long time. Then he said, 'Didn't know you were that religious.'

'I'm not but old habits are hard to break.' Luke looked at the mirror. 'How you all doing over there?'

'Luke—'

'It was given to me when I . . . when Bram, Paul, and I were

319

confirmed as teenagers. We all got the same present – a Walkman and a gold cross engraved with the name Sparks on the back. No initial, mind you, just Sparks. Our crosses are interchangeable. My parents weren't big on personalization.'

Decker was silent.

'Anyway,' Luke continued, 'mine has had a loose clasp for years. Never got around to fixing it. Maybe I secretly wanted to lose it. Not in a pile of dead bodies, but God works in mysterious ways.'

'I'm supposed to believe this?'

Luke said, 'This morning, while I was taking a shower, thinking about what I *had* to do, I noticed my neck was bare. I looked around my apartment, couldn't find it. I knew what must have happened. It came off at Decameron's place. Then I knew why you arrested Bram.'

He leaned over the tabletop.

'If Bram wears anything over his shirt, it's a Roman Catholic crucifix – a big silver thing with Jesus on it. But he also wears his boyhood confirmation cross inside his shirt. You booked him, you stripped him of his personal belongings. Go back and check your bags, Lieutenant. You'll find his cross there. Would it make sense for Bram to be wearing two identical crosses? Man, even he's not that fanatical.'

Luke grew impatient.

'Look, my brother didn't murder Decameron. He wasn't even anywhere near the house. He was with my mom in the morning, at his church in the afternoon.'

Decker was quiet.

'Yes, I know there were time gaps. Maybe he sneaked into Decameron's house between Reggie's phone call to me and before he visited my mother. That means he had to have been there around seven-thirty in the morning.'

'So?'

'Decameron had another guy there, both of them dressed in

business suits. Who the hell does business at seven-thirty in the morning? No one. Because they were murdered later on. Make sense?'

Decker didn't respond. His head was buzzing.

'I'll tell you what *doesn't* make sense,' Luke said. 'If Bram had anything to do with the murder, you'd think he'd leave porno around with his name on it? Sort of like a giveaway, don't you think?'

A setup. If so, why wouldn't Bram talk? Decker stared at the priest's twin, trying to buy time to collect his thoughts. He said, 'Leaving pornography in plain view makes about as much sense as Bram using his real name for the subscription.'

Luke didn't talk for a moment. 'No, that doesn't make a lot of sense.'

'I never saw the wrappers. So I don't know if you're shitting me or what.'

'You have the magazines?'

'We have magazines.'

'But not the wrappers.'

'No.'

'He threw the wrappers away. Why didn't he just throw the magazines away?'

'Why didn't he?'

'I don't know. Maybe he was pressured for time. He was on his way to see some kid in a hospital. Or maybe he didn't feel comfortable tossing the shit in his apartment Dumpster. Maybe he thought someone might see him. The magazines were addressed to a post office box.'

'Do you remember the number?'

'No. Course you could get it from my brother.'

'He isn't talking. Can you get it for us?'

'Me?' Luke laughed bitterly. 'No, if he's not talking to you, he wouldn't talk to me.' He paused. 'I can't in my worldly thoughts begin to fathom why Bram would use his real name. Even if he had them delivered to an anonymous post office box.'

Decker said, 'Maybe he got a thrill out of being bad. Or maybe he was about to come out.'

'That doesn't sound like Bram. He's not the bad boy type. And he's very discreet . . . or so I thought.' Luke shrugged. 'Bram's always been a mystery to all of us.'

'Why hasn't Bram told us about you being there?'

'Why do you think? He's protecting me.'

'He thinks you murdered Decameron?'

'Who the hell knows what he thinks? When Bram decides not to talk, he doesn't talk. Look, I was there. But I didn't kill anyone. You want me to make a more complete detailed statement, I'll be happy to comply. Just spring my brother. I'm tired of him being my fall guy.'

'You were willing to pin it on him yesterday. You stood by while we arrested him.'

'I was in shock, I don't do well under pressure.' He lowered his head. 'And I was mad.'

'*Mad?*'

Luke sighed. 'I always knew Bram wasn't exactly girl crazy. As a matter of fact, the guy never had a girlfriend after Dana . . . my wife. He used to date my wife. They broke up in high school and I never thought about her. We remet at our five-year high school reunion. She thought I was Bram. Bram didn't show. Anyway, we talked and one thing led to another.'

'How does Bram feel about you marrying his ex-girl?'

'He never stated an opinion on it. Truthfully, I think he feels I was stupid for marrying her.'

'Maybe he's jealous.'

'Nah, he doesn't give a rat's ass about Dana. Maybe that's why I knew that he was probably *that* way.'

'You mean gay?'

'Yes. Okay, if you're gay, okay. But be private about it, for God's sake. Especially if you're a priest! Yesterday, after seeing that shit,

I thought to myself . . . why should I fuck *myself* up over his perversions. Especially if he was going to be so careless about leaving it around.'

'So why are you here?'

Luke buried his head in his hands, then looked at Decker. 'Because, as corny as it sounds, I love my brother. I would never hurt him . . . not intentionally . . . not anymore . . .'

He looked up, spoke to the ceiling.

'A long time ago, Bram and I had a falling-out. My fault. I don't think he suffered much, but I sure as hell did. I missed him. Missed . . . talking to him. People talk to Bram. Because he truly listens.'

He made a swipe at his eyes.

'Are you going to spring him or not?'

'First, I'll have to evaluate what you've told me. Then I'm going to need a formal statement from you. Someone else will have to take it. Agreed?'

'Fair enough.'

'You're going to be detained for a while. Anyone you want to call?'

'No one.'

'A lawyer?'

'Nope.'

'You may want to call your family. Let them know what's going on.'

'They've been calling here left and right. They're furious at you.'

'No doubt.'

'I'll call Paul. Get them off your back if you want.'

'Up to you.'

'I'll do it,' Luke said. 'I owe you something for listening to me. By the way, I know why you took yourself off the case.'

Decker said nothing.

Luke said, 'Ten years ago, my parents threw us boys . . . the triplets . . . a twenty-fifth birthday party. Tons of people. I *hated* every minute of it. Actually, I think Bram and Paul hated it, too. We went along with it for my parents' sake . . . actually for my mother's. She loves playing hostess . . . showing off her cooking. Anyway . . . like I said, there were lots of people there.'

He paused, regarded Decker with arched eyebrows.

'Lots of people. But your wife's face is a hard one to forget.'

Decker was silent.

Luke said, 'I saw her picture on your desk. Recognized her right away. Her husband had been Bram's friend. I guess you knew that.'

Decker remained silent.

'Her late husband's loss was your gain—'

'You get a charge out of pissing me off?'

'It's a free country.' Luke's smile turned into a grin. 'Better behave, Lieutenant. There are video cameras on you.'

Without speaking, Decker walked out of the room.

25

'You see!' Decker yelled at Marge as he paced. 'That's precisely why I shouldn't have talked to him! Personal involvement is personal involvement no matter how seemingly small—'

'I think we should go to the jail to check out Bram's belongings.'

'Don't interrupt me!' Decker fired out. 'I'm not done ranting!'

'Sorry.'

Decker paced a few more moments. Then he stopped, took a deep breath in, and let it out. 'Fine. Let's check out Bram's evidence bags.'

'Are you all right?'

'No, I'm not all right! What a prick! Like I gave the guy a brain tumor to get to Rina—'

'I think you're making too much out of this.'

'I don't care what you think!'

Marge said nothing, calmly sitting with her hands in her lap. Today she wore a caramel-colored pants suit over an ecru top. Quite elegant except for the Nikes on her feet. Serviceability took precedence over fashion.

Decker said, 'I'm having a difficult time with this.'

'It's hard to stand on the sidelines.'

'No, I don't miss getting my hands dirty. It's the personal aspect. You know at first, I thought they might have been involved.'

'Who's they?'

'Rina and . . . him . . . Bram.'

Marge shot him a quizzical look. 'Oh, you mean *romantically* involved. I thought you were talking about *involved in the murder*.'

She laughed. 'I'm thinking, "What the heck does Rina have to do with any of this?" '

Decker wagged his finger. 'See, you're thinking business. I'm thinking about my *wife*. Not good.' He paused. 'Tell you the truth, I was relieved to find out he's gay. Not that I would have cared if he and Rina—'

'Not much,' Marge whispered under her breath.

'What was that?'

'Nothing.'

The room fell still.

'Okay. I might have cared a little.' Decker frowned. 'Or maybe the thought that he isn't still preys in the back of my mind. Because I don't really buy any of this.'

'Buy what?'

'That Bram's gay. Believe me, I *saw* the way he looked at my wife.'

'When?'

'At the memorial service.'

Marge said, 'You're telling me that Bram – a *priest*, at his father's *memorial* service, in *full view* of everyone, including *you* – leered at your wife?'

Decker sighed, rolled his tongue in his cheek. 'Okay. So maybe it was my imagination.'

'I think so.'

'That doesn't change the fact that the whole thing stinks.'

'What in particular?'

'Bram hiding the bloody clothes with the fuck mags in his apartment. Even if he was protecting someone, why would he *keep* incriminating material in his possession?'

'Like Luke said, maybe he didn't have time to find a safe dumping ground.' Marge thought a moment. 'Or if he'd been hiding magazines for someone, maybe Bram figured that the someone would want them back.'

'But Luke said the wrappers had his name on it. I can't see

Bram subscribing to that stuff for someone else.'

Marge shrugged. 'So Luke's lying. Maybe the wrappers had Luke's name on them and Bram's protecting Luke just like Luke stated.'

No one spoke for a moment.

'We should set up a polygraph for both of them,' Marge stated. 'Bram isn't talking.'

'So we'll go for Luke. One out of two ain't bad.'

'Fine. We can do it after we check out Bram's belongings.'

Marge stood. 'Is Bram still at Van Nuys or did they move him downtown?'

'No, he's at Van Nuys.'

'You want to come with me?' Marge smiled. 'For old times' sake?'

Decker smiled back. 'Sure.'

'Are we going to spring him?'

'Well, if we find the cross in Bram's belongings, and Luke swears he was at Decameron's house, it's pointless to keep Bram locked up.'

'What about the key with the ID tag of his apartment address?'

Decker thought a moment. 'It was definitely the key to his apartment. But it wasn't Bram's personal key. Because I locked the door to his apartment using Bram's own key ring.'

'So whose key is it?'

Decker wait a beat. 'If he and Decameron were lovers, Bram could have given Reggie a key to his apartment.'

'And it just happened to be in Reggie's pocket?'

Decker shrugged. 'We're getting ahead of ourselves. First, let's check out Bram's belongings. If Luke's to be believed, we should find an identical confirmation cross. You want to drive, Margie?'

'Sure.'

Decker pulled his wallet from his desk drawer. 'How're things working out with Oliver?'

'We have our rough moments.' Marge picked up her purse. 'But he's got positive attributes. He's a clear thinker.'

'Good to hear.' Decker hesitated. 'Sorry I jumped on you a few moments ago.'

Marge stood. 'I understood your dilemma, Peter. But I felt Luke wouldn't have opened up to me like he did to you. For what it's worth, I think you did the right thing.'

'The guy's a jerk.'

Marge said, 'Yeah, it was awful what he said to you.'

Decker shook his head. 'I should have just shrugged it off without comment.'

'You're human.'

Decker opened the door to his office. 'Baby, ain't that the truth.'

Rina placed the strap of her purse over her shoulder and locked the car, her heart beating hard in her chest. Because she had no idea what she was doing . . . what she would even say if given the chance to see him. As fate would have it, the situation took care of itself. She saw him bolting down the back stairs of the Van Nuys Substation. He started jogging through the parking lot away from the police complex. She had to sprint to catch up with him.

As soon as he saw her, Bram's expression turned hard and furious. 'Where's your car?'

'Right over there.' Gasping, Rina pointed to her Volvo.

He grabbed her arm, pushed her forward.

'What are you doing?' Rina shook his arm off. 'What's the matter with—'

'Give me your keys—'

'What—'

'Don't *argue* with me. Just *do* it!'

Rina flipped him the keys. She had to run to keep up with him. When he reached the Volvo, Bram opened the driver's door, got in and opened the passenger's door from the inside. As soon as Rina was seated, Bram peeled rubber before she had the door fully closed.

'What is it?' Rina asked as she shut the door. 'What happened?'

Instead of answering, Bram depressed the gas pedal. The car flew forward, the tires squealing as he turned onto Van Nuys.

Rina took a sharp intake of air. 'You're going to get a *ticket*—'

'So, you'll fix it for me—'

'Bram, slow down!' she said. 'You're going to have an accident!'

Instead, he accelerated to overdrive, had to swerve to avoid hitting a stopped car.

'*Stop* it!' Rina screamed.

The car continued racing, Bram shooting one yellow light after another. The fourth traffic light was completely red as the Volvo entered the intersection. Bram depressed the accelerator to the max, narrowly missing side impact by a eighteen-wheeler semi. The blare of the truck's horn ricocheted in Rina's ears.

Rina pounded his shoulder. '*Stop it! Stop it!*'

Bram braked suddenly, pitching them both backward. Breathing hard, he brought the speedometer down to normal city limits.

Rina covered her face, cried softly, a sharp pain stabbing her body with each intake of breath. Recovering quickly, she immediately prayed her thanks to God and wiped away tears. She held her rib cage as she spoke. 'You could have gotten both of us killed. Have you gone *crazy*?'

Bram whispered, 'Sorry.' He cleared his throat. 'Sorry.'

Rina said nothing. Signalling, he turned right, hooking onto the 405 North. Within minutes, the Volvo was going a smooth and safe fifty-five.

Rina finally managed to breathe without pain, her armpits damp with sweat. Some of her hair had fallen out of her scarf. She tucked it back in. Quietly, she asked, 'Where are we going?'

He didn't answer, didn't acknowledge her question.

She became quiet as well, too nervous to talk. Nothing to do except wait him out. As soon as he got off at Devonshire and headed west instead of east, she knew where he was headed. He wasn't taking her home. He was driving toward McCoy Park.

Years since Rina had been there. It hadn't changed at all. A time warp of yesteryear when land was still an available commodity. A velvety green lawn hugging the foothills, dotted with several picnic benches. In the distance were the outdoor tennis courts. The sky was gray, the weather was cool, and the nets were empty. Since it was a school day and the park didn't have a playground, there weren't any children around. She and Bran owned the place.

He parked the Volvo, walked away from the car without a word. If she had had the keys, she would have driven home. Instead, she had no choice but to follow.

He turned to her, his face wan, his voice a shadow. 'I am so sorry, Rina. I don't know what . . . forgive me.'

She didn't answer.

He ran his hand over his chin, surprised to find it roughened with stubble. 'Are you all right?'

'I'm alive. It's a good start.' She approached him tentatively. 'Are you all right?'

'No, I'm not.' His eyes met hers. 'What on God's green earth were you thinking, showing up like that? The LAPD doesn't have enough problems? You can't *do* things like that, Rina. If you get dragged into this mess, you take your husband down at the same time.'

'I just wanted to talk . . . to help if I could—'

'You can't.' He moved away from her, leaned against a giant, budding sycamore and looked upward. 'Go home, Rina. Just . . . go home.'

She came toward him. 'Bram, I don't know exactly what's going on, but what they're saying is absurd. You're no more capable of murder than I am.'

'You don't know anything.'

'I know you're not . . . that way.'

'That *way*? You mean *gay*?'

'Why are you torturing me?'

330

He spun around, rage in his eyes. 'Because you don't know a *damn* thing about me. And you never did. Because if you had had even the tiniest clue, you would have never told me to go to Rome.'

Rina's mouth dropped open; stunned and stung. 'So suddenly I've become responsible for your regrets?'

'I would have moved mountains for you.' His eyes moistened. 'All I wanted was some kind of . . . sign—'

'So why didn't you *ask* for one?'

'Oh believe me, I asked in a thousand ways! You just never bothered to *listen*!'

His voice was seething with bitter fury. It was hard not to respond in kind. But Rina bit back her tongue. Because a harsh word delivered couldn't ever be taken back.

There were so many different ways she could have answered his accusations. But what was the point? He was in trouble, he was hurting, and he was lashing out at her. Had she been a little less scared, a little less agitated, Rina knew she would have taken his anger for what it was – a backhanded compliment. He felt safe with her, secure enough to express himself. But she was too blinded by emotion.

Wiping wetness from her eyes, she said, 'I did what I thought was right in the past. And I'm doing what I think is right in the present. If I am wrong now . . . like apparently I was wrong back then . . . then, I'll kindly *butt* out!'

Softly, Bram said, 'I think that's a very good idea.'

They both stood in silence.

Rina said, 'I need the keys to my car.'

'Oh.' Bram rummaged through his pockets, pulled out her keys. He was about to toss them to her. Instead, he walked over to the Volvo and opened the driver's door. She sighed, dragged herself over, and scooted behind the wheel. She held out her hand and he dropped the keys into her open palm.

He whispered, 'Next time you pray, ask Yitzy to forgive me for endangering your life.'

331

She glanced at his face, blinking back moisture from her eyes. 'Did you have feelings for him, Abram?'

Bram stared at her, not believing his ears. '*What?*'

'I know you didn't do anything.' She forced herself to look at him. 'But did you have feelings for him?'

Bram's face turned stony, his voice permeated with anger. 'You can think whatever you want about me. I don't care. But don't you dare call yourself a religious woman. Yitzchak was my best friend. And a truly religious woman knows what real friendship is all about. For you to ask me such a question is reprehensible. You should be ashamed of yourself.'

He slammed the door and stomped off, leaving her alone with her thoughts, her fears, and her tears.

26

Oliver knocked on the open door, then walked inside Berger's office. Marge followed.

The place was half-empty or half-full, depending on one's perspective. The diplomas and certificates had been taken off the walls, but the books were still shelved. On the floor rested a dozen half-packed boxes. Berger was on a step stool, depleting the top shelf of its contents.

In Oliver's mind, it appeared as if Berger was planning to bolt. Which gave all the more credence to his Fisher/Tyne conspiracy theory. But Berger offered a different explanation.

'Three of my associates have been murdered, Detective. I don't plan to stick around to make it an even number.'

Marge said, 'So you're running out on the hospital—'

'Not at all.' Berger stood on his tiptoes and extracted the larger medical tomes from the highest shelf. 'I'm not running out on anyone.' His voice was remarkably steady. 'I've applied for a much deserved sabbatical. And I'm taking it whether or not it's approved.'

'Leaving the hospital in the lurch,' Marge said. 'New Christ has already lost Sparks and Decameron. Without you, it's going to fold.'

'Better that than the hospital providing me a hero's burial.' He stepped down, holding an armful of books. 'You two don't have a smidgen of empathy regarding my plight, do you?'

'I have a smidgen,' Oliver said.

The doctor shook his head, kneeled down, and placed the texts in a box. 'Figures. The police are noted for their lack of human compassion.'

Oliver said, 'Why were you and Shockley fudging the Curedon data?'

Berger jerked his head up. 'Come again?'

'You and Shockley had hacked into Fisher/Tyne's data banks and were doing funny business with Kenneth Leonard's Curedon numbers. I want to know why.'

'You're crazy. You've got no warrant. Get out of here.'

Marge said, 'We've traced a cuckoo's egg to your computer, Dr. Berger. Ordinarily, computer hacking's a federal crime. Meaning you'd plea your case to the FBI. But since we've got the rather major matter of a couple of murders—'

'I had nothing to do with them!' Berger snapped. 'Look, people! Open your eyes! I'm *terrified*! What the hell do you two *want* from me.'

'How about some answers to some questions.'

'But I don't know anything!'

'I think you do,' Oliver said. 'I think you knew that Kenneth Leonard was on to you and Shockley.'

'I haven't the slightest idea to what you're referring. You're talking gobbledygook.'

'Look, sir,' Marge said patiently, 'why don't you just start at the beginning. Because, at the very least, you're going to get hit with charges of scientific fraud.'

Berger's eyes darted from side to side. 'Get out of here! Both of you! And take your disgusting accusations with you.'

Oliver held up a dozen sheets of computer paper. 'Know what these are?'

'I don't know. And I don't care.'

Marge said, 'They're the latest Curedon data trials, Dr. Berger. Does that pique your interest?'

Berger stopped packing, ran his tongue across his teeth.

Oliver said, 'The latest report given to the FDA by *Decameron himself*. After he ran the data. *Decameron* ran it. *Not* Fisher/Tyne. Know what? These numbers looked very promising. Which is particularly puzzling. Because the numbers Fisher/Tyne had been giving the FDA hadn't been all that hot. And Gordon Shockley had told us that *his* numbers hadn't been too good, either.'

Marge said, 'Which means there was a discrepancy between Decameron's statistics and what Fisher/Tyne was reporting to the FDA.'

Berger got up, wiped his hands on a handkerchief. 'You two burst into my office, making all sorts of ridiculous claims, holding up generic data charts—'

'They're not generic. Come take a look for yourself.' Oliver proffered Berger the results.

Berger hesitated, then snatched the papers and skimmed them. He held them aloft. 'Where'd you get hold of these?'

Though he hated to admit it – even to himself – the sentiment was there: *God bless Farrell*. Oliver said, 'None of your business.'

'This is confidential information,' Berger said. 'There is no way you could have gotten this unless you did something illegal. I could have your badges for this.'

Oliver grinned. 'I don't think so.'

Again, Berger looked at the papers. 'For all I know, you could have made up some numbers—'

'We got the numbers directly from the FDA,' Oliver interrupted. 'That can be verified.'

'So . . . Reggie doctored the data. I'm not surprised. He's a worm. And to tell you the truth, I'm not sorry he's dead.'

'And why would he doctor data?'

'I guess we'll never know. Now get out of here with your horrid slander. Because we all know that both of you two aren't capable of understanding *any* results, let alone interpreting them properly.'

'No, they can't interpret the data, Myron. But I can.'

Berger whipped his head around. Elizabeth Fulton was at his door, arms folded across her chest. 'I accessed your files this morning, Myron—'

'That's illegal—'

'It's peanuts compared to what you did. Snowing all of us . . . me, Reggie, Azor. Hacking into the Fisher/Tyne data network and changing the numbers. You made them look worse to get the Curedon trials stopped.'

'You're finished, Liz!' Myron cried out. 'I'm bringing you up on charges with the medical ethics board—'

'I saw your hidden research, Myron,' Elizabeth said venomously. 'You and Shockley were working on your own chemically related T-cell inhibitor. You were trying to undercut Azor, undercut the entire Curedon project!'

'I'm a goddamn scientist in my own right. And I've got a right to work on whatever I damn well please without someone spying on me.'

'But you have no right to falsify *our* data to further your own research!' She walked up to him, spit in his face. 'How could you do such a low—'

'Fuck you, lady!' Berger shouted. 'Who do you think brought Curedon to fruition in the early years? Who do you think actually took the drug from something theoretical and developed it into something that's marketable? You think Azor developed the drug? Lady, let me tell you something. The bastard stole my research—'

'What are you *talking* about, Myron? All your research came from Azor's lab. I was there.'

'Lady, you came in after *I* handed him the drug on a silver platter. Because no one was interested in what Myron Berger had to say about T-cell inhibitors. Only what the great Azor Sparks had to say. Meanwhile, Azor didn't give a flying fuck about Curedon. All Azor was interested in was Jesus and harvesting hearts. Him and that stupid CB radio, trying to outrun the ambulances to the fatal car accidents, hoping to walk away with some poor brain-dead bastard's heart—'

'You're an asshole!'

'And you're a stupid bitch. A washed-up one at that. Because I'm filing charges on you for scientific espionage—'

'Doc, I don't think you understand the severity of the charges against you,' Marge said. 'Because you're under arrest for murder—'

'How dare you imply—'

'She's not implying, she's doing,' Oliver stated. 'Now put your hands behind your back.'

'Get out of here!'

Marge said, 'Doctor, don't make this hard on us.'

Berger screamed, flailing his arms about. 'Get out of here!' He threw a book at Oliver. *'Out!'*

Oliver flung him against the wall, kicked his feet apart, and attempted to hold him still while Marge swung Berger's arm around his back. But the doctor continued to resist, trying to break free of Oliver's grip.

Marge clamped on the right cuff, but was having trouble securing it to his left arm. 'Sir, please stop moving!'

'Get out—'

Oliver pressed his body into Berger's, trying to immobilize him. He broke into a sweat, struggling to keep Berger steady. Motherfucker was surprisingly strong. 'Got it, Marge?'

Berger screamed.

'I think you're hurting him,' Elizabeth said meekly.

Oliver was dripping rivers from his face. 'Got it?'

'Just . . . about . . . damn!' Water rolled off Marge's forehead. She jerked up Berger's left hand. 'I swear I'm gonna break—'

'Easy, Detective.'

Berger let out another shriek.

Again, Elizabeth said, 'I think you're *really* hurting him.'

Oliver jammed Berger against the wall. 'Got it?'

'I . . .' Marge heard the double lock click into place. 'Got it.'

'Oh God!' Berger moaned out. 'I swear I didn't kill anyone. I swear, I swear, I—'

'I'm gonna read you your rights,' Oliver said.

'Oh God, oh God, oh God! Liz, I swear I never killed anyone—'

'Will you kindly shut up?' Oliver said.

'Don't talk, Myron,' Elizabeth said. 'Don't say anything until you've talked to a lawyer.'

'You believe me?'

'Of course. Scientific pilfering is one thing. But murder?'

'Will you both shut up so I can Mirandize him?' Oliver yelled.

'I want my lawyer,' Berger blurted out.

'If you don't let me get this out, you ain't gonna have anything, Doc.'

Finally, Berger fell quiet. Oliver took a deep breath, then read the doctor his rights. At the conclusion, Berger again requested a lawyer.

'No problemo, Doc,' Oliver said. 'You can have your lawyer. Let's go.'

But Berger resisted walking. 'Elizabeth, please help me!'

'Let's go,' Oliver said, pushing him forward.

'Myron, who should I call?' Elizabeth asked.

'Gold and Brown,' he shouted out.

'You can tell them we're going to book their client at the Devonshire Substation,' Marge said.

Oliver shoved him forward. 'He'll probably be transferred to Van Nuys jail for arraignment—'

'Oh God!' Berger moaned. 'Stop. I'll tell you everything. Just *please* don't book me for murder.'

Oliver stopped walking. 'You'll tell us everything?'

'Yes, yes.' Berger nodded rapidly. 'I'll tell you everything.'

'So suddenly you know what I'm talking about,' Oliver said.

'Yes. Yes, I do know. And I'll tell you. Just please don't book me.'

'He asked for a lawyer,' Elizabeth pointed out. 'You can't talk to him now.'

Oliver glared at her. 'One minute you're spitting in the guy's face, the next you're his advocate?'

'He's my colleague!' Elizabeth said. 'We have our own ways

of censuring. I'm not about to let him drown in your hands.'

'Oh *please*!' Marge said wearily. 'C'mon! Let's go.'

'Wait!' Berger yelled out. 'Yes, I'll talk to my lawyer. But I guarantee you, if you wait, you won't be sorry. You'll like what I have to tell you. Just . . . please . . . hold off . . . with the . . . murder charges. Because bottom line, I swear I didn't do it.'

Oliver and Marge exchanged glances. 'Are you willing to take a polygraph?'

'Yes, of course. Right away. Just don't book me.'

Oliver shrugged. 'What exactly do you have in mind, Doc?'

'Let me talk to my lawyer. I know what you want, Detective Oliver. I know you're after the big guys. Please. Be patient. I promise you won't be sorry.'

Oliver looked at Marge. 'What do you think?'

'We should ask the Loo.'

'So we'll ask the Loo.' Oliver paused. 'Should we hold off on booking him?'

Berger looked at Marge with hopeful eyes. She shrugged. 'He gave us a rough time with the arrest—'

'I'm very sorry about that,' Berger said. 'Very sorry. Please. Let me talk to my lawyer. Then I'll talk to you.'

Again, Marge shrugged. 'Okay. You bought yourself some time. You'd better come through.'

Berger smiled. 'I will. I swear I'll make you happy.'

Oliver said, 'Last time someone said those words to me, I wound up with crabs. C'mon. Let's go.'

27

Great to be on the other side of the one-way mirror. Decker leaned against the wall, watching Myron Berger and his lawyer confer. Not that there was much to talk about. The deal had been cut hours ago. The doctor had been guaranteed immunity from prosecution by the FBI on charges of computer tempering, theft, and fraud in exchange for becoming a material witness. And though Berger hadn't been formally booked, the police had retained the right if future information and/or evidence warranted an arrest.

Marge sipped coffee. 'Is my watch fast or is it already seven?'

'Your watch isn't fast.'

'Where does the time go?'

'I don't know.' Decker rubbed his neck. 'Tomorrow night is the sabbath. I can't wait.'

Marge said, 'Are we still on for Sunday?'

'Absolutely.'

'I know Rina's strict with her kitchen, so I don't want to bring any food. How about if I bring flowers?'

'Great. Thanks.' Decker drank from a thermos, regarded the action on the other side of the looking glass. Berger had chosen Justin Dorman as his counsel, a man in his late thirties with styled wheat-colored hair and deep-set brown eyes. His regular features bore a nondescript expression. In his herringbone suit, he looked about as menacing as a model in *GQ*. But he had cut Berger a good plea. Decker had been impressed.

The doctor, on the other hand, was anything but Perma-Prest. His clothes were wrinkled and he needed a shave. More than anything, Berger was tired. Yes, he'd withstood fourteen-hour surgeries, but no endurance test could have prepared him for this.

Decker said, 'You didn't want a piece of the action?'

'Nah.' Marge threw away her plastic cup. 'The deal's been cut. Nothing to do but listen. Might as well do it here where I can make wisecracks.' She observed the scene on the other side, the door opening . . . 'And on with the show.'

Oliver came in the interview room. With him was Mitch Saugust, the deputy DA. Also young – in his thirties – but not as well coiffed nor as well dressed. Saugust was tall but not muscular. His shoulders sloped, his gut spilled over his belt. He shook hands with Dorman, then sat down. Oliver took the chair to his left.

Saugust looked at Oliver. Scott said, 'We're ready whenever you are, Doctor.'

Berger was draped in fatigue. 'Oh my.' He hung his head. 'Where to begin.'

The room was quiet.

'I've been with Azor Sparks for nearly twenty-five years. A few of our colleagues considered us a team. But most didn't. More important, I didn't. I had always looked to Azor as a boss, even though we were in the same graduating class at Harvard medical school.'

He took a deep breath.

'About ten-plus years ago, Azor went back and got a Ph.D. in biochemistry. I always felt he was a bit . . . intimidated by my own master's in chemistry. Because when we used to talk about drug structure – specifically cyclosporin A analogs – he often would be forced to cede to my knowledge, sometimes graciously, sometimes begrudgingly. Not that I was smarter, but I had been more educated in this one particular area.'

Marge said, 'I've found the perfect superhero for Berger.'

'What's that?'

'MIGHTY EGO.'

342

Decker smiled. 'Yeah, egos are something else. They make us able to live with ourselves.'

Marge laughed. 'Otherwise, we'd all crawl up and die from embarrassment.'

Berger kept talking. 'Finally, Azor did go back to UCLA and he did receive a Ph.D. Which again, gave him the formal educational advantage – at least on paper. Being involved in biochemistry years before Azor, I felt I still had the practical edge. I would have liked to further my interest in chemistry, but when Azor went back, I had to pick up the slack around the hospital. Which meant I worked long, long hours——'

Dorman tapped Berger's shoulder, whispered in his ear. Berger sighed and nodded. He went on.

'Admittedly so, Curedon was Azor's brainchild – a highly modified cyclophillin binder which seemed to be a very potent T-cell inhibitor. In theory.'

Berger stopped, regarded his lawyer, Oliver and the deputy DA. They were staring at him. He cleared his throat and continued.

'The point is Azor had developed a potentially wonderful drug in his lab, but he lacked the practical experience to refine it.'

'And that was where you came in,' Oliver stated.

Berger eyed him with suspicion. 'Yes, as a matter of fact, that was where I came in. He developed a very raw analog, I refined it into something more workable, albeit not perfect. Later on, Dr. Decameron and Dr. Fulton were brought into our club. Reggie fine-tuned the drug. Then Elizabeth set up the protocol for Curedon's animal experimentation.'

The doctor smacked his lips.

'Azor had the reputation . . . and Azor got the funding.'

'From the hospital?' Oliver asked.

'From the hospital, from NIH grants, from private donations . . . from everywhere.' Berger clasped his hands together. 'I worked over eight years on Curedon. There was extra pay for me through the grants, but the money hardly made up for the excessive time I had put into the drug. And I should remind you that I was doing this while maintaining a full-time cardiosurgical practice.'

Marge said, 'He needs to remind us, Pete.'

Decker said, 'He's pissed.'

'Doesn't justify what he did.' She paused. 'But it explains his motivation. MIGHTY EGO strikes again. Must be hard to be number two, standing in the shadows of the top dog.' She smiled. 'I should know about that.'

Decker jerked his head. 'Beg your pardon?'

'Oh, nothing . . .' Marge returned her attention to the interview. 'Nothing at all.'

Berger said, 'The finalized drug sold to Fisher/Tyne bore little resemblance to Azor Sparks's original Curedon. The Fisher/Tyne Curedon was developed after years of trial and error by four scientists working as a unit. Yet, Azor got all the credit.'

Oliver said, 'Doctor, Sparks was the . . . how do you say it . . .' He flipped through his notes. 'The primary investigator . . . the acknowledged chief, Dr. Berger. Because it was *his* drug you were refining. You knew you weren't going to get the glory at the outset, didn't you?'

'Yes, but . . . I mean . . . another—'

'You certainly must have known you weren't going to get the money,' Oliver pressed.

Berger glared at him.

Oliver said, 'True or false?'

Dorman said, 'Detective, can we keep it friendly here? My client has been completely cooperative—'

'Think so? Then next time you try to arrest him.'

'Detective—'

'Do you know how much money Fisher/Tyne paid Dr. Sparks for the rights to acquire Curedon?'

Anger flickered from Berger's eyes. 'Something in the seven-figure range.'

'Do you know if any other fees were owed to him?' Oliver asked.

Berger said, 'I was aware of something in the contract that promises him additional monies should the sales of Curedon reach a critical limit.'

Marge said, 'Why are some people so mealymouthed? "Additional monies should sales reach a critical limit." '

'Just the way academics talk.'

'You think guys like him and Sparks ever drop their masks?'

'Azor rode motorcycles.'

Marge nodded. It was a good point.

Oliver asked, 'Is that clause in the contract – the one that promises him money if Curedon has big sales – still in effect after Dr. Sparks's death?'

'I don't know.'

Saugust said, 'Detective, why don't we let Dr. Berger continue . . . do you think you might take out a little of the history, sir, and bring it back to contemporary times?'

'I'm just trying to give you the appropriate background,' Berger snapped.

'Of course,' Saugust said.

Berger said, 'Well, to make a long story short, even with all the hoopla of Curedon's arrival, there were still problems. But nothing the team couldn't hammer out.

'Since I was so instrumental in Curedon's development, Azor assigned me the role of liaison from our labs to Fisher/Tyne. Sparks also gave me a bonus when Curedon was bought. Nothing compared to what Azor had made. But it was a nice gesture.'

'Did he give all his colleagues bonuses?' Oliver asked.

'Yes, I believe he did.'

'Generous guy.'

'He certainly had enough to play with.'

The room was quiet.

'I took my job very seriously,' Berger said. 'Worked very hard with Fisher/Tyne, smoothing out the areas that needed improvement.'

'Such as?' Oliver asked.

'Primarily improving the efficacy of the drug and the honing down of the unwarranted side effects. As I worked through these problems, studying the interactions at a cellular level, specifically Curedon's propensity for human cyclophillin binding and its corrolate of immunosuppression, I discovered something very interesting. I proposed the following theory. That if one modified the drug's butenyl ring structure, you could further increase the affinity for cyclophillin binding to a fourfold level. On a theoretical basis only, of course.'

'Of course,' Oliver said.

Dorman said, 'Doctor, I think you're going to have to simplify the technical aspects of your research.'

Berger was peeved. 'On a strictly theoretical basis, I thought I discovered a better drug than Curedon.'

'Ah.' Oliver held up his finger. 'That I understand.'

'Mind you, I had nothing tangible. Just an idea. And a very abstract one at that. But I was pleased with myself. Nevertheless, I didn't think about pursuing it. I didn't have the time or the resources. In passing, I happened to mention my idea to someone at Fisher/Tyne. He got very excited.'

'Shockley,' Oliver said.

'No, his boss, Joseph Grammer. Dr. Grammer was intrigued. We met a couple of times. Talked a bit about my idea. Developing any drug is a very expensive proposition. And like they say, a bird in the hand . . .'

No one spoke.

'Grammer took the matter up with Fisher/Tyne's executive board. He came back and told me the bad news: I had almost been granted funding. But then the moment of truth. The board didn't have enough funds to support my research, and support Curedon at the same time. Since Fisher/Tyne had already spent an enormous sum for Curedon, and since it was almost ready for human trials, the board wasn't keen on going back to square one with my analog. The board voted to continue Curedon research. And I was left in the cold.'

'Made you bitter?' Oliver asked.

'No,' Berger insisted. 'I was not bitter. Disappointed, yes. But not bitter. I continued on with Curedon, figuring the matter to be dropped.'

The room was quiet.

'Oh my,' Berger said. 'Oh my, oh my.'

'Deal's been cut, sir,' Saugust said. 'Why don't you just get it off your chest.'

'About a week later . . .' Berger sighed. 'A week later, after my defeat, Gordon Shockley came to me with a proposition. How would I like to see my theoretical drug turned into a practical moneymaking venture? I asked him what he had in mind.'

Berger's hands turned into white-knuckled fists.

'He started naming numbers—'

'Who named numbers?'

'Shockley. Shockley informed me about the enormous sums of money that Fisher/Tyne was planning to spend on Curedon's R and D. He said if we could develop something even equally as good as Curedon and cut our fees by half . . . we could undersell Curedon and still make out like bandits.'

'Undersell to whom?'

'To Fisher/Tyne. It's happened before. A company will abandon a project *if* they have something better lined up. In truth, we would have sold to any drug company willing to put up cash.'

'And you agreed to work with Shockley,' Oliver said.

'We live in a country that prides itself on free market enterprise. As long as patents laws weren't violated, I did nothing illegal in agreeing to develop a new drug.'

'Maybe not illegal, but unethical,' Oliver said.

'Was it any more unethical than Azor taking all the credit for work I did?'

Oliver looked at his notes, then at Berger. He sat back in his chair. 'Correct me if I'm wrong, but Dr. Fulton – that's Elizabeth Fulton for the records – she told us that any scientific discoveries that came from Sparks's lab were *his* to publish. That's just how it is in the academic world.'

Berger was miffed. 'Do you want to hear my story or *not*?'

'Besides,' Oliver went on, 'Sparks wasn't screwing you up by monkeying with the computers—'

'I'm *getting* to that,' Berger responded fiercely.

'Rather slowly,' Saugust whispered under his breath.

Berger gave Saugust a hard glance, but went on. 'Not wanting to be accused of academic pirating, I quit the job as liaison and handed it over to Reggie. In private . . . on my *own* time . . . I began working with Shockley on developing a competing drug to Curedon.'

'Where'd you get the money? Where'd you get the *lab*?'

'Shockley provided the money, told me he'd settle the account once we sold my drug.' Berger rubbed his cheeks. 'Since I had no other source of funding, I didn't probe. As far as the labs . . . I worked on my off hours and weekends at Fisher/Tyne—'

'So that's *really* where you were the night of the murders,' Oliver butted in. 'Tustin's right around the corner from Fisher/Tyne's labs. You weren't at any *dinner show*—'

'I was there—'

'So tell me about the play, Doc. Better yet, whistle me a tune from the musical.'

Berger was silent.

* * *

'Way to go, Scott!' Decker said.

Marge shook her head. 'I should have picked up on that. Tustin being so close to Fisher/Tyne.'

'Me, too. So this time it's Scott. He did good.'

He did good.

Oliver said, 'Your wife wasn't home when we called your house. Where was she?'

'She had nothing to do—'

'I'm not saying she did,' Oliver interrupted. 'Where was she?'

Berger sighed. 'At her sister's house. When I heard the horrid news coming home from the lab, I realized I was going to have to explain why I was so far away from my house. I bought a copy of the *Orange County Register*, looked in the entertainment section, saw the listing for the dinner show. I stopped by and picked a couple of ticket stubs off the sidewalk. If I had told the truth . . . that I was at Fisher/Tyne working on a competitive drug, people would have gotten the wrong idea.'

'Or the right one—'

'I did not kill Azor!'

'Detective, please!' Dorman cut in.

Oliver said, 'Go on, Dr. Berger.'

'I went home . . .' Berger sighed again. 'Quickly changed into dress clothes, called up my wife, and told her to borrow something dressy from her sister. Then I had her take me to the hospital, to make it look like we were coming back from the theater. She was furious at me . . . having to invent this facade for me. But . . . she was also scared. She knew if it all came out . . .'

'Somebody see you at Fisher/Tyne, Doc?' Oliver asked.

'I don't know. Maybe. There are guards there. But I don't check in with them as I have my own key from Shockley.' Berger dropped his head. 'My work is very hush-hush.'

'So no one can verify—'

'I swear I didn't kill anyone!' Berger was almost in tears. 'Look, I've taken a lie-detector test. I'll take another one. I'm telling you the truth.'

'There goes his alibi,' Marge said.
  'Don't he know it,' Decker said.
  'What do you think?'
  'I think we need to question him extensively.'

'Do you want me to go on?' Berger asked quietly.
  Oliver nodded. 'Yeah, continue your story, Doc.'
  'It's the truth.'
  'Okay, it's the truth.'
  'Where was I?'
  'You were working on a competing drug to Curedon.'
  'Yes. Correct. And things were going very well. I was making incredibly good progress on my drug . . . which I named . . . Marasporin . . . which was a marriage between several known cyclosporins and Curedon. I was surprised how fast things were going. There was just one problem.'
  'What?' Oliver asked.
  'Reggie Decameron,' Berger said. 'He was working with Fisher/ Tyne on Curedon . . . smoothing out the bumps. Actually, he was ironing out the wrinkles faster than I could develop my drug. Shockley was alarmed at how scientifically facile Reggie was. The man, for all his perversions, was a brilliant thinker. And contrary to what I stated before, I am sorry he's dead.'

Marge said, 'He just gave us a reason for wanting Decameron out of the picture.'
  'Yes, he did.'
  'Stupidity or is he really innocent?'
  'He passed the lie-detector test,' Decker pointed out.
  'He is also an admitted liar.'

Decker nodded, took out his notepad, wrote down Berger's words, and underlined them.

Berger said, 'Shockley was frantic with worry. After all, he had invested money in me. Lots and lots of money, or so he told me. I, for one, suspect he had invested other people's money in me. So who knows to whom he was beholden. He suggested a way to slow Curedon's progress with the FDA.'

'Tamper with the data,' Oliver said. 'You plugged in false data to make Curedon look bad.'

'Not *bad*, heavens no. Just . . . not as *good*.'

'The higher mortality rate Decameron was concerned with,' Oliver said. 'He was right. It was a technical error. But one that was done on purpose.'

Averting his eyes, Berger whispered, 'It was a terrible mistake on my part.'

'Not a mistake, Doctor, A felony—'

'Detective, please,' Dorman chided. 'Dr. Berger has been made aware of the seriousness of his error in judgment. There's no need to remind him.'

Berger said, 'My . . . crime, I think, is a by-product of the computer age. One tampers with numbers in machines, one is never confronted with the direct consequences of one's errors. I didn't see faces, I just saw numbers.'

'All those newfangled falderah machines,' Marge grumped. 'Just suck you into sinnin'.'

'Talk about cheap rationalizations.' Decker rolled his eyes. 'Satan goes high-tech.'

Berger continued. 'Fisher/Tyne logs its computer time meticulously. All operators have to keep precise records of their machine usage. We couldn't use the computer on Fisher/Tyne's end because unaccounted minutes would show up on the log.'

'So you got to the computer on your end,' Oliver said. 'How'd you break into Leonard's system?'

Berger smiled ruefully. 'How do you think? Leonard was in on it.'

No one spoke. Finally, Oliver said, 'Leonard was in on it?'

'Yes.'

'For how much?'

'Not an even cut, but a sizable portion. Shockley arranged it all. At that point, I was already drowning in deceit. I felt I had no choice but to agree.'

'Don't tell me,' Oliver said. 'Then Leonard got greedy.'

Berger hid his face for a moment. 'It does sound like a sordid story, doesn't it?'

'Keep going, Doctor,' Saugust prompted.

Berger said, 'Kenny started whining. That he had the most to lose because he was actively doing all the illegal shenanigans. And this was true. He demanded a bigger cut and made threatening noises when we balked.'

Oliver said, 'He tells on you, he screws himself up.'

'Actually, Detective, we pointed that out to him.'

'And?'

'And we never got any farther in our negotiations.' Berger wiped sweat from his brow. 'Because a week later, Azor was murdered. Not knowing what was going on, I kept a low profile, stopped taking calls from either of them. Then yesterday . . . when I found out about Kenny and Reggie . . .'

He wiped sweat off his brow and bald head with a handkerchief. 'This should be self-evident. I became truly terrified.'

Oliver put down his notebook. 'Was Shockley the only one you dealt with at Fisher/Tyne?'

'He's the only one I know about.' Berger paused. 'Though I have no way of proving this . . . I always felt that Shockley was moving with Grammer's permission.'

'You have nothing to tie Grammer to your activities?'

352

'No.'

Oliver consulted a moment with Saugust.

'What?' Dorman said.

Saugust said, 'Would your client be willing to wear a wire to try to get something out of Shockley?'

'That wasn't part of the deal,' Dorman said. 'And since he was already offered immunity for testifying, I don't see where that would be in Dr. Berger's best interest.'

Oliver said, 'Might be in his best interest to obtain a new identity.'

Dorman said, 'What are you implying?'

Oliver said, 'Just that it's going to be hard for him to practice medicine after all this comes out.'

'Why should it come out?' Berger's voice was panicked. 'I thought I cut a deal.'

'You're associated with three dead men, sir,' Oliver replied. 'It's bound to come out.'

The room was quiet.

'Not that I can speak for the FBI,' Oliver said, 'but they might be willing to fix him up with a new set of papers so he could practice medicine without harassment.'

Dorman said, 'You don't have the power to do that.'

Oliver said, 'No, *I* don't. But the FBI does. And you know, your client is still under investigation for murder. Especially now that he doesn't have anyone who could verify his whereabouts—'

Berger interrupted. 'I had nothing to do—'

'Myron, please.' Dorman took out a pen and clicked it several times. 'I'll take the matter up with the local agents here.'

'I told you all I know,' Berger whined. 'I don't want to wear a wire.'

'Myron, we'll talk about this later.' To Oliver, Dorman said, 'Anything else?'

Oliver said, 'What was Sparks doing all this time?'

'Pardon?'

'He must have been disappointed in Curedon's mediocre results.

He must have looked over the data. Are you telling me he didn't have any idea about what was going on?'

'Azor was disturbed by the results, yes. But he had confidence in Reggie. Actually, it was Reggie who was upset. He couldn't understand why, after riding this tremendous upswing of wonderful results, his data suddenly crashed.'

Berger spoke softly.

'The team got our readouts from Fisher/Tyne. Because the company owned the drug. But I know that a couple of times, Reggie got hold of data directly from Fisher/Tyne's labs, before it went into their computers—'

'Before Ken Leonard got a chance to doctor it.'

'Yes. I knew Reggie was moving in fast. It was just a matter of time . . .'

'Yet Dr. Sparks never became suspicious.'

'Dr. Sparks had other problems to contend with – namely getting hearts. We have a severe shortage of healthy hearts. It's gotten so bad that we've been reduced to repairing hearts with minor defects and recycling them for our sickest transplant patients,' Berger muttered. 'That's what happens when the government gets involved.'

Oliver asked, 'What are you talking about?'

'What?'

'The government being involved,' Oliver said. 'Are they hoarding hearts or something?'

Berger smiled. The first smile of the entire session. 'I was speaking off the top of my head. No, the government is not hoarding hearts. What the government has done is pass *good* legislation that has done its job. Unfortunately, it's made our jobs as cardiac surgeons a little harder.'

No one spoke.

'The helmet law,' Berger said. 'Since they've enacted the helmet law, we don't get the fatal head-injury motorcycle crashes. Meaning we just don't get hearts like we used to.'

28

'So now we know why Sparks was involved with the bikers and their People's Environment Freedom Act or whatever the heck it's called.' Marge closed the door to Decker's office. 'Sparks wanted the law repealed so he could harvest hearts.'

Oliver sat in Decker's desk chair, exhausted after four hours of extensive questioning. The minutiae of Berger's activities the night of Sparks's murder. Berger had taken them through his activities in the lab step by step, giving them a plausible time frame. In the end, they had no choice but to release him. Not enough evidence to hold him for murder.

'A doctor needs a hobby.' Oliver shook his head. 'And here I thought vampires were all made up.'

'Sparks was collecting hearts, not eating them,' Marge said.

'Out of my chair, Scott.' Decker checked the clock. It was almost one A.M. Today was Friday and the evening would bring in the Sabbath, his family's day of prayer, meditation, and *rest*. As far as Decker was concerned, time couldn't pass quickly enough.

Oliver got up and parked himself in a folding chair. 'When we arrested Berger, he'd blurted out the same thing to Dr. Fulton. That Sparks was obsessed with getting hearts, used to try to pick them out of dead accident victims.'

Decker remembered New Chris's intensive care nurse talking about Sparks and his police band radio. How the doctor had raced to accidents, ostensibly to help out the victims. Had he only been interested in seizing body parts?

'I don't know if it's illegal,' Decker said, 'but preying on victims like that is major league creepy.' He sat down. 'So now we can explain why Sparks became a weekend warrior. The main question is . . . is Myron Berger telling the truth?'

No one spoke.

Decker said, 'Maybe after the Curedon meeting, after Decameron and Sparks parted ways in the doctors' parking lot, Berger came up to Sparks and invited him to Tracadero's. Then Berger jumped him in the back alley.'

'I don't see Berger taking out Sparks by himself,' Marge said. 'Too much damage, too much blood.'

Decker said, 'He's a surgeon. He's used to slicing and dicing.'

'Maybe Berger was the lure,' Oliver said. 'Once Sparks reached Tracadero's, Shockley pulled the plug on him . . . on all of them. Either Shockley or his boss, this Grammer guy.'

'But if the killings have to do with Fisher/Tyne and Curedon,' Marge asked, 'what were Bram's porno magazines doing at Decameron's murder scene?'

Oliver said, 'Maybe Decameron and Bram were lovers. Shockley found them, then left them around to put the blame on Bram.'

'Then why didn't Bram defend himself when I arrested him?' Decker said. 'Why was he willing to take a murder rap?'

Oliver blurted out, 'Maybe they were *Luke's*, Deck. Ever think that maybe Luke was having an affair with Decameron? He showed up at Decameron's house for a little morning nookie. He walked in, found Reggie and Leonard dead.'

'Then what?' Marge asked.

Oliver scrunched his brow. 'From that point on, everything happened like Luke said. He panicked, called his brother Bram. The priest, being a good guy, covered for Luke's homosexuality and took Luke's magazines. Then, in a double fake-out, Luke came back the next day and covered for Bram. Because, hell, let's face it. It's easier in life to be a gay priest than a gay married guy with two kids.

'You're using pretzel logic, Scott,' Decker said. 'He covered for him, who covered for him—'

'Isn't that what identical twins do?' Oliver retorted. 'They play mind games with people. Take tests for each other, go out with each other's dates. Decker, look at Luke marrying Bram's girlfriend. Bram's protecting his twin brother, keeping him in the closet for convention's sake.'

'Protecting your married twin's proclivities is one thing,' Decker said. 'But taking a murder rap for him is quite another.'

No one spoke.

Decker said, 'Luke told us that Reggie called him early in the morning. Decameron sounded serious, all business. Luke felt that Decameron might have been interested in blackmail.'

Oliver shook his head. 'By everyone's account, Decameron was a straight shooter.' He laughed. 'Decameron was a straight gay shooter. Why should Decameron, a brilliant doctor and a man who got his kicks out of flaunting his unconventionality, suddenly turn to a sneaky profession like blackmail? Luke, on the other hand, is lying scum—'

'He passed a polygraph—'

' 'Cause he's lying scum. Lying scum can beat polygraphs.'

Decker said, 'Maybe you're right. But let's go back to basics . . . the MO of all three murders.'

'Shooting *and* stabbing,' Marge said.

'Yes, shooting *and* stabbing,' Decker said. 'More than one person. Sounds like a bunch of bikers. Ideas?'

Marge said, 'The bikers were resentful because they found out that Sparks only wanted them for their hearts.' She made a face. 'My, that sounds awful!'

'A revenge motive,' Decker said. 'That's biker mentality for sure. These guys have been known to kill over bar stools. Imagine how they'd feel if they knew Sparks was interested in cutting out their internal organs.'

He rubbed his neck.

'That's one theory. Now, let's talk about something else. If Sparks wasn't really interested in his biker buddies except for their hearts, what was William Waterson doing with Emmanuel "Grease Pit" Sanchez up in Canyon Country?'

'Giving money to the bikers to repeal the helmet law,' Marge said.

'While Sparks was alive, I could see him giving money to the cause. But do you think he would have left money for that in his will?'

'Why not?' Marge said. 'For the benefit of future heart surgery.'

'You're both missing the point,' Oliver said. 'What do bikers have to do with Leonard and Decameron? And Myron's where-abouts are now unverifiable. He's a noted liar—'

'He passed the test twice—'

'Those tests are useless—'

'They're hard to beat—'

'I think we're all too tired to think straight,' Decker interrupted. 'Maybe something'll come in our sleep. We all got paperwork to finish up.' He stood and opened the door. 'We'll discuss this tomorrow.'

'Are we being dismissed?' Marge asked.

'Yes, you're being dismissed. I'd like to make it home before daybreak.'

Marge said, 'You're acting very brass, Pete.'

Decker grinned. 'It's lonely at the top.'

Squinting from the hot glare of morning sunlight, precariously gripping five grocery bags, Rina managed to make it from her car to the front door. She felt the weight of the merchandise in her back and shoulders, her arms aching as she rooted in her purse for her keys. Finally, she gave up, lowered the bags onto the porch, and rummaged around her handbag. She had a crashing headache, the scarf around her head choking her scalp like a vise.

What a morning! Peter and the boys had overslept, so breakfast had been fast and furious. Then Hannah suddenly decided she didn't want to go to nursery school. Her watch said half-past ten. It felt like midnight.

She unlocked the front door and picked up two grocery bags. As soon as she walked over the threshold, she threw off her head covering, shook out her hair, and headed for the kitchen.

Why did Hannah have to have a temper tantrum this morning? *Friday* morning. The busiest day of her week with the house to clean and the Shabbos cooking to do.

She laid the bags on the kitchen counter, turned around, and jumped back.

Bram laid the other three bags on the kitchen table. 'Hi.'

'You *scared* me!'

'Sorry.'

She took a deep breath and let it out. Turned her back to him, began unpacking groceries. 'You shouldn't be here. I can't be alone with you, you know that.'

'But it's okay to be alone with me in a car?'

'I can't believe you're actually equating *then* to *now*! Also, a car's a public place. My house isn't. Besides, one *aveyrah* doesn't make another one permissible.'

'Then let's take a walk.'

She faced him, trying to control her hostility. 'I don't want to take a walk. I have work to do.'

Bram went over to the back door and opened it. 'Okay?'

Rina bit back her waspish tongue, angry that he was snowing her with his knowledge of the Jewish laws. A man and a woman couldn't be alone in a closed room for modesty reasons unless, of course, they were married. Opening an outside door, turning private quarters into a public domain, made it technically allowable for them to be together. She crossed her arms in front of her chest. 'What?'

'Can I sit down?'

'Do whatever you want.' She returned her attention to her groceries. Then stopped, counted to five. 'Would you like something to drink?'

'No, thank you.' Bram sat at the kitchen table, pulled out an

359

envelope of photographs from his pocket. 'Before I forget, I was going through my closets at the rectory. Thought you might like to have these.'

Rina took the pictures, scanned through them.

Old snapshots. Ancient history. Shmueli must have been around four. He was sitting on Yitzy's lap. In front of them was a simple Hebrew storybook – a child's version of *Lech Le'cha*, the third chapter of Genesis, the story of Abraham's calling. Shmueli was pointing to a *passuk*, a line of text, his face bunched in concentration.

Yitzy's narrow face appeared serene – a spiritual glow in his eyes, his complexion pale but not pasty. His generous mouth held a small approving smile, his hand wrapped tightly around his son's waist. Amazing how sketchy he had become in her mind. How she had once been married to such a healthy, handsome man. There were three pictures of that same scene.

Then two more of another pose. A tiny Yaakov riding Yitzy's shoulders, his little hands holding on to Yitzy's sandy-colored beard. In the background was a young woman wearing a long skirt and a *tichel*.

Had she ever been that young? Had that ever been her life? She found her throat had tightened, couldn't look at the remaining snapshots. She stuffed them all back into the envelope.

'Thank you, I'll put them in the boys' photo albums. They'll appreciate them very much.'

'You're welcome.'

Bram fixed his eyes upon her. Once upon a time, the sight of Rina with her hair cascading down her shoulders, would have made him sick with desire, would have sent a raging fire throughout his body. Now, as he gazed upon her, his passions calm and controlled, he was grateful that all he felt was the fear of God in his breast and the love of Jesus in his heart. He knew it wasn't due to any physical change in Rina. If anything, she had become more beautiful. What a difference a wedding band made.

He said, 'Your hair's uncovered.'

Rina's hand reached for her head. She dashed out of the room and retrieved her scarf. Though her head was pounding, she wrapped it tightly around her hair, hiding all of it from view. She found a bottle of Peter's Advil and helped herself. Then she went back into the kitchen. Went back to unpacking groceries. 'Why'd you come here?'

'To apologize. At least, can you look at me?'

Rina turned around. Though his face was drawn, his complexion looked healthier today than yesterday. She realized it was because he had shaved and his hair had been washed.

Softly, she said, 'I could never stay mad at you. It never happened, okay?'

'But it did happen.' He locked eyes with her. 'My behavior yesterday was wretched by anyone's standards. For someone who dares to call himself a man of God, it was abhorrent. I took my frustrations out on you. I'm very sorry.'

Rina turned away. 'No need to apologize. I know what it's like to experience rotten times.'

'It's no excuse.' Bram stood, walked over to the open door, stared into the backyard. 'Rina, I have spent the entire night thinking about what you asked me—'

'Bram—'

'You asked me a question. It deserves an answer. Bear with me, all right?'

Rina was silent.

'I have tried to relive every moment I was with Yitzy ... from the time I first met him until the last time I saw him. My own mental video of the times we spent together alone ... which was very substantial.'

He ran his hand through his hair.

'I can honestly say to you that there was never, *ever*, even a wee hint of impropriety on my part. In all the time I knew him, Yitzchak was what he was. A righteous *Tzaddik* and a loving father and

361

husband. And my behavior toward him had always been above reproach. But . . .'

He swallowed hard, his eyes fixed upon the corral.

'But there were . . . as you put it . . . feelings.'

Rina said nothing.

'There were feelings,' Bram faced her. 'Vague sexual feelings.'

Rina leaned against the counter, studied her hands. 'Towards Yitzchak.'

'At the time, I had assumed so, since they came on shortly after I met him and disappeared shortly after he died.'

He shrugged.

'I didn't know quite what to make of them since they were a new experience for me. Discounting that aberrant time in both of our lives, I've always been a man of large spiritual needs and small physical appetites. I don't eat much, I'm rarely thirsty, don't drink alcohol beyond an occasional beer. I've never taken drugs, never even smoked a cigarette.'

'Nothing wrong with that.'

'Not at all.' He paused. 'And . . . also . . . I've never had much in the way of a sex drive. Something that's apparently not genetic, judging from the way my brother chased girls in high school.'

Rina looked at him, said nothing.

'So when I got these feelings,' Bram said, 'I really didn't know what to make of them. I just . . . attributed them to Yitzchak . . . then went ahead and ignored them. They certainly didn't get in the way of our friendship.'

'Did he . . .' Rina took a breath. 'Did Yitzchak ever display . . .' She turned away. 'Never mind.'

'The answer to your unasked question is an emphatic no.'

Rina covered her mouth. 'Good gracious, how could I even think . . .' She started ripping through her grocery bags, placing items on the counter.

'Can you stop?'

'I don't want to.'

'You're making me nervous.'

She spun around. 'What!'

'Why are you killing the messenger? I'm not even giving you bad news. There was never anything between us except fraternal love. Yitzchak was not gay. So calm down.'

She flopped into a kitchen chair. 'I'm not handling this right.' She looked at him. 'You know, Bram. I don't think I ever really thanked you—'

'You thanked me.'

'No, I didn't—'

'We're getting sidetracked. I spent an entire night in tortured self-reflection on this. Can you please let me finish?'

'I'm sorry. Go on.'

'Mazel tov. Where was I?'

'Your vague feelings didn't get in the way of your friendship with my late husband.'

'Right.' He continued his narrative. 'It wasn't until later . . . after Yitzy died . . . during that too brief time we saw each other . . . that I was able to interpret my sexual feelings for what they were.'

He sat back down at the table, avoided her eyes. 'With all my heart. I believe in Jesus' words as holy. I wouldn't be much of a priest if I didn't. Both of our religions forbid adultery. It is the sixth commandment of my law, the seventh of yours. The Savior, Jesus Christ . . .'

He hesitated.

'My Savior, Jesus Christ, has also amended the commandment to condemn *desire*. He teaches us that lusting for another man's wife is equivalent to adultery of the heart. And back then, as a newly graduated seminarian, His words were something I took very *seriously*.'

He paused to collect his thoughts.

'I know that in this day and age, it's fashionable to minimalize . . . even romanticize adultery. Follow your heart, and damn be the consequences. In truth, betrayal is a horrible, destructive beast . . . damaging everything in its path . . . those who betray . . . and those betrayed.'

He glanced at her, looked away.

'It absolutely destroys self-esteem . . . crushes and flattens it like asphalt under a steamroller. In my case, it was particularly hurtful . . . because I was two-timed by my identical twin. I don't know what Dana's motivation was. But I did know her problem with me couldn't have been lack of a physical attraction. Because she traded me for my mirror image. So I was left to think that there had been something terribly wrong with me personally.'

'There was nothing wrong with you, Bram,' Rina said gently. 'You were all kids. And kids do dumb things.'

'Of course. And I absolutely bear no ill will to Dana.'

He stood, again walking over to the open door.

'As far as Luke goes, I love my brother very much. I'd do anything for him. Forgiveness was never the problem. It's the forgetting. Because try as I may to forget, I can still viscerally remember how much it hurt.'

Rina sighed. 'You always talked about it in such a detached way. I never knew how much you were suffering.'

'I don't even know why I told you about it in the first place. It must have just . . . slipped out during one of our marathon discussions. The hurt might have come and gone had the situation not been complicated by Dana's pregnancy, which necessitated a confession to my folks.'

'What a mess!'

'A mess, a disaster, a fiasco, an ordeal . . . all of the above.' He raised his brow. 'Up until then, I had always thought that, no matter what, I was safe from my father's wrath. So there I was, too embarrassed to admit to *anyone* that I'd been screwed over by my own brother, ashamed that I wasn't the kind of guy I thought I should have been, taking the blame for something I didn't do. And there was my father . . . ready to throw me to the wolves.'

Bram let out a small laugh.

'Imagine what Dad would have done to Luke had he found out the truth. The Doctor's vituperative tongue gave me a lot of empathy for what my brothers had been going through.'

'Your father adored you.'

'Yes, in the end, I believe he did. And for all his faults, I adored him as well. But this is all beside the point.'

He licked his lips.

'Like I said, these hazy sexual feelings came on after I met Yitzchak and left after he died. But, in fact, what I'd experienced hadn't been exclusive feelings for him. They were feelings for you, Rina. But being as you were a married woman, and the thought of adultery – even adultery of the heart – was so odious to me back then, I simply transferred them onto what I perceived was a less sinful target. Which was your husband. Easier for me to think of myself as gay than as an adulterer.'

Rina looked at him. 'And I'm to believe that?'

'You know how much I loved you . . . God, how I loved you.' As he smiled, his cheeks pinkened. 'Hard to fake that kind of ardor.'

'You loved Yitzy as well.'

'Yes, I did.' Bram appeared thoughtful. 'I'm a priest. I'm allowed to have a confused sexual orientation.'

Rina started to talk, but laughed instead. 'Abram Matthew, I don't believe you said that!'

'I'll wash my mouth out with soap.' Bram was pensive. 'It's all irrelevant now. Since taking my orders, I've remained a faithful servant to my Lord, Christ. And what I feel in my heart toward you, Yitzchak, my family, or anyone else is strictly between God and me.'

She eyed him. 'So what about the magazines?'

Slowly, Bram fixed his gaze upon her face. 'The press has inferred a gay angle because of Reggie. But even they don't know about the magazines. How'd *you* find out?'

Rina blushed, looked away.

Bram said, 'Your husband wouldn't have told you. What'd you do, Mrs. Decker? Put your ear to the keyhole?'

'Actually, I just picked up the phone extension . . .'

No one spoke.

Rina said, 'You were in trouble. I couldn't just . . . look the other way. You wouldn't have done any less.'

'I appreciate it.' Bram laughed. 'You know why God fashioned woman from Adam's rib—'

'I know the story. I don't need an ethics lecture.'

'Especially not from a murder suspect.'

'That's not funny!' Rina locked eyes with him. 'You *didn't* murder Reggie. But do you know who did?'

'If I did, why would I hold back?'

'You're protecting someone.'

'I'm a priest, Mrs. Decker. I've an out called a sacramental seal. Believe me, I'd hide behind it if I could.'

'So you don't know?'

'Didn't I just say that?'

'Not exactly.' She kept eye contact. 'The magazines, Father Sparks. Whose are they?'

He didn't speak for a long time. Then he said, 'I wish I could tell you differently, but the magazines are mine.'

'I don't believe you.'

'That's your prerogative.'

'Who are you covering for?'

'It's a CIA conspiracy.'

'Why do you have a safe in your apartment?'

Bram furrowed his brow. 'You must have listened in for a *long* time.'

'Sorry, but I left my guilt back at the market. Father, *heal* thyself. *Talk* to me, for goodness sakes!'

Bram was silent, pushed hair out of his eyes.

'I'm *waiting*,' Rina said, tapping her foot.

'Why do I have a safe . . .' Bram's voice was a whisper. 'Because

366

I got held up at gunpoint three years ago—'

'Oh my God, that's awful!'

'It was on a Friday night, after one of our big church fund-raisers. There was a lot of cash and I was alone in the rectory, the veritable sitting duck. Afterward, I figured cash was more secure in my apartment safe than in a church. Sign of the times.'

'I never heard about it, read about it.'

'I never told anyone. I replaced the cash from my own pocket and kept quiet. Hard enough bringing people into the fold. I'm not about to broadcast news that scares people away from God.'

He looked at his watch.

'I know Fridays are busy for you. Thanks for being so generous with your time.'

'Cut the formalities, please. You're always welcome in my home, Abram. You will always be welcome in my home. Anytime, anywhere. No matter *what*!'

'And you, Rina Miriam, are a righteous woman. More than that, you're a spectacular friend whom I dearly love. If I had more time, I'd get all mushy on you.'

'Stay for a moment. Have a cup of coffee.'

'Unfortunately, I can't. I have a meeting with my parish board. My regional bishop is going to be there.'

Rina sighed. 'What do they want?'

'Explanations, I imagine. In theory, they're entitled to them. Too bad they're all going to walk away disappointed. So be it. I humbly submit to God's will.' He smiled. 'Thank you for listening to me ... far less painful than true confession.'

Rina paused. 'Are you sorry you became a priest?'

'No, Rina. I'm not sorry at all. Yesterday I was crazed. I blurted out things in frustration. Going to Rome – becoming ordained – was the best thing that had ever happened to me.'

He looked down, his face rosy with heat.

'One of the best things. And I'm so grateful that you were an instrumental part of it. We both had other destinies to follow. I pray that you're as happy with your choice as I am with mine.'

She looked at the priest. 'I love him with all my heart, Bram.'

'I know you do. And everyone knows the feelings are reciprocated. The Lieutenant isn't very subtle.'

Rina stared at him. 'Are we talking about the same man?'

'Yes, we are.'

'*My* Peter?'

'Yes, *your* Peter. Trust me, Rina, I know these things. If he were any more overt about his love for you, he'd be wearing his heart on a sandwich board instead of his sleeve. I'm very happy for you. For the boys as well. Your family is a gift from God.'

'So we both have things to be thankful about.'

'True.' But his face was pale, sketched with worry lines. Rina wanted to hold him, comfort him as he had done with her. But that was impossible. Different places, different times.

'Are you going to be all right, Bram?'

'Who knows?' He shrugged. 'God gave Abraham ten trials. Let's see how Abram does with one.'

29

If the way to a man's heart was through his stomach, Rina had a monopoly on cardiac tissue. By five o'clock Sunday evening, the entire house had become aromatic with the scents of savory herbs, onions and garlic. Evocative smells. Of Decker's bimonthly childhood Sunday dinners. A rotating affair with the relatives. His mother toiling in the kitchen, wet with heat, a starched apron covering her best black dress, a small strand of pearls around her upright neck. The men in her life – Decker's father, his brother Randy, and him, sitting at the table, stiff in ill-fitting suits. Grandparents, aunts, uncles, and cousins. As soon as the food was served, things began to loosen up. The adults conversing, kids acting like kids, good times . . .

He entered the kitchen. Rina's face was damp, her hair falling down her back in a neat, compact braid. She wore a free-flowing cotton maroon dress that ended midcalf, with midelbow sleeves. Her feet were housed in flats. Though simply dressed, she was still a stunner.

He said, 'Look like you only made enough for the U.S. Army. What do I tell the Navy when it shows up?'

'Funny.' Rina stirred a pot of soup. 'I know I cooked too much for five adults. But it'll freeze.'

'You need a taste tester?'

'You're volunteering for the assignment? What a jewel you are, Peter.'

'It's a nasty job, but someone's got to do it.'

Rina gave him a spoonful of soup. Split pea with beef marrow bones. Decker's taste buds were in heaven. 'Good.'

'Thank you.'

'This looks like enough for me. What are the others going to eat?'

Rina hit him, returned her attention to the rack of lamb in the oven, basted the riblets with a mustard seed and honey sauce. She stood, wiped her hands on a towel. 'Why did you invite Marge over?'

'Just to be friendly. Why?'

'You weren't planning to discuss your cases?'

Decker paused. 'Maybe something'll come up in passing. But that wasn't the purpose of the invitation. Are you worried we'll say things in front of the boys?'

'No, of course not.' She checked the pilaf and turned down the fire.

Decker approached her from behind, wrapped his arms around her waist, kissed her neck. 'No talk about work tonight, okay?'

She turned to him. 'I've got a confession to make.'

He loosened his grip on her. 'This sounds ominous.'

'I saw Bram last Friday,' she said. 'Actually, I saw him on Thursday, too. But that was a very short visit. First time, I came to see him. Second time, he came here.'

Decker looked at her. 'Here.'

Rina nodded.

'Here meaning the house,' he said.

'Yes.'

'Entertaining a murder suspect on the chief investigator's premises.' He dropped his arms to his side. 'That'll sit well with my boss.'

'He's not a suspect. You released him.'

'I did nothing of the sort,' Decker snapped. 'He posted bail.'

'Well, you're the one who lowered his bail.'

'Rina, he's still a *suspect*! You had *no* right—'

'Please don't be mad.'

'You promised *no* interference!' he said.

'Yes, I did.'

'You broke your promise, Rina! How could you do that?'

'You know, according to Jewish law, a husband can nullify his wife's promises.'

'What?'

'A husband can nullify vows and/or oaths made by his wife. Which means you can absolve me of my promise.' She frowned. 'I don't really know if you can do it *ex post facto*.' She smiled. 'But I'm willing if you're willing.'

'Stop it. I'm not in the mood for games.'

'You can be mad. Just say you nullify my oaths. At least, I won't have the sin of breaking my vow – my *shevuah*. Or is it a *neder*?'

'Oh, for chrissakes!' Decker stomped out the back door. Rina followed him to the stables. Decker picked up a pitchfork.

'Peter, you're in good slacks and a white shirt.'

'The animals won't mind if I go formal,' he said angrily.

'Peter, *c'mon*!'

Decker ripped open a bale. 'Uh, excuse me. Could you kindly move unless you want a face full of hay.'

'Can I just talk to you?'

'First move.'

Rina moved. 'Can you put down the pitchfork?'

'No.'

'I'm really sorry.'

'Fine.' He jabbed the fork into the packed bundle and loosened the yellow reeds. 'You're absolved of your promise. Now, can I get a little solitude, please.'

'Don't you even want to know why I went to see him?'

'Not particularly.'

'Don't you want to know what we talked about?'

Decker began tossing a fresh layer of hay over the stalls' floor, trying to feign apathy. But he was curious. In a bored tone, he said, 'If you talk, maybe I'll listen.'

'I can't talk to you while you're working.'

'Then you'll wait.'

'Oh, you're impossible!' She turned on her heels and marched back into the house.

Decker threw down the fork and trailed her footsteps. 'I'm impossible? *I'm* impossible? Last I heard, *I* didn't break any promises. *I* didn't compromise anyone's job—'

'I didn't compromise your job—'

'Yes, you did, Rina. The long and the short of it is yes, you did.'

'This is what I get for being honest.'

'No, this is what you get for being dishonest and breaking a promise.'

She turned to him, eyes blazing with passion. 'I couldn't let him . . . *sink*, Peter! You don't do that to a friend!'

'Your loyalty is to me—'

'Loyalty to your job versus the life of a human being? Thank you very much, I'll pick a human being.'

Decker lashed out. 'Why are you putting yourself and *my* job on the line for this guy? Traditionally, you only do things like that for people you love.'

She crossed her arms over her chest, her eyes boring into his. 'Just what are you really asking me, Peter. Why don't you just spit it out?'

Decker took a deep breath, held it, let it out slowly. 'I'm not asking you anything, all right?' He looked at his shirt, soaked with sweat. 'I'd better go change.'

Rina licked her lips. 'Wait a second. I'm not done. I've got another confession.'

He stared at her, mouth agape. 'There's more?'

'Unfortunately yes. I eavesdropped on one of your phone conversations . . . the one where you conferenced with Marge and Scott Oliver. I know about Bram's safe . . . and the magazines.'

Decker continued to stare. 'Anything else?'

'No . . . that's about it.' She smiled weakly. 'Looks like I'll have a busy Yom Kippur.'

Decker closed his mouth, ran his tongue along his cheek. 'Whatever your reasons were, your behavior was inexcusable, Rina.'

'I'm sorry.'

'It doesn't cut it, babe.' He walked away.

Rina turned to her cooking, her eyes wet with tears. She shoved open the oven door and painted the meat with more sauce. Everything looked wonderful, smelled delicious. She had no appetite.

The doorbell rang.

Great.

She took off her apron, but left her hair uncovered. It was only Marge. She opened the door and tried to keep the smile on her face. At Marge's side was Scott Oliver.

'He followed me home,' Marge said. 'Think you can throw him a bone?'

'I think we can actually feed him,' Rina answered. 'Come on in. Both of you. Delighted to see you, Detective.'

'Hello, Mrs. Decker.' Oliver held out a bouquet of spring flowers. 'Thank you for your gracious hospitality.'

Rina took the flowers. 'Well, thank you.'

Marge handed her a bottle of wine. 'I hope this kind is okay. It's got that Circle O-U on it.'

Rina looked at the bottle. 'This is fine.' A two-year-old Cabernet Savignon. 'I'm going to age this one. I've got an older bottle in storage that Peter'll pop open. Come sit down. Peter's just changing his shirt. I'll go get him.'

She disappeared into the other room.

Oliver took a deep whiff, smiled, then rubbed his hands together. '*Laissez les bontemps rouler.* You know how long it's been since I've eaten home cooking?'

'She's a great cook.'

'Man, she's a great everything. I'd cut off a nut for a chance to do her.'

Marge glared at him. 'You are so . . .'

'Rude? Crude? Tasteless? Disgusting? Horny? Pick a card, any card.' He sat down on one of the buckskin chairs. 'I know you did it out of pity. But thanks for asking me to come.'

'No problem.'

'I must have sounded really pathetic over the phone.'

Marge sat on the leather couch opposite the chair. 'Just a little lonely.'

Oliver said, 'It's these Sundays. Used to be family day. Sometimes, I miss the noise.' He exhaled. 'Anyway, it was nice of you to ask me along. Nice of the missus to be so welcoming.' He looked up, saw Decker. 'Ah, the host with the most.'

Decker shook hands with Oliver, kissed Marge's cheek. 'What's up, Scotty?'

'She felt sorry for me.' Oliver jerked a thumb in Marge's direction. 'Hope it's not a problem.'

'Not at all,' Decker said. 'Sit down. Get either of you something to drink?'

'Beer's fine,' Marge said.

'Ditto.'

'I heard it,' Rina called out. 'I'll get it.'

Decker sat on the couch, smiled. But it lacked warmth. 'So . . .'

'So how 'bout them Dodgers?' Marge said.

Oliver leaned forward. 'You know, I've been running this whole thing over in my mind and—'

'What thing?' Marge asked.

'What *thing*?' Oliver threw up his hands. 'Decameron's murder scene! I've got a real good fix—'

'Scott, this is a social visit,' Marge chided.

Oliver drew his head back. 'You can't be serious.'

'She's right,' Decker said. 'This is a social dinner. No shop talk. I promised Rina.' He flashed a smile of ice. 'And *I* keep my promises.'

Marge looked at Decker. What was wrong with him? They sat

in silence. A moment later, Rina came back into the room, balancing a tray of drinks. She had covered her hair. 'Did I interrupt anything?'

'Not a thing,' Oliver said. 'Thank you, Mrs. Decker.'

'It's Rina.' She handed him a drink. 'How's life, Detective?'

'It's Scott,' Oliver took a swig of his beer. 'Life is fine . . . well, passable. Thank you for having me.'

'It's really no problem. Like Peter said, I cooked enough for an army.' She handed a glass of beer to Marge, then to Peter.

Decker took it, nodded. He knew he was exuding tension. Rina, on the other hand, was acting perfect hostess. Galled the heck out of him.

'Sit down, Rina,' Marge said.

'Yeah, sit down,' Oliver echoed.

Rina looked at Peter's stony face. 'In a minute. I have some goodies in the oven. I'll be right back.'

She scurried out of the room.

To Decker, Marge said, 'Is this a bad time, Pete?'

Decker glared at Marge. 'No, it is *not* a bad time.'

Oliver said, 'You're pissed at her. You might try hiding it a little better. You're embarrassing her.'

Decker said, 'Who invited you?'

Oliver sat back. 'Sorry.'

'What's going on, Pete?' Marge said.

Oliver said, 'They got into a tiff—'

'She eavesdropped on me!' Decker said. 'Worse than that, she invited him over to the *house*, for chrissakes!'

'Who?' Marge said.

Decker lowered his voice. 'Bram Sparks, can you believe that? She invited *Bram Sparks* – a murder suspect in one of the city's biggest cases – over to *my* house.' He downed his beer. 'I swear I don't know what goes through that woman's mind.'

'Did you ask her?' Marge said. 'I'm sure she had her reasons.'

'I don't care about her reasons—'

Oliver said, 'What did she and Bram talk about?'

'How do I know?' Decker was annoyed.

'You didn't ask her?'

'No, I didn't ask her.'

'Loo, if she's good enough friends with this guy to invite him into the house, she may have learned something germane. You gotta pump her—'

'Scott—' Marge interrupted.

Oliver said, 'Don't Scott me, Marge. Rina could be sitting on the entrance to a gold mine. We've got a murder to solve here.'

'Rina should be locked up with a zipper on her mouth,' Decker said.

Marge regarded him, said nothing.

Rina returned with a salver of hors d'oeuvres. She started with Marge. 'I had mini-hot dogs. Before I turned around, they had been consumed by marauding teenaged boys.'

Marge said, 'Where are the boys?'

Rina served Oliver. 'In their room, I think.' She raised her eyebrows. 'I don't go in when the door's closed. Don't want to get my head bitten off.'

'And the baby?' Marge asked.

'The baby, *Baruch Hashem*, is sleeping.'

'How's she doing?' Oliver asked.

'She's a great kid. Very, very active. I'm always running after her. I'm too old for her.'

'*You're* too old?' Decker said.

Rina brought the tray over to Decker. She kissed the top of his ginger head. 'You're only as old as you feel.'

'Then I must be rivaling Methuselah.'

'Have a cracker, Peter.'

He took a smoked salmon with an olive on top and glared at her. 'Thank you.'

'You're welcome.' She put the tray down on the coffee table. The phone rang. Decker stood, but Rina motioned him down. 'It's probably my mother. I'll get it in the kitchen.'

Decker watched the sway of her rear as she disappeared behind the kitchen door. He remained standing, ate his smoked salmon. 'Will you excuse me for a moment?'

He followed her into the kitchen.

Marge blew out air. 'I didn't know I was walking into Virginia Woolf. He's overreacting to this Bram thing.'

'Nah, he's being a guy,' Oliver said. 'See, he tells us his wife spoke to Bram because he's a friend, we get excited. Maybe she knows something that'll help out the case. But all Deck's thinking about is whether or not she ever fucked the guy.'

Marge didn't answer.

Oliver lowered his voice. 'I don't know too much about women. But I know enough to never, ever ask a woman about her past. You force it out of her, she tells you, you go crazy. What does it matter anyway?'

Marge nodded.

Oliver twiddled his thumbs. 'At some point, we need to know if Bram said anything important.'

'Maybe Pete doesn't want to pry.'

'Oh believe me, Deck wants to pry. But into the personal stuff. That's a dead end.' Oliver leaned over. 'Suppose Bram had a past with her. And suppose he came to her, looking for help? Couldn't you picture it, Margie? He's in the shits and a looker like Rina is there, giving him all her tea and sympathy. Hell, it's enough to make even a priest slip up. Tell her things. Deck's gotta pump her.'

'Scott, even if Bram did tell Rina things, I'm sure they were said to her in confidence.'

'So what?' Oliver said, sipping beer. 'He's a priest. He talks, he violates his vows. But *she* isn't under any oath. She shoots off her mouth, she's just acting like a woman.'

They must have made up. Because when Rina called everyone to the table, she and Pete were all lovey-dovey. Cute, Marge thought, but nauseating. Smiling at each other, little love pats on the rears when they thought no one was looking. Marge almost wished they were still fighting.

As expected, the food was excellent. First course was a thick pea soup with diced carrots and thick marrow bones. It was followed by a butter lettuce, mandarin orange, slivered almond, and green onion salad. The entrée was rack of lamb served with a timbale of rice pilaf and a crookneck squash puree.

Copious amounts of comestibles. Marge had seconds, Decker and Oliver had thirds. Rina's sons didn't just eat, they devoured. Nice kids, Marge thought. Polite and attentive. Still, it was clear they were anxious to leave. As soon as they finished clearing the plates, they excused themselves, saying they had errands to run.

Rina poured coffee. Oliver eyed the cup and saucer with suspicion. 'Can you die by eating too much?'

Rina said, 'You know, I once read about a knight who died of a burst bladder.'

'Lovely,' Decker said.

'I'll pass on the coffee,' Oliver said.

'Nonsense.' Rina placed the cup in front of him. 'A little decaf never hurt anyone.'

'Tell that to the knight.'

Rina said, 'I think the story went like this. The knight had been at a king's banquet, had been drinking gallons and gallons of wine. Apparently, back then, one wasn't permitted to excuse oneself from the table for any reason until the festivities were over.'

Oliver said, 'Too bad trains hadn't been invented. Otherwise, he could have gotten himself a brakeman's companion.'

'I've got dessert coming,' Rina said.

'No more,' Oliver pleaded. 'No more. No more.'

'Everyone can use a little sweetness in his or her life.' Rina stood at the kitchen door. 'I'll be back.'

After she left, Marge said, 'She's awfully chipper.'

'She's a pain in the neck.' Decker smiled. 'But a good kid down deep.'

'She don't look like a kid to me,' Oliver said.

'Watch your tongue,' Decker said.

Oliver gave Decker a forced smile. 'Now that you two are in good graces, think you might want to ask—'

'No.'

'Deck, she might know something.'

'It's Loo to you and she doesn't know anything.'

'So you asked her.'

'No, I didn't ask her,' Decker replied. 'But she doesn't know anything. If she did, she would have told me.'

'Deck, how does she know what's relevant?'

Marge said, 'He's got a point, Pete.'

Oliver said, 'I'll bring it up—'

'No, you won't.'

'Just let me ask her—'

'Ask me what?' Rina said, carrying in a layer cake.

'Ask you nothing,' Decker said.

'Ask what you and Bram talked about,' Oliver said.

Decker turned red with anger, held his tongue. Rina set down the cake.

To Oliver, she said, 'I was willing to tell him. He wasn't interested.'

'Rina, that's *enough*!'

'She isn't talking to you,' Oliver said. 'She's talking to me—'

'You're in my house, Scott!'

Rina said, 'Let's not ruin a nice dinner. I'm sure Peter has his reasons for wanting to change the subject.' She kissed her husband's head. 'Would you like some cake, dear?'

Decker glared at her, eyes sweeping over his colleagues' faces. He groused, 'Tell us what you talked about.'

'Unfortunately, there's nothing much to say.' She cut Peter a slice of cake. 'Just some personal talk. About my late husband . . . Bram's feelings toward his siblings.'

379

Oliver said, 'He didn't talk about the murder charges against him?'

'He didn't murder anyone,' Rina said. 'He's not capable of murder.'

'Yeah, he's a saint,' Decker said. 'That's why he had bloody clothes in his safe.'

Marge looked at Decker, put her finger to her lips.

Decker grumped, 'She knows about the safe, Marge. I told you she eavesdropped on our phone conversation.'

Marge's eyes widened. 'Rina, that's low.'

'Yeah, sounds like something I'd do,' Oliver said.

'Sorry, but I'm not remorseful. My friend's life was at stake, so too bad!'

'Think you might fake some humility for my sake?' Decker snapped.

'Peter, I'm—'

'How about some cake, Mrs. Decker?' Oliver piped in.

Rina served Oliver a wedge of cake.

'Too big,' Oliver said.

'Just eat what you'd like.'

'I'm gonna eat the whole thing, that's the problem.'

'You only pass through once in your life, Scott.'

'You're right. Leave it.'

Rina said, 'Marge?'

'Half that size, Rina.'

Rina cut a piece for Marge, filled up the coffee cups. 'Bram didn't do anything. He's clearly protecting someone.'

'He said that to you?' Oliver asked.

'No,' Rina admitted. 'Bram's a priest. He'd never reveal anything confidential. But I did find out why he has a safe in his apartment.'

'Why?' Oliver asked, taking out a notepad.

'He got held up at gunpoint several years ago in the rectory. Since then, on weekends, when the chapel's empty, he keeps the church's cash and valuables in his safe.'

'Valuables?' Marge asked.

'The gilt chalices used in Mass,' Rina answered. 'Silver candlesticks, incense holders and trays . . . things like that.'

Oliver smiled. 'Yeah, I didn't think he was referring to the porno magazines.'

'They're not his,' Rina stated.

Decker said, 'He told you that?'

Rina paused, then shook her head no.

Decker took a forkful of cake and appraised her. 'What are you hiding, dear?'

Rina sighed. 'He told me the magazines were his. But I don't believe him. He's protecting someone, Peter. You know it and I know it.'

'I don't know anything,' Decker said.

'I know I've said this before.' Marge swallowed a mouthful of devil's food. 'But why would Bram leave explicit magazines with his name on the wrappers at the scene of a murder? It doesn't make sense.'

'I don't know why,' Decker said. 'But Luke said his name was on the wrappers.'

'My opinion?' Oliver said. 'I think *Luke's* name was on the wrappers.'

'What are you talking about, Scott?' Decker said. 'Bram just told Rina that the magazines were his.'

'I don't believe it,' Rina said.

Decker said, 'Fine, Rina. Don't believe it. Can we change the discussion?'

Marge thought a moment, then said, 'So let's assume Bram's name was on the wrappers—'

'Marge,' Decker said. 'Please.'

Rina cried out, 'Peter, this is *important* to me! How can I make you understand that?'

Decker rolled his tongue in his mouth. 'What's important to you, Rina? Proving Bram innocent or hearing the truth?'

Rina paused. 'I'll accept the truth. As soon as you can prove him guilty.'

'I don't prove guilt or innocence, Rina. I just collect evidence. And right now, the evidence collected from your friend's safe is incriminating.'

'He's protecting someone.'

'And you're repeating yourself.'

'Peter, how do you know the wrappers had Bram's name on them? Did you see them?'

'No.'

'We're taking Luke's word for it,' Oliver said. 'A big mistake.'

'Except that Bram admitted they were his,' Marge said.

'He's lying,' Rina stated formally.

'Rina—'

'So Luke *claims* he saw wrappers with Bram's name on them,' Rina said. 'So what? That's not conclusive. Someone could have *made* those wrappers, put Bram's name on them, stuffed them with the magazines, and left them at the murder scene.'

Marge said softly, 'Rina, if that was the case, why would Bram tell you they were his?'

Decker said, 'Darling, what difference does it make whether the magazines were Bram's or not. It's the clothes that are incriminating. They tell us he was there.'

'Either he or Luke,' Marge added.

Rina said, 'It's just that Bram owning *those* kinds of magazines—'

'Especially *that* kind of magazine,' Oliver said.

'You mean the gay stuff?' Rina said.

'No, it's not the gay stuff that makes me wince,' Oliver said. 'It's the sadomasochism and body piercing.'

'*What?*' Rina shrieked.

'Thank you, Scott,' Decker said.

Oliver turned red. 'I figured she knew—'

'No, she didn't know.'

'*Body* piercing?'

Oliver said, 'Needles through everything imaginable.' He held his crotch. 'Ouch!'

Rina threw up her hands. 'Bram would *never* have anything to do with that kind of stuff!'

Decker said, 'People have secret lives, Rina.'

'No way!' She shook her head vehemently. 'No, I don't believe it. He would never be into something so . . .'

'Kinky?' Oliver said with glowing eyes.

Decker said, 'Rina, why are you obsessing on the magazines? They're not the important issue here.'

'Because I know Bram. He'd never own things that glorify hurting people – gay or straight! He's protecting someone. Either that or he's being framed.'

'You're turning this discussion into a screed for his innocence.'

'I'm trying to make sense out of the illogical!'

The room was quiet. Rina poured more coffee. 'Okay. So I'm biased. What's the harm in that?'

'Nothing,' Decker said. 'But because you're biased, you can't help us. Doesn't Jewish law state that judges may not be biased.'

'I'm not his judge, I'm his advocate.' She sat down. 'I'm his friend. Friends need advocates.'

Decker said, 'Can we drop the discussion?'

Rina was quiet. But a moment later, she started up. 'Luke *told* you he saw Bram's name on the magazine wrappers?'

Decker stared at her. 'Yes, dear.'

'He said he *saw* Bram's name.'

'Yes, dear. Luke said all the wrappers had Bram's name on them.'

Rina said, 'Luke told you, "I saw the magazine wrappers and they had the name BRAM SPARKS on them."'

'Rina, for goodness sakes,' Decker said. 'He said he saw magazine wrappers with his brother's name on them.'

'Luke said the wrappers had his *brother's* name on them, right?'

Marge said, 'Do you have a point, Rina?'

'Luke didn't say they had the words BRAM SPARKS on them.'

'Rina, you are beating a dead horse!'

'Can you just hear me out?'

'Go on,' Marge said.

Rina said, 'Luke told you that in the back of his mind, he thought Bram was gay, right?'

Decker nodded.

'So what if the magazine labels just had SPARKS on them. Luke assumed they belonged to Bram. But maybe they belonged to another brother.'

Decker said, 'Rina, you're stretching—'

'Bram would protect his brothers.'

'Rina—'

Rina's eyes got big. 'Maybe, Peter, the labels said "*A*. Sparks." Or even "*A. M.* Sparks." You know there are more than one A. M. Sparks in Bram's family.'

As soon as she said it, Decker knew she had hit pay dirt. 'What's Bram's middle name?'

'Matthew.'

'Oh my God!' Marge slapped her forehead. 'The *father*!'

'Azor Moses!' Oliver said. 'They're *his* magazines?'

Decker buried his head in his hands.

The *father's* magazines.

And that was why a Fundamentalist like Azor Sparks hadn't fired Decameron even after he had been convicted of picking up male hookers. Excusing Decameron because the old man had been wrestling with his own similar demons. Azor Sparks had either been latent or led a *very* secret life.

Had Bram known? Good chance of that. Because Azor had confided things to Bram. Perhaps he'd confessed his desires to his son. Especially after that fateful Sunday night dinner when Bram refused to equate evil thoughts with evil action.

Giving Sparks a license to fantasize.

Perhaps Sparks took it one step further and began with fantasy magazines. After all, Bram had relieved him of the guilt.

At Sparks's memorial service, Bram had spoken to Decker about his father's distinctions between the homosexual and the homosexual act. Decker thought about that brief interchange in the Sparks's kitchen. His discussion about Decameron's moral charges, about Azor's loyalty to his colleague despite church rumblings. And about the religious way one copes with homosexuality.

Either celibacy or sublimation *in a legitimate heterosexual union.*

The fifth commandment spoke of honoring one's father and mother. By enlarging upon the precept – what honoring one's parents might mean to a man of the cloth – Decker began to put the pieces together. Abram Matthew Sparks, the priest who put God before American law, took the magazines as his own to protect his father's name. Just as important, he was protecting his mother from postmortem embarrassment.

Marge said, 'Luke told us that Decameron had called him up, early in the morning, wanting to talk about the family. But not over the phone. Right?'

'Right,' Decker muttered.

'Maybe that's what he wanted to tell Luke. That it may come out that his father was gay.'

'He'd bother calling Luke up to tell him *that*?' Oliver said.

Marge said, 'Maybe he wanted to spare the family some embarrassment and/or ridicule.'

'Then why would he call Luke?' Oliver said. 'Why not Bram?'

Rina said, 'Maybe Dr. Decameron felt Luke was more worldly about human foibles . . . being as Luke had been a user.'

'Or the answer could have been much more pedestrian,' Decker said. 'Bram had been occupied that morning. Very busy. First with mass, then with his mother. Decameron knew Dolly Sparks hated him. He wouldn't have called up the house.'

'Aha,' Marge said. 'Maybe that's why she hated him. She found out that her husband and Decameron were having an affair.'

'Nah, I don't buy that,' Oliver said.

'Why not?'

Oliver said, 'Margie, why would Decameron call up Luke to tell him about their affair?'

'Blackmail,' Marge suggested.

'Nah, Reggie was a good guy,' Oliver said.

'You keep saying that,' Marge answered. 'That don't make it so.'

Rina said, 'So how did Dr. Decameron come to have Dr. Sparks's magazines?'

'Could be that after Azor died, Decameron went through Sparks's office . . . to clean things up.' Oliver shrugged. 'Maybe he found the magazines.'

'Christ!' Decker was disgusted with himself. 'The Fisher/Tyne data you two had requested. At Sparks's memorial service, Decameron *told* me he was going to look through Azor's files to find the most updated numbers. Could be he came across the magazines by accident.'

Marge said, 'Then Decameron took them home with him, intending to give them to Luke . . . to dispose of them as he saw fit.'

'The magazines which had *A. M.* Sparks on the wrappers,' Rina said pointedly. 'Having found them in his boss's file cabinets, Decameron knew that A. M. stood for Azor Moses. But Luke didn't know. He just assumed they belonged to his unmarried priest brother Bram. So I'm not so stupid.'

'No, darling, *you* are not stupid.'

Rina smiled. 'You're a good sport.'

'I'm a lousy sport,' Decker said. 'I'm pissed as hell. You know, Decameron may have also found Bram's apartment key in Azor's files. Maybe he thought his boss had a secret hideaway for his activities.'

'What would Azor be doing with Bram's apartment key?' Marge asked.

'I've got a key to my daughter's apartment in New York. In case of emergencies.'

Marge said, 'I still don't understand why Bram would have kept his dead father's porno magazines in his safe.'

Decker frowned. 'Because he was on his way out to visit a sick kid and didn't know what to do with them. Because you don't toss magazines like that in your apartment Dumpster. You hold them until you figure out how to get rid of them.'

'You know what I don't understand,' Oliver said. 'I don't understand why Dr. Azor Moses Sparks – Mr. Austere, By the Book, Elder, Pillar of the Christian Community – would have subscribed to those kind of magazines using his real name.'

'Arrogance,' Decker said.

'Or he wanted to get caught,' Rina said. 'Maybe he was planning to come out.'

They all looked at Rina. Oliver said, 'You know, Loo, she's real bright—'

'Yes, I know that, Scott.' Decker sat up. 'So . . . if Azor Sparks were suddenly to come out of the closet . . . who would that impact on the most?'

'His wife, of course,' Rina answered.

'His wife,' Decker echoed. 'Say she found out about her husband's preferences. Say she confronted him. Maybe he denied it. But maybe he admitted it, even told her he was going to leave her. Think about it, guys.

'Here's a woman who put in forty years with a man. Bore him six children, lived her life around him, developed her identity on the basis of being his wife. His parties were her parties. His dinners were her dinners. Through him, she had a role – as a wife, as a mother, as a leader in the church, as hostess of dinners and parties. She thought he was her soulmate, her heavenly match from God.'

'Hell hath no fury,' Oliver said.

'You'd better believe it,' Decker said. 'What if he decided to leave her – sort out his feelings, wrestle with his inclinations, make his own peace with God. Maybe he took it one step further. Maybe he had someone watching in the wings—'

'Decameron,' Marge said.

Oliver said, 'No way.'

'What difference does it make?' Rina asked. 'We'll never know so let's move on.'

Oliver was taken aback. 'She's tough.'

'Tell me about it,' Decker said. 'The point is that we're assuming Sparks was going to leave his wife for a lifestyle she considered odious and sinful. He was making a fool out of her, making a mockery out of her Fundamentalist religion, out of God. Most important, without Azor, Dolores had no role in life. If that was the case, if she had lived her life around this sinner of a man, what do you think she might have done?'

The room fell quiet.

Marge broke the silence. 'It's a big leap, Pete.'

'It's logical,' Oliver said. 'She ices the old man, then maybe ices Decameron because she *thinks* he's having an affair with her husband.'

'Throwing the magazines around the bodies,' Rina said. 'Like you always said, Peter. It looked like a calling card.'

'That was me,' Marge said.

'Oh, sorry,' Rina replied. 'Anyway, someone was angry and wanted the world to know who Azor Sparks really was. I could see a spurned, unbalanced wife doing that.'

'Why do you say *unbalanced*?' Decker asked. 'Bram mention something to that effect to you?'

Rina looked down. 'Just that she had been a bit nervous when they – the triplets – were growing up. She couldn't seek professional help because it would have been an embarrassment to her husband. So she turned to barbiturates. Dr. Sparks prescribed the medication himself, but left Bram in charge of dispensing them

388

to her. She was addicted to them for a while.'

Decker tried to keep his voice soft. 'Might have helped if you would have *told* me all this in the beginning—'

'Peter, are you saying I should have implicated Dolly in her own husband's murder based on her past drug use?'

'I'm just saying—'

'Besides, I couldn't mention Bram without you having a fit—'

'That's nonsense!'

'Is this really important now?' Marge asked.

'No, it isn't!' Rina stated. 'What is important is Dolores Sparks hated Decameron. She probably felt he had stolen her husband. Either directly – as in they were having an affair – or indirectly – as in Decameron being a bad influence on Azor.'

Marge gloated. 'And like I always said, Kenneth Leonard was just an innocent bystander. He came to Decameron's to clear his conscience about the fraud. Instead, he wound up with a bullet in his head.'

Oliver said, 'I think it still could be Fisher/Tyne.'

'It could be,' Decker said. 'I haven't ruled out anyone . . . including Bram.'

Rina folded her arms across her chest. 'He would never, ever *hurt* anyone. He probably knew what was going on. He was protecting his father's name, Peter.'

Marge said, 'Sounds to me like he's protecting his mother from a murder rap.'

Oliver said, 'She couldn't do it by herself.'

'So she had help,' Marge said.

'Who?'

'Someone who's been spending lots of time with the family.' Decker stood up from the table. 'It's time we pay Dolores Sparks a visit.'

30

'She's unavailable.' Michael was hostile. 'Next time call before you harass us.'

'Sorry, but it's important.' Decker sidestepped around him, entered the house, Marge and Oliver keeping pace behind him.

Stunned, Michael hesitated before shutting the door. 'You just can't barge in here like that.'

'Fine,' Decker said. 'Kick me out. Make it obvious to everyone that you have something to hide.'

Michael's mouth dropped open. 'I've got nothing—'

'Where's your mom? Upstairs?'

'You pester my family, you arrest my brothers, you throw around ridiculous charges, you—'

'Save it for the judge,' Oliver said.

'Sorry about the intrusion,' Marge said.

'I don't believe this!' Michael raised his voice. 'I'm calling my lawyer.'

'You mean Waterson?' Oliver asked. 'I wouldn't call him if I were you.'

Decker started up the stairs, Michael at his heels. 'Detective Oliver is right, son. You *don't* want to do that.'

Michael said, 'And why's that?'

'Ask your brother, Bram. Bet he knows.'

As Decker opened the door to the master bedroom, he was instantly attacked by a pair of burning green eyes. Bram was kneeling in front of his seated mother, his hands clasped around hers, a hunk of shiny metal between their interlaced fingers.

A Beretta semi automatic.

391

Decker stopped at the threshold. With a hand signal, he told everyone behind him to halt. But Michael paid no attention, storming past Decker.

'He just barged his way in, Bram. I—'

Abruptly, Michael stopped talking when he noticed the gun. Eyes darting back and forth. Quietly, he asked, 'What's going on, Bram?'

The room fell quiet. A cavernous place in beige and white, eerily lit by a couple of reading lamps posted on either side of the king-sized bed. In the corner was a desk piled high with papers. The drapes had been drawn – old, ecru things – worn and frayed.

Dressed in a flowing caftan, Dolly Sparks looked at her youngest son, then returned her eyes to her lap. She was seated in a cream-colored wing chair, her shoulders hunched, her hair bedraggled. Bram was in his usual black garb. His voice was soft . . . controlled. He directed his words to Decker.

'She's suicidal. Can you please leave?'

Decker whispered to Marge to call for backup. Oliver placed himself at Decker's side, but kept the door wide open.

Bram said, 'Please, Lieutenant. A tragedy serves no purpose.'

The priest's face held a sweaty sheen. Decker said, 'I can't leave you two alone, Father. Not as long as she has a weapon.'

Bram said, 'Do you have an arrest warrant?'

'No.'

'Then please go.'

'Under these circumstances, I can't. I'd be negligent in my duties if I did.'

'You're hearing privileged conversation. You cannot use it against her. Because she wants a lawyer.'

Michael said, 'Should I call Mr. Waterson, Bram?'

'No, don't do that.' To Decker, Bram said, 'Do you hear what I'm saying? She wants a lawyer. A real lawyer.'

'I understand.' Decker paused. 'So she told you everything. Or maybe you figured it out after Decameron was murdered—'

'What difference does it make?'

Tears ran down Dolly's face, her fingers gripping the gun. 'They're coming for me, aren't they? They're going to take me away—'

'Please, Lieutenant,' Bram was pleading. 'If you won't leave, at least don't make matters worse.' He held his mother's hand, pointing the gun away from her stomach. 'Mom, I'll take care of everything. I'll take care of you. I'll be there for you. You know that—'

'It's too late,' she sobbed.

'No, it's not too late. Never lose faith, Mom. You taught me that.'

'Did I?'

'Yes, you did. You taught me everything. You taught me that our Savior died for our sins. So that we may remember Him in our time of need, and remember His eternal love for us. He loves all of us, Mom, sinners as well as saints. He loves *you*.'

Dolly was quiet. Decker's hand moved imperceptibly toward his service holster. He undid the strap, his fingers tightening around the butt of the gun.

Bram said, 'The commandments teach us to love our parents, both our physical parents and our Father in Heaven. I love you very much, Mother. We'll go through this together. But first, you have to give me the gun—'

'The police know—'

'Shhh—'

'They know, Abram. They know!' Her watery eyes met Decker's face. 'I'm going to die!'

Bram said, 'No one's going to die—'

'It was all my fault—'

'Mom, it wasn't anyone's fault—'

'I wasn't a good enough wife—'

'You were a perfect wife,' he cooed. 'A perfect wife and a perfect mother. We all love you very, very much. Your pain is my pain. Please let me help you.'

'Why did he do this to us? Why did he do this to *me*?'

'I don't know, Mom—'

'After all these years of devotion. I never strayed . . . not even in my heart. I never wanted anything else but to be a good wife to him.'

'You were a perfect wife.'

'Then why did he turn out *that* way?'

Oliver crept up behind Decker, whispered in his ear, 'Backup's coming.'

'Mom?' Michael said.

Dolly raised her eyes to her youngest son.

'Mom, I love you, too.'

Dolly didn't answer.

Michael said, 'Mom, please give Bram the gun. We'll take care of you. Please.'

Dolly returned her eyes to Bram. 'Why would he desire such a vile thing, Abram?'

Michael's eyes were questioning. But Bram's were full of understanding. 'I don't know why God makes people the way He does. We're not meant to know.'

'Why did you give him your *blessing*, Abram?' Dolly blurted out angrily. 'How could *you*, of all people, give him permission to sin so gravely?'

'I never gave him my blessing, Mom.'

'You gave him permission by saying it was healthy to fantasize. You told him it was okay—'

'Never, Mom.'

'That's what he told me.'

'I never gave him permission to sin, Mom,' Bram said quietly. 'I never gave him my blessing. What I did say was . . .'

He cleared his throat.

'I told him I'd love him no matter what path he felt he had to take.'

'By your acceptance, you encouraged him!' she said vehemently.

'You encouraged him to sin and you damned him to hell! You damned *me* to hell!'

'I see that now,' Bram said gently. 'I see I did the wrong thing. I see that this is all *my* fault—'

'Oh my beautiful golden boy!' She cried out, grabbing his hands, the gun resting between their digits. 'My chaste, wonderful, precious son. He was so cruel to you.'

'Give me the gun, Mom. Just let go—'

'If *he* hadn't sent you away, this never would have happened. You would have become a minister – a real servant of God – instead of a priest. You would never have left the true faith to worship idols and statues. You would have stayed with me, protected me from his evilness. Protected me as you've always done. Oh Abram, I should have seen so long ago what kind of man he was. He sent you away as surely as the Jews closed the door on the baby Jesus—'

'Mom, I left on my own accord—'

'No!' Dolly shook her head. 'No, you didn't. He sent you away! *Drove* you away with his harsh words and unforgiving disposition. And all the while he carried the gravest sin in his despicable heart.' Out loud she orated: ' "*Let he who is innocent cast the first stone.*" '

'Give me the gun, Mom.'

'Men are beasts,' she said fiercely. 'They come to you with soft words and sweet promises, then snare you into their evil traps of lust and carnage, use you until you're old and tired—'

'Mom—'

'He was evil, Abram. How could you give him your blessing?'

Slowly, Decker inched forward.

'I was wrong, Mom,' Bram purred. 'Give me the gun.'

'Mom, please give Bram the gun,' Michael pleaded, stepping into the room. But Oliver grabbed his arm, pulled him back into the doorway. Decker took another step forward, his hands still tightly wrapped around the grip of his holstered gun.

Dolly liberated her left hand, stroked Bram's face. She ran her hands through Bram's long hair. The leonine mother grooming her cub.

'Ah, but how beautiful you are to me. So chaste and pure with the face and body of an angel.' Her smile turned into a sneer. 'So unlike Lucas who wasted his attributes, wasted his life on whores and vices. Two faces, both the same, but so different. Jacob and Esau. You, devoting yourself to the service of God even if it's in the wrong way.'

Tears streamed down Dolly's cheeks. 'How could you give him your blessing, Bram? How could you *do* that to me?'

'I was wrong.'

'Especially knowing what was in his heart. Seeing the filth and perversion in his lusts. Why? *Why?* How could you condone him?'

'I never condoned him, Mom. But forgiveness is another matter. Our Lord forgives us all of our grievous sins. Should we do any less to each other?' His voice was a hush. 'Give me the gun, Mom. I'll take care of you.'

'William said he'd take care of me,' Dolly snapped angrily. 'Look what he did, the stupid, stupid fool. Look what happened! Men are *beasts*!'

'Let's not think about him now, Mom.'

'William knew of your father's filth. Your father told him one day . . . blurted it out with pride. Then William told me, planted evil in my heart—'

'I know, Mom. It was his fault. Give me the gun.'

To Decker, she said, 'That's the monster you should be arresting. Not us, *him*!'

Decker nodded. William Waterson – the man who had been hanging around the house, painting himself as a family friend, and mysteriously visiting bikers with big checks drawn from Dolly's account. A quick call to Farrell and his computer had verified that plus a few other interesting things.

Just how much was Waterson involved in his mess? Did he orchestrate the whole thing?

Decker regarded Dolly intensely. Her eyes were rolling and unfocused, her mouth slightly agape, tiny rills of drool amassing at the corners. Her body held a slight twitch. Unnatural. As if on strong, strong medication. Too zonked out to plan something like murder on her own.

She must have had help. Once she had been a user. Maybe Waterson had known about the addiction. Prodding her along, keeping her dazed and confused, because the lawyer had had a vested interest in keeping Dolly's checkbook open for consumption.

The woman wept. 'Oh my cursed life. And all I ever wanted to be was a good wife.'

She squeezed Bram's hands with both of hers, the hard gun between them pressing deep into her fleshy palms. Decker took a step toward them.

'William sowed evil in my soul, Abram,' she continued. 'He used the anger in my heart for his own wretched purposes. He enticed me to do evil . . . like Eve did unto Adam. He swore sweet words of God and everlasting love. William is a vile, vile man. Abram, I swear I never meant for anyone to die—'

'Mom,' Bram said quietly, 'if you love me . . . if you want me to help you, please, please, give me the gun.'

'Don't leave me, Abram.'

'Never.'

'Don't ever go back to Rome.'

'It's not even a consideration,' Bram spoke soothingly. 'I'll stay here and be with you. We'll work things out. But first you have to give me the gun.'

Decker crept closer, looked over his shoulder. Oliver gave him the thumbs-up sign. Backup had arrived.

Dolly said, 'You won't go back to Rome? You'll be here with me?'

Bram said, 'For as long as you need me.'

'Forever?'

'Yes, forever and ever,' Bram whispered. 'Let go of the gun, Mom. Just loosen your grip . . .'

Decker saw the priest's slender fingers working their way into his mother's hold on the gun, prying her hand from the grip.

'That's a good girl,' Bram encouraged. 'Just relax your hand.'

Slowly, he managed to wriggle his fingers around the weapon, extracting the gun from her with much deliberation. As soon as he freed it from her grasp, he placed it to the floor, gently pushing it toward Decker's direction. Kneeling, Decker retrieved the semi and took out the magazine clip. For the first time, he realized how wet his hands were, face and body drenched with sweat.

Bram held his mother's hands. As he stood, he brought her up from the chair.

'I love you, son,' she said, crying.

'I love you, too.'

'You'll never leave me?'

'Never.'

'You'll stay with me forever?'

'Yes, Mom. I'll stay with you forever.'

'But what will happen when they come for you, Abram? When those idol-worshipping bishops call you to Rome?'

'I won't go, Mom. I won't leave you.'

No one spoke.

Bram inched his mother forward. 'We have to go to the police now, Mom. We'll get you a very good lawyer. Then you and he can talk about Mr. Waterson . . . what he told you, what he did.'

Dolly stopped walking. 'He's an evil, evil man.'

'Yes, he is. And we'll tell the police that.' Bram glanced at Decker. Decker nodded back. The priest continued. 'Once your lawyer arrives, you can tell them all about Mr. Waterson. The lieutenant here? He'll want to hear what you have to say. Right, Lieutenant?'

'Right,' Decker answered.

Bram said, 'And I'll be with you when you talk to the lieutenant. I'll be with you, your lawyer will be with you . . . isn't that right, Lieutenant?'

'Absolutely,' Decker replied.

'You love me?' Dolly asked her son.

'Yes, Mom, I love you very much.'

'Hug me, Abram. Hold me, please.'

The priest embraced his mother.

'Big bear hug, gorgeous.'

Bram squeezed his mother tightly.

'I love you, Abram,' Dolly said. 'I want to be with you. I want to be with you, forever!'

The way she spoke sent chills through Decker's spine, sent his reactions into overdrive. As soon as he saw her hand dip into her caftan, he charged her.

But a fraction too late.

Fire exploded from Dolly's hand, Bram slipping from her grip, hitting the floor. Decker flew into her, knocking her down as the gun went skittering across the floor, firing as it hit the wall.

'Shit!' Decker screamed as he raced toward Bram. 'Shit, shit, *shit*!'

Oliver wrestled Dolly to the floor. 'I got her, Pete.'

'Oh my baby!' she moaned. 'I'm supposed to die, too!'

'Get her out of here!'

'Oh my God!' Michael shrieked. 'Oh my God, oh my God!

A pair of uniforms ran into the room.

'Call Emergency *now*!' Decker yelled, turning Bram onto his back. He tore open the priest's shirt while blood spurted from inch-round bullet holes in his chest and stomach, dousing Decker's face and clothes. Decker placed pressure on the priest's chest with one hand, fished for his keys with the other. Attached to the ring was a Swiss army knife. He unlatched the blade, sliced into Abram's flesh and inner fascia. His fingers dove into a blind hole of viscera, searching desperately for the ruptured arteries. He shrieked out, 'Somebody call it in?'

'It's been called in, Pete,' Marge answered.

Decker screamed, 'Michael, get over here!'

Immediately, the med student leaped into action.

'Hold this spot,' Decker said, guiding his hand into the priest's insides.

Bram whispered, 'Your father was a good man, Michael. Don't let anyone tell you diff—' He was suddenly seized with uncontrollable cramps. 'Oh God have mercy!'

In Oliver's hands Dolly wailed, 'I want to die. I'm supposed to die! Please let me die!'

'Get her *out* of here!' Decker barked.

Again, Bram attempted speech. 'A . . . tortured man . . . even so, he remained faithful to Mom to the end . . . He swore to me . . .' His body writhed in agony. 'Oh sweet *Jesus*!'

'Just hang in there, Abram,' Decker whispered. 'You're going to be—'

'A *good* man, Michael . . . and Mom's a good wo—' He cried out as searing pain swept through his body.

'Shhhh,' Decker purred. The priest's body was still spewing blood. Decker frantically tried to staunch the flow. 'Press down right here,' he ordered Michael. Out loud, he said, 'I need more hands. Marge, get over here!'

Marge froze with indecision, regarding her ungloved hands.

'*Move it, Dunn!*' Decker ordered.

She ran to him. Decker grabbed her hand. 'Press here.'

Bram looked at Marge. 'My blood's clean. I haven't . . .' His body broke into spastic convulsions.

'Hold his legs with your knees, Michael.'

'I hurt, Peter.'

'Shhhh,' Decker cooed. 'You're gonna be all right—'

'No, I'm not—' More spasms. His face sweating profusely, blood seeping from the corner of his mouth. 'Rina had faith in me.'

Decker's fingers found another ruptured vessel. He tightened his grip as best he could around the slippery, wet cord. 'She had unshakable faith in you. Don't talk, Abram.'

His voice was barely audible. 'Tell her—' He began shaking uncontrollably.

'Shhhh.'

'Do you know . . . Psalms, Peter?'

'Not by heart, Abram. I'm sorry.'

'Rina knows Psalms . . . *Tehillim*.' He broke into a series of spasmodic coughs, hacking up gobs of blood and sputum. 'Tell her . . .'

'I'll tell her, Abram.' Decker gently wiped his mouth 'I'll tell her to say *Tehillim* for you.'

The priest nodded. 'I'm cold . . .'

Michael's face was wet with tears and blood. He stuttered out, 'He's going into shock.'

Decker yelled out, 'Someone get a fucking blanket! Elevate his feet.' His hands remained deep inside Bram's chest. Everything was flooded with body fluids, seeping and oozing from the open cavity. At least at present, arterial blood wasn't actively squirting.

The priest's face had turned gray, his legs and arms a series of random twitches and tics.

Decker whispered, 'Hang in there, Bram. We all need you to hang in there, buddy. I need you to do it, Rina needs you to do it. Everyone needs you, guy. Just hang in there.'

Marge's hands began to tremble. She willed them to be steady. Her eyes welled up with wetness.

Words forming on the priest's cyanotic lips.

'*Our Father who art in heaven.*
Hallowed by thy name.
Thy kingdom come.
Thy will be done on earth, as it is in heaven.'

'Ambulance is here,' Oliver yelled out.

'Thank God!' Marge whispered.

'Nobody move until they get here!' Decker said to Marge and Michael. A group of paramedics raced over to the scene, meticulously relieving the cops of their tenuous positions as medics. Immediately, Marge walked away. But Decker and Michael remained kneeling at the priest's side. Michael took one hand, Decker took the other.

Bram's complexion had turned pasty, his skin temperature cold and clammy. He managed to squeeze his brother's hand. 'Finish . . .'

Michael's voice trembled, his eyes clogged with tears. There was panic in his voice. 'Finish?'

An oxygen mask was placed over Bram's face, a needle scanning the priest's arm for a vein. His breathing remained choppy, and shallow.

He whispered, 'Give us this day . . .'

'Oh, the Lord's Prayer . . .' Michael said. 'Yeah . . . uh, give us this day our daily bread . . . uh . . . uh . . .'

Decker said, softly, 'And forgive us our trespasses . . .'

Michael cleared his throat. 'And forgive us our trespasses, as we forgive those who trespass against us . . .' He paused as the IV was hooked into Bram's deflated vessels, an instrument buried into his collapsed lungs.

Decker said, 'And lead us not . . .'

'And lead us not into temptation,' Michael sputtered out, 'but deliver us from evil.'

Bram nodded, whispered between labored breaths,

'*Deus, qui inter apostolicos sacerdotes famulum tuum Abram Matthew Sparks et Sacerdotali fecisti dignitate vigere: Praesta, quaesumus; ut eorum quoquo perpetuo aggregetur consortio. Per Dominum nostrum.*

'*Te amo, Jesu Cristo.*'

The priest shut his eyes and went slack. Michael looked at Decker with frightened eyes.

'His chest is moving,' Decker said.

Michael bit his lip, continued to squeeze his brother's limp hand.

A paramedic said, 'You're going to have to move so we can transfer him to the gurney.'

Decker nodded, helped Michael up onto shaky feet. Both of them were covered in blood. 'Clean yourself off. Start calling your siblings.'

Tears were running down Michael's face. 'I don't know if I . . .' He staggered on his feet.

Decker grabbed his shoulders, steadied him. 'I'll ride in the ambulance. But *you* have to call your brothers and sisters, Michael. No one else can do it except you. Understand?'

Michael stood unresponsive, paralyzed with shock.

'*Understand?*' Decker repeated.

Michael nodded vigorously.

'Tell him to meet us at . . .' Decker turned to one of the paramedics. A skinny kid with a big Adam's apple. 'Where are you taking him?'

'New Chris.'

Decker swallowed hard. 'Tell him to meet me at New Chris.'

The paramedic looked at Decker. 'You know you got a bullet wound in your right arm?'

Decker pulled back his sleeve, regarded the shredded fabric of his suit jacket. He quickly removed it. As expected, his shirt was torn as well. He rolled up his sleeve. Next to his bicep was a round patch of raw meat.

The kid said, 'C'mon. I'll patch it in the ambulance.'

The wound was leaking blood. Suddenly, it hurt like hell.

31

'We've been going at this for over an hour,' Martinez said. 'You're making life difficult on yourself, Mr. Waterson.' The detective leaned across the table in the interview room. 'Dolores Sparks shot her son, hoping to make it murder/suicide. He's been on the operating table for the last three hours, hanging on to life by a thread. The woman wants to *die*, Waterson.' He snapped his fingers. 'She turned you in like that!'

'You're gonna fry, sir,' Webster jumped in, 'unless you do something to help yourself.'

'If you talk to us,' Martinez said, 'tell us what happened . . . give us the triggerman . . . and then maybe Mr. Kent over here will deal.'

Mr. Kent was John Kent, a fifty-five-year-old Fundamentalist Christian who had put in over twenty years with the DA's office. Fight religious with religious – Decker's idea.

Kent smoothed his tie and said, 'You talk to us honestly, Mr. Waterson. Then maybe I can save you from the chair.'

'How many times must I repeat myself. Dolores Sparks is a very sick woman.' Waterson's eyes darted about the interview room, deep, wet circles under the arms of his suit jacket. He ran his hand through white, thin hair. 'She's been on medication for years. She's not a credible person. No jury will believe anything she says.'

'So y'all willing to go to trial,' Webster said. 'Good luck to you.'

Martinez said, 'You know, Mr. Waterson, if you don't start talking—'

'I didn't *do* anything,' Waterson insisted. 'I killed no one.'

405

Webster said, 'But you know who pulled the trigger because you hired them.'

'All you have is Dolores's word against mine. Is it my fault that some demented lady mistook my kindness for craziness?'

Kent said, 'Sir, you don't stand a chance.'

'I wish I had a nickel every time a lawyer said that to me.'

'Spare your life, sir. Then use it to repent to Jesus to spare your soul.'

'My soul . . .' Waterson looked away.

Farrell Gaynor folded his arms. 'You make a good living, Mr. Waterson. You want to tell us how you got so far in the hole?'

Waterson gave Gaynor a steely glance. 'I don't believe I have to answer that. I don't believe I have to answer any more of your questions.'

'You're going to talk to us one way or the other. You want a mouthpiece . . .' Martinez handed him the phone. 'I've always said, be my guest.'

Waterson looked at the phone, but didn't move.

Gaynor said, 'You won't tell us about your financial woes, I'll tell you about them. Your wife, Ellen, underwent treatment for renal cancer. Unsuccessful treatment. Eventually, both kidneys came out. She had two transplants that failed. You blamed Azor for that, didn't you?'

'*Never*—'

'Then your medical insurance topped out,' Gaynor continued. 'Four more years of expensive out-of-pocket dialysis. And during this terrible time in your life, Azor's just raking it in—'

'You're despicable.'

'Are you sure you don't mean Azor's despicable?'

Foam gathered at the corner of Waterson's mouth. 'He was despicable – a sinner and a pervert.'

Webster said, 'I was taught Jesus loves all His children.'

'Not those who mock His words. Pray fervently in public and debase in private.'

Kent's voice was soothing. 'I know it's hard, Mr. Waterson. Hard to watch the wicked prosper while the righteous suffer.'

The room went quiet.

'You did what you thought was right,' Kent said. 'In your eyes, in God's eyes. But the law doesn't see it like that, sir. And the law's going to punish you severely. You might lose your life unless you do something to help yourself.'

Tears spilled down Waterson's cheeks. 'I don't need help. I didn't do anything.'

'You did do something, Mr. Waterson,' Martinez said. 'We all here know you did do something. You contracted murder—'

'No . . .' Waterson shook his head. 'No, it wasn't supposed to happen like that.'

'But that's how it happened.'

Martinez said, 'How much did you pay them?'

Waterson was quiet.

'I got receipts from your account,' Gaynor spoke up. 'Which match up nicely with money that had been withdrawn from Dolly Sparks's account. Ten grand in and out right before Azor died. Ten grand in and out right *after* Azor died. And for good measure, a final ten withdrawn just last Friday – the day after Dr. Reginald Decameron died.'

Waterson wiped tears from his cheek. 'Abominations before the Lord. Both of them.'

'How'd you find out about Azor's inclinations?' Webster asked.

Waterson lowered his head. 'Azor had called me . . . to talk about estate planning. At least, that's what he said. A strange call because his affairs seemed to be in order.'

A long pause.

'He told me he had some changes in mind. Setting up separate accounts for Curedon once it hit the market. Accounts in his name only. Separate property . . . as opposed to community property. Naturally, I asked him why.'

Another hesitation.

'Then he just . . . blurted it out. I was . . . stunned . . . repulsed.' He looked beseechingly at Kent.

'What really disgusted me was his complete . . . *lack* of remorse. He told me he was going to drop out for a while to think over who he was. He was planning to do evil in the form of an abomination . . . and he spoke as if he needed a simple vacation.'

Waterson's eyes became hot flames.

'He was going to leave her . . . just like that. Forty years of marriage and suddenly, he was going to desert her. How could he *do* that?'

Webster said, 'Must have pissed you off. Especially since you stuck with your wife through thick and thin.'

'You'd better believe it *pissed* me off,' Waterson spat. 'But that was Azor. An egotist who thought he was God. I couldn't let him do that to Dolly. At the very least, I had to warn her.'

'So you told her Azor's plans to drop out,' Martinez said.

'Of course, I told her. She was entitled to know.'

'What'd she say?'

'She was in shock. Utter, complete shock!' Waterson's lower lip trembled. 'I couldn't stand to see her in such pain. He was going to *ruin* her life, everything she worked so hard for. Don't you understand anything!'

'Of course, we understand, Mr. Waterson.' Martinez nodded encouragingly. 'Whose idea was it to kill him?'

Waterson was silent.

'Mr. Waterson, whose idea was—'

'I heard you.'

The cops waited for him to continue.

Waterson said, 'That was never the plan.'

'Then what was the plan?' Webster asked.

Waterson buried his head in his hands. 'What difference does it make? I told her I'd take care of things.' Again, he looked at Kent. 'Dear God, what is to become of my damnable soul?'

'You want a lawyer now, Mr. Waterson?'

Waterson didn't answer.

Kent said, 'Let's give you some representation, sir. Then perhaps I can help you.'

Waterson looked at Kent. 'I'm a sixty-three-year-old man. Even if you'd plead it down to life in prison, eligible for parole in twenty, what does that make me . . . eighty-three? Assuming I can last that long.' His eyes were filled with tears. 'I've had enough hardship. I think I'd rather die.'

'What about the monsters who killed without remorse?' The DA sat next to Waterson. 'Don't let the real sinners go unpunished. That's a crime even Jesus could not forgive.'

'What kind of a life do I have in prison?'

'A chance to serve God, sir. A chance to do penance. Do penance here on earth, sir. And Jesus will forgive you. Take you into His bosom and save you from eternal damnation.'

The room fell silent. Slowly, Waterson nodded. Kent summoned someone from the PD's office. Within an hour, everything was set into place.

The public defender was Gilda Rosen – thirtysomething, tall and dark, and dressed in a red power suit. She had Waterson sign on the dotted line. For turning state's witness, he was spared the death penalty.

Waterson spoke in a monotone.

'I have known Azor Moses Sparks for many, many years and had always regarded him as a pillar of our community. A leader in his field of medicine, an active and forceful member of our church, a devoted father of six children, and a loving husband.'

He looked at the glass of water in front of him. Made no attempt to drink.

'When my wife . . . got sick, I looked to Azor for support both emotionally and medically. And he seemed generous with his help. Set up appointments for me with the best doctors, reviewed their opinions, informed us of our options, assured us both that everything was going to be all right.'

He sighed deeply.

'And we believed him. After all, he was one of the top physicians in this country. We believed him, all right.'

Waterson stared into his water glass.

'Even when my wife's kidneys failed, he said that everything was under control. He said not to worry.'

He looked up, tears in his eyes.

'He lied to me . . . everything was *not* all right. Nothing was *under control*.'

The room was silent.

Waterson said, 'I know there's only so much man can do. But why didn't he just *tell* us that! Instead, he chose to represent himself as God . . . giving us false hope . . . lying to us day after day after day. Meanwhile, Ellen was deteriorating. She needed a transplant.'

He wiped his cheeks.

'Azor found a donor. But he didn't do the surgery. Instead, he sent us to someone else who charged exorbitant fees. Sent our insurance rates sky-high. By the time the second surgery came around, our insurance company canceled on us.'

'They can do that?' Martinez asked.

'Oh yes, they can do that.' Waterson perked up, had found a sympathetic ear. 'Enough to make your blood boil. You pay out premiums and then when they've had enough, they cancel on you.'

'Terrible,' Webster agreed.

'That doesn't even begin to describe it, Detective,' Waterson said. 'I was a desperate man. I begged Azor to do the surgery himself. Because I couldn't afford another surgery without bankrupting myself. But he wouldn't do it. He just *refused* to do it!'

Waterson growled with anger.

'He made excuses. Said it wasn't his bailiwick. Said he had

misgivings about operating on such a close friend.' The lawyer thumped his fist against the table. 'Don't you see? It was all a frameup because he knew he had failed.'

'Failed?' Webster asked.

'He knew from the beginning that she was going to die.'

'Mr. Waterson,' Kent said, 'we all die—'

'He gave me hope only to let me down. He failed *my wife*. He failed *me*! When he was going to fail his own wife, it was just too much . . . the pain this man was spewing into the world.' Waterson wagged a finger. 'Enough was enough.'

No one spoke for a moment.

'I was appalled when he told me he was of *that* persuasion. He told me he had never acted out, that he was leaving to sort out his feelings. But I didn't believe him for a second.'

'Not a second, huh?' Webster said.

'Not a single second!' Waterson snapped back. 'After what he did to my wife and me, Azor had zero credibility. Besides, one only had to look at whom he kept in his employ even after the man was shown to be a pervert. At that point, it was obvious why Azor remained loyal to such an abominable sinner.'

He stopped speaking.

Gilda said, 'You may continue, Mr. Waterson.'

Waterson seemed suddenly deflated. 'I just couldn't let her down.'

Again, the room fell silent.

Kent said, 'Who down?'

'Dolly.' Waterson looked up, eyes wet, nose red, lips trembling. 'I have sinned. I've had adultery in my heart.'

Kent said, 'You love her, don't you?'

'I had always loved her from afar. Yet, for the sake of God, I kept my passions in check. Even after my wife died, I hid my true feelings. Almost an insurmountably difficult task. Because I saw her wither and suffer from emotional neglect day after day after day after day.'

His eyes moved downward.

'After Azor confessed his evilness to me, I knew I had to tell Dolly. Because she was a frail thing and had to be handled with utmost sensitivity. Something that Azor knew nothing about.'

'So you told her,' Martinez said.

Waterson nodded.

'Then what?'

'She cried to me . . . she cried to *him*. She begged him to reconsider. But just as God did to Pharaoh, Satan had hardened his heart. He turned obstinate, refused to hear her pleas. I mean, would it have been so hard for him to live out his life with her . . . at least for decency's sake? That's all we were trying to do. He could do whatever he wanted as long as he . . . kept quiet about it and stayed with her. I swear murder was never part of the plan.'

Webster said, 'What was the plan, Mr. Waterson?'

'They were supposed to convince him not to leave her . . . and to keep his mouth shut.'

'Who are they?' Webster pressed.

'Stanislav, aka Sidewinder, Polinski and his group,' Waterson said. 'He'll tell you different. He'll tell you I said vile things, told him to do vile things. But this isn't so.'

'Who are Polinski's accomplices?' Martinez asked.

'I never asked. I just told him to take care of it for me.'

'Take care of what?'

'Of Azor,' Waterson said. 'Convince him to stay with her, to pray harder, to try to rid himself of these demons. And to make sure he kept it to *himself*. That was all I said!'

Gilda said, 'Mr. Waterson, you know the deal has been cut. No matter what you say, things can't get worse for you.'

Webster said, 'Why don't you level with us?'

'But I am—'

'You can hide behind your lies with us,' Kent broke in. 'But you can't lie to God. He knows what was in your heart.'

Martinez said, 'Where did you know Polinski from?'

Waterson gulped down water. Again, he covered his face, then dropped his hand on the table. 'Azor had me deliver some checks to him.' He paused. 'To him and a man named Emmanuel Sanchez, aka Grease Pit. Checks for this Peoples for the Environment Freedoms Act that Azor was hepped up on. I never understood it. But I was his lawyer. He asked me to cut a check for him. I cut a check for him.'

'You delivered the check personally to Polinski?' Webster asked.

'Yes, either Polinski or Sanchez.' Waterson's face had turned red. 'Azor gave me a percentage for . . . cutting the checks and personal delivery.' The old lawyer bit his lip. 'Pocket money. Like I was some errand boy.'

'It must have been more than pocket money,' Webster said. 'For you to agree to do it.'

'It was . . . generous, I suppose.'

Webster stared at Waterson, his expression neutral. *So much resentment that this man had built up in his mind and Azor never knew. No doubt he thought he was doing Waterson big favors.*

He said, 'Did you ever talk to Emmanuel Sanchez about taking care of Azor?'

Waterson shook his head. 'No, I never spoke to him about the job. But I did deliver money to him afterward on Polinski's orders.'

Sweat broke from his brow.

'I didn't want Azor killed. Just scared. Scared enough to abandon his evil plans and heinous ways. Scared enough to keep his mouth shut. Scared enough to go back to God and ask His forgiveness for his wicked thoughts. *They* went crazy. Not me. That was *not* part of the deal!'

'But you still paid them off,' Martinez said.

'Of course, I paid them off! At that point, seeing what they were capable of doing, I was too damn scared not to!'

'Polinski do it for the money?' Martinez asked.

'What do you think.'

'I thought he was a friend of Azor's.'

Waterson laughed bitterly. 'You're talking about *monsters* who cut their own mother's throat for money. Of course, with Azor being of *that* kind, they didn't need much convincing. They don't tolerate faggots in their ranks.'

Webster said, 'So you called Sparks up, told him to meet you at Tracadero's?'

Waterson nodded.

'On what pretext did you get him over there?' Martinez asked. 'Redoing his papers?'

'Yes.'

'How'd you get him to park in the back alley?'

'He always parked in the back. Too cheap to use the valet.'

Webster stated, 'So you got him there, arranged to have the bikers jump and murder him in the back alley—'

'I swear they weren't supposed to kill him!'

'But they did,' Webster said softly.

Waterson went quiet.

'Why Decameron?' Martinez asked. 'What did he have to do with Azor leaving his wife?'

Waterson loosened his collar. 'Dolly hated him.'

'She told you to pop him?' Martinez asked.

Waterson shook his head no. 'I took it upon myself to have that pervert properly punished. Because it was all *his* fault. He was vile, the evil serpent of Eden spreading lies, influencing men like Azor to sin. I figure it didn't make much difference to the world if there was one less faggot.'

'How 'bout one less distinguished scientist?' Webster said.

Martinez said, 'How 'bout one less human being with a heart and a soul?'

'He had no heart, his soul was damned. He was a filthy animal!' Waterson grew rigid. 'He deserved to die.'

'That wasn't for you to decide, sir,' Kent said.

Waterson said, 'Obviously it was. Because that's what happened. I decided it. And poof! He was dead.'

32

Answering the page at two in the morning, Decker had no choice
but to tell Rina. He called her from the hospital's waiting room,
used a pay phone off the corridor, manipulating the money slot
and the keypad with his left hand. His right arm was confined to
a sling, the bullet still visibly lodged in his arm. The resident had
offered to remove it under a local. Decker had told him he'd have
it done later, after he found out about the priest's progress. But as
the hours dragged with no news from the operating table, he
wondered if he hadn't made a mistake. Mind-numbing and nerve-
wracking watching a family grow old before his eyes.

A twist of irony: Myron Berger was doing the surgery.

Decker leaned against the wall of the nearly deserted lobby,
keeping a respectable distance from the family. They were
congregated around two brown couches and a pair of orange arm-
chairs. The glass sofa table held glossy in-house hospital
magazines, Azor gracing a couple of covers. In the corner of the
room a coffee machine bubbled thick, walnut liquid. An occasional
lackluster page wafted through the PA system.

The waiting. Purgatory on earth.

Eight of them total – five siblings and three spouses, all of them
weathered and worn as if wrung out to dry. Luke was sprawled on
one of the couches, his blanched face showing the effects of his
blood-letting. They had taken the most from him – three pints; the
other two brothers, had each donated two pints. The two remaining
sisters weren't correctly type-matched. By last count, Bram had
gone through two transfusions.

Dana sat by her husband on the arm of the couch. Her eyes were veined with red. She offered a paper cup to Luke, encouraging him to drink more Coke.

He pushed the cup away with his arm. 'If I drink any more, I'll throw up.'

'You're still pale—'

'Of course, I'm *still* pale. I'm goddamn sick to my stomach. Leave me alone.'

Lids fluttering, Paul's eyes swept over the scene. He paced, checked his watch for the thousandth time. His wife, Angela, was blond and plump, a floral muu-muu covering her body, doughy arms popping out of the short sleeves. She wore no makeup, her face was haggard.

The minutes crawled along with the fear of the unknown.

Michael regarded Decker. 'You should . . .' His voice cracked. 'Your arm . . . you should take care of it.'

Paul turned his glazed eyes toward Decker, as if looking at him for the first time. No doubt that was the case.

'What happened to your arm?'

'Mom . . .' Michael cleared his throat. 'Mom did it.'

'Oh God!' Paul sank into a chair. 'Will this nightmare ever end?'

Pink-eyed, Angela said, 'Do you want more water, Paul?'

'Nothing.' He lowered his head between his knees. 'I think I'm going to throw up.'

But he remained hunched over, arms wrapped around his head.

Angela kneaded her hands. She had bitten a couple of her nails past the quick, trickles of blood oozing over the fingertips. To Decker, she said, 'Is your arm okay?'

'It'll keep.'

She said, 'Mama's really not an evil person . . .'

Angela stopped talking, waiting for someone to corroborate her position. When no one rose to Mom's defense, Decker said, 'Somebody should be paying attention to her needs . . . go down to the jail, talk to her and to her representation. Right now, they've assigned someone from the PD's office. Eventually, you might want to hire your own lawyer.'

Nobody said anything, nobody moved.

Eva's husband, David, tapped his foot. Dark, Semitic-looking. Sleepy brown eyes, thick black hair, a long face, and a prominent nose. Handsome though, because his features were strong. He was wearing an untucked linen shirt over a pair of old jeans. 'You want me to go?'

Nobody answered him. He looked to Decker for help.

'It would be a good idea,' Decker answered.

Eva had curled herself into a ball and pressed herself against the corner of the couch. Maggie was next to her, head on her shoulder, eyes closed, mouth open, snoring slightly.

'Then I should go, Eva?'

Eva glanced at him, looked away. Her eyes held no emotion, dead to the world. 'Do whatever you want.'

Paul raised his head, looked at his watch. 'You said they brought him here around ten, Michael?'

'About,' Michael answered by rote.

'So it's been four hours,' Paul said. 'Don't they say the longer the better?'

He had addressed his question to Michael. But the med student didn't answer.

Paul said, 'Did anyone hear me?'

Luke said, 'I don't know, Paul. I guess no news is good news.'

Paul surveyed his brother's face. 'You're gray, Luke. You need to drink.'

'I'm too nauseated,' Luke said. 'Goddamn room feels like a boat in a storm.'

'I've got a crashing headache,' Paul said. 'Anyone have an aspirin?'

Michael said, 'Paul, you just gave blood. You can't take aspirin for at least a week. It makes you bleed.'

'I've got a Tylenol,' David said.

'Tylenol doesn't work on me.'

Michael said, 'No aspirin, no ibuprofen – Advil, Motrin, Ecotrin. Didn't you read the handout they gave you?'

Paul said, 'No, Michael, I didn't *read* the handout.'

'*Please* don't fight,' Dana said.

'No one's fighting,' Paul said. 'Last thing I want to do is fight. I'm sorry, Michael.'

Michael smiled weakly, tried to speak but couldn't. Instead, he paced. A minute later, he turned to Decker with wet eyes. 'I never did thank—'

'Not necessary,' Decker said.

'Some people can think on their feet.' He shook his head. 'Others just stand around like stunned idiots.'

'Michael, I was a medic in the army. I didn't think, I just did.'

'You saw action then?' Paul asked.

Decker nodded.

'Vietnam?'

'Yes.'

'A survivor,' Paul whispered. 'More power to you. That'd been me, I would have shriveled up and died.'

Decker said, 'Self-preservation kicks in, Paul.'

Again, the room fell quiet.

To Decker, Luke said, 'He talk to you at all, Lieutenant?'

'A little.'

'What'd he say?'

Michael said, 'He prayed, Luke.'

Luke said, 'Say anything to you in the ambulance?'

Decker shook his head.

'Unconscious?'

Decker nodded.

'So, he wasn't in pain, right?'

'No,' Decker lied. Because he really didn't know one way or the other.

Tears fell down Eva's cheeks. 'You should go see Mother,

David. The sooner the better. You should leave now.'

David rocked on his feet. 'If that's what you—'

'Yes. Go.'

He threw his wife a surprised glance. Decker gave them the address of the jail as well as the name of a contact person. David thanked him and left. As soon as David was gone, Eva uncoiled an arm, placed it around her sister's shoulder.

Maggie sat up abruptly, rubbed her eyes. 'Oh my God! I dozed off.'

Eva said, 'That's good.'

'No, it's not,' Maggie cried. 'It's horrible! How could I sleep when . . . I'm so *terrible*!'

She burst into tears. Eva hugged her. 'You're not terrible. I'm terrible.'

'No one's terrible,' Luke said.

Eva blurted out, 'I was always *yelling* at him.'

'Eva, everyone was always yelling at him,' Paul said. 'That's what we did. We yelled at Bram. Do this! Do that! Get this! Go here! Take care of Mom! Fix up my life!' He lowered his head into his hands. 'You want regrets? I've got enough to fill a bank vault.'

Dana said, 'You know, everything might be okay . . . I mean, he . . . we . . .'

Her voice faded to nothing.

Maggie said, 'How could I fall asleep at a time like this?'

Luke said, 'Maggie, honey, you didn't do anything wrong. If Bram were here, he'd tell you to sleep.'

'We'd all sleep if we could,' Paul said.

Luke said, 'Only reason why you can sleep and we can't is your conscience is clean.'

'Amen,' Paul said.

'I don't understand what you mean,' Maggie said.

'It means, like Paul and Eva, I'm wracked with guilt and filled with "I should haves." ' Luke's eyes watered. 'You know, I don't want or expect miracles. I don't need the Red Sea to split or to walk on water or to see Lazarus rising from the dead. All I want is a chance to *talk* to him again. Is that asking too fucking much?'

'Amen,' Paul answered.

Dana said, 'You came to his rescue, Lucas—'

'No, Dana, he came to my rescue—'

'You know, he's not . . .' Dana held back tears. 'Stop talking like it's . . . final!'

Luke's eyes shifted upward, over Decker's shoulder, across the empty lobby. Decker turned around.

Rina.

She wore the same maroon cotton dress she had on for last night's dinner. Light years ago.

He started toward her, meeting her in the middle of the room. She stared at her husband, lip quivering. The hospital had given him a clean top, but he still had on blood-stained pants. He expected her to explode into tears.

Instead, she said, 'What happened to your arm?'

'It's nothing—'

'Peter—'

'I got shot—'

'Oh my *God*—'

'Rina, I'm—'

'Can you move it?'

'The arm? Yeah, no problem.' He lowered his voice. 'They just have to take the bullet out.'

'They haven't taken the bullet *out*?'

Decker sighed. 'I was waiting for some news first.'

Rina was quiet, regarded her husband. 'Nothing?'

Decker shook his head.

Rina kneaded her hands, remained silent.

'You tell the boys?' Decker asked.

'Nothing specific. I told them I had an emergency and to listen for Hannah on the rare chance that she might wake up.'

'What'd they say?'

'They were half-asleep. I told them to go back to bed. I left their door open.'

Abruptly, Rina embraced her husband.

'Oh Peter, I can't *take* this anymore! Learn in a *kollel* all day. Start your own dog kennel or riding stable. Do anything except what you're doing. Find another *job*! I need to sleep at night.'

'This is very unusual—'

'Once burned, twice shy. Twice burned, you pick up your cards and go home.'

'Rina—'

'I'm *serious*! I can't take it! I can't take . . .' Rina sighed, whispered, 'Is he going to pull through?'

'I don't know, Rina.'

'What do you think?'

'Honey, I wouldn't even attempt a guess.' He kissed his wife's head, looked intently into her puffy blue eyes. 'He appreciated the faith you had in him. He also asked if you could say *Tehillim* for him.'

'He actually said that?'

'Yes.'

'Oh my, my . . .' Rina gazed upon her husband with faraway eyes. Her hands reached into her purse, pulled out a thin Hebrew book. She held it up. 'I don't know why I bothered bringing it.' Her eyes spilled tears. 'I practically know all the Psalms by heart.'

Decker's eyes watered. 'I'm sorry, Rina. I did the best I could, but it wasn't enough. The sad part was I felt it coming. As soon as I saw Dolores Sparks's hand disappear into her robe, I jumped her. But it wasn't soon enough. If I had only gotten to her a second earlier—'

'If you had gotten to her a second earlier, it might have been you instead of him.'

Decker paused, realizing the gravity of her statement.

Without a word, she opened her book, wondering whether or not gentiles said *Tehillim* for one another like the Jews did. And if they did, how did they choose which psalms to say? Tradition had it that Jews recited the psalms that corresponded to the letters of the Torah-given name of the person in need. Obviously, Bram didn't have a Torah name. But since Abram Matthew had a Hebrew equivalent – *Avram Matisvahu* – she plowed ahead.

She hadn't gotten very far when Myron Berger walked into the waiting room. From the look on his face, it was clear she needn't have bothered to start.

She closed the book and recited, '*Baruch atah adonai elohenu melech haolam dayanj haemet.*'

'Blessed are you, Hashem, our God, King of the universe, the true judge.'

The Jewish blessing upon hearing distressing news.

Decker closed his eyes and opened them, dread in his stomach. Berger's blue gown was soaked with blood, his mask dangling over his scrubs like a pinafore. His eyes skittered across the sea of beaten faces as he tried to find the right words.

'I'm sorry . . .' The surgeon averted his eyes. 'I did what I could . . . but he was too far gone . . .'

The silence was crashing.

Berger said, 'Maybe, if I had been your father . . . with his skills, I could have . . . I'm terribly sorry.'

Paul got up, walked over to Berger, and placed his hand on the surgeon's shoulder. He retreated a few steps, then erupted into silent tears. Michael reached out to him, the two brothers fell upon each other's necks, choking back sobs. The sisters embraced and cried out loud.

Luke remained by himself. Bram's twin, covering his face with his hands, wails emanating from the heart, deep moans of despair. His wife held him in her arms, rocking him while he wept. But Dana was ill-equipped to console his bitter misery.

And so it was that Decker saw the sorrow – the unbridled grief he had expected to find when he had originally come to them announcing Azor's death. For all their professed love and respect

424

of their parents, their honest love and true despair came out in Bram's death.

Because in fact, with Azor being a punitive, unapproachable figure in their lives, and Dolores, a fragile, imbalanced mother, they had turned to Bram for nurturance and guidance.

Abram Sparks – the golden boy.

Decker looked at Rina.

Stoically, she took his hand. 'We need to take care of your arm, Peter.'

Decker nodded, leaving the family alone to grieve. Out of deference to their needs for privacy and more than a little of his own fear. Because witnessing such abject pain was a very hard thing to do.

33

'Are you sure you want to be here?' Marge asked.

Decker flexed his elbow, wriggled his fingers, and winced. 'I'm not saying I feel great. But since I can write, I might as well work.' He shook his head. 'Better here than being at home. It's been hell this past week.'

'How's Rina?'

Decker thought about the question. 'She's . . . functioning.'

'Should I send her a condolence card or something?'

'I think she'd appreciate a call. You go to Polinski's arraignment yesterday?'

'No, I didn't go. Tom and Bert went. Scott and I spent the day going over Waterson's confession tape.'

'Everything okay?'

'Seems to be pretty clean,' Marge said. 'I think he'll be a very credible witness for the state. I think the DA's going for the death penalty for Polinski.'

'Fine.'

'My opinion? Waterson and Dolores deserve it as much as Polinski does. Maybe even more.'

'Maybe.'

'They might not have pulled the trigger physically, but they arranged the murder . . . murders. At least, Waterson did. Calling up Polinski, telling him to meet Azor in the back alley of Tracadero's. Asshole set the whole thing up.'

'True.'

'And Dolores . . .' Marge shook her head. 'What a cold-blooded bitch. Sets up her husband and his colleague, then literally shoots

427

her own son. *Two* guns on her, mind you. An extra in case the first one jams, the psycho. The kids have hired some hotshot psychiatrist to the tune of God knows how much money . . .' She paused. 'I guess they can afford it. Anyway, the court sends her to a *hospital*. I say, in lieu of electroshock, how about the electric chair.'

Decker ran his left hand through his hair. 'She might agree with you.'

'Bullshit. They all start off remorseful. Within a very short period of time, it's "I don't want to die. Save my fucking ass!" I wouldn't lose any sleep if they fried her.'

Decker nodded.

'Fried her big time.'

'Whatever.'

Marge paused. 'You're being rather mysterious.'

'I'm in pain.'

No one spoke for a moment.

'Why don't you call it a day?' Marge said.

'No, I'll slug it out. I'm a man. I can't admit weakness.'

Marge smiled.

Decker said, 'When's Berger going before the grand jury?'

'Originally, they had him down for next week. But the FBI keeps finding stuff. Apparently, Fisher/Tyne has not only been monkeying around with data – which is federal offense because they've been hacking into computer data banks cross-country – but the company's also been covering up dubious results and negative side effects of their test drugs.'

'How?'

'They discount side effects as anomalies or just plain disregard the data. Ignore it. If a doctor says anything about the outrageous practice, the company hits the MD with a slander suit. Keeps the doc tied up with expensive litigation that encourages others to keep their mouths shut.'

'That's not illegal?'

'Nope. But bribing is. FBI's uncovered incentive bribes for

looking the other way. Shockley is up to his *ears*. Scott has had the last laugh.'

She paused.

'Course that doesn't bring Kenneth Leonard back to life. Poor guy. He finally decides to do the right thing and gets mowed down. Talk about bad timing.'

'Ironic,' Decker said. 'Whole thing might never have been discovered if Azor hadn't been murdered.' He exhaled forcefully. 'And his murder had nothing at all to do with Fisher/Tyne.'

'It always boils down to a personal thing, doesn't it?'

'Usually.'

Marge's eyes met his. 'Are you mad at me, Pete?'

'Mad at you?'

'For crapping out on you.'

'What are you talking about?'

Marge sat down at Decker's desk, across from him. 'When you called me over to help Bram, I hesitated. I didn't want to do it.'

'It's understandable. You weren't gloved.'

'Neither were you.'

Decker shrugged. 'Thinking about it later on, I wondered if I did the right thing by yelling at you to come over. There'd been rumors that he was gay. Suppose he was HIV positive.'

'Yet you didn't think twice about it, did you?'

'Rightly or wrongly, no I didn't.'

'I really admire you.'

'Nothing to admire. Like I told Michael Sparks, I didn't think, I just did what I'd been trained to do.'

'I don't believe that.'

Decker smiled. 'You're imparting undeserved nobility to my character.'

Marge said, 'His blood was clean.'

'Thank God,' Decker said. 'I'm not saying Bram's death has a silver lining. In fact, the whole thing is simply an ugly, useless tragedy. But . . .'

He swallowed.

'But it does give you pause for thought. Life is short. When Rina feels like joining the human race again, I'm going to take a few days off.'

'Don't be too radical, Pete.'

'Nah, never. I'm Joe American Dad, Margie. Mr. Straightlaced, Middle-aged Fart.'

'You're not *that* bad.'

'No, actually, I'm not. But I gotta act the part.' He grinned. 'Otherwise my boys'll have nothing to rebel against.'

Ginger's barking woke Decker up from a luxurious Sunday nap. He arose from his living room couch, rolling his shoulders to relieve them of stiffness. Stretched a moment. It hurt. He gave his hair a cursory comb with his fingers, then answered the knock on the door.

Eerie seeing Luke. At present, garbed in black, his weight loss, his longer hair, and his glasses, he looked indistinguishable from Bram. As if that entire ordeal had been just a terrible nightmare.

'Did I wake you, Lieutenant?'

'Uh . . . no, the dog did.' Decker smiled. 'It's okay.'

'How are you feeling?'

'Not too bad.'

'Sorry to bother you at home.'

'How's your family?'

'Fucked.'

Decker said nothing.

'Sorry, but it's the truth,' Luke said. 'I could lie, say that Abram's death made us closer, made us appreciate one another. But the sad thing is . . . we're the same people. Worse. Because we lost our family glue. And the world lost a truly good man.'

He looked down, then up.

'Ain't a day that has gone by . . . when I haven't looked in the mirror . . . and pretended my reflection was him. Most of the time, when I reach out at it and feel that cold, slick surface, reality just slaps me across the face. But then there are times . . . times when my fingers melt with his . . .'

Luke rubbed his green eyes under his glasses. He smiled coldly. 'Maybe that's drugs talking.'

Decker waited a beat, then said, 'What can I do you for, Mr. Sparks?'

'Actually, I came to see your wife. Is she home?'

Decker paused. 'I'll go get her. You want to come in?'

'No, thanks, I'll just wait here.'

Luke tore into his thumbnail as he waited. A moment later, Rina appeared, a child of around three riding her hip. A real looker that woman was even with the scarf covering her hair. Made her even more desirable. He had a sudden urge to rip it off and see what was underneath.

'Hello,' Rina said.

'Mrs. Decker . . .' Luke's eyes moved sideways. 'Thanks for seeing me.'

Rina waited. Her husband was still with her. Luke glanced at him and said nothing.

Decker relieved Rina of the baby. 'Come on, Hannah Rosie. Let's go play in the orchard.'

'Your shoulder, Peter. Let her walk.'

'I'm fine.' To Luke, Decker said, 'Excuse us.'

'Can I pick the oranges, Daddy?' Hannah asked.

'Yes, you can pick the oranges.'

'Can I throw the oranges, Daddy?'

'No, you may not throw the oranges.'

'Can I throw just . . .' The little girl held up a lone finger. 'Can I throw just . . . one orange?'

'Maybe one. If you walk.'

'I walk.'

Luke watched them go. 'Cute kid. Got a couple of my own that age.'

'I know.'

Luke was momentarily thrown off-kilter. 'Bram told you?'

'Yes. And I met your son at the memorial service.'

'Oh . . . oh yes, that.' Luke looked away. 'I've been going through my brother's things . . . I came across this.'

He reached into his jacket, pulled out a small wrapped package and an envelope. He handed them to Rina. 'These were meant for you.'

Rina fingered the envelope, noticed the gum seal had been broken. 'It's been opened.'

'I opened it,' Luke said. 'To see who it belonged to.'

Rina smiled softly. 'Of course. That makes sense.'

He closed his eyes and opened them. 'Actually, I did more than just read the name, Mrs. Decker. I read the entire card. I shouldn't have, but I did.'

Rina took out the card and scanned Bram's compact writing. Dated years ago. It had been written while he'd been in residence in Rome right before he was due to be ordained. Obviously, he had nixed the idea of sending the card. She wondered why he had kept it. Whatever the reason, she was glad he hadn't thrown it away.

Emotional words, filling her soul with a bottomless ache. Too much to absorb in front of a stranger. She'd reread it carefully when she was alone, able to break down in private.

'It was a personal note.'

'I know. I apologize. I was just so . . . shocked. I never thought of my brother as an emotional being, much less being in love.'

Rina looked at him, said nothing.

'To tell you the truth, I'm not sorry I read it. Because it made me feel good . . . to think that Bram had experienced love and passion and fire and all that good stuff.'

He looked at her.

'I hope his feelings were reciprocated.'

Rina rubbed her wet eyes. 'Thank you for bringing this over. It means a lot to me.'

'Does it?'

'You couldn't possibly know how much.'

Luke stared at her. 'Enough said then. I won't pry.'

'Thank you.'

He paused, then said, 'Do you know I was very jealous of your husband?'

'Jealous of Peter?'

'No, your first husband,' Luke said. 'Bram and I had had a falling-out, weren't talking much when he had hooked up with Isaac. I always felt we would have gotten back together sooner if your husband hadn't gotten in the way. Because Bram loved him like a brother.'

'They were very close.'

'Anyway . . .' Luke clapped his hands. 'I'm sure Bram would have wanted you to have the package. Even if it's late.'

'Thank you.'

Luke bit a nail. 'Pooch is his kid, you know.'

Wide-eyed, Rina stared at him, not knowing what to say.

'My son Peter . . . he's Bram's kid. My daughter too. I had chicken pox when I was twenty-two. An odd allergic reaction left me sterile. My wife and I tried all sorts of procedures for a long time. When nothing worked, I went to my brother.'

Luke looked away.

'He wouldn't agree to artificial insemination . . . against his Catholic religion to mix seed or something like that.' Luke swiped at his eyes. 'But apparently, nonvital organ transplants . . . or in our case, organ exchanges . . . were permissible. Which didn't make a lot of sense to me . . . or maybe he got permission from the Pope. I never knew much about Bram's affairs or his religion.'

Rina waited for him to continue.

'He donated one of his . . . you know.'

Rina couldn't hide her surprise.

Luke said, 'He would have given me both. Said they weren't doing him any good. But my father put his foot down . . . wouldn't allow it.'

'Your *father* did the surgery?'

Luke nodded. 'Yeah, Mister Cutting-Edge Surgeon. Excuse me . . . Doctor Cutting-Edge Surgeon. He didn't want Bram to do it. But my brother . . . once he got a bug in his head . . .'

Rina was silent.

'Dad did it after hours, in secret, off the record. No one knows. No one. Not even my wife. She thought I went in for a hernia. Anyway, with my dad holding the knife and Bram and I being identical, the exchange took. Eye for an eye, tooth for a tooth, etcetera, etcetera.'

Rina remained silent.

Luke said, 'I bunked in at Bram's apartment for about . . . four, five days. Dad did a good job. We healed up, both of us. Lo and behold, we still had beards and talked like men. Three months later, my wife became pregnant. Lucky all the way around. God only knows what my own DNA looked like after ten years of using.'

'That's a beautiful story.' Rina stared at him. 'Is it really true?'

Luke blushed. 'Honest injun. Some endings are happy, Mrs. Decker.'

'More like bittersweet.'

'Yeah, more like bittersweet.' Luke's eyes watered. 'But we take what we can get. I don't know why I told you. I guess I wanted to know that he didn't die empty.'

'Thank you, Luke.' Rina smiled sadly. 'Thank you very much for telling me. It does make me feel better . . . for whatever that's worth.'

'Thanks for your time.'

'I'll walk you out.'

'Nah, don't bother.'

Rina watched him go. As soon as his car motor faded to nothing, Peter and Hannah reappeared from the orchard. Peter was carrying a handful of oranges.

'Your daughter has an arm,' he said.

'How many did you let her throw?'

'Let's change the subject. What did Luke want?'

Rina showed her husband the package, but not the card. 'This was apparently meant for me . . . a belated birthday present that never arrived.'

'From Bram?'

She nodded, tore open the wrapping. Inside a box was a pair of tortoiseshell hair combs. She showed them to Peter. 'He bought these a long time ago. It's good he chose combs instead of a mood ring.'

'Very good. They're beautiful.'

'Yes, they are. Bram always loved my hair.' She smiled at Hannah, lifted her into her arms. 'Come on, pumpkin. Let's go make some juice.'

'Can I throw the oranges, Mommy?'

'No, but you can squeeze them.' She kissed Peter. 'Go back to sleep.'

'Good idea.' Decker lay back on the couch, stared at the ceiling, thinking about Rina's words, that Bram had loved her hair.

Which gave Decker significant insight into their relationship. Which had to have been very personal. Because how else would Bram have known about Rina's long, luxurious hair, which she usually kept covered for public consumption?

From the very beginning, Decker knew intuitively that Rina had loved Bram, knew that her love had been returned in spades. Maybe they had physically consummated the relationship, maybe not. What did it matter anyway? He had once heard a Jewish proverb stating that jealousy rots the flesh off the bones – the reason why man disintegrates after death. He could believe that.

It was a petty, trivial emotion – a waste of time and precious breath.

Decker thought about his wife's closeness to Bram, examined the feelings in his heart. They felt warm, very good indeed.

FAYE KELLERMAN

GRIEVOUS SIN

FICTION/THRILLER 0 7472 4116 X

More Thrilling Fiction from Headline Feature

FAYE KELLERMAN

'WIFE OF THE MORE FAMOUS JONATHAN
BUT . . . HIS PEER' *TIME OUT*

GRIEVOUS SIN

Minutes after Sergeant Peter Decker witnesses his wife
give birth to their first child his policeman's instinct tells
him something's wrong, something the doctors are not
telling him. He is right, and in the midst of his wife's
trauma he begins to suspect something else is awry in
the hospital. The disappearance of a new-born baby,
together with that of the nurse in charge of the post-
natal unit, confirms once again that Decker's instincts
were correct – but this time *he* is the professional best
qualified to deal with the potentially tragic crisis, a task
to which he takes with a vengeance.

The early signs look bad – the missing nurse's burnt-out
car, together with some charred remains, are found in a
remote ravine. But as Decker and his partner Marge
delve deeper, they start to uncover the network of
family tragedy and betrayal that led to the frantic
kidnapping of an innocent baby girl.

'Faye Kellerman creates powerful, unhingeing characters and
her narrative leaves you sweaty-palmed' *Jewish Chronicle*

'Painfully touching as well as taut with suspense'
Mystery Scene

'A marvellous melange of complex family feuds . . . satisfying
denouement' *Scotsman*

'Tautly exciting' *Los Angeles Times*

'The most refreshing mystery couple around' *People*

FICTION / THRILLER 0 7472 4118 X